023

Sarah Pinborough was born in 1972 in Stony Stratford, Buckinghamshire, where her family still have their home. She spent much of her childhood and adulthood travelling all over the world — her father, now retired, was a diplomat, and so her early years were spent roaming the Middle East before, at eight years old, she packed her trunk and headed off to boarding school for a ten-year stretch, the memories of which she says still provide her with much of her material for horror stories. She now lives about five miles from where she was born, with her cats, Mr Fing and Peter. She is a member of the British Fantasy Society, The Horror Writers' Association and, along with fellow horror authors Sarah Langan, Alex Sokoloff and Deborah LeBlanc, is part of the writing collective-known as MUSE.

You can discover more about the author at https://sarahpinborough.com

CROSS HER HEART

Someone is very angry. The letter he's reading has sent him into a rage. He starts to make a plan — he wants to destroy the woman who's rejected him . . . Lisa lives for her daughter Ava, her job, and her best friend Marilyn. But when a handsome client shows an interest in her, Lisa starts daydreaming about sharing her life with him too. Maybe she's ready now. Maybe she can trust again. Maybe it's time to let her terrifying secret past go. Then her daughter rescues a boy from drowning, and their pictures are all over the news for everyone to see. Lisa's world explodes, and she finds everything she has built threatened. Not knowing who she can trust, it's up to her to face her past to save what she holds dear . . .

Books by Sarah Pinborough
Published by Ulverscroft:

13 MINUTES

SARAH PINBOROUGH

CROSS HER HEART

Complete and Unabridged

CHARNWOOD
Leicester

First published in Great Britain in 2018 by
HarperCollins*Publishers*
London

First Charnwood Edition
published 2019
by arrangement with
HarperCollins*Publishers* Ltd
London

A catalogue record for this book is available
from the British Library.

ISBN 978–1–4448–4187–9

Published by

(Publishing)
cestershire

Graphics Ltd.
estershire

Great Britain by
, Padstow, Cornwall

on acid-free paper

For Irvine, thank you for having the faith!

1

AFTER

HIM

Bitch.

He grips the edge of the paper so tightly the neat lines of carefully written words twist into odd zigzags that crunch some sentences but highlight others, taunting him.

I can't cope.

You're too angry.

You frighten me when you hurt me.

I don't love you any more.

The world is shaking and his breath comes heavily as he scans to the end.

Don't come after me. Don't try and find me. Don't try and find us.

He reads the letter three times before it sinks in. She's gone. They're gone. He knows it's true — he can feel the fresh emptiness in the house — but still he rushes through the rooms, pulling open hollow cupboards and drawers. There is no trace of her, however; no passport or driving licence, none of those important things that frame her life.

Don't try and find us.

He returns to the kitchen table and crumples the letter, suffocating her words in his clenched fist. She's right. He is angry. More than angry.

1

He's raging. It's a white heat inside him. He stares out through the window, the battered ball of paper damp in his sweating palm. Vodka. He needs vodka.

As he drinks, a seed of a plan takes hold in the dark soil of his mind and starts to grow.

She has no right to do this to him. Not after everything they've been through.

He will destroy her for it.

PART ONE

2

NOW

LISA

'Happy birthday, darling,' I say, from the doorway. It's only six thirty and I'm still bleary from sleep, but my kitchen hums with teenage life. It's like a surging wave hitting me. I don't remember *ever* having this much energy. It's a good feeling. Full of hope and confidence.

'You didn't have to get up, Mum. We're just leaving anyway.' She's smiling as she comes to kiss me on the cheek, a cloud of apple shampoo and pink deodorant, but she looks tired. Maybe she's doing too much. Her GCSEs are coming up and between morning and evening swimming training several times a week, spending time with these girls, and going to school, I barely see her any more. Which is, as I keep telling myself, how it should be. She's growing up. Growing *out* from me. I have to learn to let go. But it's hard. For so long it was us two against the world. Now the world is nearly hers to grasp for herself.

'It's not every day my little girl turns sixteen,' I say as I fill the kettle and wink at her. She rolls her eyes at Angela and Lizzie, but I know she's happy I still get up to see her off to school. She's at once grown up and still my baby. 'And anyway,' I add. 'I've got my big presentation at work today so I need an early start.'

A phone buzzes. All three heads drop to screens and I turn back to the kettle. I know there's a boy called Courtney in Ava's life. She hasn't told me about him yet, but I saw a message come in when she left her phone on the kitchen table last week, a rarity in itself. I used to check her phone occasionally, when I could, but now she uses a passcode, and as much as it pains me to admit it, she deserves her privacy. I have to learn to trust in my bright daughter's sensible mind to keep her safe.

'Do you want your presents now or tonight at Pizza Express?' I ask.

Ava's clutching little gift bags with coloured tissue poking out the top, but she doesn't share with me what her friends have bought her. Later, perhaps she will. A few years ago she would have run to show me. Not any more. Time flies. Somehow I'm nearly forty and Ava is sixteen. Soon she'll be flying my nest.

'Jodie's outside,' Angela says, glancing up from her iPhone. 'We should go.'

'Tonight's fine,' Ava says. 'I haven't got time now.' She smiles at me and I think that one day, she'll be quite beautiful. For a moment, I have a sudden pang of loss in my chest, so I focus on stirring my tea and then check my presentation printouts are still on the kitchen table while the girls gather up their coats, swimming kits, and school and college bags.

'I'll see you tonight, Mum,' Ava calls over her shoulder as they disappear into the hallway and I feel a gust of damp air as they flood outside. On a whim, I get my purse and take out twenty pounds and go after them, leaving the front door on the latch.

'Ava, wait!' I'm only in my thin dressing gown but I follow her down the path, waving the banknote at her. 'For you and the girls. Go for a nice breakfast before school.'

'Thank you!' Ava's words are quickly echoed by the others and then they're tumbling into Jodie's car, the tiny blonde girl at the wheel, and I'm left behind at our open gate. They're barely all in before Jodie pulls away, and I flinch slightly as I wave after them. She's going quite fast and she can't have checked her mirrors. Has Ava got her seatbelt on? *Worry worry.* That's me. They don't realise how precious life is. How precious they are. How can they? So young and with blessed lives.

It's the cusp of summer, but the sky is heavily grey and threatening more rain, casting a chill in the air. I watch until Jodie's turned the corner and I'm about to go back to the warmth of the house when I see a car parked on the bend of our quiet road behind me. My skin prickles. It's unfamiliar. Dark blue. Not one I've seen before. I know all the cars in our street. It's become a habit to note these things. This car is new.

My heart thrums in my chest, a bird trapped against glass. I don't move an inch; this isn't fight or flight, but a cold dread. The car's engine is turned off and there is someone behind the wheel. Thickset. It's too far away to see his face. Is he looking at me? There's a sound like buzzing flies in my head and I try to catch my breath. As

7

my panic threatens to overwhelm me, a man, still pulling on a suit jacket while trying to wave at the driver, comes down his front path. The engine starts. Only as it moves do I see the small strip down one side. *EezyCabs*.

The flood of relief makes me almost laugh. Almost.

You're safe, I tell myself as the taxi drives by, no one inside glancing my way. *You're safe and Ava's safe. You have to relax.*

Of course it's easier said than done. I've learned that over the years. The fear never truly leaves me. I've had lulls where I can almost let go of the past, but then a random moment like this triggers a panic and I realise it will always be there, like hot tar glued to the lining of my stomach. And recently, I've had this feeling, an unsettled disquiet, as if there's something off-kilter I should see but I don't. Maybe it's me. My age. Hormones. Ava growing up. Maybe it's nothing. But still . . .

'Penny for them?'

I gasp and flinch and then laugh in the way everyone does when goosed, even though the shock isn't funny. My hand is at my chest as I turn to see Mrs Goldman standing at her front door.

'Are you all right?' she asks. 'I didn't mean to make you jump.'

'Yes, sorry,' I say. 'Lost in the day ahead. You know how it is.' I walk back down towards my own front door. I'm not sure Mrs Goldman *does* know how it is. She's careful as she bends to pick up the single milk bottle from the step and I see

8

her flinch. What does her day hold? Daytime TV? *Countdown? Pointless?* Her sons haven't visited for a while either.

'I think there's going to be a thunderstorm later. Do you want me to grab anything for you from the shops? I've got to get some more bread and bits anyway. Although I won't be back until quite late because I'm taking Ava for pizza after work. It's her birthday.' I don't need bread but neither do I like the thought of Mrs Goldman having to go out in the rain. Her hips are bad and the roads can be slippery.

'Oh, if it's no bother,' she says, and I can hear the relief in her voice. 'You are lovely.'

'It's fine.' I smile and I feel an awful ache I don't fully understand. A kind of empathy for someone's fragility. For everything people hold inside. Something like that anyway. I listen as she gives me her small list of items. Everything just enough for one. I'll add some Battenberg to it. A little gift. I should try to pop in for a cup of tea with her at the weekend too. Her days must be long and it's so easy not to notice the lonely people in this world. I should know. I was lonely for a long time. In some ways, I still am. I try to be kind to lonely people now. I've learned that kindness is important. What else is there, really?

⋆ ⋆ ⋆

Since PKR opened a second branch, we've been moved to a smaller but more stylish office and even though it's a while until Simon Manning is due to come in, when I get there at eight I feel

9

slightly sick with nerves and my hands are twitchy and trembling. I tell myself it's just about the presentation, but that's rubbish. It's also about Simon Manning. Simon has moved into some strange limbo between potential new company client and something *other*. A flirtation. An attraction. The way he looks at me has changed. I don't know how to deal with it. It's a low-voltage hum in my head.

'This is for you.'

I look up from checking through my presentation pages and see Marilyn holding up a pack of three Ferrero Rocher chocolates. 'For good luck. And this,' she takes her other hand from behind her back to reveal a single glass bottle of bubbly, 'is for when you've nailed it.'

I grin at her, flooding with warmth. Thank God for Marilyn. '*If* I nail it. I know he's been speaking to other recruiters.'

'Oh, don't worry, I've got vodka in the drawer for if you fuck it up.'

'Gee, thanks.'

'What are best friends for?'

The great thing about this new open-plan office is that my desk and Marilyn's are facing each other's, a little island of two. Marilyn designed the whole layout and it works well. She's got an eye for spaces. Maybe comes from being married to a builder for so long.

'Look at Toby,' she says, nodding across the room. 'He's like a pig in shit with these new girls.'

She's right. We lean against her desk and watch as he preens himself. The new women all look under twenty-five, and at thirty Toby probably seems like a sophisticated older man. He's certainly playing up to it. Breathless nervous giggling wafts over as he says something obviously hugely entertaining while explaining the photocopier.

'They'll learn,' I say. It'll be entertainment for us for a while at any rate. It's good to be at work, under the bright strip-lighting and with the uniformity of desks and red office chairs and smart clothing. It makes my momentary unease from this morning fade like the remnants of a bad dream.

At nine, Penny, our glorious leader and the PK in PK Recruitment, calls us all together. We gather in a semi-circle around her office door and Marilyn and I hang a little bit back, like sheep herders perhaps, or nannies. I like Penny. She's brisk and efficient and doesn't feel the need to be too familiar with her staff. I've worked here for over ten years and I don't think we've ever socialised personally, only the two of us. Marilyn finds it odd, but not me. Even though Penny's about my age, she's my boss. I don't want her trying to be my friend. It would make me uncomfortable.

'It's so lovely to be able to welcome our new team members at last,' she starts. 'It's wonderful to have Emily, Julia and Stacey joining us and I hope you'll be very happy working here.'

The three young things, tanned and fully made up, beam at her and then exchange sideways happy glances with each other. I hope they'll all stay as friendly with each other as they are today. I met Marilyn on my first day here,

11

and I can't imagine my life without her. Colleague and best friend rolled into one. She suffocates my loneliness.

'Also, I owe a big debt of thanks to Toby, Marilyn and Lisa for holding the fort so well in this transition period. Marilyn and Lisa are senior staff here. If you have any problems, don't hesitate to ask them for advice — they probably know more about the day-to-day running of this agency than I do.'

Marilyn smiles as curious eyes fall on us, whereas I look down at my feet and wish their gaze away. If only I had Marilyn's poise and confidence. She takes everything in her stride.

'Anyway, there will be cakes in the kitchen later and drinks in the Green Man on the corner after work for those who want to come along — which I hope will be all of you.'

She disappears back into her office and our little cluster fragments. I glance at the clock. Still a while before Simon gets here and the importance of this meeting kicks in, all thoughts of ridiculous attraction evaporating. My stomach churns and I take a couple of deep breaths. I can do this, I tell myself, only half-believing it. I have to do this. The commission alone is worth this anxiety and I'm bound to get a better annual bonus on the back of it. Maybe even a pay rise. I need to save for Ava potentially going to university. I don't want her starting her adult life with baggage and I'm determined to help. I'll protect her from the world however I can.

I have to. I know how terrible it can be out there.

3

AVA

The cafeteria is like the changing room at the pool, hot and moist, and the windows are misted up as the summer rain pelts at the glass outside. I don't mind the rain so much. Ange does because her carefully straightened hair starts to frizz as soon as the first drop falls, but unless the sun is properly baking, I prefer spending our lunchtimes indoors. It's how I always spent them before, when I used to hang out with Caz and Melanie, which feels like a lifetime ago now. It's the only thing I really miss about them. Angela is more of an outdoor girl so we have lunch on the benches normally. Not in this downpour though. Today we're safely inside with everyone else.

'So, what do you reckon?' she says. 'For Saturday? Crash at Jodie's? We could go to the pub first and then make a punch or something. See if anyone else is around?' One thick black eyebrow, filled in with pencil, wriggles like a slug on her olive face as she tries to raise it suggestively. If I did mine like that I'd end up rubbing brown all over my face. Angela is way better with make-up and clothes than me. When she's all dressed up she looks about twenty. I just look about twenty stone. I'm the ugly duckling of our group, I know it. Please God, let me one day turn into a swan.

'Yeah, sounds good,' I say. 'If the others can come.'

Angela's fingers fly over the keypad of her phone, and I know mine will buzz in a minute once she's sent out the message to our *MyBitches* WhatsApp group. Lizzie came up with the name. We *are* each other's bitches after all, she'd said, and we'd laughed. She was right. I can't believe I've only been at Larkrise Swimmers for a year. I've only known these girls for about ten months. It feels like we've been friends forever. Well, I *kind* of knew Angela before because we're in the same school, but we've never been in any of the same sets so she was only a face in a crowd, like I was to her. Now look at us. *MyBitches*. It still makes me smile. But I think I prefer *The Fabulous Four*, as our coach calls us. We're his winners. We may compete as solo swimmers but we drive each other to be the best. We clicked right away, from the first morning practice, like jigsaw pieces slotting into place around each other, coming together to make a brilliant picture and put Larkrise on the competitive map.

We're different ages, and in a lot of ways, it's better. Gives us more to talk about. Me and Ange are the only ones at King Edward's Grammar, Lizzie is in sixth form at Harris Academy, *Arse Academy* as it's known, the shithole school in the middle of town, and Jodie is a first year at Allerton Uni. She's nearly twenty-two and competes with the adults but she's one of us really and she doesn't seem to care we're younger than her. She trains with us because her lectures clash with the adult sessions and she says she prefers mornings. She doesn't stay in halls but at her mum's house here in Elleston and so she hasn't really got into uni life. She helps us with our techniques and she's pretty cool. She never makes me feel like I'm way younger than her. Not that five years is *that* much younger, but the sixth formers at KEGS make you feel like they're thirty or something, constantly looking down at us.

'Lizzie's in,' Ange mutters, focused on her phone, as if I can't read my own pinging matching messages. 'Jodie says her mum's not back this weekend. She'll double-check but she's pretty sure.'

Another bonus to having a friend at uni — much more relaxed parenting. Jodie's mum does interior design or something for big posh houses, and she has a boyfriend in Paris where she's currently living while she works on some project. It all sounds very glamorous, but more importantly means she's hardly ever home. I've never met her and Jodie pretty much has the place to herself.

'Cool,' I say. I want to check my Facebook, but I've told myself I won't until the end of lunch. I pick at the dregs of my cold jacket potato instead. My shoulders ache from the butterfly this morning — not my best stroke — and the gym session last night. We push hard, but I've been slacking a bit recently and I'm feeling it. I need to get my shit together or it will start to show to the others, or worse, I'll start letting the club down. I've always had to work harder than them to stay fit. Lizzie is naturally toned and runs like a gazelle. Jodie is only five foot three, but she's all muscle, lean, angry and boyish in her swimsuit and Ange has the curves. Her own *personal floats*, as Lizzie would put it. Not that her boobs stop her cutting fast through the water. All her femininity dissolves as soon as she dives under the surface. I'm not quite sure how I fit into the pack. *More ass than tit* is how I overheard twatty Jack Marshall talking about me last term — it still stings badly — and he probably had a point. I've inherited my mum's pear shape. Any extra weight goes straight to my thighs, and they're big enough even when I'm barely eating.

I may tell Mum that Jodie's mum is back this weekend, just to stop her worrying. I feel a flash of guilt. Of all of our families, my mum is the most protective. I never noticed it much before. It's always been us two together — and Auntie Marilyn — and I know she loves me more than anything, and I do love her too, but I'm sixteen now and I have to have my own space, like the rest of my friends do. *Text me when you get there. Text me when you're leaving. I'll come and pick you up, no, really, it's no problem.* I know she means well, but no one else's mum does that and I can't help but feel embarrassed. It makes me feel like a child, and I'm not. I'm pretty much a woman. I have my own secrets now.

Our phones buzz again and we laugh in unison

at Lizzie's message. A gross spunking dick gif.

'So, are you gonna?'

Ange always does this weird half-American accent whenever the subject is sex. She breaks off a piece of doughnut and pops it in her mouth, but her brown eyes are sharp on me as she chews.

I shrug, casual, although my heart trips. Am I? I said I'd do it when I was sixteen, and part of me wants to — at least used to want to — but I don't see why it's so *urgent* I do it straight away. But Courtney is hot, and he's totally different and more than anything he's cool. Cool boys have never really liked me before and I kind of feel I owe him now. He's probably not used to waiting, even though we've only been sort of seeing each other a couple of months.

'Probably,' I say, and Ange breaks into an excited grin.

'Oh my God, I bet he's totally experienced. Way better for your first time.'

'He's been pretty good so far.' I stick my tongue out at her, wiggle it crudely, and wink.

This time she shrieks loud enough to make several girls at other tables turn and stare.

The banter comes easily and I know I probably *will* do it with Courtney this weekend, if only to get it out of the way, and it's not like we haven't done most other things anyway apart from *that*, but I don't feel the way I used to about him any more. I'm not overwhelmed by him like I was at the start. Not since . . . well . . . not since the messages started. I've got a new secret now. One I haven't shared even with the

17

girls. I can't. It's something which is entirely mine and it's making Courtney and all his *cool* seem like teenage-boy bullshit.

My new Facebook friend. Someone I can *really* talk to.

The bell rings out overhead signalling the end of lunch and my heart races. I made it through the hour without looking at Messenger. I don't like to check in front of Ange or the others and I've turned my notifications off. We have sharp eyes as well as strong muscles. We demand to know everything of each other. If it pinged, I'd have to share. We are *one*.

As Ange disappears off to Geography, I clear our trays before going to English revision. Only then do I click into FB Messenger. My heart thumps, but quickly falls. No new messages. I can't believe how disappointed I feel. It's my sixteenth birthday. It's important. I thought he *cared*.

Maybe later, I tell myself, as I pocket my phone, determined not to be too upset. To believe in him like he said I should. There'll be a message later.

4

LISA

It's gone way better than I expected, and two hours after our meeting starts, the deal is done. I'm still trembling, but this time it's with pride, exhilaration, and general relief at not messing it up. I walk tall as I lead Simon through to Penny's office, and all heads turn towards us, even Marilyn's. It's not only that I've obviously negotiated the contract and it's a big one, it's also that Simon Manning is not a man you can ignore. He's not handsome in a smooth estate agent way like Toby, all hair product and overpowering aftershave, but he exudes something attractive. Handsome probably isn't the right word. His nose is slightly misshapen as if it's been broken a few times and he's got the thickened out body of someone who used to play rugby but maybe doesn't so much any more. Still physically fit, but with less intent. There's grey hair at his temples, and he has a confidence about him which is alluring and friendly. But then he *should* be confident, I think, as I shake his hand and say goodbye for now, trying not to enjoy the feel of his strong grip, and leave him with Penny. He's about to open his fifth hotel and health club. He can't be much more than forty and he's well on the way to building an empire.

I close Penny's office door behind him, leaving them to it. I can feel the heat in my skin and I know I'm glowing. I can't believe how well it went. He needs cleaning staff, catering staff and hotel staff and he's happy to let PKR — me — manage it all. If I'd known after my first approach how many people he was interested in taking on, I'd have gone straight to Penny to handle it; it's her company and this is a big deal, maybe one of the biggest contracts the company has ever had. I'm so glad I'd been oblivious. I'd been nervous enough thinking he was going to want maybe thirty workers, I'd have had a breakdown knowing the real figures. But it's done. And brilliantly. I can't keep the smile from my face as I emerge into their office chatter.

'Oh, I always try to walk to work and back wherever I am,' Julia, the new one with the brunette bob, is saying. 'Keeps me toned.'

'Go well?' Toby asks, looking up at me, the girls' conversation no longer interesting. I can see a glint of envy in his eyes. He's so desperate to get on and succeed. He likes the slick IT clients, the ones who want graphic designers or web developers on one-year contracts for fifty or sixty thousand pounds, and yes, they probably do give him bigger chunks of commission when he places someone, but those jobs don't come along every month. I've always liked the other end of the market. Helping people who really *want* a job, whatever it is. Those who need the sense of self-worth a weekly pay cheque brings in. I know how they feel. I felt it once.

'Better than well, in fact. Turns out it's going to be a pretty big contract. At least one hundred and fifty people.' I sound like I'm bragging — and I am, but I can't help it. Pride and falls spring to mind but I let myself have this small moment.

'Wow, well done!' It's one of the new girls. Stacey. Long blonde hair, acrylic nails. Her words could sound patronising but they don't. Under her veneer of make-up and tan, I can see she's nervous and desperately wants to be liked, to fit in, and get on with her job.

'Thank you.'

'Definitely drinks on you tonight.' Julia again.

'I won't be there, I'm afraid. I'm not much of a drinker and it's my daughter's sixteenth birthday. I'm taking her out.'

'That's nice,' she says. 'Normally at sixteen they only want to be with their friends, don't they? I certainly did.'

There's something sharp in the way she talks and I smart. She's a little cocky for someone on her first day.

I look more closely at her. She's not as young as I thought she was, however much she's trying to appear otherwise. She's over thirty definitely. Botox probably.

'We're very close.'

She smiles, sugar cubes dipped in cyanide, and shows perfect white teeth that are reminiscent of a shark. She makes me nervous and it annoys me.

'I'll never have kids,' she says. 'I'm too

career-focused. Couldn't do it as a single mum, either. Hats off to you.'

It's an insult wrapped in a compliment and Stacey's eyes widen at Julia's nerve, and Toby — obviously the one who's been talking about me — has the good sense to keep his gaze on his screen as if reading some hugely important email.

'Thankfully, Lisa is a superwoman who can manage everything and more. If only the rest of us were so capable.' Marilyn has appeared alongside me. Shark smile meets shark smile and this time Julia shrinks slightly in her seat. 'Lunch?' Marilyn finishes. The last is addressed to me as if the others aren't there; flies she's already swatted away.

'There's always one,' she mutters as we get our handbags and jackets. 'In any gaggle of women. There's always one you have to watch. At least we know which it is in this bunch.' She casts a dark glance back at Julia. *Why does there always have to be one?* I wonder. *Why can't things just be nice?*

★ ★ ★

'He's gorgeous, too.' Marilyn has our drinks, two glasses of Prosecco, and I'm clutching the cutlery as we grab a corner table. 'In a rugged kind of way. And it's so obvious he likes you. All those unnecessary meetings. The way he watched you walk when he followed you through the office.'

'Oh shut up,' I say.

'I don't see why you don't go for it.'

'Oh, can you imagine Penny's reaction? Mixing business and pleasure. And anyway — no.'

She watches me, thoughtful. My lack of a man comes up at least once a year in a *serious* way, and she peppers our conversations with it throughout the other months. I wonder if this is going to be another probing lecture. Thankfully, it's not. Instead, she holds her glass up. 'Cheers and congratulations!'

We clink and sip our bubbles. I like the way it fizzes in my mouth. I prefer to drink at lunchtimes because it's only ever one glass.

'Oh, before I forget' — she leans over and rummages in her oversized handbag — 'I've got something for Ava.' She pulls out a small wrapped gift. 'From me and Richard. God, I can't believe she's sixteen. Where have the years gone? If she's sixteen, how old are we?'

'Old,' I say, but I'm smiling as I drink some more.

I take the present and tuck it in my own bag. It's not only me who's lucky to have Marilyn. Ava is too.

I skipped breakfast because I was so nervous and although I've barely had half a glass, the wine is going to my head. The tension in my shoulders begins to unknot. Then I see Marilyn's face and I know what's coming. I was too quick to think she wasn't going to pry today.

'Nothing from Ava's dad?'

'No.' I bristle, though she's asking cautiously. Quietly. She knows how this goes. Another conversation that rolls around too often for my liking. 'And I'm not expecting anything either.' I need to change the subject. 'Anyway, how are *you*? You seemed a bit quiet yesterday. A bit off. All okay?'

'I had a headache. It was nothing. You know I get them sometimes.' She looks over at the waitress heading towards us with our food. Is she avoiding my gaze? It's not the first time she's had a headache in the past few months.

'Maybe you should go to a doctor.'

'And maybe you should go on a date with Mr Manning.'

I scowl at her.

'Okay, okay. I'm sorry. But Ava's nearly grown up. You need to get back out there.'

'Can't we forget this and concentrate instead on how brilliant I am?' I try to lighten the mood, and am relieved when the barmaid arrives with our sandwiches and chips, distracting us with food. How could I ever tell Marilyn anything? She knows it wasn't a one-night stand like the lie I told Ava, but she doesn't know the truth of it. The *whole* truth of it. She wouldn't understand. Marilyn of the charmed life, the great husband, the nice house, the good job — happy, lovely Marilyn. If I told her, it would change how she saw me. Don't get me wrong. I wish I could tell her. I've dreamed about telling her. Sometimes I find the words sitting right in my mouth, wanting to spill out, but I have to swallow them down like bile. I can't do it. I can't.

I know how words spread. They catch fire and pass from one person to another to another.

I can't risk being found.

24

5

AVA

The rain has almost stopped by the time we get home, but my coat is damp from getting caught in a downpour running to the car earlier and I stamp my feet quietly on the pavement feigning more cold than I feel to hide my impatience.

'We can watch a film if you like,' Mum says when she finally gets out. 'It's still early.'

'I've got to revise.' It's only seven and I'm not planning on going to sleep until at least midnight, but I want to get to the privacy of my bedroom. She looks disappointed, but she's the one who's always going on about my exams. It doesn't stop the squirm of guilt in my guts. We used to always have sofa blanket and movie nights sharing bowls of microwave popcorn. I used to love them. I *do* love them. But life is more complicated now. He's waiting. I *have* to talk to him. Sometimes I feel like I'll die if I don't.

'Oh flip,' Mum says suddenly, with a groan. 'I forgot to pick up Mrs Goldman's shopping. I'll have to pop down to the little Sainsbury's. Will you be okay on your own? I'll only be ten minutes? Or you can come with me.'

My irritation rises and I prefer it to the sad guilt of forcing cracks into our relationship.

Every time she goes out and leaves me she asks this. *Every time.* What does she think is going to happen? I'll stick my finger in a plug socket because she's not here? 'I'm sixteen,' I snap. 'You've got to stop going on at me like I'm a kid.'

'Sorry, sorry.' She's in too much of a rush to get offended and that suits me. I don't really want to upset her. I don't actually like upsetting her but she's becoming so *needy* now she can't control everything I do like when I was little. Our pizza hadn't been too terrible and I know she'd been trying to make it a fun time, but all her questions are so cloying and clingy and intrusive. She wants to know everything about me all the time and somehow now I can't tell her. I don't *want* to tell her. Whenever I think about talking to her about something — like Courtney and the sex thing — it all gets tied up on my tongue and I get moody instead. Everything is changing. I need my own space. Now more than ever.

But still, she gave me great birthday presents. An iPad mini and an underwater MP3 player, way more expensive than the one I wanted. I love the necklace Marilyn's given me too — thick silver coil with a dark purple glass centrepiece. It's chunky and cool and perfect for me. Sometimes I wish Mum was a bit more like Marilyn. She's relaxed and fun. If Mum was more easygoing maybe I *would* talk to her about stuff. Not everything, I think, as I try not to rush up the path to the house. But some stuff. I couldn't talk to her about *this*. She'd go crazy.

'Up for a chat tonight, Birthday Girl? I'll be around for an hour or so if you're not out having fun!' The Facebook message had come in when I'd checked my phone in the loo before the puddings arrived. I said I'd get home as soon as I could and to please wait. I hadn't realised how needy *I* sounded when I sent it, but it does sound a bit lamely desperate and that makes me worry I'm turning into my mum. But God, why can't people just install Messenger on their phones? Like everyone's data isn't already out there in one way or another? Anyone under twenty-five has made their peace with it. It's only adults who think anyone cares. What's the point of having a message service you only use from your computer?

A different kind of privacy.

The thought worms into my head. It's the kind of privacy you need when keeping secrets from those closest to you. A wife maybe? Whatever *his* reasons it's the kind of privacy that has made me turn off notifications.

We all have secrets.

I'm beginning to realise maybe secrets are great.

★ ★ ★

I'm trying not to be disappointed when I come downstairs for a drink twenty minutes later. Our chat was brief and all his replies were short. Distracted and not really answering my questions. I don't want to be upset — at least we had *some* time — but I guess I'm mainly frustrated.

27

Courtney is all over my WhatsApp *now*. But I know what he wants. Funny how he's pissing me off with it a bit. A few weeks ago I'd have been so happy to have him chasing me and making me feel pretty and sexy. Now, he's simply another irritation.

I'm quiet on the stairs in my socks and when I turn the corner to head to the kitchen, I stop. Mum's there. She's standing by the kitchen table, staring at nothing, and there's a stiffness to her that's all wrong. The whole thing looks weird and I'm not sure why, but my heart is racing and my stomach churns. After a moment she reaches into her bag for the small bottle of Prosecco Marilyn gave her, twists the lid off and drinks it straight from the bottle.

I freeze where I am, confused and alarmed. Is this my fault? Is this because I've been so shitty? I hover in the hallway, unsure of what to do. Do I ask her what's wrong? I feel small again. I go to take a step forward, but then hesitate. There's something about the way she's standing — the stillness — which makes me feel as if I'm watching something private. Something where I don't belong. Are the cracks in our relationship coming from her side too? Does she have secrets she's not sharing? I find it hard to believe. She's an open book, my mum.

It's unsettling though. Those little bottles only hold one glass or so, but who doesn't pour wine before drinking? What would make you drain it in basically one swallow? In the end, my stomach in knots, I creep back upstairs. I can live without a cup of tea.

6

LISA

It's pitch-dark outside, no hint of a comforting grainy dawn grey yet, but I sit, wide awake, with my knees up under my chin and stare out at the bleak night, my stomach in terrible knots. It wasn't Peter Rabbit. I know that. Peter Rabbit is long gone. It would be impossible for it to have been Peter Rabbit, *the* Peter Rabbit, but I want to run down to the recycle bins at the end of the road and root it out again to be sure. I take a deep breath. It's not Peter Rabbit. It's just a coincidence.

When I'd seen the soft toy out there in the rain, slumped dejected against Mrs Goldman's gate, my heart had almost stopped. It was grubby and sodden, dropped maybe hours before, but the bright blue trousers stood out against the greying white fur. It wasn't the same bunny, that was clear when I'd picked it up with trembling hands and a scream trapped in my throat, but it was close. *So* close. I wanted to hold it against my chest and wail, but the front door opened and Mrs Goldman appeared and instead I forced an air of idle curiosity as I asked if she knew whose it was. She didn't, of course. Why would she? Her hearing isn't great and her days are spent staring at the TV, not out of the window.

I gave her the bag of shopping and tried to smile and chat but the bunny was heavy and wet in my hand and the soft fur was cold, and all I could think was how the blue dungarees were exactly the same shade and style as *those* dungarees and *those* dungarees had been hand-made, and my head started to swim and I felt sick. Once Mrs Goldman had finally gone back inside, I forced a confident walk down the path and then, out of sight of both her house and mine, I finally held the toy close as if it were a dead animal my body heat could somehow bring back to life.

I took several deep breaths, years of therapy having drummed the technique into me as if steady oxygen could make anything better when most of the time I wished I didn't have to breathe any more at all, and walked swiftly to the big bank of recycling bins at the end of the road and threw it inside. I could still feel the ghost of damp fur against my fingertips though, and I wasn't sure my legs would carry me home without crumpling.

In the kitchen, for once grateful my daughter was finally becoming the kind of surly teenager who hides in her room, I grabbed the small bottle of Prosecco Marilyn had given me from my handbag and twisted the lid off, drinking it straight from the bottle in two goes. The acid bubbles made my chest burn and my eyes sting but I didn't care. Anything was better than the awful pain and fear at the core of me, in the place I try hard to pretend is at best empty now, until something like this happens and the scab is ripped away and all the terrible terrible hurt crammed inside is exposed once more and I want to curl up and die.

I gasped and choked as I swallowed the last of the wine, leaning on the breakfast bar and using the physical discomfort as a distraction to calm my thinking. Slowly the buzzing in my ears faded. It was a coincidence, it had to be. Lots of children have toy bunnies. Some poor toddler was probably crying for the one I'd so ruthlessly tossed away at the end of the street. So what if it was wearing blue dungarees? There were probably thousands of soft toys in dungarees. It *wasn't* Peter Rabbit.

I repeated that one sentence over and over in my head, glad I'd thrown the bunny away in the communal bins rather than the ones in our garden, too far to keep running to look at it without drawing attention to myself. It *wasn't* Peter Rabbit. Yes, it had upset me, but it hadn't been put there on purpose. It was harder to reconcile myself with the second sentence. It isn't a statement of fact. It's highly unlikely it's been put there on purpose, but I can't for definite know it in the way my sensible brain *knows* the toy I found wasn't Peter Rabbit.

It's this *unease* I've felt recently. The sense something isn't quite right. What if it's more than my usual paranoia? What if I'm wrong to steer away from it? I get up and creep down the corridor to Ava's room. The lights are all off and the house is silent and I twist the handle as carefully and slowly as I can, not wanting to make any noise.

I watch her from the doorway, my perfect girl. She's on her side, facing away from me, curled up small, exactly how she slept as a toddler. She is so precious. So wonderful, and looking at her calms me and reminds me that I have to stay alive, I have to keep breathing. For *her*. She gave me back my desire to live, and I will always protect her. She will never know what I keep inside. Not if I can help it. I want her to be blissfully free. It must be a wonderful thing to be blissfully free.

I stay for a few minutes more, the sight of Ava far better for me than any amount of deep yoga breathing, and then reluctantly leave her to sleep in private. It's nearly three a.m. Taking sleeping pills now is a bad idea, but so is facing the day with no rest at all, and so I compromise and only swallow one instead of the usual two I need when these fearful, sad moods have me gripped tight. I'll feel terrible all morning tomorrow but at the moment two or three hours of oblivion is what I need. I *can't* keep going round in circles of fear and grief. I'll go mad by dawn if I do, I'm sure of it. The bad feeling is only my anxiety. The bunny wasn't Peter Rabbit. The words bang at my skull, trying to knock sense into me as I crawl back under my covers.

I want oblivion, but instead I dream. It's *the* dream, in glorious, vivid technicolour, and while I'm there, it's wonderful.

In the dream, I'm holding Daniel's hand. It's soft and small and warm and his fingers grip tight in the way toddlers do as he looks up at me and smiles. My heart bursts in rainbow showers of joy and I bend over to kiss him. His chubby cheeks are all smooth, creamy skin, tinged pink from the outside air, and he giggles in surprise as my lips smack loudly against his face, but his eyes are lit up by love. His eyes are like mine, blue flecked with grey and green and in them I can see how I am his *everything*.

Peter Rabbit is in his other hand, and he holds him maybe even more tightly than he holds on to me. He cannot imagine me not being there, but he's had some near misses with Peter Rabbit. Once left on a bus but remembered in the nick of time. Another time, on a counter in the corner shop. Daniel has the fear that Peter Rabbit might one day *not be there* and the thought alone is enough to make him cry. He's two and a half years old and Peter Rabbit is his best friend.

I feel something tapping against my subconscious, a dark truth which won't be ignored, not even in a dream — *It is not Peter Rabbit who will one day not be there. This little hand in mine will be cold and still and will never reach for me again* — but I push it away and take Daniel to the small park with the tatty swings and roundabouts where the paint is so chipped the rust from the metal below stains clothes on a damp day, but he squeals with joy at the sight of it. He's two and a half and he doesn't see rust and decay and something unloved. He only sees the good things. He *is* the good thing.

His hand is out of mine and he and Peter Rabbit run to the swings. I run after him, staying slightly behind because I love watching the way Daniel's small body moves, so cute and clumsy, bound up in the constraints of his coat. He looks over his shoulder at me and I want to hold this picture of sweetness forever to remember when he is grown into a boy and then a man and this *everything* I am is gone.

It is a perfect dream. An afternoon in the park. The love is overwhelming. It's pure. It's so strong it almost suffocates me, bubbling out through my pores there's so much of it. It's unrestrained. No barriers are up around it. There is nothing wicked in the world in that moment and I think, if I let the love take me, I shall transform into a pure beam of light shining on Daniel.

I wake up, gasping painful breaths into my pillow and clutching at fragments of fading images, hoping in vain to grasp one and follow it back and hold his small hand forever. It's always the same after the dream. It hurts so much I want to die, the aching need to go back and *save* him. I try to think of Ava, my perfect girl, the child who came *after*, oblivious, free and wonderful and untarnished by the world. She is here and alive and I love her with all of what's left of my heart.

Perhaps my love for Ava makes it all worse, if it's at all possible. I think of the bunny rabbit in the bin. It is *not* Peter Rabbit. I know that. I know where Peter Rabbit is.

Peter Rabbit was buried with Daniel.

7

AVA

I'm not sure exactly what's in the punch but it's some crazy mix of shit. Fruit juice, lemonade, the vodka Ange brought and a bottle of Bacardi Jodie added from her mum's booze cupboard. Jodie reckons her mum won't miss it, but I'm not so sure. There was a fierce look on Jodie's face when she poured it all in that made me think her mum would *definitely* notice when she gets back from France. Like Jodie wanted to get in some shit. So weird, how our mums are such opposites. Jodie's is never here and mine is becoming way too clingy. Weird mums club, is what we call it. We haven't told the others. They wouldn't understand.

My head buzzes. We had cider in the pub earlier and this is my second glass of punch. I'm well on my way to getting wasted, which is probably the best way for doing it. *Losing it.*

I lean back on the bed, half-lying down, my head resting against the wall. My mum would lose it if she could see me now, on my friend's bed with my sort-of boyfriend. She's already texted once to check we're all at the house. I've put my phone on silent. Imagine if she texted right in the middle? At least she's gone out tonight. She doesn't go out much which makes me feel more guilty about wanting my own life, but I've been stretching the umbilical cord for the past year or so and I want it to snap, even though I can feel her constantly trying to pull me back.

I'm still a bit freaked out by the other night. The weird drinking in the kitchen thing was bad enough, but then she came into my room in the middle of the night and watched me while I pretended to sleep. Why would she do that? It's made me uncomfortable, as if the world is suddenly unsteady.

I take a long swallow of my punch as, down the corridor, the toilet flushes. My heart speeds up a little. Fuck. I'm actually going to fuck. For a moment, I have a totally irrational longing for my mum. It makes me drink some more. She's the *last* person I need. I'm not a kid any more. I'm a woman. *He* always says so.

'You all right?' Courtney asks, as he comes back into Jodie's spare bedroom and starts fiddling with his phone to play some tunes. I smile at him, nod, and drink some more. It's too sweet but I don't care. I want to get smashed, and the booze and lack of food is obliging. I wonder if he's nervous. Probably not. If all the stories are true, Courtney's done it loads.

I'm not as anxious as I thought I would be. It's been a busy day, I'm tired, and I could happily curl up and go to sleep. I started at the gym early this morning, and then, once my legs and shoulders were trembling and aching, I forced myself to swim for an hour. I'd met Ange at ten so she could buy something new to wear. Something skin-tight, obviously. Angela's been served in pubs since she was about twelve. With her tits and all dressed up Angela often looks older than Jodie.

Courtney's mouth is hot and wet on my neck and his hand slides on to my hip. This is it. I feel detached, here but not here. My body's in the moment, but my mind isn't, like I'm watching us from above and thinking, *just get on with it*. I can hear my breath getting heavier, although I'm not really turned on. It's a mechanical reaction. Being with Courtney means I can't help thinking about *him*. I've heard nothing today. He said he was going to be busy, but surely everyone has time to send one little 'hello'? Something so I'd know he was thinking about me.

Courtney's mouth meets mine and I obligingly part my lips and let our tongues explore each other. He's a good kisser compared with most of the other boys I've been out with, but tonight it feels like an invasion.

Why hasn't he messaged me?

He's grinding hard against my thigh. I have to do it. I haven't got a choice — everyone's expecting it. They'll be laughing and chatting and dancing downstairs, but inside they're all wondering if we've done it yet. Is it going to hurt? Am I going to be different *after*?

I'd thought about backing out somehow, but then that woman in the pub knocked my bag off the table and sent all my stuff flying everywhere. The girls saw the condoms and Ange went all weird American for a while. Once the laughter

37

and teasing had died down, she said black boys don't use condoms, and we'd all called her a racist, but she insisted it was true before Lizzie said it wasn't only black boys, it was all boys if they could get away with it, which is why she's on the pill. I laughed with them, but Jodie must have seen how uncomfortable I was feeling because when we went to the loo she whispered that there are only a couple of days in the month you can get pregnant in anyway and so not to worry.

'You okay with this?' Courtney's got my bra hitched up over my boobs and his eyes look all funny and the words are breathless. *Needy*.

I nod, even though I am *not* all right with this any more. He's already pushing my skirt up. Everything's clumsy. Not like it was when I imagined it.

What would he think if he knew what I was about to do? Would he be jealous?

The condom is still in my bag on the other side of the room. A continent away. How am I supposed to mention it? I should have said about it before. His jeans are undone and yanked down and he grabs my hand and pushes it into his crotch. He groans as I touch him, and his shaking hands yank at my knickers but we get caught up in a tangle and our teeth clash together. I take control and there's a pause as I wriggle my pants off, and as I do, he looks at me properly.

'You know I really like you, don't you?' he says. 'I've never gone out with a girl like you before.'

It makes me feel slightly better about all this, and so I take the moment to tug my top off too. He might not be naked, but I am. If I'm doing this, I'm not doing it being half choked by my own bra.

'You're beautiful.'

This time when he kisses me, I try to be in the moment even though beautiful is *his* word, not Courtney's. Courtney normally calls me *hot* despite the fact I know I'm not. Not really. I think of the condom again but it's too late to mention it now. He's poking and prodding and nudging, trying to get it *in*, and I realise that maybe he's not quite so experienced at this either.

And then we're doing it. Or rather, Courtney's doing it. I'm just lying here and trying not to think about how different it would be with *him*.

8

LISA

'Hey, everyone! Smile!' It's Emily, face glowing, a mobile phone held up in the air over us. I turn away automatically, one hand flying up across my face. 'No photos,' I say.

'It was only for Facebook.' Emily sounds hurt. 'So my boyfriend and family can see who I work with.' She's very sweet but very young.

'I don't want photos of me on your Facebook either,' Julia says. Her voice is sharp, a cutting blade that takes no prisoners. She's late, arriving only moments ago, and I wonder if she's irritated because she looks hot and bothered rather than her usual cool self, but I'm still surprised — and relieved — by her interjection. Marilyn knows I hate having my picture taken, but this time I've been saved from having to explain myself to new people. Maybe Julia and I have something in common after all. 'And anyway,' she continues, 'it's hardly professional, taking selfies at a work do. This isn't some cheesy club.'

'More of a celebration than a work do,' Marilyn cuts in, seeing how stung Emily is. The poor girl looks like she might cry. 'But you may have a point. Not everything in life has to Facebooked and Instagrammed.'

She's saying all this as much for my benefit as anything else. I don't have any social media accounts even though Marilyn swears you can set your profile to completely private. I still wouldn't trust it, and who would I have on there? Only Marilyn probably, and I see her most days as it is. 'Oh shit, I sound old.' She groans over-dramatically, lifting the mood as only she can. 'Come on, Lisa, let's grab us all another wine before the money behind the bar runs out.'

We separate from the others, leaving Toby to continue his obvious hot pursuit of Stacey, and make our way to the bar. I didn't want to come tonight. No matter how much I've tried to shake it, my stomach has been a river bed of slithering eels since finding the rabbit, and the past clings like an oil slick on feathers, breaking my heart all over again. It's taken everything I have not to spend my time following Ava around to make sure she's safe, which I've worked really hard at not doing now she has more freedom. Trying to hide how I'm feeling is exhausting and if there was any way. I could have got out of coming to the party, I would have, but there was no way I'd have got away with it. This is Penny's once-a-year company and clients drinks and nibbles, and with the new staff, the second branch opening, and my new contract, she wouldn't have been happy.

In that respect, Julia was right. We may be in a salsa club, but this isn't a girls' night out. It's still, in some ways, work. However, as I lean on the bar next to Marilyn, I'm surprised to find I'm feeling better for coming out. The music is full of life and the words are foreign so I can't get snared by lyrics of love or loss.

'God, I could use a tequila shot,' Marilyn says, and I laugh although I'm a bit surprised. Marilyn drinks more than me — but everyone does. I know what too much alcohol can do to people and none of it is good. I can't stay alert when I'm drunk and I have Ava to protect. Still, Marilyn's not a *drinker drinker*. I can't remember the last time she did shots. Her eyes shine a little too bright. How many wines has she had?

'You okay?' I ask. She doesn't answer.

'Well, well, well,' she says, as she looks at something over my shoulder. 'Look who's showed up. Mr Millionaire himself.'

I glance back. Simon Manning is standing in the doorway, dressed down in dark jeans and a V-neck T-shirt. My wine glass is suddenly too big and slippery in my hand and it feels like the party pauses for a moment. It's rare for major clients to come to these things. Penny always invites them but it's mainly staff who turn up — now two branches' worth — and some of our longest-serving temps. Penny does a separate private dinner for the top-level clients.

The room is quite dark and he probably doesn't realise he's 'making an entrance' as he stands there, backlit, and peers around trying to recognise anyone. Finally he moves. My breath catches.

'What a surprise,' Marilyn drawls. 'He's coming this way.'

I look behind me, expecting to see Penny

42

nearby, but she's over by the side tables where Julia is talking to James from the new office.

'Lisa.'

I have no choice but to look at him. He's standing close, barely a foot away, and my nerves jangle and I feel awkward as his aftershave and body heat fill the gap between us. I'm no aftershave connoisseur, but he smells good. Fresh and citrussy, but not overpowering. I hate myself for noticing.

'Hello, Simon.' She reaches forward and shakes his hand, as ever saving the day for me as I flounder. I take the moment to try and gather myself. I need to stop behaving like a stupid teenager. 'Welcome aboard, I hear.'

I wish I found it as easy to talk to people. Marilyn is so confident. Friendly without being flirtatious. An open book. I *can't* be like that. I don't think I've ever been like that.

'Well, Lisa sold the company so well I couldn't say no,' he says. They're both looking at me, expectant. I can't stay silent forever. Where is Penny?

'I'll be sending some more figures over to you on Monday.' It's all I can think of and sounds so bland even I'm cringing.

'It's Saturday night.' He takes the glass of wine Marilyn has somehow spirited out of thin air. 'Let's forget about work. Can you salsa? I'm terrible but willing to give it a go if you are.'

My feet are suddenly glued to the floor. There are a few people taking advantage of the expert on hand on the dance floor, but not many. Not enough to stop us being the centre of attention if we joined them. My mouth opens and closes silently as I panic, a drowning fish, trying to find a way to say no which won't sound rude, although a part of me thinks it would be fun to let myself go to the music if I was a different person. If I was Marilyn maybe, or Stacey, or Julia. But I'm not. I'm me, and I don't want him to want to dance with me. And yet, even as I think it, I know it's a lie. I hate the snake in my belly that wants all of life's excitements.

'Simon!' Here she is, Penny, breezing through us. I could cry with relief as I take a step backwards, giving her space. 'How wonderful of you to come!'

Marilyn smiles and gives him a shrug, pupils as the teacher arrives, but I'm already walking away on shaking legs.

'Told you he likes you,' Marilyn says as she catches me tip.

'Leave it alone.' My words come out with more bite than intended and she doesn't follow me when I go to the table at the rear of the room where we left our things, but instead goes to join Eleanor who used to sit opposite us before she went to the new branch.

I should apologise. I don't though. I want to text Ava. To check she's okay. I want to stay here, hiding at the back in the dark. I want the earth to open up and swallow me whole. To bury me in the cold and damp. To be with Daniel and Peter Rabbit in the ground.

I sit down before my legs give way, and I take deep breaths. I can't keep texting Ava. I've already sent three. I have to let her be free and be young. I *have* to. But it's so hard. Exhausted as I am by my fear, it refuses to leave me.

While breathing slowly, I focus on the present. Marilyn and Eleanor are laughing about something. Toby has dragged Stacey on to the dance floor. They're both good dancers, but she's keeping a distance between their bodies and I feel a wave of something close to maternal pride. She may not be the brightest bulb in the pack, but she knows better than to be a notch in his bedpost.

I grow calmer, knowing I'm lost in the shadows. No one is seeking me out. I can't see Penny and Simon from here, but I know she'll be attached to him for the rest of the evening. I push away the memory of his body heat and aftershave, intent as it is on clinging to me.

A glint of metal distracts me to my right. Someone crouching down by the tables along the side. Julia? Yes. Rummaging in her bag. Lines tighten across my forehead, my instinct for *wrongness* kicking in. That's not her bag. It's Penny's. The Dolce & Gabbana gold clasp is flashing as lights from the dance floor catch it. Julia's bag is smaller, barely big enough for a wallet, phone, keys, perhaps some lipstick. Not an expensively practical middle-aged woman's bag. I can't remember how I know this, but I do. I always take in the details of a person. My brain is trained that way.

Definitely Penny's bag.

I can't see what Julia's doing and so I work my way round the edge of the room until I'm closer. She gets up and glances around, unaware I'm watching her, before striding confidently to the bar. I follow, moving faster to catch up, and when I'm only a few feet behind I see the crumpled twenty-pound note in her hand. My heart thumps, banging a truth into me. *Money stolen from Penny's purse.* It can't be. Surely not. I want to doubt the instinct I have for both detail and trouble. I don't want to know this rotten-apple worm of fact which will squirm inside me every day at work. But if it's Julia's own money, why has she taken it out of her purse already? She's got her little bag with her — with her own wallet in it — so why is she holding a twenty-pound note?

Penny and Simon are still talking at the bar and although he's smiling at her and laughing, his eyes move away from hers as I come into his sightline. I don't so much as glance his way. I have no time for him right now. I'm absorbed in Julia's confidence as she flashes the barman a smile and orders a bottle of Pinot Grigio.

'It's for the lady over there,' she says, pointing out Penny. 'Can you tell her it's a thank you for the great job opportunity? From Julia? I don't want to interrupt them.'

I'm standing beside her and she notices me watching but doesn't offer to buy me anything. She can't anyway. The wine she's chosen is exactly twenty pounds.

'Diet Coke,' I mutter to the barman as Julia moves away, joining Marilyn and Eleanor near the dance floor, far enough away for Penny to have to seek her out and thank her, and also, perhaps more importantly, on the other side of the room from the Dolce & Gabbana handbag she was so recently digging around in. I watch her insert herself as if they've invited her to join them and I don't know what to do. I should say something to Penny. But what? I *think* Julia stole your own money to buy you a drink? It's dark. I wasn't that close. It's a big accusation to make.

Penny leaves the bar and rushes over to gush a thank you at Julia, who does a fine impression of embarrassment. She's not fooling me though. If she didn't want a fuss, she wouldn't have given a thank you gift in such a public place. I'm an expert in not wanting to be fussed over. I wouldn't have given a gift at all. If I say something, will people think I'm somehow jealous of the new girl? Julia *shines*. I don't. Maybe I didn't see it right anyway. Maybe I'm making a wild assumption. I feel sick.

Over to my right, Simon Manning half waves at me, but I'm saved by Marilyn, who's fled Eleanor now Julia's there. 'God, butter wouldn't melt,' she says. Marilyn's not fooled by her either.

'Sorry I snapped. About Simon.' Ava may be my heart, but Marilyn is my rock. I should tell her what I think I saw. No, not what I think. What I *saw*. She wouldn't doubt me and she'd be able to handle it much better than I can. I've had two glasses of wine, and I'm feeling braver than normal. But still I can't bring myself to speak. Marilyn would *act* on it and then there would be confrontation and who knows where that would lead? Julia is trouble. I can sense it.

Thankfully, Marilyn is staring down at the

bright screen of her phone. 'I didn't realise the time,' she says. 'Richard's outside, if you want a lift home.'

My instant relief is almost overwhelming. 'Yes, please. I'm done. Let's sneak out. I can't be bothered to do the circuit of goodbyes.' I'm trying not to sound too eager, but I want to get out of here, away from Simon Manning and Julia and the noise of it all.

'Sounds good to me,' she agrees.

I don't fully relax until I'm strapped into the back of Richard's Saab.

'Good night, ladies?' he asks.

'Yes, thank you,' I say.

'It was all right.' Marilyn is less enthusiastic. 'The music was too loud, and you know, work people.' She rolls her eyes and he smiles.

'Present company excepted, I hope,' I say, and we all laugh a little in the polite way people do with a predictable joke. I stare out at the night as we drive away, zoning out Richard's questions as the two of them chat. It's nice to be in their company. Money. Julia. Penny. I don't want to think about any of it.

When I get home, my resolve breaks and I send Ava one last text.

I'm home from my party but I'm sure your sleepover is still going strong! Give my love to the girls and I'll see you tomorrow xx.

Even as I send it I know how passively needy it is under the chirpiness and wish I could call it back. I doubt the other mothers text nearly as

48

much as I do. But they're not me. They haven't had my life. When the handset immediately pings I'm so sure it's going to be Ava snapping at me — *but at least I'll know she's safe* — that it takes a moment to register I'm staring at an unknown number. I feel sick. The bunny rabbit. A strange number. The past tumbles towards me, and I tremble as I click to open it.

Hey, Lisa, it's Simon. I know this is wholly inappropriate and I can always pretend it's about work, but I wondered if you'd like to have dinner with me next week? Anyway, no need to reply straight away. Think about it. (before you say yes;-)). Enjoy the rest of your weekend. Sx

My emotions have raced from anxiety to calm to anxiety again and I don't know quite how to process this. The memory of warm citrus scent fills my head.

No. I can't. I can't let a man in again. I can't.

I delete the text and climb the stairs in the dark.

9

MARILYN

We wait, as we always do, until Lisa is through the front door, give her one last wave goodnight, before Richard pulls away.

'Sorry if we kept you hanging about,' I say. 'I didn't realise the time.'

'It was that good a night?'

'Ha, no.' I look at him, a comedy bored expression on my face. 'A Penny company night out. You can imagine. All work talk and pretending to be enjoying myself. I'd rather have been at home. I almost called you to come early, but I didn't want to make Lisa feel she had to leave too.' I'm over-explaining, despite my attempt at humour. Richard has always worked for himself. He doesn't understand the whole office politics thing, no matter how many years I've had this job. He thinks it's all some social whirl all day.

'Isn't it Lisa's birthday soon?' he asks, his eyes on the road. 'The big four-o?'

'A couple of months I think.'

'We should do something for her. Organise a party. You could ask all the people at work along. Any other friends she has.'

I stiffen. Invite work into my home life? I can

think of nothing worse. 'She's not a party person.' Outside, the night flashes by. Where would we have it? Somewhere expensive? Somewhere to show off at? Regardless of everything else that screams at me this is a bad idea, we can't afford to host a party.

'Maybe not, but she's changed over the years. She's not the little shy mouse she was when you first started working together.'

He's right, she isn't. It's still there sometimes, the unsettled edge which used to come off her like electricity, but it's not an everyday thing. She walks with her shoulders back now and laughs easily. I became friends with her at first because I felt a bit sorry for her, not that I'd ever tell her so, but then I saw the person behind the shyness, wry, clever and kind, and things changed. Best friends. We're there for each other. I love her. It's as simple as that and I love her new confidence. It's part of why I keep my secret from her. She doesn't need any more shit in her life. I figure she's had enough in her past one way or another. Plus, if I tell, I have to admit it to myself. I can't face that.

'We've all changed,' I say, the words heavy, and as he glances across at me, I add, 'It's been ten years. My thighs have *definitely* changed.'

'Your thighs are gorgeous.' He looks back at the road. 'But she'll only be forty once and she doesn't have anyone else to organise something for her. Ava won't do it. She can't arrange her own fortieth birthday and we're her best friends.'

The thought is sweet, sometimes he is so very sweet, and my words come out too fast, my

51

tongue loose after one glass of wine too many. 'She may have a boyfriend to celebrate with by then.'

'Oh?' Now he's looking at me properly, the road ahead empty of cars. 'Come on. Spill.' He smiles, white teeth in the darkness.

I fluster. I shouldn't have said anything. This isn't his business. This isn't my business. Lisa would hate me talking about it. 'Oh, it's nothing really. Just someone at work.'

'There's a hot new man in the office? You didn't say.'

The seat feels warm under me. 'He's not staff. He's a client of hers. He owns a hotel chain or something.' I sound disinterested. Maybe *too* disinterested. It's hard to get the balance right. 'He's opening a new one in town.'

'A hot new boyfriend for Lisa? Sounds great. She's been single too long. About time she got back out there.'

'He's not good-looking.' Houses go by outside, lights still on in some, and I wonder at the lives inside, all the truths people hide behind those walls. Private lives. 'But they like each other.'

They *do* like each other, however defensive Lisa might have been tonight. That was just nerves and embarrassment because she doesn't know how to handle it. I wish I could tell her to relax. She deserves some happiness. Some fun at least. It's been lovely to see her in the delicate dance around each other that comes at the beginning of something. The glow she has after their meetings, the endless meetings no client needs to have so many of, the smiling she doesn't know she's doing. I'm full of joy for her. Simon has the potential for a *happy ever after.*

'Maybe we should go out for dinner with them,' Richard says, as he pulls into the drive. 'There could be some work in it for me.'

'That would be nice,' I answer. I've got no intention of setting up a foursome dinner with Lisa and Simon. They haven't had a date yet, and Richard would push for work, I know he would, and then Simon would either offer him something out of pity or have to awkwardly ignore all the hints. Either way, it would be terrible.

'But let's see if they actually go out together first, okay?'

'Okay. It's sweet how you look after her.' He kisses me on the forehead before unlocking the front door.

I watch Richard go inside before following, taking one last breath of clean night air. So many times I've been tempted to tell Lisa what's going on, and I'm glad I haven't. She needs hope. She's had something bad happen in her past, that much is clear even if she closes down when I ask her about it. I can't burden her with my problems. And maybe it will get better. Maybe it will go back to how it was at the beginning. We all need hope, me included.

Richard says nothing more about it until we're getting ready for bed. I'm taking my make-up off, suddenly tired, when I see him looking at me in my reflection in the mirror.

'What?' I ask, a smear of cold cream across my cheeks.

'What did you mean when you said he wasn't good-looking?'

And so it begins.

10

AVA

I'm glad Courtney didn't stay over. I just wanted to wash him out of me. It's not him I think about all the time. The first thing I did *after* was check my phone for a Facebook message but there was nothing. I wanted to cry.

By the time we came downstairs, everyone was drunk and Ange was snogging Darryl in the kitchen, but after ten minutes or so, Jodie told the boys it was time to go. It felt clinical. *Done what you came here for, now fuck off.* I didn't argue. It suited me when they left although after that came the interrogation as the girls wanted all the details. *Did it sting? It stung me the first time. Did he get it in okay? Oh my God, how big? How was he after?* I'd tried to stay excited about it but I felt hollow and sad. My first time shouldn't have been like that. So nothingy. There wasn't even any blood on the bed.

This morning it all feels like something that maybe happened in a dream, but the slightly dull ache between my thighs reminds me it was real. Can I dump him now? No. I'd look like such a tramp, and he'd be upset and who knows what he'd do, what he'd say or tweet or whatever. Call me fat and ugly and all that shit. I remember all the Snapchat crap that happened with Meg in Year Ten when she'd sent Christian pictures of her tits. At least I was never that stupid with Courtney. Anyway, I do like him. I don't want to hurt his feelings. It's all a mess.

I lean against the door frame as I puff on the cigarette. We don't smoke much or often — it's shit for our lung capacity — but there are times. And this is one of them. Jodie's mum, Amelia, apparently smokes occasionally and Jodie found the packet last night, after which Lizzie insisted we smoked to celebrate the death of virginity and one more girl being safe from vampires in the night. Weird punch and a cigarette. What a way to celebrate. I'd spent most of the time going to the loo — *I think he's burst my bladder with his big cock* — to check my messages, and coming out with a big fake grin on my face to cover my disappointment at my empty inbox.

The tobacco tastes horrible now I'm sober, and I don't inhale. Only Jodie and Lizzie inhale. Does he smoke? I haven't asked him. I mentally add it to the list of things I want to know about him. If he ever messages me again. Was he having sex last night? Was he thinking about me?

'I'll have to shower before I go,' I say, as a breeze blows my smoke back at me. 'If my mum smells this on me, she'll go apeshit.'

'Tell her my mum was here and smoking.'

'It's not worth the hassle. You know what she's like. She forgets I'm growing up sometimes.'

The others have gone. Ange had to get home for some family lunch and Lizzie's mum collected her half an hour ago. She'd offered me a lift too, but I can't face my mum yet. She'll want to talk, for me to tell her all about my night, and I'm going to have to come up with something to placate her or just storm up to my bedroom and hide under my duvet, which is what I really want to do. She makes me moody and then my being moody hurts her feelings. Anyway, it's not ten thirty yet. If Angela hadn't had to get up, we'd all be lounging in bed.

'Did she never smoke?' Jodie asks.

'Nope. She doesn't drink much either. And she was probably a total loser when she was my age.' It feels disloyal but it makes me sound cooler when really I'm the mouse of our group — the most *ordinary* one. Maybe that's what bothers me. Maybe me and Mum are too alike. Both boringly average.

'At least she's there for you.' Jodie doesn't look at me, but stares out into the garden before throwing her butt down on the path. She nods at me to do the same. 'I'll clean up later.'

She makes us huge cups of milky coffee and we go into the lounge, slouching into the furniture. Her home is like a show house — beautiful but impersonal. It never fails to surprise me.

'I don't know why we moved here,' Jodie says, curling her small frame up in the armchair. 'It wasn't so bad in our old house, but now she's always in Paris. She comes home once a month for a night if I'm lucky, and I'm sure that's just to check I haven't wrecked anything. She needn't have bought a house at all.'

It sounds like heaven to me, but then I see

Jodie's face and realise maybe it's not as good as I imagine.

Jodie shrugs. 'You know I've never met her new man?' She pauses. 'She used to at least be home at weekends, but now she doesn't even bother with those. Got to stay in France to see him apparently. God forbid she should want to see me. It's not as if I even really want her here, but I want her to *want* to, if you know what I mean.'

It's only me Jodie opens up to like this. We've splintered from the others a bit. She's older and recently I feel older too. Because of him.

'But then she's always been weird,' she continues. 'Like I'm not really here. Not a real person. A pet maybe. She makes sure I have everything I need, but that's it. I can't say I know very much about her at all. She had me really young, did I tell you that? I didn't live with her for years. Until I was about eight. She paid some people to look after me, how wrong is that? She was off travelling or working or both.'

'How often do you see your dad?' I know her dad's not around but that's it. Swimming, clothes, music, sex, bitching, booze, those are the things we four, the Fabulous Four, talk about most.

'I don't,' she says. 'He left when I was born. My mum gave me a photo once to show me what he looked like, but you know what, I'm not even sure it was him.'

We've been getting closer over the weeks but suddenly I feel a surge of proper unity with her. As if foundations are being set underneath us.

58

This is something the others can't be part of.

'I don't care who my dad is,' I say. 'I totally honestly don't.' I pause. 'A while back someone at school said maybe my dad was a rapist. You know, like he raped my mum and she didn't abort me? And that's why she's never had a boyfriend or anything.'

'Wow.' Her eyes have widened. 'That's some messed-up shit.'

'Yeah. I mean, I don't believe it, but it's the only time I've ever cared about who he was. The rest, well. It's hard to miss a ghost. I don't even have a photograph.'

'Did you tell your mum about the rapist thing?'

'Yeah. She was horrified. She was fussing around me, reassuring me.' I laugh. 'How fucked up is it to be reassured that your dad is just some bloke your mum shagged round the back of a pub after drinking too much.'

I see her face.

'I'm exaggerating. It wasn't round the back of a pub, but she says it was a drunken one-night stand.'

'At least she can't have a go at you for anything to do with sex.'

I laugh again, but I'm thinking of last night. My first sex. The only sex I've had. Shit sex. I can't imagine having any one-night stands. 'I haven't told her about Courtney yet.'

'Are you guys a proper thing now?'

I stare down at my cooling coffee. 'He wants it to be. I'm not so sure.'

'I thought you were crazy about him. Was it

the sex? First time's always bad, so don't judge him on it. Unless it was you who was shit.'

I half-heartedly throw a cushion at her. 'Shut up. It's not that. It's complicated.'

'Someone else?'

She sits up straighter, curious, and I know I should have lied and said everything was fine. I need to shut this down. 'Maybe.' Everything I say is potentially making it worse. I wish I hadn't opened my mouth. If Jodie tells Ange I'm interested in someone, she's going to presume it's someone at school and be on my case all the time to know who. I'll have to make someone up. Pick some boy at random. I can't think of anyone I fancy in Year Thirteen. 'But it's only a crush.' My face is flushing with worry. 'It's not going to *be* anything.'

'Don't worry. I won't say anything to Ange,' Jodie says, reading my mind. 'I love her, but she's got a big gob and I wouldn't want her knowing my secrets, if I had any.'

'Or the others?' I ask. 'I don't want it to be a thing. I'm sure me and Courtney will be fine.'

'I swear,' she says. 'Your secret's safe. But if anything happens, you have to tell me first. Deal?'

'Deal.'

For a moment I'm tempted to tell her everything. To tell her what's really turned me off Courtney. The friend request. The messages. Everything about *him*. But suddenly, she's up on her feet and saying I should grab the spare room shower and she'll use her en-suite, and then we should go.

* * *

'Shit,' I say when we get back to mine and I'm rummaging in my bag. 'I've lost my keys.'

'Check the car floor,' Jodie leans over. 'I always find stuff down there.'

I scrabble around under the seat, but they're not there. My house key, swim-locker key and school-locker key, all on a key ring with a pair of big red Mick Jagger lips. Gone.

'Nope. Fuck it. Where can they be?'

Jodie roots around but comes up empty-handed, and then it dawns on me. 'That dumb bitch in the pub who knocked my bag over.'

'What about her?'

'I don't remember picking my keys up.'

'You must have.' She looks in my bag as if maybe my eyes aren't working properly. 'She was helping pick stuff up. Maybe she put them in a side pocket.'

I let her look, but I've already searched everything.

'Your mum's in though, right?' she says.

'Yeah, but I'll take the spare from down the side. She'll want to change the locks if she thinks I've lost mine, even though there's no address or anything on them. You know what she's like.'

'You don't have to explain your mum to me, remember. The weird mums club, that's us.'

I grin and I want to say a thousand things to her but I think they'll all make me sound lame, so instead I say, 'I hear ya, sister,' and climb out of the car. 'See you at training on Monday. But text me, bitch.'

'Happy revising!' she calls out, and I groan. Three exams this week, and I can't find a shit to give about any of them.

She toots her horn as she pulls away, and I hurry down to the side gate and lift the loose brick on the wall, peeling away the taped key underneath. I know Mum will have heard the car. She'll be waiting for me.

11

LISA

It's pouring summer rain, but it's so good to be driving Ava to school again. This used to be our everyday routine until Year Ten, when it became cooler to get the bus. It's wonderful that my daughter is so independent and busy, but I still have a sneaky delight when she needs a lift, even though the journey takes me the wrong way to work through rush-hour traffic.

There's no swim training this morning — and I'm glad because Ava has two exams today — and in this weather a ride with Mum is definitely preferable to waiting for the bus. For all her sportiness, Ava has never liked bad weather. She feels the cold too much, and now there's the added worry of how it will affect the way she looks. They make me smile a little, these worries of her youth. I like how she's preoccupied by such things, because it means her life is relatively carefree. I've done a good job in that regard. I don't pride myself on much, but I do think I am, in my own way, a good mother.

The radio is on at my usual station. It's the local one which tends to play more music from the eighties and nineties but Ava doesn't complain. She's head down over her phone, texting or whatever it is they do to talk to each other.

'Everything okay?' I ask as her fingers fly over the keyboard. I keep my tone light. It's dangerous ground, showing any interest in Ava's life these days. In the wrong mood — and those come more frequently recently — she can bite my head off. I know it's normal. I've seen enough TV shows with surly kids in them to know I've had a good run before we got here, but it still stings when it happens.

'Yeah. Last-minute nerves and stuff.' She glances up at me. 'Is it okay if the girls come round after my afternoon exam?'

I almost say no, there's still a week or so of GCSEs left, but after two papers today she'll probably need to relax. I've studied her exam schedule and she only has revision sessions tomorrow, so a few hours with her friends might be nice. Also — and I hate myself for thinking it — if they're in the house, I know where she is.

'Sure. Have they got exams today too?'

'Lizzie has Geography AS I think. Ange is in History this afternoon with me, but she doesn't have double Science this morning. Jodie's all done. Her term is pretty much over.'

Her phone goes silent and she looks away, out of her water-streaked window at the headlights that dance in the muggy morning. 'Her mum's back in Paris again,' she says. 'New boyfriend there as well. I used to think it was cool her mum was away so much, but I think it pisses Jodie off a bit. Must be weird to be in that big house on her own all the time, looking after it for her mum when she could be having a great time in halls.'

I don't know Jodie's mother. I've met Angela's a few times at parents' evenings, and I think I saw Lizzie's once from a distance at a swimming event, but Jodie is older and her mother obviously has her own busy life. Our girls are too old for us to have become friends through them, but we all know a little about each other. I wonder what they know of me. *Worrier. Doesn't go out much. No boyfriend.*

'She didn't even live with her till she was about eight. Not properly. How odd is that? She's always working away. There's some cleaning woman who comes in, and there's always loads of easy food in the fridge and freezer, but it must get boring to live off posh pizza and microwave meals all the time.'

Ava's nonchalant, but she doesn't fool me. A warm tingle floods my veins. This is almost a compliment. She might not be coming right out and saying it, but maybe my daughter is realising it's not so bad to have a mum who's there for you. I say nothing, but tap my hands on the steering wheel along with the end of Salt-N-Pepa's 'Push It' as she goes back to her texting.

The windscreen wipers cut through the rain and along with the beat of the song, the rhythm is almost comforting. Apparently there are only a few more days of this terrible weather and then we shall all be bathed in glorious summer sunshine. Perfect timing for the end of Ava's exams. Maybe I should suggest we go away for a weekend somewhere when they're all done. Just the two of us, like we used to. Paris, perhaps.

'And now for a request!' I don't know who this DJ is but he hasn't quite mastered the voice they all do on national radio. The ease with which they speak. 'We haven't done one for a while, but this one appealed to me. The caller apparently wanted to remain anonymous — obviously shy — '

'Or married, Steve.' The cheeky co-host. Every show has one.

'Oh, you're a cynic, Bob. I'm sticking with shy. Anyway, not only did the caller want to keep themselves a secret, but they also wouldn't give up the name of who this song was for! All they'd say is that the person would know. It was their song. And two people never forget their song.'

We're coming up to the roundabout and I flick my indicator on, peering out to my right, waiting for my turn to go.

'Since we have no names, I'm making this everyone's song. All of our listeners out there so, if you're stuck in traffic in the rain, this one is for you.'

I pull forward with the traffic, and, half smiling at the cheesiness of the DJ, reach to turn the volume up.

'It's a classic of 1988. Frankie Vein and 'Drive Away, Baby'.'

My hand freezes and I stare at the radio as the oh so familiar tune, one I haven't listened to in years, breaks in. I feel sick.

Leave with me baby, let's go tonight,
You and me together, stealing into the
*   night.*

*Is that a deal, is that a deal? We can make
  it all right.
Drive away with me, drive away, baby,
  let's take flight.*

The words assault me.

Me. It's meant for me. It was our song.

An anonymous caller. The bunny rabbit. The strange feeling I've had of something being not quite right, that someone's watching me, and now here's the song, *our song*, requested in secret, and I think my heart might explode in my chest with the fear of it all. Frankie Vein's husky voice fills the car, and fills my head and the years vanish and each lyric is a knife in my brain.

'Fucking hell, Mum!'

I start suddenly as Ava grips the dashboard, and from outside, a dim and distant place belonging to other people beyond my panic, comes the squealing of brakes and blast of horns. The car stalls as I stop too quickly, my feet leaving the pedals and my breath coming in gasps as I pull myself back into the present as best I can.

Beside me, Ava's eyes are wide. 'What are you doing?'

I've come to a stop halfway on to the roundabout, and in my daze, all I can see is the anger and road-rage hatred in other drivers' contorted faces as they go by.

'Weren't you looking?' Ava barks.

'I . . . I didn't . . . I thought it was clear.'

Frankie Vein is still singing and making my head throb. I want to turn it off but I can't let

Ava see my shaking hands.

'I should have got the bloody bus,' she mutters. There she is, my surly teenager. Her disdain kick-starts me into action, and I force myself to turn the key again and move on, watching each exit this time, thankful that we're so close to the school. The song finally fades out.

'Great song,' Steve's disembodied voice says. 'Whatever happened to Frankie Vein?' he asks. 'Where is she now?'

I can't turn it off quickly enough. *Where is she now?* The question makes my face hot and I press my back into the seat as if I can hide inside the fabric.

'Good luck,' I say, the words thick in my mouth, as Ava gets out. She looks back at me, and I expect some form of reproach, but instead she looks concerned.

'Drive carefully, okay?'

I nod and give her a weak smile. My daughter is worried about me. Worried or fearful? Did I frighten her? Of course I did. I nearly crashed the car. For all my secret terrors, I could have been the one to harm her. As soon as she closes the door, I pull away, trying not to race over the speed bumps. I turn a corner and keep going until I'm away from the prying eyes of other parents and then stop at the kerb. I lean out of my door and retch violently as the rain soaks me. My vomit is hot and burns my chest as I expel my breakfast and coffee and stomach acid and I wait until I feel entirely empty before flopping back in the car.

My whole body aches and trembles. I'm

purged but it's a false emptiness. I can't get my fear out by vomiting. My terror will never leave me. Nor the grief I keep hidden like a precious jewel, a hard diamond made from the black carbon of my burnt-up heart.

The toy rabbit.

The song.

The feeling I've had of something being just a little bit wrong.

How much of it can be coincidence? Random events? None of it? All of it? Am I going mad?

I stare out of the window at the ordinary world and wonder how much of my make-up has run. I have to look presentable for work. I've got a jacket on, so my blouse is relatively dry, and my hair doesn't have enough life to get wayward after some rain. I can always stick it under the hand-drier at the office and put it up in a bun.

Eventually I push all thoughts of the past aside — not *away* though, never that — and check my reflection in the rear-view mirror. It's not as bad as I thought. I won't have to go home and re-do it all.

At least I'm not a crier, I think as I start the car again. I've never been a crier. In the silence the song lyrics echo in my head and I know they'll stay there all day. I can't wait to get to work. I don't care about Julia and the money. I don't care about Simon Manning. I only want to be somewhere I feel safe.

12

AVA

My bedroom is more like a bedsit really. I've got my double bed, my desk with a little drinks fridge under it, and there's even a sofa up against the wall — one of those reclining ones you can slob on and watch TV. It all came as part of my bedroom revamp last year. We only got mine done, not Mum's. She said it was because she loved her room and didn't want to change it and I was growing up and needed something different. I was young and I believed her. Now I know she could probably only afford to do one room, and by making mine so cool I might spend more time at home. It was around the time I started going out more on my own. Being a proper teenager. It's kind of backfired because recently we spend most of our time at Jodie's rather than here.

'Thank fuck no exams tomorrow.' Lizzie is stretched out on the sofa, Ange is lounging on the bed with me, on her side, all hips and curves, and Jodie's sitting against the wall on the old beanbag I had when I was little. Coke cans and crisp wrappers are strewn across the coffee table.

'But we're nearly done,' I say. 'And then freedom.'

It's not only the long hot summer holidays waiting for me this time, it's a sense of a new future. Even though Ange and I are staying at KEGS for sixth form, it's still going to be like going somewhere new. Different rules and freedoms. Being *above* everyone else. Crossing a new boundary. Another step towards the adult world. It makes me think of Saturday night. I crossed a boundary then. In some ways, staying at KEGS feels a bit lame, but the college is too far and our A-level pass rate is high.

'Swimming tomorrow?' Ange says. 'We should train even if we don't have any proper meets coming up.'

'It's so lame they won't let us race during exams.'

My phone pings. Courtney. Again. Do I want to meet up tonight?

'Him again?' Lizzie asks, and I nod, chewing my bottom lip, trying to think how to respond.

The lethargy in the group evaporates and I'm sure Angela purrs. We're on heat all the time. Sex is everywhere in the summer, and we're like dogs waking up to it, sniffing it in the air. We're nearly adult. Sex is part of that. It's what adult *is* in many ways. I hadn't wanted to do it with Courtney on Saturday, but I had wanted to *do it*, and I get a strange thrill remembering the feeling of him inside me and the sounds he made when he came, and it all seemed so different to the things we'd done before, even though I liked that stuff better. I spend so much time thinking about sex. Just not sex with Courtney. Sex with *him*.

'He loves you, he wants to kiss you . . . ' Ange mocks.

'Oh, shut up.'

'When are you going to do it again?' Lizzie says, blunt. She's always so direct. 'It's better the second time.'

'Like you'd know,' Ange says.

'Better than you.'

It's probably true. Lizzie is a year older and is on the pill. Ange figures it's only to regulate her periods, but at Christmas when Lizzie went out with Chris or whatever his name was for a couple of months, she swore blind they'd done it. She went into pretty graphic detail, and Lizzie isn't a liar. Maybe I should talk to her about what pill she's on. Just in case. Not that I'm worried. My period is due soon and my boobs are getting sore like they always do, so I'm sure it's fine.

'I can't see him tonight. My mum won't let me out in the week while the exams are on.'

'Your mum never wants to let you out past eight,' Ange says. 'Like primary school.'

'She's got better,' I answer. It's true, she has. And as much as she drives me mad, I still have pangs of loyalty to her. It's always been just us and now I'm growing up and abandoning her. I don't mind slagging her off myself but it bothers me when Ange does it.

'Ava!' The voice sounds distant through the door but instantly recognisable.

'Jesus, what is she, psychic?' Jodie says and smiles. It's not malicious like Ange was. She gets it. Weird mums club.

'*Ava! Can you come down here for a second?*'

I groan and roll my eyes as if this is the biggest pain in the arse, but actually I'm pleased to get off the topic of Courtney. I know I'm not behaving as they expect so I'm trying to cover my tracks. I made some comment to Ange at lunch about him being needy, so while I'm out of the room she can share that snippet with the others. We're best friends. We talk *about* each other almost as much as we talk to each other. *MyBitches*. Sometimes the WhatsApp group name is too true. The group is like a hub, but then we splinter off to discuss the things one of the others says that pisses us off.

As I slouch down the stairs I wonder if boys' friendships are the same as girls'. Do they give a shit about the minutiae — a look or comment or a pound of weight or two put on — the stuff we so obsess about and judge each other on? I don't think so. I don't think they have the same high expectations of each other that girls do. We *demand* everything of each other and it's impossible to deliver.

Still, when it comes to the crunch we may be bitchy at times, but we have each other's backs.

'Did you knock this off?' She's standing by the hall table holding a broken photo — it's a picture of the two of us from a few years ago. Alton Towers? Marilyn took it, I think. The glass is smashed in the frame.

'Nope.' I'd forgotten it was even there.

'What about the other one?'

'What other one?' She looks angry, her soft, doughy face pinched and tight, and I feel

73

suddenly defensive. She never gets angry. Disappointed and hurt and all that shit, but rarely angry. My loyalty of moments ago fades.

'There was another picture here. Of you. Your first day of Year Eight. It's gone.'

'You must have moved it.' I don't know what the big deal is. They're just old photos.

'I didn't,' she snaps.

'Well it's nothing to do with me!' I bite back; it doesn't take much to light the touchpaper between us.

'What about your friends? Could they have done it? By accident? Maybe thrown the other one away?'

'No. They'd have said. They're not idiots.'

She's looking down at our younger faces through the broken glass as if this is some major deal.

'Can I go now?' I'm surly. All my guilt, the sex, *him*, bubbling out in moodiness. He tells me she's too clingy. She should let me be free. He's right. He understands me. She wants me to stay a little girl.

'If it was you, tell me. I won't be angry.'

And there it is. The pleading tone along with the pathetic facial expression that makes all the fine lines on her forehead and around her mouth crease and deepen.

'For God's sake!' I explode, as if she's accused me of stealing or something. My jaw tightens as rage surges through me. My fingers curl into claws. I feel more animal than human. 'I've already told you! No! Anyway, they're just stupid old photos, so who cares! Maybe it's a poltergeist or something!' I don't wait for her response but turn and stomp back up the stairs.

'Oh, and my exams went fine — thank you for asking!' I send the words down to her with enough venom to make them poison arrows in the heart and leave her there, clinging to the old photo frame. Maybe that's why I'm so angry. She misses those days. I know she does. And I do too. Life was simpler then, with no tits and no sex and no becoming something new, but I can't help growing up — I *want* to grow up — and she needs to let me get on with it.

'Everything okay?' Ange asks when I close the bedroom door firmly behind me.

'Yeah. Exam stuff. You know.' I force a smile. It's a lie, and I have a feeling Jodie knows it because as I pass her she flashes me a sympathetic look the others can't see. Weird mums club. That, or they all heard me shouting.

'Jodie was telling us how she likes old men.' Lizzie snorts as I flop on my bed. 'So gross.'

'I said *older*, not old.'

'I don't think it's gross.' I try to sound nonchalant. 'A lot of older guys are hot.'

'I don't think she means like thirty.'

'Neither do I. Brad Pitt's still hot and he's fifty or something.'

'I don't care what you say,' Jodie lets their mocking disgust wash over her. 'It's true. Older men have something.'

'Experience,' Lizzie says and giggles. 'And cash.'

'Your dad's pretty hot, Lizzie.' Jodie leans forward, enjoying the conversation. 'How old is he? Forty-four? Forty-five?'

'God, you're disgusting!' Lizzie shrieks.

'He's in shape though.' Jodie wiggles an eyebrow. 'I bet he looks good naked!'

Lizzie looks so appalled we all lose it and soon we're trying to outgross each other with how Jodie could fuck Lizzie's dad until our sides ache with the kind of laughter that makes your eyes water and your breath catch. We're laughing so hard I forget to text Courtney back and I don't care. I don't need anyone but these girls. *MyBitches.* The Fabulous Four.

13

LISA

This has not been my day.

The thought is so comical I let out a snort of a hysterical giggle. It's the kind of thing the old me would say. Before all this. Before Daniel. Back when I was funny. The laugh turns to a choked sob and although it's still hot, I pull my duvet up to my chin like a child scared in the night.

You and me together, stealing into the
night.
Is that a deal, is that a deal? We can make
it all right.

Round and round in my head all day.

There was no respite at work either. Marilyn was off sick with one of her migraines and didn't text back when I checked on her, which left me with more unease — something's going on with her she's not telling me about — and then Julia had gone out this afternoon for a first client meeting and come back smug and flushed and with cakes for everyone. It made me think of the money again and I missed Marilyn.

I had a meeting with Simon to finalise some job specifications, and found myself saying yes to having dinner with him when Ava's exams are over, because I was too weak — too weak at the knees — to say no. It was easier to say yes. Less confrontational. That's what I told myself. It was *easier*. It's not true though. I said yes because I wanted to. Because I'm lonely. Because he makes me throb in ways I thought were lost to memory. Because being near him is like peeling back layers of delicate crepe paper wrapped around a treasure you've packed away somewhere to keep safe and forgotten about.

Alive. He makes me feel alive again.

But I got home and there was the broken picture and the missing photo and my first thought was *That will teach me to try to be happy* and my stomach cramped in that way from *then*. Sharp, acid pains as if two sides of my gut have been glued together and someone is trying to tear them apart again. I'd had to wait five minutes, doubled over, before I could call Ava down because I could barely breathe, let alone speak.

Above me, in the grey of the night, the ceiling swirls like dangerous eddies in a river. I want it to suck me up and drown me and break me into nothing.

It wasn't Ava or her friends who smashed the picture of us and took the other of her. After I confronted her and she stormed upstairs, I feverishly searched all the bags the girls had dumped in the kitchen, no doubt while ransacking the cupboards for snacks. There was no glass, no picture frame, nothing. Neither did I find anything in the kitchen bin or the larger ones in the garden. I even forced myself to check the recycling container where I'd thrown the not-Peter Rabbit. Though I knew it had been emptied days ago, I still half-expected to see the sodden, dirty toy looking balefully back up at me. He wasn't there. Neither was any hastily hidden evidence of broken or stolen pictures.

Drive away with me, drive away, baby,
  let's take flight . . .

Maybe I am going mad.

When the girls were leaving — all tight clothing, nothing hidden there — I asked Jodie if she wanted to stay for tea. She's the one I know least, and although she's older I didn't like the thought of her going back to an empty house and a microwave meal. Also I didn't want to fight with Ava any more. I thought maybe my edginess was what was making her moody and if I showed willing with her friends she'd calm down. But as it was Jodie scurried out fast, head down, and I felt worse about whatever Ava must have been saying about me.

I made us dinner, my hands on autopilot and my mind numb, but my gaze kept stealing off down the corridor to the empty spaces on the hall table and so we sat in near silence, her still rankled at my accusation, and me in the grip of some paranoid fear. It was, in the end, a relief when Ava took her plate and went to the sitting room to watch something on MTV and I was left to sit staring at my own reflection in the kitchen windows.

One photo missing, one broken. Was one left broken to draw attention to the missing one? Is it a message of some kind? A picture of my little girl taken, and the one of the two of us looking happy, smashed. It doesn't take a genius to figure out what that means, does it?

Ava. My baby. I must keep her safe.

My breath is hot and sour against the covers as I try to stay the right side of hysteria. I checked all the doors and windows. There was no sign of anyone breaking in. The kitchen door was locked. How could someone have got in and out without leaving a trace?

Maybe it *was* Ava. The thought is a tiny buoy to cling to in the dark ocean of fear. Maybe the evidence is hidden in her room somewhere. It's the only place I haven't been able to search. Maybe it was Ava, I repeat over and over but I'm not convincing myself. I keep seeing her face on the stairs. She was confused. She didn't know what I was talking about.

My eyes burn, tired, despite my racing mind. They want to close, to rest, to sleep, but I can't allow it. I dread the dreams. I can't face Daniel, not tonight.

And I know he'll come, because I can't let him go. How can I ever let him go?

You have to learn to live in the present. Focus on every day. On Ava.

I thought it was crazy bullshit the first time a therapist said it to me, and I've tried, God knows I've tried, but it remains impossible. The past is my shadow, always there, clinging to me.

Maybe I should ring Alison. She'd listen to

me. *Listen to what?* my inner voice sneers. *I have an odd feeling? A photo has gone missing? I heard a song on the radio?* I know what she'd say. I've rung her too many times recently. She probably thinks I'm crazy. It's only my imagination. Take deep breaths. Let it go. I should cancel dinner with Simon. Maybe then all this will stop. It was stupid to think I could go on a date. I should know better.

I'm withdrawing, a snail pulling back into its shell.

We're gonna live wild and free, on the
  road, you and me,
It's a deal, a done deal, now drive away
  baby . . .

Maybe it's nothing. Maybe I am just going mad. Maybe I broke the photos. Maybe it's me who's broken.

14

AVA

My room is dark, except for the glow from my iPad and iPhone screens, like two moons in the night. Facebook is open on my iPad and I stare at it, waiting. I'm always waiting for him and it's like an itch on the inside of my skin that I can't reach. I think about him all the time. More when he's like this — in a hurry or stuck doing something in his boring real life. He said he'd be back in ten minutes but it's been nearly twenty.

Have I driven him away by ranting about my mum? Was it teenage and childish? The skin on my bottom lip is sore where I've been biting it. He didn't *seem* to mind. In fact, he was so understanding of how embarrassed I'd felt when she invited Jodie to stay for tea. She hadn't invited the others so it was totally obvious I'd been talking about how Jodie's mum is never here. I really like Jodie and I felt like I'd betrayed her somehow — sharing her weird mum's behaviour with my own. Thankfully, Jodie didn't mind. Or if she did, she didn't say anything and seems pretty normal.

I look down at our last WhatsApps on my phone.

So, is it a teacher? Your crush?

I'd answered: *Kind of.*

She hadn't asked more. It's what I like about Jodie. She knows when not to push. If it was the other way round, I'd be nagging her to tell me. I make a mental note in my *how to be a better person* endless list to try not to do that any more when someone has a secret. In a lot of ways, it's made me want to tell her more. I want to tell *someone.* I'm bursting with it.

My WhatsApp has three unanswered messages from Courtney too — even though he's probably seen I've been online. I sent one to him earlier saying my mum was being a bitch about going out while my exams were on and he seemed to believe it.

It made me feel a bit bad because he's being so nice but I don't want anyone here in the evenings. Not past around nine or ten when *he* might be around to chat.

It's midnight. Jodie went to bed an hour ago and Courtney's given up on waiting for a reply, so I shut my iPad down and relax against the pillows, opening Messenger on my phone. Once, a while back, I sent a text to Lizzie meant for Angela. Thankfully, it wasn't bitchy, but it made me paranoid about having too many conversations on the go at once on one device. I'd hate to send something meant for him to someone else.

In the silence of the house, I find myself listening out for sounds in the corridor. What if Mum comes in my room again like she did the other night? Maybe I should go under my covers.

You there, Beautiful?

All thoughts of anyone else vanish and I sit up in my bed, my heart racing. He's back.

Yep. Right here, in bed. Waiting for you.;-)

I feel hot and awkward about my words, but I press send anyway. I'm trying to sound sexy and flirty but at the same time I don't want to go too far down that road — to pictures and videos and things. He asked before, once, last week, and I said no. I was too shy. He hasn't asked since, and apologised. He said he'd had a few drinks and was thinking about me and got carried away. I kind of liked it though. Him thinking of me like that. I wonder if I'm in his head all the time like he is in mine?

Still, maybe I should have sent something. In my underwear. Not with my face in it, obviously — I'm not stupid like Meg — but something to show him I'm a woman not a girl. But I hate my body and I can't imagine it looking good at any selfie angle, like all those girls on Instagram do in their bikinis. My thighs would look awful. Maybe that's what stopping me. My own embarrassment.

Can't chat long. Just wanted to say goodnight.

My disappointment burns through me, a flame consuming curling paper.

I've only got a few minutes. I'm sorry I'm so shit at this. I will make more time, I

84

promise. One day we'll have all the time in the world.

I don't say anything. I don't want to sound moody and I need a moment to get myself together. He's always saying he'll make more time and in the future it will be different, but what about *now?*

I thought you might have been with Courtney tonight. I'm glad you weren't.

My skin tingles and I feel the power shift. I told him Courtney was there for my birthday. He knows we're sort of going out, even though I've said I'm probably going to end it.

I thought about it, I type. He keeps texting me. He really wants to see me. I don't know what to do.

I hadn't thought about it. I haven't answered Courtney's messages but there's no need for *him* to know that. Not while he's clearly worrying about it. This isn't how I expected love to be when I was little. I thought people fell in love and everything was perfect. I should have realised that wasn't the case from my own family, but no one ever told me how selfish love is. How it eats you up. How many games you have to play to get what you want.

I don't want you to see him, but that's not fair on you.

My heart leaps.

Why? Are you jealous?

It's too direct.
I'm annoyed at myself but I have to know. I don't want him thinking I've been trying to make him jealous, which obviously I have.

A bit. He seems too young for you. You're too mature for a boy like him. He's not going to make you happy.

No, I answer. You make me happy. But you're not here. We've never met. Courtney's here.

I'm proud of myself. I'm making this his fault.

We should meet.

The words shock me so much that for a minute the screen blurs slightly. My palms sweat with a surge of adrenaline.

When?

Does that sound too demanding? But I want to know. I want to meet him *now*. I'd get out of bed and go anywhere he asked to see him in the flesh and talk to him and all the other stuff.

After your exams are over. About ten days? I'll sort out a time and place and let you know. Will have to be at night, though. Is that okay?

Is that okay? I'm grinning so hard I think my face will split.

Yes, yes yes! xxxxxxxxx

I'm too excited for any more games. And it's good for him to know how happy this makes me.

But keep it secret okay? Just us. It'll be fun. No pressure.

My heart is exploding.

I promise I won't tell a soul.

And I mean it. I won't. Maybe afterwards I'll tell the girls — if there's something to tell — but not before. They'd probably want to come with me, and no way is that happening.

For a few moments he says nothing and then:

Sorry, gotta go. Miss you, Beautiful. See you soon. Xx

I sign off with about a hundred kisses and flop back on my pillows. We're going to meet. We're actually going to meet.

This is the best thing ever.

15

LISA

It's been over a week and though I've started each day with a horrible worry about what it might bring, there's been no more Frankie Vein, no more soggy rabbits in the street, no more missing pictures. For a few nights I upped my sleeping tablets, drowning myself in darkness and leaving my mornings fuzzy, but now, at last, the glue in my stomach is slowly coming unstuck. The weather has improved too, the rain making way for bright, warm sunshine. In this light and joy of summer it's easier to convince myself it's all been a coincidence.

Life has also settled down here at work with the new staff at PKR. It's odd how quickly a set of people can become the status quo. Those gone to the new branch are like ghosts in my memory now and it's quietly comforting — how easily people can be forgotten.

A giggle — quickly covered up — comes from across the room. Despite my initial thoughts that Stacey was too smart to fall for Toby's smooth patter, it looks like I was wrong and their flirting is becoming quite obvious. Heat fills the spaces between them, a warm ocean undercurrent if you walk through it. Still, I can hardly comment, given that I'm going out for dinner with Simon tonight.

Dinner with Simon Manning. I feel sick with nerves. Not just nerves. It's excitement too. A distraction from this unease — this fear — which has gripped me. But now I still have the fear and also all *this*. All this emotion. I'm not used to it. I have lived a dampened life. It's been easier that way.

I haven't told Marilyn yet and I should. I will. But I know how excited she'll be which will add to the pressure for it to *be* something when I'm telling myself it's only a friendly meal. Plus, the last thing I need is for any of the others here to pick up on something. I'm not keeping it exactly a secret, but I'm not telling anyone. I don't think he has either.

I look at the clock. It's nearly two o'clock. Ava will be in her final exam now — the last of her GCSEs. I still find it hard to believe my baby is nearly a sixth former. I imagine after the past few days she can't wait for those last two years to fly by. It's not been a good week for us. I've been too clingy — that song going round and round and round in my head tightening like a vice on my nerves, and I've been terrified every time she's left my sight. I tried to look at her phone and iPad while she slept, but she has passwords on both. In return, she's bitten my head off at every opportunity. I can hardly blame her.

I get my phone out and send her a quick text.

Hope the last exam went well! I've got some money for you in case you want to go out and celebrate with the girls. Remind me when I get home. Xx

I'll give her fifty pounds. It's a stupid amount, I know, and I ignore the voice in my head warning me that at her age it's more likely to be bottles of vodka she'll spend the money on. At least this way she and her friends can line their stomachs with a cheap pizza first. Anyway, they're sporty girls. They wouldn't risk their swimming by doing anything stupidly unhealthy. This is what I tell myself. The floating branch I cling to in the energetic uncontrollable torrent of my daughter's life.

It's the festival tomorrow. She'll probably save a lot of the money for that. I'm going with Marilyn and Richard — the days of Ava holding my hand are long gone — and I'm looking forward to it. Live music, a funfair, sunshine, hot dogs and candyfloss. Everything I need to dispel my lingering disquiet.

'Brownie?'

I look up, slightly startled. Julia is holding out a Tupperware box of roughly cut chocolate squares. 'You made them?' I sound incredulous, my words coming too quickly to hide how at odds I find the idea with what I think I know of her.

'I find it relaxing,' she says.

I have no choice but to take one. 'Thanks. I'll get a coffee and have it in a minute.' It feels moist and heavy, exactly as it should. She bakes well. Of course she does. She holds the box out to Marilyn and I look at her delicate nails and

90

try to imagine her in a kitchen covered in flour.

She brought flowers in the other morning to 'brighten the reception area up'. They were lilies; beautiful and expensive and stinking of grief. Penny loves her which makes me feel worse about what I saw. I can't prove anything so I've tried to forget it. But Julia's a strange one. Even with these friendly gestures that scream out for approval, there's a coldness to her, as if she's ice at her core.

'I'd be huge if I ate everything I baked myself.' Her face tightens and there's the hint of a line around her mouth I haven't noticed before. *Detail, detail, that's me.* Her Botox or fillers or whatever she uses to make herself look younger must be wearing off.

'I'll get the kettle on,' Marilyn says. 'Thanks, Julia.'

'I'll help,' I say. 'Let's make one for everyone.' I need to tell Marilyn about the dinner — the *date*. I don't want to keep any secrets from her if I don't have to. If I can trust *anyone* in my life, it's her.

16

AVA

'Thank God it's all over!' Ange says as we slam our cubicle doors. We've beaten the rush out of the sports hall at the end of the exam, everyone else still squealing at each other about what was good and what was bad.

Ange's happy sigh is accompanied by the sound of her urgent piss hitting the toilet bowl. She has no inhibitions. She'll walk naked around the changing rooms after swimming while the rest of us try to pull our clothes on under damp towels.

'Yeah,' I say. 'Thank fuck.' I'm not really listening. I'm staring down at my clean knickers. I was sure, *sure*, I'd felt the first twinge of my period an hour ago. What is it? A week or so late now? I wish I kept a better track, but who does? Periods just *are*. They turn up. It's what they do. For the first time this week I'm not exactly worried about it, but I'd feel better if it came. I force out a half-hearted wee I don't need and then check again as I wipe, willing the paper to be streaked with blood. It's not.

Outside, doors bang and more girls turn up and so I flush and escape to the sinks. Ange is already there, plumping up her full lips with shiny gloss and my phone pings a couple of times as I turn it back on. Courtney and Mum. I tell Courtney we'll be out tonight and then I open the text from Mum.

'The cash machine is paying up,' I say as I scan through the message. I feel mean calling Mum that, but Ange came up with the nickname for her back at the start of Year Ten, and it kind of stuck. 'I told you she would. Plenty for tonight and the festival tomorrow.'

'Is Courtney around tonight?' Ange isn't using her stupid faux American accent, but the question does sound as if she's bored, which means she's curious. I wonder if Ange slightly fancies him herself. She's the one who asks the most.

'Yeah, I figure we can all meet up, maybe.' I don't mind the idea of seeing Courtney. We can celebrate together and I can plead the period I don't have if he tries anything too heavy. I do miss him a bit, weirdly. Not in *that* way, but it was fun when we were all hanging around together at the start. Having the boys there breaks up our intensity. Our Fabulous Four-ness. *MyBitches*.

Plus, Courtney isn't such an issue now. He's simply a distraction to fill in the days until I meet *him*. A little over a week to go. One week. I can't believe it.

My period better bloody come before then.

17

MARILYN

'So, how was your day?' Richard asks, flicking through the channels, no doubt looking for sport or some home repair show to fill the time before bed. I don't mind what he chooses, to be honest. All I want is to eat my dinner, maybe have a long hot bath, quickly check in on how Lisa's evening went, and then bed.

'You know, the same as usual. Still getting the new girls up to speed.' We've slumped on the sofa with plates of frozen lasagne and oven chips with a smattering of peas as an attempt to make it look like a balanced diet. I worked through lunch so me and Lisa could leave early to get her a new dress, and I'm starving. I have a sudden pang of envy at Lisa's evening. A beautiful restaurant. Charming company. A new dress. New beginnings. It's only a gentle envy. I can't be jealous of this. I'm getting joy from her joy. It's about time she dated, although a little part of me is worried he'll whisk her away and then what will I do? You don't make new best friends in your forties. I don't think I could. Especially not now.

I scoop up a forkful of lasagne and it's surprisingly good and I didn't have to get all dressed up for it either. There are small pleasures to be found in sofa living.

'You said you were going to make a curry.' Richard is looking at his plate as if I've stuck a steaming dog turd on it and for a moment I want to shout, *Oh just fucking eat it*, but I don't. I'm shattered and it's not worth it. Anything for an easy life.

'You like lasagne better. And I thought maybe we could go for a curry or something after the River Festival tomorrow if you fancy it? Ask Lisa along? They've got a banquet-night offer on at the Bekash in the high street. Ridiculously cheap.' I smile at him. 'We may need it after beer in the fresh air.'

He doesn't smile back but picks at a chip. 'I was driving through town this afternoon. Went to get some supplies for the outside office I'm doing for the Grange couple,' he says. 'I saw you and Lisa. Pretty sure it was you. Going into that underwear shop.'

My heart sinks. For a start, I know the Grange job was cancelled. They decided they couldn't afford it. He's forgotten he told me.

'Oh yes.' Only room for one liar on this couch. I stare at the TV, my hunger fading. I'm too tired for this tonight. His moods. 'She's going out for dinner with that client. You know, the one I told you about. The one who likes her.'

'You didn't say they had a date.'

'I didn't know until today.'

He doesn't believe me, I can tell. 'And you thought she needed new underwear for it?'

'It was only for fun. So she'd feel sexy.'

95

He laughs. 'What, if she's dressed like a slut, she'll act like one?'

I flush. I can't help it. 'Lisa's not a slut and you know it. She's a nun, if anything.'

'I didn't say *she* was. I'll bet it wasn't her idea to tart herself up.'

My hunger evaporates. 'Are you saying I am?'

His eyes scan me. 'It would take more than new underwear to sort you out. You've put on weight. Too much wine and crap food with the wankers you work with probably. Turning you into a fat cow. Still, at least I don't have to worry about rich clients trying to fuck *you*.'

So it's going to be one of these nights. *Another* one of these nights. More business problems that are somehow all my fault. We used to laugh together on this sofa. Seems a lifetime ago now.

My lasagne grows cold. Untouched and unwanted. I know how it feels.

18

LISA

There is no way I'm going to be able to eat anything. My stomach has folded itself up into a tiny square and while I don't have the awful cramps of last week, it's a whole different kind of anxiety. I must look ridiculous too. When I'd quietly told Marilyn about the dinner she'd looked so stunned I thought she was having some kind of haemorrhage but then she burst into life and insisted we get away early and go and buy something new to wear.

At least she didn't go crazy with the shopping, I think as I get out of the taxi and walk on shaking legs towards the restaurant door. A black dress which is slightly too clingy for my taste but way better than the shorter one she originally picked out, and a pair of black patent heels I don't trust to carry me. She also made me buy a new underwear set. 'Not for him,' she'd said. 'For you. It's like wearing a disguise.' That unnerved me. Hiding. Always hiding. The bra strap is cutting into me, but I'm wearing it anyway. Maybe she's right. I do feel slightly more confident with the lace next to my skin. I feel like somebody *not me*.

'This is the best time,' she'd said, wistful,

97

linking her arm in mine as if we were teenagers. 'The flirting. The promise of the future. The perfection before you truly know each other.' I couldn't see how this could be the best time. I was too busy fighting a panic attack of nerves and excitement and fear of letting someone get to know me, and wondering if it was too late to change my mind.

But here I am, and as I see him get up from where he's waiting at the elegant bar, it feels very much like whatever a date should be. My hands tremble. I feel ridiculous. Clumsy. Ugly. Obvious. He doesn't seem to notice.

'I was worried you'd cancel.' He leans in to kiss me on the cheek and I smell the citrus and warmth mixture that has such a stupid effect on me. It doesn't help my nerves as I mutter a hello.

'You look beautiful,' he says, standing back. I want to shrink into myself. I don't look beautiful. I still have dumpy thighs and the shifting skin tone of an ageing woman. My hair could use highlights. All those things. His words make me think of how Ava had stared at me as I was going out the door. She'd called me 'pretty' and she was shocked enough to have meant it. It made me feel warm and happy and sad all rolled into one. Pretty is only luck or effort and yet it can have such an effect. No one should trust pretty, not really. Not just for itself.

He's not wearing a tie and his fitted shirt is undone at the top button and the suit is expensively stylish enough to be something like Paul Smith. In fact, I'm pretty sure it's Paul Smith. A suit that is not office wear. Ava would

98

be surprised at me. She thinks I have no real interest in clothes. She'd be wrong. When I was her age and younger I was obsessed with fashion, poring over the pages of any magazine I could get hold of until the colour and gloss of the favoured pages had worn away. And for a while, before she was born, I would go into the big designer stores simply to touch the different fabrics and breathe in the wonder of the design. Even if I could have afforded to, I wouldn't have bought any though. Those clothes weren't for someone like me.

A waiter takes us to our table and Simon orders bread and olives and some sparkling water. I sit, happy to be off my trembling legs, and glad the lighting is soft.

'How did Ava's last exams go?' he asks as a waiter hands me a large menu. The words all shimmer on the surface of the card as if they might slide off at any moment.

'Oh, good — I think.' I sip some water. My throat is rolled sandpaper. 'She's sixteen. Getting a full analysis out of her is never going to happen. But she didn't slam any doors and she seems happy enough.'

'Is she going out to celebrate?'

I nod. 'And it's the River Festival tomorrow, so I'll barely see her. She has a good group of friends. I don't worry too much.' The lie comes so easily. I worry all the time. All I do is worry. 'It's hard to know how much freedom to give her,' I continue. 'They're so grown up at sixteen and yet not grown up at all.'

He glances down at his menu and I realise

how dull this must be to him. 'Sorry, I forget you don't have children.'

'No, I don't. But I like hearing about yours.'

'Why?' I try not to sound defensive.

He smiles. 'Because I like you, Lisa. I want to learn more about you, but you're hard to get to know.'

'Oh, there's really nothing to know. I'm quite dull.' I try to make it sound fun and flirty but I fall short. *Daniel.* My heart aches with the weight of him.

'I don't believe it for a second. Still waters and all that.'

'Well, it's true.'

Thankfully, the waiter returns and I randomly choose the scallops and the sea bream and a glass of Chablis.

'I'm not much of a drinker,' I say. 'So only order a bottle if you're prepared to drink the rest.'

He laughs. 'I have to drive to Kent tonight for a meeting at my Grainger House Hotel in the morning. No rest for the wicked. So, a single glass for me too. If I'm honest, I'm not a great fan of getting drunk either. I'm too old and too busy for the hangovers.' This sends a dual wave of relief through my nerves. He's not a big drinker, and he won't be trying to get me into bed tonight. It's a ridiculous thought anyway, that he would want to have sex with me, but I still fear it. I haven't been naked with a man for years. I haven't been anything with a man for years.

'So,' he says, and I know from his tone what

100

question is coming. Some variation on *Tell me about yourself.* 'You said you've been at PKR for about ten years. What was before that?'

'Ava,' I say, simply. Oh God, where would I start? There is so much before that. Too much. A universe of existence. How nice it would be to be able to condense my life into a pat paragraph or make the years thus far into a hugely entertaining anecdote. I can do neither.

'Ah.' His eyes are full of quiet interrogation. Marriage, divorce, Ava's dad, other boyfriends — all the information men are interested in. Things that boil down a woman's relevance in relation to other men, rather than anything in and of themselves. The *inside information* comes later. Those talks are for the middle of the night, heads on pillows, faces only outlines in the darkness. That's when people surrender their weapons to each other and hope they don't end up stabbed in the night by them in the future.

Our wine arrives, and I take a sip. He's still waiting, expectant. 'Someone once told me,' I say, 'that the human body replaces its cells in their entirety over the course of seven years. So in essence we are all completely different people than we were seven years ago, and that person was different to the one seven years before. This makes me wonder why everyone is always so fascinated by other people's pasts, because none of us are those people any more.'

He sips his own wine. 'I've never heard that. Do you think it's true?'

I shrug. 'I don't know. I should probably Google it, but if it's made up, I lose the magic. I like to think it's true.'

'Me too. It's a very liberating thought.' He looks at me then, properly. Two adults rather than a man and woman dancing around each other in the grip of chemistry. 'I did some things when I was younger that I'm not proud of,' he says. 'It's nice to think maybe I can leave them behind with all those old cells.'

'I won't ask about the other yous, if you don't ask about the other mes. Deal?'

'Deal.'

Life is a series of deals, that's what I've learned. Most get broken. I just need this one to hold for the next couple of hours. After that, I'll regain my sanity and we won't do this again. We clink glasses. Dear God, but he's sexy. A heart-breaker. What the hell is he doing having dinner with me?

By the time eleven thirty rolls around and we've finished I'm almost completely relaxed and my smile is coming naturally. In fact, I'm enjoying myself so much I'm not sure I can *stop* smiling. We've talked about so many things without crossing the border into the past, I'm starting to think maybe it *is* possible to focus on the present and find it satisfyingly full. We talked about movies and TV shows we both loved or hated, pet peeves, I told him about Ava's swimming and how bright she is and all the things I hope for her. He talked about the hotels and how his dream was to retire from the UK business in about five years and open a resort in the Caribbean — a small one focusing on diving and water sports and fine local food. The kind of relaxed place he could pretty much leave to run itself and spend his time on the water, or painting. Maybe even write a book. He looked embarrassed saying these things, but I thought they sounded wonderful.

He offers me a lift, but I say I'll get a taxi. He has a long drive ahead of him as it is. The restaurant orders one for me, and we go outside and wait in the cool summer night.

He stays with me until the cab pulls up. 'Can we do this again?'

'Stand outside in the cold?' I smile. 'Sure.'

'Very funny. This. Dinner. Drinks.'

Although the other D word, *date*, hangs in the air, I find myself nodding. 'I'd like that.'

He beams and leans forward. I turn my head sideways at the last minute and his lips land on my cheek. They're soft and warm. 'Goodnight,' I say. My heart is all panicked wings, but it feels good. 'Drive safely.'

'Have fun with Ava at the River Festival tomorrow.'

'Ha!' I get into the car. 'I doubt I'll see too much of her.'

'Well, have fun with Marilyn. I'm sorry I can't be there.'

The door closes and I sink back against the leather.

'Good night?' the driver asks as we turn out on the main road.

'Yes,' I answer, as I realise I can't stop smiling. 'Yes, it was.'

19

AVA

The River Festival is one of the highlights of the town's year. Everyone at school always bitches about how lame it is, but we love it really, under the skin. Like us though, it's changed over the years. Where it used to be a few stalls and games and maybe a canoe race, it now covers the fields on both sides of the river, the two old footbridges serving to connect them, one to go one way, one to come back. There's a full funfair, several music stages, clowns and fortune tellers, art displays, stalls to buy stuff, a huge cafe marquee run by the WI that only the old people use, several beer tents and loads of vans serving any kind of fast food you could want.

I love the festival. We all do, though we would rather die than admit it. We swagger through the crowds, hips thrust forward, glossy lips slightly parted, eyes locked behind our mirrored shades. The air is filled with the shrieks of kids and mums. The past couple of years I haven't come down until about four when the little ones are being dragged home, but after too much cheap wine last night, I — we — needed to get out in the sunshine to blow away the clinging cobwebs of hangover. The boys brought the wine and after a few glasses I didn't even mind snogging Courtney. I told him my period was here — it still isn't — but I gave him a handjob to get him off my case. Lizzie and Jack got off together but I think that was just the drink. Jack's not her type at all. They're all so immature anyway. I feel a fizz in my lower belly. A week until I meet *him*.

'Let's find somewhere down by the riverbank,' Jodie murmurs, 'where we can laze in the sun for a bit. What do you think?'

We all agree. None of our stomachs are quite ready for the rides yet. We'll need some food and Cokes first.

The boys are coming down later, but I'm glad of this time of only girls. We're not even sure we'll meet up with them. After last night, Lizzie's not keen, and I'm finding the glamour of their roughness compared to the KEGS boys is wearing off. We come from different tribes. Under the skin we might not be so different, but at our age it's only everything on the surface that matters. We get up early and swim. They go to bed late and smoke weed. They watch football. We watch *Glee* reruns. Maybe it's only sex that draws us together, I think as we wander closer to the river. Maybe it will be the same way with *him*. Once the lust wears off, I'll be bored. It's an alien thought. The girls make the boys seem immature, he makes *MyBitches* seem immature. *One week. One week to go.*

It's hard to keep the smile off my face. Me and Mum are almost back to normal today. Her weird mood of last week seems to have faded and she was almost glowing this morning so her work dinner must have gone well. She gave me an extra twenty quid and for once I said I didn't need it, but she insisted I take it anyway in case everything was more expensive this year. It made me feel warm inside. Close to her again. Me and her against the world, even as the world pulls me away from her. She's still my mum. I do love her, cautious and careful as she is.

Picnic blankets are everywhere, like quilt patches laid out for sewing. The festival is busy although it's not officially being opened until one. These days people arrive well before eleven and if all the rides aren't quite open, there's food and drinks and stalls to wander through. This year's official guest is that hot guy from *Hollyoaks* who won *Strictly Come Dancing* last year and constantly seems to be in every magazine ever. It said in all the flyers he'd be signing pictures and doing photographs too. Lizzie wants one. We told her she could queue alone.

We find a spot a little way from the families where the bank is a steep drop to the water and the kids can't paddle, and I flop to the ground, the grass cool and ticklish against my bare legs.

'I'm hungry,' Jodie says.

'Starved,' Lizzie agrees. 'We should've stopped at Maccy D's. I'm also busting for a wee.'

'I can't be arsed to move,' I say. It's true. I just want to sit and let my thoughts drift in the sunshine for a while. 'But if you're getting some food, I'll have some.' I drag the twenty from the tight warmth of my denim pocket. 'Whatever you're getting. And a Coke. I'll keep our spot.'

'I got money,' Jodie says, getting her bearings before heading off towards the food vans, her tiny frame quickly lost in the sunshine. Lizzie drifts off in search of the Portaloos and Ange sits down cross-legged beside me as I lie back and close my eyes.

'I could fall asleep,' I say.

'I know what you mean.'

'Wake me up when Jodie gets back with my food.'

I don't close my eyes, but lie there looking up at the branches through my shades and thinking about him. Is it possible to love someone you've never met? Is that crazy? I know everyone always goes on about how you shouldn't talk to strangers on the Internet, but this is different. For a start, I'm not a kid — it's not like I'm Internet stupid. And secondly, he's not weird. He's wonderful. He makes me feel wonderful.

I glance sideways. Ange is hunched over, absorbed in something on her phone and her fingers fly over the keys. I haven't heard any pings so she must have it on silent. Has she got secrets too? I wonder if it's Courtney. I don't mind her texting him, we're all friends after all, but it's weird if she doesn't mention it. She hasn't talked about anyone else and Ange is a talker. Maybe she does fancy him. Perhaps I should encourage them. If they got together, I might not look like such a bitch when me and *him* are out in the open.

I take a deep breath and let all the tension out of my neck and shoulders as I close my eyes. I still have the dregs of a headache and so I let my thoughts drift like wisps of cloud on a clear day. The sun is hotting up and even in the breeze my skin doesn't prickle. It's a beautiful, perfect day.

⋆ ⋆ ⋆

At first I think the shrill noise is my alarm. I've dozed into a half-dream of exams and school and being late, and suddenly this awful sound is cutting into my chase for the bus, and when I open my eyes and sit up, it's a moment before I realise where I am. *The festival. Saturday. No more exams.* It's not an alarm though, it's screaming, and even though I'm bleary behind my sunglasses, and my mouth is dry, I find I'm on my feet. My heart races me awake.

'*Oh God! Someone! My boy! Ben! Ben! Someone, please! Do something!*'

I look around for Ange, but she's gone, and I see the crowds gathering at the bank. An overweight man is pulling his shoes off. I look to the water. *A small hand. Panicked splashes. A tuft of hair. Skin. Close to the other bank. The overweight man won't get there. The currents are strong and there are weeds and his feet will hang too low and by the time he makes it across to the child he'll drag him down as likely as save him.*

I have all these thoughts as well as *Where the fuck is Ange?* as I run the few feet to the bank and jump in, my legs pulled up under me like a bomb in case it's shallow here. The shouts and screams muffle. The water's fucking freezing and stinks and I can taste the dirt in my mouth but my strong legs straighten and kick out, cutting across the current that will drag the child to the weir. I break the surface and swim.

20

LISA

I'm still smiling. The sun is out and the weather glorious, and Ava was in such a good mood this morning it was like a glimpse of a future where my adult daughter and I are friends who talk and laugh together. It was lovely.

Simon texted at breakfast to say how much he'd enjoyed our dinner and was *not* looking forward to spending this beautiful day indoors in meetings while he could be out having fun with me. When I read it I felt my usual knot of anxiety but then an overwhelming rush of excitement. It could be the weather, or the fact Ava's exams are over, but I *do* feel better. I still have *the* fear, I'll always have that, and I haven't quite shaken off the anxiety of last week — *it was not Peter Rabbit, and the song was just a coincidence* — but I feel tougher, more resolute. I can learn to live in the present. Maybe allow myself to be happy again.

'Here,' Richard says, and hands me an ice cream with two wafers in it. 'I didn't get us sprinkles because we're grown-ups.' He winks at me, and I smile. The ice cream is already starting to drip down the side in the heat and I lick it from the cone.

'Oh God, I shouldn't,' Marilyn says. 'I've put on two pounds somehow this month.'

'Don't talk rubbish.' Richard slides a strong arm around her waist. 'You're gorgeous.'

After a moment's hesitation, she takes the cone. 'Oh go on then.'

Her smile is bright and I find myself imagining Simon and me on a foursome date with them. Would he put his arm around me like that? Protective and caring? Marilyn hasn't asked how the dinner went — she must be keeping that private from Richard for me. For me or for her. She wants me to be happy more than anything and she knows me well enough to know how quickly I'm capable of closing myself off. Any more pressure on this to be a *thing* might make me run after all these years of being defiantly single.

As it is, I'm bursting to talk to her about it. Maybe we'll be able to sneak off later and I can tell her. Not that there's much to say, but I just want to relive it. Get her opinion on him, on me, on everything. God, I'm like a teenager, all nerves and jittery excitement over a boy.

'What the hell is going on over there?' Richard's smile turns to a frown as he looks at something beyond my shoulder. 'Down by the river.'

I turn, as does the rest of the small crowd around the ice-cream van. It's like ripples in water, the sense of something *off*, spreading from one person to the next. I squint, the brightness of the day too much. In the distance the riverbank is busy. Where people had been lying or sitting on blankets, they are now on their feet, all facing the other way. Mothers hold their toddlers close. I can feel it from here; the relief and guilt in the tightness of a grip that screams thank God it's not my child.

Child . . . river . . . girl gone in . . . has some-one got the ambulance men . . . Jesus where was the mother . . . what is wrong with people . . .

The words drift back at us, Chinese whispers passing through the field, and suddenly I know, I just *know*, Ava is somewhere beyond all those people, she's central to whatever has happened.

I drop my ice cream as I start to run.

'Lisa?' Marilyn calls after me, confused. I barely hear her through the wall of my panic. This is my fault, all my fault, and pride and falls and happiness and loss and I run and I run, pushing hard through people as I force my way to the epicentre. Please God, let my baby be all right, please God let my baby be all right . . . my brain screams the prayer at a God I know isn't listening and my eyes water with the kind of tears that come from terror.

As I break through the final row of people, the first thing I see is the St John's ambulance men, big figures in green uniforms blocking my view. Sunlight flashes from the silver foil of a blanket and for a moment everything sparkles, distracting me, and then she stands up and I see her. My baby. Soaking wet but alive.

I run to her, wrapping my arms around her, burying my face into her stinking hair. Oh God, she's alive. She's safe. My baby is safe.

'It's okay, Mum. I'm okay.'

She gives me a half-smile and I half-laugh in return, but it's nearly a sob. And then suddenly her friends are there too and we're a huddle of love around her, all their young voices high-pitched in my ears: *What happened, I was just, oh my God I can't believe, Jesus Ava, you saved him, this is mental* . . . I cling to her, to all of them, not trusting myself to speak as relief makes my limbs tremble.

A woman's arm breaks through, reaching for Ava, and we splinter outwards. I see my own fear and relief reflected in the young woman's face. She can only be about twenty-five. Something has settled into her face today, I think. Something that wasn't there before.

'Thank you,' she says, through her tears. 'Thank you. I don't know how he got over there. He was supposed to be with the others . . . '

She's holding him tight. A little boy, wrapped, like my little girl, in a silver blanket. His big eyes peer out. He's not crying. He's too busy trying to process it in his young head. The danger. My heart stops for a moment. How old is he? Two or three? The same age as Daniel. As Daniel *was*. The world fractures around me again, my seeds of happiness blowing away through the cracks. *This is what happens when you relax*, my inner voice tells me. *This is what happens when you let yourself be happy*.

'Look this way please!' The voice is so commanding and I'm so lost in my relief for Ava, and the reminder of Daniel, that I do as I'm told. We all do.

I'm blinded by the flash.

21

Local teenager saves toddler from drowning in dramatic river rescue...

Tragedy was averted at Elleston town's annual festival when plucky sixteen-year-old Ava Buckridge saved two-year-old Ben Starling from the River Stour. Ava, pictured below, was enjoying the sunshine when screams alerted her to the horror of two-year-old Ben struggling in the water. The quick-thinking teenager dived in without hesitation and pulled the boy to safety.

The toddler had been playing with his cousin and older children but wandered off, and, unknown to his young mother, found his way across the bridge where he slipped on the steep riverbank. Thankfully, Ava, who swims at county level with Larkrise Swimmers at Elleston pool, was on hand, and Ben was returned to his mother safe and well.

The pretty sixteen-year-old is humble as well as brave, commenting, 'I saw the little boy in the water and a man was pulling his shoes off to jump in. I swim every day and knew I would have a better chance against the currents, so I just ran. Honestly, it wasn't a big deal. But it was a bit cold!'

22

LISA

I tell myself I won't look, but my eyes drift to it every time I have to pass the front desk. Marilyn had one newspaper article laminated to keep, but Penny had this one framed. She says it reflects well on the company. Marilyn has all the press reports cut out in an envelope. So does Ava. I don't even want to touch the paper. I feel as if my face shines out from each picture, though in truth I'm half turned away in most.

The mug scalds my hand as I come back to my desk. It's almost comforting, this pain that keeps me in the present.

'You must be so proud,' Marilyn says, for about the thousandth time this week, as I put her drink down. She's got a new Internet page open. It's the Larkrise Swimmers and Ava's coach. He's put a piece up about her and how all children should learn to swim. My jaw aches from tension. Why can't they all shut up and go away?

'Of course I am, how many times can I say it?' I hold my mug tighter. 'To be honest, I'm just happy the little boy is okay.' Ben. His name is Ben, but when I see his face in the paper my breath catches as if he is Daniel. He's not

Daniel. Ben is alive. Daniel is dead. There are more pictures of Ava than there are of Ben and his mother. I'm not surprised. She looks like some American starlet in all of them. Denim cut-off shorts and her soaking T-shirt slick against her body. She loved the fuss too, as I cringed and tried to pull her away. I stood no chance. She and her friends were happy to pose. Too many pictures. Too many with me skulking in the background.

It's only local news, I tell myself, over and over. No one pays it any attention. It will fade. They're Alison's words. I called her on Sunday, breathless and panicky and apologetic for disturbing her weekend. Her voice was soothing and reassuring. It dripped cool and professional into my ear. I would be fine, she said. It would blow over, she said. She told me to call again if I felt my anxiety getting too much. She told me to do my breathing exercises. I heard children in the background. It's hard to imagine her with a life of her own. Funny how we put people in boxes. She's always only professional with me.

My calmness lasted for about five minutes after putting the phone down and then the fear and worry crept back in, and I haven't been able to expel it as I've crawled through each day. If anything, my tension has got worse. It hasn't helped that some reporter from the largest of the local rags got hold of my mobile number yesterday and called wanting to do a mother-and-daughter interview. I turned it off after that and haven't turned it on since.

My hand red raw from the hot mug, I try to

116

focus on the mail-merge job contract letter I'm composing, but the musky smell of the Stargazer lilies in the vase on the table by my desk distracts me. Most days I would find it lovely, but Simon bought these, and when I think of Simon it's a reminder of how stupid I was to think I could relax into happiness. He brought a bouquet of these for me, and a small, funkier one made of bright unusual flowers I couldn't name for Ava. They're in a vase in the office kitchen. I didn't take them home. There's enough going on without having to explain him to her as well. Penny didn't send her flowers, after all, so why would a stranger? Ava would know there was something not entirely professional about it all.

I wanted to get her something myself to show that I am proud of her. I want to try to tell her she is my everything, and pride isn't a big enough word for how she makes me feel when I see her being kind and sweet and selfless. But all of this is bound up so tightly with the truth of everything inside me, that even if I *wanted* to tell her, I could never undo the knots.

'Have either of you taken any money from the petty cash box?'

I've been so busy staring at my screen while my thoughts race I didn't notice Penny coming out of her office. Her voice is low, her back to the rest of the room.

'No,' Marilyn says.

'Not me,' I add. My mouth is dry. Suddenly what I saw this morning is making more sense.

'It's twenty pounds short, I think,' Penny says. 'It's happened a couple of times now.'

'How many times do we have to tell you to lock the cash tin?' Marilyn should have been a mother. She has the perfect tone for it. 'The cleaners are probably having it.'

'I lock my desk.' Even as she says it, Penny's face is half-admitting the lie. 'Well, when I remember.'

'Make sure you do from now on,' I say.

'I probably took it myself,' Penny mutters. 'Brain like a sieve these days. Bloody hormones.'

As she walks away, I see Julia heading over to the photocopier. Penny smiles at her; a warm expression of open fondness. Julia, the new golden girl. I should say something. I really should.

'You okay?' Marilyn asks.

'Oh, it's nothing,' I say. 'Just trying to figure out what to cook for tea.'

'Rock'n'roll, Lisa.' She grins at me. 'Our lives are so rock'n'roll.'

I stare at my computer screen and force deep breaths into my lungs. It's all too much. The world is starting to choke me, fingers tightening around my throat.

23

AVA

It's been weird since the thing at the river, but I have to admit, the attention has been nice. Better still, I look okay in most of the pictures printed, which is a major result. My Facebook has gone crazy. So many new friend requests — seems like everyone at KEGS wants to know me now — and there are so many posts about how great I am. A little bit of me is pissed off the exams are over and so I can't go into school and revel in all this glory, even though I know that's really shallow.

The only person not fawning all over me is Courtney. He's gone a little cool and I think he's sussing out that I'm going to ditch him. Or maybe he's jealous of all the attention I'm getting.

Maybe that's why Mum's being a bit of a moody cow too. Could she be jealous? *He* tells me she's a drain on me. That she's selfish to want me to stay her baby forever. He says she's dragging me down and I shouldn't pander to her. I think maybe he's right. He's been amazing though. He said he wasn't surprised at what I did at all because he knows that's the kind of woman I am. Brave and strong and beautiful, and he's such a lucky man to have me. He called me a *woman*.

It makes me shiver to think about it. Not a girl any more. A woman. His woman. I'm the lucky one. When he calls me beautiful, I feel it. Normally, if someone pays me a compliment it has the opposite effect. I feel clumsy and awkward and so aware of all the things that are wrong with me. Not when he does it, though. Perhaps that's what love really is. And in a few days I'm going to see him! I can't wait. I'm so excited. There's just one other thing to sort out beforehand.

I stare down at the Boots bag on my bed. I should do it. Maybe after tea. It's not going to be positive, that would be crazy, but still there's a nugget of fear in my stomach. I'll feel better when it's done and I *know* either way. And as Jodie says, even if it *is* positive — please God don't let it be positive — it can be sorted out. *Taken care of.* At least it's the summer holidays. If I need an abortion I can do it while Mum's at work. She'll never know.

24

LISA

'I couldn't get hold of you. Your phone's going straight to answerphone. Richard's out for an hour doing a quote, so I thought I'd pop over.'

I can't decide if I'm happy to see her or not. I've just finished washing the dinner plates after a less than pleasant chicken salad with Ava, who grunted answers to my questions and has now locked herself away in her room, her friends no doubt on their way over, only ever fleeting figures on the stairs. I'm not sure I have the energy for Marilyn now. I'm emotionally exhausted. It takes everything I have to stay in this state of nervous anxiety alert.

'What's up?' I ask, boiling the kettle.

'Nothing's up with me.' She slings her bag over the corner of a chair before flopping into it. 'But you were a bit off this afternoon. Something on your mind?'

I can feel her eyes on my back as I busy my hands getting mugs and tea bags and milk. I have to tell her *something*. She knows me too well if also not at all. She knows my tics. I need to give her something and I can't tell her about my worries from the weekend so I choose the lesser of two evils.

'I think I know who took the petty cash.'

Her eyes widen. 'Who?'

I pour the hot water and join her at the table. 'Julia,' I say. 'It's Julia.'

For a moment Marilyn says nothing, and then she exhales loudly. 'I should have known. The way she's always sucking up to Penny with little gifts for the office, or cakes for everyone. How did you find out?'

'I got in to work early today.' I've been in early every day since the weekend. Anything is better than lying awake with all my worries and it's not like I have to get Ava up for school now the exams are done. 'Sorting out the details for the Manning contracts. When I got there, she was coming out of Penny's office. I startled her.'

'Did she say what she was doing?'

'Putting some invoices on her desk.'

'Maybe she was?'

'I checked when she went to get coffee and she had put some papers in there. But this is Julia. She wouldn't be so stupid as to go in there without a *reason*.'

I see a flicker of doubt on Marilyn's face.

'There's more,' I say. 'Something happened at the salsa club night. You know, the office party. Something I saw.'

'Go on.' I start to tell the story and she leans forward as I speak as if sucking in my words from the air, to savour and swallow them, until finally I finish and we both sit back.

'Why didn't you say something?'

'What could I say?' I shrug. 'I didn't have any proof. It's not like I caught her red-handed. I was on the other side of the room and by the time I realised what she'd done she was halfway to the bar. It would have been my word against hers, and you know what Penny's like, she probably wouldn't have known how much cash she had in her wallet, let alone if twenty pounds was missing from it.'

'We need to tell Penny,' she says. Decisive. She's always decisive.

'But there's still no proof.'

'Then we get some. We can set a trap. Mark the notes in the box or something and do a spot check.'

'We're not the police, Maz.' I half-laugh. 'We can't go around demanding people show us what's in their wallets.' The relief of *telling* is being consumed by the anxiety of potential action.

'We've got to do something. Penny thinks the sun shines out of that girl's arse.'

'She's not a girl. Look more closely. I bet she's not far off our age.'

'You think?'

I shrug.

'Thank God I'm married, eh? I can let it all go.'

I almost laugh. Marilyn has never let herself go. Me, maybe, but I never had *it* in the first place.

'You're not doing so bad,' I say. 'For an old bird.'

'Cow.'

We both smile and it feels good, even with the constant nausea and ache in my stomach.

'We need a drink,' she says, decisive again. 'I'm

driving but I can have one. Sod it. Get your bag. Let's go to the pub.'

'But Ava . . . ' I mutter.

' . . . Is sixteen,' she finishes. 'I keep telling you — you've got to give her space. Now sort yourself out while I have a wee. Let's go.'

★ ★ ★

It's past eleven when I crawl into bed. I feel better than I have all week. The pub was good, old-fashioned and cosy and no one paid us any attention at all, which reminded me how this whole business with Ava and the river is only important for the bubble of our social circles, such as they are. No one else cares, they're all getting on with their own complicated lives. We bitched about Julia, she quizzed me about what Ava was going to do over the summer and in sixth form and then we talked about Simon — who texted while we were out, asking for another dinner, and she made me answer yes. It was a good escape but as soon as I relaxed I felt shattered and couldn't stop yawning. Relief and release. The sheer exhaustion that comes from having been wound tight for days and the comedown from living in fight-or-flight mode. I'm out of practice.

I haven't said goodnight to Ava, my tiredness too much to face any more confrontation. I'm clinging desperately to this wispy ribbon of calm. If I can get to sleep before the anxiety creeps back I've got a chance of a good night's rest and everything will seem better in the morning. Rest does that. Sunshine does that. I'll let Marilyn take the lead on Julia. And like she says, we won't make any real accusations until we have proof. Evidence. I don't want to think about evidence. It leads me back to worry.

Even though it's warm I leave the window closed and pull my duvet and knees right up to my chin. I make myself small. I close my eyes and take deep breaths. I imagine myself as the last person in the world. It makes me feel safe. The last person. Only me. Alone. I drift.

★ ★ ★

'Mum?'

I'm dead to the world and when Ava shakes my shoulder and I startle awake, I'm not sure where I am, or when I am, and I leap out of my bed as if my life depends on it. I squint in the bright light. Is that daylight? No, my curtains are drawn. She's turned the light on. Blue-white creeps through the edges of the fabric though, so it *is* morning.

'It's crazy, Mum.' She's all energy and excitement, still in her shorts and T-shirt from bed. I can't catch up, but my heart is racing. *No No No*, it drums against my ribs. *Please no.*

'I mean, it's just crazy.' She's almost at the window and I want to pull her back, pull her under the covers and hide us both there. She laughs. 'Who'd have thought all these people would be interested in what I did? It's not that big a deal. But look, Mum, look!' She pulls back the curtains. 'See?'

I hear them through the double glazing. The shouting. The clicking of bulbs. The chatter of the hyenas. I don't move.

Ava's face is full of sparkle and light as she turns to me. 'Look.'

I don't move. I'm frozen. Downstairs the doorbell goes. Hard. Long. The phone starts ringing. Noise. All the noise is filling me up, choking me like quicksand. My breath comes in pants.

'Mum?' Ava frowns. She's on the other side of the universe from me. 'You okay?'

'Come away from the window.' A harsh rasp. Not me at all.

'What's the matter?' She comes closer. I want to hold her. I want to tell her how much I love her. I don't though. I can't. Not now. Instead, I simply tell her the truth. I hear the calls outside.

'They're not here for you.' I swallow hard as the world darkens and the noise drowns me and I surrender myself to it. All of it.

'*Charlotte! Charlotte! How long have you lived here, Charlotte? Is Ava your only child?*'

My world crumbles as if it had never existed.

'They're not here for you,' I repeat. 'They're here for me.'

PART TWO

25

AFTER

Life Licence Conditions for release of
Charlotte Nevill 1998:

1. She shall place herself under the supervision
   of whichever supervising officer is nominated for this purpose from time to time.
2. She shall on release report to the supervising officer so nominated, and shall keep in
   touch with that officer in accordance with
   that officer's instructions.
3. She shall, if her supervising officer so
   requires, receive visits from that officer
   where the licence holder is living.
4. She shall reside initially under whatever
   conditions are laid down by the General
   Manager, and thereafter as directed by her
   supervising officer.
5. She shall undertake work, including volun-
   tary work, only where approved by her
   supervising officer and shall inform that
   officer of any change in or loss of such
   employment.
6. She shall not travel outside the United
   Kingdom without the prior permission of
   her supervising officer.
7. She shall be well behaved and not do anything which could undermine the purposes

of supervision on licence which are to protect the public, by ensuring that their safety
would not be placed at risk, and to secure
her successful rehabilitation into the commu-
nity.

8. She shall remain under the clinical supervi-
    sion of Dr [   ] or any other forensic
    psychiatrist who may subsequently be
    appointed to provide such supervision.

9. She shall not enter the Metropolitan County
    of South Yorkshire without the prior written
    consent of her supervising officer.

10. She shall not contact or attempt to associate
    with [   ].

11. She shall not reside or remain overnight in
    the same household as any child under the
    age of 16 years, without prior written
    permission of her supervising officer.

12. She shall not have unsupervised contact or
    engage in any work or other organised
    activity, with children under the age of 12
    years, without the prior written permission
    of her supervising officer.

26

LISA

It all has to come out somehow.

It is worse than I could have imagined. It is worse than last time. It is terrible and I deserve it. Nothing for me will ever be as bad as my own guilt, my own dreams, my own need for punishment. I deserve this pain, and I can cope in my own way. I absorb it. I earned it. Not Ava though. Not my baby. She doesn't deserve this. Her world has crumbled too and she has only ever been *good*.

I have never thought of Ava as having my blood. It's been the joy of her, that she's so different to me, to *Charlotte*. She liked school, from day one. So proud in her little uniform. She's focused. An achiever. She was never any trouble, not really. A bundle of goodness from her first giggle. She was sweet, always ready with a smile, her bad moods only light breezes not dark thunderstorms. *She was like Daniel.*

Now, in this rage, now that she *knows*, she is all mine and it breaks my heart all over again.

At first there was too much happening to talk, we were stunned zombies as Alison and the others swept in moving us like mannequins — *What's going on, Mum, why are they calling you Charlotte, who's Charlotte* — bundling us out in separate cars, blankets over our heads, our lives evaporating in the darkness, and then, finally arriving at this small damp flat which reminds me of the first one, the past all jagged edges cutting into me from all angles.

I stand still as she screams at me. I wish I could cry. They've told her what I did. How can I explain it to Ava when I can't explain it to myself? I think of my fairy tale, my shed cells, my *new me*, and I almost laugh hysterically. The dirt. The guilt. Charlotte can never be shed. She's there, always, under the layers I've housed myself in.

'You disgust me!' Ava *is* crying, but these tears are something feral and wild, her face blotchy red and her hair, still bed-scruffy, like brambles around her beautiful head. 'How can you say you love me? How can you love anyone? You disgust me! You make me disgust me! Why didn't you abort me?'

I take a small step forward into the gale of her fury. I want to hold her. I want her to punch me. I want to do something, anything, to try to make this easier for her.

'Don't come near me!' Her shriek makes me flinch. Alison hovers in the doorway. They know Ava needs this. I know she needs this. 'Stay away from me! I hate you!' And then she's gone, storming away, a door slamming.

I don't move. I can't. Is this my justice at last? My baby, my one good thing, my chance at a small redemption, hates me. She wishes she hadn't been born because of me. I have ruined her life. I ruin everything. How can I tell her how I wish I could unravel it all, take it back? To stop myself. To kill myself *before*. How can I tell her how I dream of him, always, and each time it destroys me? How can I tell her anything without it sounding like a pathetic attempt at an excuse? A plea for forgiveness, even though I know there can never be any forgiveness. I will never *want* forgiveness.

I don't mind so much that she hates me. I have always expected that to come *one day*. All those fears, the worry, knowing how easy it is to be found, it was a fantasy to think Ava would get through life blissfully ignorant. I hoped it would come later. When she was grown and had a life of her own that couldn't be taken and changed just to protect me. I hate that she hates herself. I can't bear for her to hate herself. Was I so wrong to have a child? To want someone to love? To be loved by? Oh selfish, Charlotte. Always wanting.

'She'll calm down,' Alison says, coming in and turning the TV on as if this can distract me and establish some kind of normality. 'We'll get her some help. Help for both of you.' She looks at me with pity, but I barely see her. I'm already drifting deep inside myself. My own personal hell. 'I'll make you a cup of tea,' she says.

I don't think Ava will calm down. I know this rage. It reminds me of Charlotte. She's my girl after all, and that terrifies me more than anything. I know how that rage can lead to terrible things. Can leave someone with regrets like tombstones which have to be carried through life, back-breakingly heavy and deserved. *It all has to come out somehow.*

27

NOW

MARILYN

The bright office lights have given me a headache and my sleepless eyes throb. It isn't a migraine — I haven't had a real one of those since I was a teenager, whatever I tell Penny when I need a day or two off — this is complete emotional exhaustion. I feel numb, as if the synapses in my brain aren't quite connecting and I have a constant queasiness in the pit of my stomach.

I turn the radio off and drive in silence. Sitting here in the traffic is the closest I can get to some actual peace and quiet. Some alone time to breathe. To try to process everything. Even when no one was actually speaking at work I could feel the hum of it. All the news tabs open behind work documents. These youngsters who can't even remember 1989 poring over every detail. The whispers. The gasps. The sideways glances at each other when they found something new. This horrible piece of history that is now part of their lives.

No one sent me the links, of course. I imagine Penny told them not to. She probably meant well, but it's only made things worse, separating me from the crowd. And it's not as if I haven't searched it all myself at home, scouring the Internet until my eyes burn. It's different though — Stacey, Julia, those new staff, and even Toby just have the thrill of excitement. It's not *real* to them. Lisa — I must stop calling her Lisa — wasn't real to them.

Still, I didn't let any of them see how terrible I feel. Years of practice at hiding things. I look the part. Always together. Nothing fazes Marilyn. Skin of steel, that's me.

The only glitch in my armour was arriving late this morning, but they hadn't expected me to turn up at all. The news had hit us all, but it had frozen me. Then I'd thrown up. I have a vague memory of crying almost hysterically and trying to ring Ava — *Oh God, poor Ava* — before Richard had realised what I was doing and pulled my phone from me. It was going straight to answerphone anyway. I heard it click in before he hung up. By the time we'd finished *discussing* that, I was over an hour late, didn't get Penny's message to take the day off if I wanted it, and when I got there she'd already briefed the office in no uncertain terms not to speak to the press when they inevitably started calling, to pass any concerned clients her way, and to try to carry on as normal. I came through the door in time to hear her final remark that she would not tolerate anyone bringing the company into disrepute.

You've got to hand it to Penny, she's at her finest under pressure, but she still looked at me funny when I came in, although nothing compared to the glances the others gave me. The way you look at someone you almost feel sorry for but who might be contagious. Everyone's smiles were too tight and their concern too shallow. They were more curious than worried. *How awful for you. You must feel terrible.* Underneath it all was the lingering, unspoken *Did you know?* Well, fuck them if they have to ask. I have a bubble of anger. It's a good feeling. Better than the rest, anyway.

In the end, Penny gave us all a half-day while she fielded phone calls from Lisa's client list and did her best to reassure others. I didn't ask her about Simon Manning and she didn't mention him, as if by us staying silent he'll stay too busy to notice. But Penny doesn't know that Lisa — *Charlotte. Charlotte, not Lisa* — has been for dinner with him. Been on a date.

I asked Penny if she wanted a hand with the calls and she'd said no, it was best coming from her. It was probably true but she'd looked away awkwardly in a way that made me want to scream, '*I am not Charlotte Nevill! I got fooled as much as all of you! I got fooled more!*' Only when I was gathering my coat and bag did she come out again.

'I need to do a DBS check for you.' She was hovering close to her door, clearly uncomfortable. 'I never did a CRB when you and Lisa started here. I was so busy setting all this up, and I didn't have any reason to . . . well, she was a single mother. Well-spoken. Good CV.' She'd shrugged and I knew why she was so keen to lay all this to rest at work quickly. She could have prevented this. I felt sorry for her. She's just opened a second branch, taken a financial

137

gamble, and it could all get damaged because she didn't do *one* criminal background check.

'Sure,' I'd answered. 'I'll do the form in the morning.' As if there was no doubt that I'd come in. Good old reliable efficient Marilyn. Gold star for me.

'Are you okay?' she'd asked me. What could I say? I nodded and told her I was in shock like everyone else.

Up ahead, the light turns green but it takes someone angrily beeping their horn behind me until I move the car forward. My shock *isn't* like everyone else's. Not everyone else was Lisa's best friend. I think again about that missed CRB. One small form would have changed everything. Lisa would probably never have taken the job — surely a fake identity still wouldn't allow for a faked criminal record check. I would never have met her. Ten years of friendship would never have happened. *This* would never have happened. I try to unravel the past, removing Lisa from it, as I pull into the drive. I can't. She's so woven into me it's impossible.

There are no press here yet, thank God. They're probably still all over the school and Ava's friends. *Oh, poor Ava.* They haven't torn Lisa's life far enough apart to get to me yet, but they will. Even as I mentally try to distance myself from her, the past floods back — Ava's birthdays, laughing over *Strictly Come Dancing* while eating Chinese takeaways, wine after work. All so ordinary, and yet I loved it. I needed it.

Hot tears sting my face. How much of it was a lie? Where did Charlotte end and Lisa start? I

138

can't put them together as the same person. The evil child who did this terrible, shocking thing and the shy woman who quietly became so important to my life. Charlotte and Lisa. *Lisa never existed.* I tell myself again and feel a fresh wave of grief. No, she did exist but she wasn't real. Now she's gone and I'll never see her again. I can't help but mourn that, no matter how hard I pretend I'm fine. The illusions may be false, but the love is real.

Lisa was my best friend and I loved her. But what am I supposed to do with that? What does it say about me?

I shouldn't be surprised, I think as I get wearily out of the car and see Richard's Audi still parked up in front of the garage. I've made a habit of loving illusions. My ribs hurt. They're not cracked this time, only bruised. Experience teaches you the different kinds of pain, but my back aches and a dark purple butterfly is forming on my left side.

You told Lisa your own lies, a little voice inside my head says. *This perfect marriage she so admired.* I silence the voice. That was different. That was private. I take a deep painful breath before opening the front door.

* * *

Only when Richard is fully asleep do I creep downstairs. He's given me my phone back and the kitchen is spotless where he's washed up and cleaned after the dinner he cooked. My nerves are zinging. Something here doesn't add up. He

139

doesn't calm down this quickly — the hot rage is normally followed by at least twenty-four hours of the cold silent treatment. Only afterwards does the remorse and regret come, along with the turning around of events so that it's somehow my fault because *you know what I'm like*. This is all far too quick.

It should concern me, but I'm too tired to think about what he might want as I put the kettle on. My head is filled with Lisa and my own shame at being the best friend who should have known. But as I stare at the knife block and think of Richard upstairs, I wonder how much it must take to drive a person to murder. God knows I should be close, but even with how much he's beaten the love out of me, I couldn't kill him. I notice there are more final demands in the bin as I tip the tea bag away. No, he shouldn't be this calm yet.

I keep one eye on the stairs as I try Ava's number again. I love Ava as much as I can imagine loving a child, a child I could never have, and I may not be able to love Lisa any more, but Ava can stay in my heart. I need something in my heart.

This time though, there's no answer message. Just a dead tone. Like she never even existed.

28

AVA

That moment keeps going round and round in my head on a loop. Mum staring at me. Me staring at her. *Why are they calling you Charlotte? Who's Charlotte?* The wide-eyed frightened-rabbit look on her face.

Even after the brick through the window and being bundled out into the back of a van to go to the police station and then out again, unseen, and driven to this pokey flat, I hadn't quite figured out what it all meant. Now I block it all out and hide behind my wall of anger and hurt and fear and a thousand emotions in between.

I hate this flat. It smells wrong. Not like home. I miss my bedroom. No reclining sofa in the box room I have here. It's a strange place filled with strangers and *she's* the biggest stranger of them all. Everything has changed. My whole life is being evaporated and it's not fair. None of it's my fault. I didn't do anything. I hate it. I hate them. I hate *her*. I miss my mum who I thought was a bit wet and needy but she was my mum and we'd laugh together sometimes and I knew she loved me. Not this woman. Not this stranger. I don't want her blood to be part of mine. I don't want to be part monster.

When I have my door shut, which is most of the time, I can still hear their voices and the creak of the floor under their sensible shoes as they move about. It's probably only about four or five people but it feels like more. A couple are police. At least one is a head doctor — I know because she tried talking to me but I refused. I'm not the crazy one here. She spends a lot of time in the sitting room with Mu — *Charlotte*. Not that *she's* doing much talking beyond yes or no answers. She's like a zombie, sitting there staring at the too loud TV. Still looking pathetic, as if she's got Mum's skin on. Well, I'm not buying her routine any more. Why should anyone feel sorry for her? She's the one who did it. She's the murderer. She's the one who — I can't even bring myself to think it aloud — did that *thing*. Why am I having to pay the price?

I want my phone and iPad back but Alison said I can't until they've sorted out what's going to happen with *her* identity. And mine. They've clamped down on any more papers printing my face but from all the hushed talking outside my bedroom door it would seem that this whole thing is a mess. They don't know what to do with us.

I don't want a new identity. I want to be me.

Alison is *Charlotte's* probation officer. I hate them all, these strangers, but if I didn't, then I'd probably like Alison a little bit. When I rage at her, demanding to see my friends, she looks at me with a weird blend of kindness and pity. She keeps telling me to be patient. Easy for her to say.

I feel sick. But then I always feel a bit sick right now. That's the other thing I can't deal with telling anyone yet. How the fuck am I supposed to get that thin blue line sorted while I'm caged up here?

I know it's all worse because of what I did. Technically it all started with what I did. Someone, an anonymous caller, somehow recognised *her* face in one of the pictures with me by the river. Alison says it was simply bad luck. A million to one shot. That doesn't make me feel better. What I did gave all the newspapers and stuff an angle. *Devil mother, angel daughter. Child killer, child saver.* They're picking our lives apart. I kind of always wanted to be famous in that *X-Factor* way that everyone does, but I never imagined it would be like this. What do my friends think? Do they miss me? They must do. I bet they wish they could see me as much as I want to see them. I think of Jodie and imagine her saying, '*Well, this takes weird mums club to a whole new level!*' It almost makes me laugh and almost makes me cry. I wrap myself up in my rage and avoid doing either.

My Facebook account has been deleted. And my Instagram. When Alison told me, her face pretty much said my chances of being allowed another were pretty shit. Hardly likely, is it? Someone would find me and then they'd find *her* and that would be another huge chunk of government money flushed down the toilet.

No more social media. It's like staring into an endless darkness. Why am I being punished? It's all right for *her*. She didn't have any friends anyway apart from Marilyn, who probably hates her right now too. She barely used her phone let alone the Internet. Not like me. I *lived* on mine. We live on it. No more *MyBitches*. No more Fabulous Four. I'll probably never see them again. Not until I'm eighteen or whatever and by which time we'll all have changed. I can't quite get my head round that, but I can almost, almost accept it as a fact I've got to get used to.

But not no more him. Not that. I want to wreck this place with all the pent-up frustration of not being able to contact him. What must he think of all this? Will he still love me? Think I'm some kind of freak? Or is he going out of his mind worrying about me? What about our meeting? We had it all set up. What now? I have to be there. I *have* to. I'll do whatever it takes. I need to start thinking cleverly about this. Like a grown-up. A woman, not a girl.

From the kitchen I hear the sound of voices before there's a quiet knock on my door. Alison pokes her head in. 'Cuppa?' she asks.

I nod and smile. 'Thanks.'

She looks surprised at my lack of sullenness and smiles back.

'I'll be out in a minute,' I say.

When she's closed the door I lean back on my pillows and stare up at the awful swirling plaster patterns in the ceiling. What I need is for them all to go away. Just for a bit. One night in fact.

The TV twenty-four-hour news is loud in the other room as if she can drown it all out by drowning herself in it. I swallow the anger and

144

hurt that makes me want to go in there and scream my rage at her again. Shouting won't get me anywhere. I need to be nice. I can do that if it means I will get to see him. I'll do anything for him. He's all I have left.

I love him.

29

AFTER

2000

He always comes in on a Tuesday and she walks to work more quickly on those days as if by getting there earlier she'll see him sooner, which she knows is stupid but she does it anyway. It's not as if she talks to him. Not properly. She doesn't know what to say, so she mutters answers to his polite questions and blushes and clumsily sets whatever he needs to print. Still, she likes Tuesdays best. Tuesday is her Saturday.

Some days, when the winter sun is shining and the sky is bright and clear, days like today, she can almost believe the past doesn't belong to her at all. She imagines her *legacy life* as Joanne, her probation officer calls it, as an invisible tattoo imprinted on her skin, slowly soaking through and becoming part of her. She looked up 'legacy' in the dictionary. A gift. A gift of a new life. She likes to think of it that way. It makes her feel special. *She was in care since she was small. A series of foster parents. She doesn't like to talk about her real parents and has no contact with them.* It's all so close to the truth she can almost believe it herself.

Sometimes, when a moment of old daring comes back to her, she embellishes her new life with stories made up from the photos she develops. The pictures are part of why she likes this job so much. Seeing all those happy memories coming through the machine. Pictures of lives she'll never know. Holiday snaps from the seaside. Children's birthday parties. Teenagers out having fun in bars and clubs. She studies those sometimes. The make-up, the clothes, the smiles. Arms flung around each other. Bright shining eyes. She practises the poses in the mirror at home even if it makes her feel silly.

She found some 'other' photos once — very different pictures. Mr Burton told her there was nothing illegal in them however *distasteful* they might be and to package them up like the rest. He marked the envelope though, and made sure he served the customer when he came in, and she knew he'd had a 'quiet word' about how he didn't like his young assistant having to see things like that and to perhaps invest in a digital camera where he could print his own photos at home. Mr Burton is a good man.

Her days are routine and she likes that too. Even the overwhelming terror of the first few months of trying to catch up with the world has faded, and she's been in her small flat above the video rental shop for a year and she pays her rent and manages her money and hasn't asked for a single handout. Everyone is, apparently, 'very happy with her progress'. Even the Home Secretary. He's a dark cloud. She doesn't like that the Home Secretary has a special interest in her progress. It reminds her who she is in the meat of herself, the sticky red flesh under the skin. Under the legacy life she wears like the invisibility cloak in *Harry Potter*.

She loses herself in the routine and likes the blandness of it. Up, work, home, tea, bed, repeat. She likes the budgeting of what's left of her meagre wages when the rent's paid. What she can spend on food. Deciding which tin to take from the shelf. Adding it all up. Counting the pennies left over. There's a solid satisfaction in it.

She hasn't woken to wet bedsheets in nine whole months, although she keeps the plastic sheet on the mattress. She's not sure she could sleep without the familiar rustle. She's nearly twenty-three and she's finally stopped wetting the bed. Of all things; the job, the college certificates, these markers of her new self, this is the one she's most proud of. Joanne says it's a very good sign that she's integrating into her new life. Integrating. Like the world has shuffled up to make space for her, Lego squares locking her in.

She likes Joanne. Is she a friend? She feels like a friend. She's been there through all the ups and downs since her release. Joanne getting a new job or moving away is one of *the fears*.

The fears are worst in the days after the dreams come. She has the dreams more now that she's trying not to take any of the pills they gave her. Pills to keep her calm, pills to help her sleep, pills that all left her half-empty. She didn't have the dreams so often in those days, but although she now wakes from them filled with horror and dread, she also thinks it's what she deserves. She can't imagine not having the dreams. It would be worse than having them. They're a reminder of the past, yes, but they're also like photographs she doesn't have. A way of seeing Daniel that isn't from a newspaper picture. A way of holding his hand.

Oh, but they leave her with so much fear, like clingfilm across her face. Always *the fears*. Joanne leaving. Being recognised. Letting something slip. Becoming Charlotte again. Doing something terrible again, even though she's sure she wouldn't, she couldn't.

At the beginning, when each step outside of the sheltered accommodation made her freeze and tremble, and she hesitated every time she went to open a door herself, Joanne told her something that made the fears ease. It's become her talisman. Joanne said the cells in the human body are constantly regenerating. She said it takes seven years for all a person's cells to be different than they were before. So basically, by the time she was released, she was an entirely different person from when it happened. She clings to that in the dark moments. She is *not* the person she was then.

Today is Tuesday though, and not a day for dark thoughts. Today is a different kind of knot in her stomach. Not the slicing pain of her worries, but bubbles like Babycham. Tuesday is his day. Ten minutes of bright colour in the bland greys of her life.

This time, when he comes in for his flyers, he lingers a little at the desk. She can't bring herself to look at him directly as he tries to make polite conversation and she nods and mutters her answers while worrying at a strand of hair behind her hot ear. She can see Mr Burton watching from his office. He's not concerned though, or annoyed. He's smiling indulgently. Like he's known this was coming, which is a shock because she didn't know *at all*. He asks her then, when the tension between them has become almost unbearbable. Nothing big. Just would she like to go for a drink sometime. Fireworks go off in her head. He doesn't ask her for dinner and she's glad about that. That would be too much and she's not sure she'd know how to do 'going out for dinner'. A drink is fine. She's done that before with Annie, who comes in on a Saturday to help. Her skin burns bright as a beacon as she nods. Her blush fits into the colours of the world. He smiles and his eyes light up and they set a time for Friday.

She doesn't stop smiling for the rest of the day. These are all new cells, she tells herself. It's the start of a new century. She needs to embrace the gift of her new life. New beginnings. For the first time in such a long time, she feels happy.

30

NOW

MARILYN

Simon Manning's a charmer, not like Toby wants to be, but the kind of man who smiles because on a subconscious level he knows how to make other people feel good. At ease. It's a rare skill. But today, when he comes out of Penny's office, every crease in his face is visible. He doesn't look at anyone, although he must know all our eyes are on him. It wasn't a scheduled meeting. Penny would have booked a meeting room to keep it out of the way of prying eyes as best she could. He's caught her unawares with this visit.

He's already in the lift by the time I make my sudden dash to go after him, but the second one is empty and waiting and on our floor. I grab it and hit the ground-floor button. The doors take an age to close and my heart thumps. I'll probably miss him. I don't know what I'm going to say if I do catch up with him, but I need to say something. The lift pings and I rush out and across the shiny tiled floor to the rotating doors.

'Wait!'

He's about to get into his car when I stop him. It's a sleek Jaguar. The kind of car Richard would love. Richard would hate Simon Manning. He's everything Richard would want to be. Charming. Rugged. Successful. *Please God don't let Richard be watching me today. Don't let him see this.*

'Wait!' I say again and he turns. I feel like I might burst into tears. Chasing after him has made my ribs ache and I'm so tired of keeping up this *front* of cool calm. As if everything is A-okay. If anyone can understand how I feel, it's going to be Simon. He's had a sliver of it. Inside. A splinter of dirt that's wormed its way in.

'I've got to get to a meeting,' he says.

'Bullshit.' The word's out before I can stop it, but fuck it. If he's taking his business from PKR, then he's taking it. My swearing isn't going to change that. 'I don't blame you for not wanting to hang around here — God knows it's no fun for me right now — but don't bullshit me. You've got time to talk.'

'I really *do* have to be somewhere.'

'Are you cancelling the contract with us?' My stare is as direct as my question and he has the good grace to look uncomfortable. 'Because if you are, it's not fair. It's not fair on Penny, it's not fair on the company and it's not fair on all those people on our books who were looking forward to a decent working contract. It's tough for them out there. A lot of them are people who've fallen through the cracks. And to be fair to Lisa, she — '

'To be fair to Lisa?' His eyes are wide and I'm not sure if it's shock or anger or both and I cringe at my own words.

'I mean in this context. A lot of those people

wouldn't have been taken on by anyone else. She fought for them. Persuaded them to take all the free courses. And they've become some of our most reliable workers.' I pause, the heat in me draining away. 'Look,' I say. 'I know you liked her. I know you guys had been flirting for a while and she told me about your dinner date.' I see the flash of anger in his eyes as if I'm about to blackmail him and I hold my hands up in supplication. 'I have no intention of telling anyone. Trust me, I don't want to talk about her *at all.*' Tears sting my eyes. 'Because I'm not actually sure how to. Ten years of friendship have been ripped away from me and I feel like she's fucking died or something, and yet everyone is looking at me as if I should somehow have known, like she maybe even told me or something. But Jesus, how could I have known something *like that*? Who thinks a real person can do something like that?'

He slumps back against his car as I wipe the threatening tears away. 'I always pride myself on not being conned,' he says quietly. 'I can smell it coming, you know? I've got a past myself. I can sense a conman. It's why I'm good at what I do. I can read people. But this time . . . I didn't think . . . I feel like a fool.' He's bitter, that much is clear. His mind has fast-forwarded through all the *what if*'s. What if he'd married her and this had come out? What would it have done to his business? Everything he'd worked so hard for? Would she have told him? How would he have felt if he'd fallen in love with her? What if, what if, what if.

'I don't think I'll ever trust a friend again,' I say. It's an awful thought, dark and lonely, but how could I get so close to another person now? How could anyone fill the hole Lisa has left in my life? 'And the worst part is,' I say without looking at him, 'there are moments when I really miss her.'

I pull myself together and straighten my shoulders. I didn't come out here to cry about my own miserable lot. 'We all have our own shit to deal with in this. Penny, me, you. But what we have to remember is that it's none of our fault. That's what I keep telling myself. When I feel everyone looking at me funny. It's not my fault.' I meet his eyes. 'And it's *definitely* not the fault of all those people who are excited at the prospect of a long-term contract with a weekly wage packet. None of this makes you a bastard or an idiot. This is a one in a million situation. A one in thirty million situation. This is not something you can plan for. We were just unlucky for being in Lisa's world.'

'Charlotte's world,' he says.

'No,' I'm adamant. 'Lisa's. She may not have been real, but she was real to us. The fact that you liked her doesn't make you a bastard. But taking out how you feel about yourself on all those strangers? That would.' I let a moment of silence hang between us. 'Anyway, that's all I wanted to say.' I'm tired and bruised and I don't even know why I'm out here. 'You do whatever you've got to do.'

I turn and head towards the building.

'Marilyn?'

I look back at him.

'I'll think about it, okay?'

They all look at me when I get back to my desk, but I ignore them as if I've just been to the loo or something. My steel plating is back on, but I'm lighter for having talked to Simon. To know that someone else is feeling at least a little of what I am.

Penny calls me to her office after lunch. Up close under the bright lights I'm surprised at how tired she looks, but I don't comment. Glass houses and stones.

'Thank you,' she says. I don't have to ask for what. The relief is palpable.

'It was nothing.'

Penny nods towards the door. 'How is it out there?'

'Gossipy,' I say. 'Pretty much as you'd expect. It'll calm down.'

There were more homemade cakes today — *we're a team, we must all pull together* — and although Julia could maybe still pass as a twenty-something, she's taking on the mother role with the others since I'm now an outsider. Stacey has pulled in closer to Toby, who's oh so happy to look after her. At least Stacey showed some sadness. She's sweet enough to be able to say, 'But I liked her,' out loud and have nobody judge her. It's the power of youth, I suppose. No one will give me that leeway. I'm too old. Past it. *I should have known better.*

'I still can't get my head around it,' Penny says. She's been so busy firefighting, she probably hasn't had any time to think until now.

155

'Tell me about it.' I smile at her. Maybe she's realising now that it's no different for me. In fact, it's *worse* for me. I'm the one next to the empty desk, a desk I was so keen to have alongside mine when we were planning the new office layout. She doesn't look at me, but instead stares at the door as if she can see through it to the others.

'I bet it was her who stole the petty cash,' she says sharply.

My mouth opens and closes like a goldfish. In all this, I'd forgotten what Lisa had seen at the party. What she'd told me the last time I saw her. What she thought about Julia. Had it all been a cover? Had it been Lisa who'd been stealing all along?

'Maybe,' I say, but my disagreement slithers inside me. 'But then why did it only start going missing now?'

Penny gives me a sharp glance. 'Maybe I only started to notice now. Things have been hectic.'

'True,' I concede quickly. 'And it was Ava's sixteenth birthday and I know she bought her expensive presents. She always does.' *Poor Ava. Has she told Lisa?* I wonder what she's going to do and I wish I could talk to her. I wish I'd said something that last night. Gone to her room and spoken to her instead of pretending I hadn't seen it.

Penny's gaze softens now I'm onside. There's no way I'm going to mention the 'Julia suspicions'. I don't have the energy for more conflict and why should I consider defending Lisa? I'm here on my own while she's headed off to another new name and new life. No doubt where she'll make another mug of a best friend, ignorant that she's a child-killer.

And not just any child, I remind myself. *Her own two-year-old brother.* Eleven is old enough to know what you're doing. My best friend was a monster. My anger takes hold again and it's a good feeling. A rush of energy that gives me strength.

'Do you fancy grabbing a glass of wine later?' I ask. 'The old pub we used to go to?' I haven't been for a drink with Penny in ages — not since she decided to expand the business. She's quite caustically funny after half a bottle of Sauvignon Blanc and I could use a good laugh.

'Oh, I can't.' Her eyes slip away and discomfort radiates out from her. 'I've still got so much to do.'

'No problem.' My smile is too wide. 'It was only a thought.'

'Another time?'

'Sure. Whenever.'

She looks grateful I haven't pushed it and I keep my walk confident as I leave her office and go back to my desk, my emotions simmering under the skin. I should have *let* Simon Manning take his business elsewhere. Ungrateful bitch. And fuck you, Lisa. Fuck you for swanning off and leaving me tarred with your guilt.

Richard's hanging up the phone when I get home, and he does it a touch too quickly, as if he didn't want me to see and hadn't heard me coming in. His eyes are bright and he's grinning. Handsome. I used to think it was wolfish, but now I see the hyena. Now he's started to *show* me the hyena.

'A new job?' I ask. It's delicate ground. Work has been thin, and that's a generous view. The housing market has slowed and no one seems to need reputable builders any more. Of course I never paid any attention to what he was doing with money during the good times, and he failed to ever mention there were bad times until it had all got out of hand. It's such a mess. Our marriage is showered in a confetti of final demands.

'Something like that. Could be things are looking up!' He winks at me. 'Get your lippy on, lovely wife. Let's go out to the Peking Palace.'

All I want to do is take my shoes off, drain some wine, go to bed and pass out, but I can see that's not an option. He's already pulling his jacket on.

'We can walk down to the Navigation for a drink first. Make it a date night.' He leans forward and kisses me. I don't trust this good mood. I don't trust it at all. He's up to something. My nerves sing and my bruises throb in harmony as I follow him out and close the door. And it won't end well.

31

AFTER

2001

His face is an outline in the darkness. They're both hidden in the night, only the rustle of cotton sheet betraying their existence as she talks. She loves him, she knows that. He says he loves her. He says they're going to be together forever. He takes care of her. He wants her to move in with him. Joanne is happy she has a boyfriend but says she should take it slowly. Be sure. Joanne wants her to keep her flat on for a little while, so there's no pressure. Joanne says living together is a big step.

She still loves Joanne and can't imagine life without her support but she wishes she'd stop treating her like a child. It's true she's only been with Jon for a few months but they're inseparable and she's a woman in her twenties. It sounds older than twenty-three. But still, twenty-three is hardly a baby.

Jon makes her laugh. No one has made her laugh like that since . . . well . . . since *then*. But her body is now made of different cells. She's a different person. The sheets beneath her are damp, but with adult sweat, not shameful urine. This is her new life.

She leans back against the pillow, the world

swimming a little. They've been drinking — him more than her — he drinks far more than her but that's what men do, isn't it? Get drunk? She likes it when his eyes are hazy and he looks at her with so much love and a big boyish grin on his face. In those moments she thinks she'll explode with happiness. And sometimes, just sometimes, when they're sitting together on her little sofa in front of some comedy film and eating sweet-and-sour pork and chicken chow mien and he apologises that they can't afford to do more while she's thinking she's in heaven, sometimes, she can forget the secret she's keeping from him. For so long she's been worried about people knowing but now she feels she'll burst if she *doesn't* tell him. How can she say she loves him and not be honest? How can he be sure he loves her if he doesn't know?

The dark shape of him moves beside her and he leans up to take a swallow of red wine from the tumbler by the bed. He holds it out to her and she does the same. It dries her mouth but it's warm and makes her head sing. The buzz reminds her of *before* too. When she was a different person. She's been thinking about the past far too much. Worrying at it like a tiny splinter under a nail that she can't get out. But it's always there, between them. Even here in the echoes of their love-making.

'Jon,' she starts, before hesitating. He tries to pull her back in to lie on his chest but she doesn't want the reassuring beat of his heart right now. Not until she's sure it belongs to her. 'I have something to tell you.' Her voice is

160

disembodied, floating in the dark. His face is grainy and for once she's glad of the thick curtains that block all brightness from the street-lamp outside. Normally, when she can't sleep, the darkness chokes her, but tonight she's using it as a comfort blanket to hide within.

'You sound serious.' He laughs a little but there's an edge to it and she realises he thinks this is about *them*, that perhaps she's done something, perhaps there's another boy. It astounds her to think he could ever worry she'd leave him. She'll love him until the day she dies.

'It's something I need you to know. But something you can never ever tell another person.' He quietens, cowed by the seriousness of her words. 'Do you promise?' she asks.

'Cross my heart and hope to die,' he says. His words suck the life from her for a frozen moment as her nerves jangle and her palms sweat. Was this a bad omen? Him saying those words that have haunted her for so long? Should she say nothing? Joanne has told her to stay silent. Joanne said it was human nature to want to tell. People want to share things but some things you have to carry on your own. If at some point in the future they had a baby, apparently that would be different. Then, perhaps, he'd have to know. But then he'd also have a reason not to tell anyone else.

He's waiting for her to say more and her mouth moves guppy-like, opening and closing silently. There will *be* a baby, so why not tell now? Babies are what happen in the world when a girl and a boy fall in love, and it's not as if

161

they've always been careful. She should have made sure they were careful, but she found herself not bothering. She knows what that means. There's been far too much analysis over the years for her not to see her motivations clearly. She *wants* a baby. It's a thought that both excites and terrifies her. The idea of it is too fragile and precious to examine.

She opens her mouth again, still wondering how to begin. Once upon a time? Turn it into a dark fairy tale? Try and frame it all in something sugar-coated? It's a stupid thought. However she tells it, it will be shocking. He may never speak to her again. He may strangle her right here in their bed as so many strangers have said they'd like to do.

She will tell him. But she won't talk about the actual event. She's never talked about that. She *can't* talk about that. She did it, what more is there to say? As it is, she starts with her name. Delivers the punchline first. Her cells might all be new but there has not been so much time passed that her real name isn't at the very least a familiar ringing bell in people's heads. A bogeyman to scare small children with. *Be home for tea or Charlotte Nevill will get you.*

She speaks into the gloom, stilted quiet sentences which belie their weight, and although she's oh so aware of him lying beside her, his body inadvertently tensing with her words, she doesn't turn to look at him once, but spills her story out until it's an added layer of darkness, an extra sheet across them both.

When she's done, and it really doesn't take

long to tell, the truth rarely does, there is only silence. He sits up and reaches for the wine glass. She hears him swallow. Everything stops. She's made a terrible mistake. She wishes she could cry. The silence is endless as it all whirrs about in his head. She looks up at him and wonders if this dark silhouette is the last she'll ever see of him. Her legacy life suddenly seems to be an origami horse, like the ones Mr Burton makes with left-over paper. Beautifully constructed. So easily crushed.

'I'm sorry, Jon,' she whispers, and although her eyes are dry, her voice cracks. 'I'm so sorry.'

But then he's telling her it's all right and that he loves her and he presses his naked skin to hers and they kiss. He loves her. He loves *her*.

In the weeks that come after, when she realised the sickness and tiredness and constant hunger weren't anything to worry about and that their two was about to become three, she thinks she knows when their baby was made. In that special, open, honest night.

It was as if maybe, maybe, God had forgiven her.

32

NOW

AVA

Finally, finally I got them all to go. To give us 'some time to ourselves'. It wasn't easy. They act like we're kids no one trusts to be safe alone, but after being all sweetness and light for a while I got my way. Some time alone with Mum. One night without any of them around.

It was weird when they all left. This tiny flat suddenly felt so big. Alison put a load of contact numbers on the fridge, which looks so normal until you remember they're not for cleaners or babysitters, but police and psychiatrists and probation officers. Still, my stomach fizzes with excitement and nerves. Not my life any more. Not after tonight. Even if he doesn't show up — *he will show up, of course he'll show up* — I'm not coming back. I've decided. Mum's trying to be more normal but we haven't talked about *it*. What she did that day. Alison says she never has. I think they're hoping that maybe she'll open up to me, but that won't happen. I don't want to know and I don't want to hear her speaking with my mum's voice. She's not Mum any more, just some twisted freak from the newspapers.

Alison wasn't her probation officer when I was

born. That was some woman called Joanne. Alison came along when we moved areas when I was small. It's a past life. Not mine. My life is in my future. Soon Mum will be a memory. History. She already is after all this. How can I try to love her or understand her, however much I might wonder about the years before I was born? She's a stranger. She's a *lie*. It's easier to remember that now we look so different.

I didn't want my hair cut but I gritted my teeth and let them do it and I actually think the bob suits me. They razor-cut it and it's quite cool. Ange would fucking love it. I'm also a redhead now — not ginger but a deep auburn — and they gave me brown contacts. It's weird how such small changes make me look like a new person. I've practised doing my make-up differently too. Bigger lines around my eyes. Confident colours. With slightly different clothes on I'll look like a totally new person. Mum looked like she was going to cry when she saw me. She didn't though. She's not a crier — that's what they say about her. She didn't cry *then*. Not in court or anything.

I told her I liked my new look and then she was okay about it. She says sorry all the time for everything. *I'm so sorry about this, Ava.* As if it's a dress ruined in the wash, not our whole lives down the drain.

They've changed her too. She's blonde now. Not properly blonde or anything hot, but a kind of sandy run-of-the-mill colour. She looks younger, although that could be because she's lost some weight. Alison and the police are less worried about how *she* looks. There are hardly any pictures of her for people to recognise her from. The papers aren't allowed to print them, and now all her privacy and hating herself in photos and *what would I do with Facebook anyway?* comments are making sense.

We didn't really talk at all on this night to ourselves I'd arranged. Alison left a supermarket version of a Chinese takeaway in the fridge and I heated it up and we ate it on our laps in front of the telly. I said I liked her hair and she started to apologise all over again. I said it didn't matter and we'd get through it. She looked so relieved. How can she think it's that easy? Like we can get back to how we were before? That life was a pack of lies anyway.

Yesterday, when I had started my campaign of *niceness*, she came into my room, picking at the edges of her fingers as she sat on my bed. She told me to write down any questions I had for her. It was Alison's idea. Not questions about *it* — she can't bring herself to say what she did — but about her life and our lives and anything else. She said she'll answer them all as best she can. I told her I would, but I didn't mean it. I don't want to know any of it *now*. Okay, maybe I do want to know — *tell me about my dad* — but what good would it do? It doesn't matter. Not any more.

We watched more TV and drank cups of tea as if this was some normal evening at home, and I quietly clock-watched, desperate for the time to pass, wondering if he was feeling the same.

Eventually Mum took her sleeping pill — I

wonder how many pills they've got her on right now — and I made a big deal of yawning and saying I was tired, and I kissed her on the head before going to my room. It was the only freaky moment in all this. Something about the smell of her scalp made my stomach cramp, and for a second I wanted to climb on to her lap like I did when I was small. When she was my world. It was a funny, horrible feeling and I slammed the lid on it hard. I don't know if she's capable of loving me — if she could love, she'd never have done what she did — and I can't understand why she even had me. These are the sorts of questions Alison wants me to write down. But fuck them. I'm not going to be here. She's not part of my new life. He's my world and he'll be waiting. He has to be.

I lie in my bed in the dark, my clothes on under the duvet that's pulled up under my chin. What will he think of my new look? I'll have to change it again, anyway. The hair colour at least, because no doubt the police will look for me. But I'm sixteen. I'm not a child. They'll think I've run away, and they'll be right. I'm going to leave a note. It says. 'Don't come and look for me.' It's short but does the job and I didn't want to mention him. It's not his fault this is such a fucked-up situation.

Has Alison noticed the money missing from her wallet? I took thirty when she was in talking to Mum before she left, and I took a twenty from the psychiatrist yesterday. She hasn't been back today so fuck knows whether she suspected.

Anyway, fifty should be enough if I can find a

phone box for a cab or a bus still running. I've got to get to the country lane where we're going to meet. Where no one will see us. It's further away now, but still doable. We said four a.m. so I've got plenty of time. If he's not there I'll go to Ange's or Jodie's. But he *will* be there. He loves me. When we're safely away, I'll message my friends and tell them not to worry. I'll have to deal with the other thing too, the thin blue line Jodie was going to help me sort out, but he'll deal with that. I know he will. He's been so understanding about Courtney, even though he got jealous. Will having an abortion make me feel more grown up? Will I seem more grown up to *him?* Maybe one day we'll have children of our own but right now, I just want this thing *out* of me. Maybe it will go away all by itself. When I'm not feeling sick, I can almost pretend it's not there.

I wait until the flat is completely silent. My heart thumps. My mouth is dry. *He will be there, he will be there*, I tell myself. *He won't let me down.* I push my covers back and quietly stand. I don't put my shoes on yet. They can wait until I'm out of the flat and in the corridor.

I gather my things and check my pockets for my money before creeping out the front door.

This is it, I think. And then I'm gone.

33

MARILYN

'Look. There. You see?' Richard holds the magazine out in front of me. '*She's* done it.' Mrs Goldman, the old bird who lives — *lived* — next door to Lisa stares out at me from the cover. She looks frail. Did someone bully her into this? It's a lurid magazine, the gossipy kind found in dentists' and doctors' waiting rooms, and aimed at the more 'settled' woman than *Closer* or *Heat*. I glance at the headline above the photo of Mrs Goldman on her front step: *Charlotte Nevill's neighbour tells all — the secret life of the child killer*. I take the magazine and drop it on the side, flicking to the relevant page. A quote stands out. *I always knew she was odd. A loner.*

'It's bullshit,' I say, turning away to stir my coffee. 'And she should be ashamed of herself. Lisa used to buy her bloody shopping for her, *and* add extra treats. She checked on Mrs Goldman more than her own family ever did.'

'That's not the point.' I hear it then. The anvil hardness. He's running out of patience with me and playing nice hasn't worked. 'If she can peddle this shit to a national magazine, we can probably up the *Mail's* offer. It's *your* story they all want. You knew her best.'

'Given how things stand, I'd say I didn't really know her at all.' I don't have time for this. I have to go to work so I slide past — *gently does it* — to get my coat and feel the tension radiating from him as he tries to keep his rage under control.

'I don't understand why you won't do it.' He follows me into the corridor. 'It's money for nothing. It could sort all our financial problems out.'

Not my problems, I want to say. *Yours.* 'It's not for nothing. It's dirty. Sleazy. You've always said that about anyone who sells a story yourself.'

'It's like you're protecting her,' he growls. 'Always defending her.'

'Don't be ridiculous.'

'You did it just then. About the old woman.'

I pause at the front door. 'I wouldn't want Ava to read it. Me talking about them for money. She has no one to trust at the moment.'

'You're never going to see her again so why does it matter! Why can't you get that into your thick head?'

I let the front door slam behind me. There are still a couple of reporters — for want of a better word — dirt-diggers, maybe — loitering at the end of the drive, but I don't look at them, let alone answer as they call out to me. I get in my car, put my sunglasses on, and drive — too fast for our 20 mph speed limit — until I'm free of them.

If only it was so easy to escape all of it. I think about the £40,000 the *Daily Mail* have offered.

Richard said they got in touch with him, but he hasn't knocked so much sense out of me this year I'd buy that. He called *them*, of course he did, and told them all about Lisa and me and our friendship and how much insight I'd have into her day-to-day life. His face was a picture when I said no. He couldn't believe it. Especially when he realised how powerless he was in this. No one wants *his* story — it's not worth a fraction of mine. How did I ever think this man was love? Even in the early days, when I'd help him with his work, study the shapes and spaces of houses with him, give him ideas for clients, I should have known it would come to this eventually. *Why are you wearing red lipstick? Who are you wearing it for?* The little accusations should have been my first clue, so many years ago.

My phone starts ringing. Him. I let it ring out and when I stop at the traffic lights I send a short text: *I'll think about it.* I really should think about it. I don't owe Lisa anything, and Ava probably isn't looking at the papers anyway. Given everything else, I doubt it would matter to her. But it would matter to me. I'm angry at Mrs Goldman, because she should know better. *She's lonely.* I hear the words in Lisa's voice. *She's probably just enjoying the attention. At least she can afford a cake now and then after this.* I shut the voice down. Lisa doesn't get to be Mother Teresa in my head now. *She's* the fucking problem. Even now she's gone I'm still left carrying the can for her.

The atmosphere in the office is different and I

feel it before I reach my desk. They're all slightly hyper, like young pups let off a leash. A pack for sure, and one I'm not quite part of any more. Stacey glances my way, as does Toby, and the noise settles as my arrival registers.

'What?' I ask. 'Have I missed something? I'll have a coffee, if you're making, Emily. Thank you.' All bright smiles as I throw my handbag down under my desk. Unfazeable Marilyn. Confronting things head on.

'It's about Lisa or Charlotte or whatever,' Julia says, after a Mexican wave of knowing glances passes around the room. I bristle. What now?

'Oh yes?'

She perches on the edge of my desk, proprietorial. 'Well, we all went for a drink last night, and Penny said — '

'Penny?' I cut in before I can stop myself.

'We thought she needed a break from everything.' She says *we* but she means *I*. She is teacher's pet, after all.

'That was nice of you.' My tone matches hers, sweetness and light, although my heart is racing. They all went to the pub without me. Worse, Penny said no to me but yes to them. Sure, it could be that she simply changed her mind, but it doesn't ring true. She's not comfortable with me any more. I'm too *close*.

'Anyway, Penny said money has been going missing from the petty cash. She thinks Lisa took it.'

'Really?' It all plays out behind my eyes. Julia buying wine, Penny drinking too quickly, needing to relax, and then opening her big mouth.

172

'You didn't know about the money?'

She's good. She knows I know. 'Oh, I know about the money.' This is my shot across her bow, a hint of accusation in my tone, and I don't know if it's my imagination but I'm sure I see a flash of something in her eyes. *Careful*, I tell myself. *How much do you actually care?* 'Penny told me.'

'Did you ever see Lisa do anything suspicious?'

They're all listening now, little flicks of heads in my direction. What else was discussed last night? Me, obviously, but in what capacity? What conclusions did they draw? What path did Julia lead them down, the sneaky little thieving bitch? The aggression in my thought shocks me into acknowledging that I believe what Lisa said. Julia is a wolf among sheep in our office.

'No. If I had, I'd have said something.'

'Of course you would.' She smiles, the slashes of blood red on her lips highlighting her perfectly white teeth. Bleached, no doubt. Another trick to appear youthful. Lisa wasn't wrong about that either.

The blinds in Penny's office are shut and I wonder if it's because she's hiding from them or me or all of us. Maybe she's got a hangover. Whichever, I can't believe how ready she is to lay the guilt at Lisa's door. *She's a child-killer*, I want to storm in there and tell her. *Not a bloody petty thief.*

'I suppose we'll find out soon enough if she had money problems,' Julia purrs. 'It's all coming out in the news.'

173

My stomach knots. What if they find out Richard has dug me into a financial hole and we're living off credit cards? Will that make me suspect number one? 'Or maybe she did it just because she could?' I say. Julia's smile twists, triumphant. She knows what I'm doing. Trying to worm my way back in by agreeing with them. How will they react if I do what Richard wants and sell my story? My job would be over. Would anyone else hire me? A woman in her forties in this job climate who tells all for cash?

'Marilyn Hussey?'

I hear my name being called before I've even noticed the man and woman standing a few feet away from my desk. The office falls silent, everyone alert and watching.

'Yes?' All professional as I die a little inside. *What now?*

'They told us at reception we could find you here. Could we have a word?'

The woman flashes a badge as she introduces herself as Detective Sergeant Bray, but with the dark suits and sensible shoes they're wearing along with the dour serious expressions, it wasn't necessary. It's obvious they're police.

'Of course,' I say. 'Let's go to a meeting room.' I don't bother to ask what it's about. It'll be Lisa. What else could it be? Lisa, Lisa, Lisa. I'm so sick of Lisa.

★   ★   ★

It's not about Lisa. Not directly, anyway. It's about Ava, and I'm not steeled for that. As they ask their questions — *Have you seen her since her mother's identity was exposed? Have you heard from her last night or today?* — alarm bells ring in my head and they say nothing to reassure me when I point out they must know where Ava is better than me. She's with Lisa, surely?

Their polite smiles and expressionless eyes meet my concerned ones. I ask if she's run away and they don't answer, but instead parry with questions of their own. *Are there any other adults, other than those at her school, she might be close to? Anyone she might contact?* I rack my brains but I can only think of that swimming club of hers. Their coach maybe? Lisa didn't have any close friends other than me, and therefore, by default, Richard. But Ava doesn't really know him other than to say hello to.

They thank me, though it's clear I've given them nothing, and it's only when they're about to leave I remember the one thing I know about Ava maybe no one else does. The thing I spent the whole of the last evening wondering if I should tell Lisa about.

'If she's missing,' I say, hoping to get a reaction out of them that may give me some snippet of information, 'you may want to try any local abortion clinics. I saw a bit of wrapping in the bathroom bin at their house. Only the corner, but it was from a pregnancy test, I'm sure of it.' I should know, I've done enough of them in the past. 'I think Ava might have been pregnant.'

They thank me again — this time with more

175

sincerity, their visit here no longer wasted time — and DS Bray gives me her card. Her name is unfortunate, I think, as she walks away, feet heavy in her solid shoes, no elegance in her gait. She's like a donkey.

It's a mean thought and I realise what a bitch being under so much stress is making me. If Lisa were here we'd probably laugh at it, but alone it's just bitter and mean. But if Lisa were here none of this would be happening at all.

Ava's run away. The thought hits me as I turn back to the office to face the pack's curious, hungry looks. My worry ties itself in knots. Little Ava out there somewhere in the world, angry and alone. I hope she's not alone. I hope one of her friends knows where she is and will crack under police pressure. She's sixteen, I tell myself. She's not stupid. She'll be somewhere safe. The thought is hollow. The world is full of bright but angry sixteen-year-olds who run off and end up on the streets or worse. Dragged out of rivers. Never heard of again. Ava's stubborn and she always has been. She wouldn't go back, however bad it got.

Maybe she *has* gone to get an abortion. Maybe she'll turn up afterwards. I never thought Ava getting knocked up would be a comfort, but now it's like an emotional anchor. She's gone to get an abortion somewhere. The police will find her.

I go straight to the kitchen to make a coffee — the one Emily left on my desk now too cold for my taste — and it's Stacey who joins me like a skittish cat, and asks what they wanted. She at least has the decency to look a little embarrassed and I wonder who pushed her in here, Julia or Toby or a combination of the two.

Fuck you, Lisa, I think for the millionth time since she ceased to exist. *Fuck you very much for all this.*

34

AFTER

2003

There are no fairy tales, no happily ever afters, no matter how many cheap Disney videos she plays in the afternoons to keep her daughter settled while she cleans and tidies and tries to make their lives look normal and under control. Not for her at any rate. She was stupid to ever think there could be.

She aches as she gathers up the empty beer cans and cheap vodka bottles and throws them away. What is the point, she wonders. There will only be more to throw away later. Later. She can't face any more *later*.

Upstairs, in her cot, Crystal starts crying. Crystal. She hates their daughter's name. One of their many, many big arguments was about that name. *Ava* was what she'd wanted to call her. A name which spoke of elegance and charm and better things. Crystal sounds cheap for trying so hard not to. Crystal is breakable. Crystals can be smashed into a thousand pieces. The thought of any harm coming to her baby terrifies her. It fills her every waking thought, humming in her blood. Someone taking some terrible crazy revenge. She should never have told Jon who she really is. She should probably have never got involved with him, never have dared to think she could have a love that survived her past, but without him she wouldn't have her daughter so she can't wish for that.

Little Crystal is two now. Her turning three can't come quickly enough. To be three would mean she was past Daniel's age. Maybe her dreams of him will then fade. Maybe this sense of terrible dread will go. She doesn't believe it. The dreams and the dread will be with her forever, and they're so much worse since Crystal was born. At first she thought the dreams were Daniel's ghost wanting to punish her more from beyond the grave, but in her heart she knows that's not true. Daniel was a good boy. And he was only two and a half.

She goes upstairs and cradles Crystal to her thin chest, soothing her. The little girl's clothes need washing, as do most of her nappies, and the whole of their small house smells vaguely of shit and warm milk, but Jon hasn't left her any money again and she's out of washing powder. This cannot go on. She needs to call Joanne. She has to. *She* may deserve this awful life with a man who drinks too much and calls her a killer and says she revolts him whenever she tries to appease him, but her Crystal, *her Ava*, doesn't. If they stay here, who knows how it will end? What he'll do?

Last night was a wake-up call and she needs to act. To finally show some spine. Every time she closes her eyes she sees it: the bottle smashing against the wall to the right above her head. Little Crystal, sitting on the floor, shocked into stopping crying at her parents' fight for a moment, covered in broken glass and alcohol.

It killed his anger in its tracks. He loves their daughter, she knows that, but she knows violence and what he did was enough to chill her to the bone. To make her realise how he blames her for everything through his alcoholic haze. She's grown up a lot in the past three years, the long years since the perfect night when she told him her secret. She's learned a lot about people. She knows he loves her, but she knows he hates himself for it. He can't look at her most of the time and when they have sex she can feel his disgust. It's worse since Crystal came along. Her sweet innocence is a constant reminder of what *Charlotte* did.

You're a monster. That's what he said last night. *How can I love a monster?* His words are worse than blows, but the blows can't be far off. She's had to gauge these things before. It's all building to some awful conclusion, and she's terrified he'll take it out on Crystal, however much he says he loves her, because she knows how easy it is for things to go horribly wrong.

She holds the pudgy little girl too tightly, until she starts to cry. She doesn't scream or wail, but lets out a gentle sob as if she can pick up on her mother's anguish. She can, of course, and maybe she's afraid to cry loudly now, even when Daddy's out of the house.

Jon won't be back for hours. He's not at work, he's at the pub or the bookie's or round a mate's house. He only works a few hours a week now and that won't go on forever. His drinking is too out of control to hold down a job. She used to be able to see the man she fell in love with still inside him, but not any more. Not now it's all turned to shit. Worse than shit. This awful loathing that emanates from him.

She has to call Joanne. This is the end of the line. Failure has to be faced. Maybe it will be fine, maybe she'll be able to stay who she is now and move to a little flat in the same town — maybe even her old flat. She won't be able to work until Crystal goes to school, but it could maybe be almost like before she met him. She'd have routines like when she was happy.

It won't be that way, of course. Joanne's already unhappy about the situation. She thinks it's 'precarious'. Jon's 'highly unpredictable right now'. And she's right. He should have taken the counselling he was offered when they came clean about him knowing. But he didn't. He said he was fine. He loved her. That was before the pressures of fatherhood and the pressure of carrying her secret every single day for years and years.

This is the other thing she's learned over these years. The secret is her own. It's her burden and sharing it doesn't lighten the load, it simply doubles it. She can't stay here if she leaves Jon, that's just wishful thinking. Joanne, and the police, and all those people who make her decisions won't let her. Jon's threatened often enough that if she takes Crystal away, he'll ruin everything. Tell everyone. Finish her. When he's sober, he says he's sorry, but how often is he sober? You can't trust a drunk, she knows that too.

Crystal is crying and she has to do what's best for her. She burns with shame when she finally calls the probation officer, but Joanne is nothing but professional and suddenly it's all out of her hands. Plans are put in motion. It would seem they were readier for this than she is. All that's left for her to do is leave him a letter. She tries to write how she feels, and also to be cold with him. He needs that. He needs to start again as much as she does. Her hand shakes as she writes. She doesn't love him any more. This is true. She's afraid of him. This is also true. She writes one final line before folding the paper and leaving it on the kitchen table.

Don't come after me. Don't try and find me. Don't try and find us.

Calm now, she was always calm when someone else took control, she gathers what she needs and the pieces of her legacy life — passport, NHS certificate, everything that made this ghost of a person real. They're useless now, a skin that will soon be shed, but Joanne will want them back, and even if she doesn't, Jon shouldn't have them.

She takes a moment to stand in the house, the flimsy walls of her playing card castle, and then she's ready when the car comes. She doesn't cry, she never does, but her heart empties as she closes the door.

Goodbye, Jon, she whispers. *I'm sorry.* She doesn't look back as they leave. She's so tired of looking back. Instead she holds her tearful daughter tight and points at buses out of the window. 'Don't cry, Ava,' she says, sucking in the smell of her child. 'Don't cry.'

35

NOW

MARILYN

I'm on autopilot, watching my movements from the inside, in awe of my body's ability to get all the shit I need doing done. Despite the awful pain — this time a rib or two are definitely cracked — I get up, get dressed and head into work. On my way I stop at the bank on the high street and wait outside until they open. I'm the first customer through the door and I hear myself speak. 'I'd like to empty these accounts, please.' I smile, confident. There is barely five hundred pounds in one, but there is a thousand in another. Money I've been squirrelling away as an emergency fund, never thinking I'd actually use it. An illusion that I may one day be brave enough to break away.

When I first found out about Richard's debts I'd considered telling him about it, but my thousand wouldn't touch the sides of the well of his poor financial judgement, and once his gratitude had faded he'd want to know why I'd been hiding money from him. And what would I say then? *Because when I vowed to love you until death do us part, you beating my ribs into my spleen isn't what I had in mind . . .*

I don't close the account — I'll need it for

Penny to pay my salary into, somewhere Richard won't be able to get his hands on it — and then when I get to work I go straight to her office and tell her Richard and I are 'having problems' and that I need a couple of days to sort myself out. She doesn't ask any questions — she probably thinks it's all down to Lisa, and in some ways it is, but this fire was smouldering before the petrol of Lisa and Charlotte was poured on it — but tells me that she won't take the days out of my holiday. I say I'm going to stay with a friend and I warn her Richard might call looking for me so I won't tell her where. I also give her the new bank details for my wages. I see her pity. *That bad?* If only she knew. I'd hate for her to know. It makes me cringe that I've become this beaten woman. This is not who I am. It's who *he* is, nothing to do with me, but if I find it hard to see the distinction sometimes, then there's no hope for other people. I nod, not trusting myself to speak, and she impulsively gives me a hug that almost makes me shriek in pain.

I tell her I have my mobile if they need me for anything. I would have left that at home too — God, I want some peace and quiet — but I can't bear the thought of the police not being able to get in touch about Ava. I've blocked Richard's number because I have no intention of answering any of his calls, and I'm not a fool, I've turned the 'find my iPhone' setting to off. Let him stew.

Before I leave, I turn on my 'out of office' email and quickly get the number I need from Lisa's files. It's barely ten in the morning but I

185

haven't slept and I'm in so much pain all I want to do is go to Tesco, buy a bottle of wine and neck it in the car. But that can wait. Instead, I swallow what little pride I have left and make the call. I speak quietly, sounding like a powerless child. It's how I feel too, even though technically this is the first step in getting the power *back*. Right now, it seems more like straightforward running away.

He's awkward on the other end of the line, and he doesn't agree straight away, but then from nowhere, I'm sobbing, every hitching breath causing my fractured bones to grind together, and he tells me he'll get it sorted and it will be in his name. I'm still thanking him repeatedly when I realise he's already hung up.

I have nothing with me, not even my toothbrush, just a bare minimum of make-up in my handbag and a tube of hand cream. I couldn't risk sneaking anything out of the house during my getaway, but I can buy a spare set of cheap clothes and the hotel will have toiletries. I keep looking in my rear-view mirror, but there's no sign of Richard following me. Still, I don't begin to relax until I've checked in and when I get up to the room — a junior suite, God love him, not some claustrophobic single — he's waiting there for me. Simon Manning.

'What the hell is going on?' he asks. There's no edge or growl as there is whenever Richard asks the same question. Instead, he's concerned and curious why a woman he barely knows would need him to let her stay anonymously in one of his hotels. 'Marriage problems,' I say, my eyes filling again. I'm so tired and sore. His face tightens, and I don't blame him for feeling a shift. No good ever comes from getting in between warring couples. 'He wanted me to sell my story. To the *Mail*. I said no, obviously.'

'Oh.'

The wheels are whirring in his head. *Must have been some fight.* I drop my handbag on the bed. How much is this room anyway? Why should he let me use it? How long before he picks up the phone to Penny and pulls his business from her because we're all barking mad in one way or another and this was not what he signed up for. I need to explain and I don't have the words for it, so I simply lift my blouse and sweater to show my midriff. I don't worry about the fat there. He's not going to notice it against the blooming colours. I see his eyes widen.

'Jesus Christ.'

'Yeah.'

'You should call the police. Get to a doctor.'

I shake my head. 'It's bad, but it's not that bad. I've been here before. And I *really* don't want any more of the police.'

There's a long pause and I carefully tuck my shirt in again.

'Do you need anything?' he says. 'A change of clothes maybe? A toothbrush? That kind of stuff?'

'I've got some money,' I say. I don't want to leave the hotel. It feels safe here.

'Don't be stupid. I'll send someone out. And if you're hungry order room service.'

I'm so grateful my tears spill again, and my

187

nose is thick with snot. 'I didn't have anywhere else to go.' The enormity of that realisation is driving my self-pity more than anything else in this godawful situation. It's made me realise how much Lisa and I depended on each other. All my other friends are joint ones with Richard. Penny is awkward around me and I can hardly see myself pouring my heart out to Stacey or Julia. Without Lisa, I am entirely alone.

'Please don't tell Penny,' I ask. 'I know it's crazy, me calling you like this. But I thought maybe I could have the room and then pay you back at some point, and I'll get something else sorted . . . ' I'm babbling, repeating myself. I said all this on the phone already.

'I won't tell anyone. Don't worry about it.' He checks his watch. 'But I'm sorry, I have to go. I'll get someone to send some clothes and pyjamas up. And some painkillers. What size clothes do you take?'

'Twelve. Thank you.'

It's only when he's almost through the door that I tell him Ava's missing. He pauses for a moment saying nothing, before curtly commenting. 'I hope she turns up.'

His back stiffens and I feel a waft of coolness as he closes the door quietly behind him. I stare at the wood. I've been stupid to mention anything to do with Lisa. I'm a charity case — God, I hate that — and he doesn't need reminding of her any more than I do.

36

LISA

Even though the sheets have been washed and changed, the whole flat stinks of urine, the mattress still sodden.

Once a bed-wetter, always a bed-wetter.

A change of name can't cure that. Not really. I should have put a plastic sheet on it. They'd have given *Charlotte* a plastic sheet. But, as it is, no one cares about the smell or the fact I pissed myself like a child. It's nothing in the hive of activity the flat has become. Noise. So much noise I have to strain to hear the television.

Ava is gone. The thought alone is a knife in my heart and I bite my cheek to stay focused. It's been twenty-four hours, although for me it's been one wet mattress and a lifetime. I'm submerged in my loss. They're worried I've drowned completely. I was close, that is for sure, but now I can see a tiny splinter of hope, a branch to cling to. I've been staring at the TV screen for so long my eyes are burning. They want to turn it off so they can speak to me, but I won't let them. I may miss something the next time the news report runs. I need to hear it over and over again to make sense of it. To add it to the pieces of the puzzle. It's making me feverish.

'Lisa, we need to — '

'Shhh,' I hiss. Angry. Sharp. 'After this.'

The snippet of a report is back on. The mother of the boy Ava saved claims her son, Ben, says he was pushed into the water.

Pushed. Pushed.

'We know you didn't do that, Lisa.' Alison sounds frayed. They think I'm crumbling, the madness dormant within me eating its way outwards. 'We know you were with Marilyn Hussey and her husband when Ben went into the river.'

Marilyn. Oh, for Marilyn.

'I need the radio on,' I say. There is too much electricity in my head. I'm trying to make the links too quickly. *Drive away, baby. The boy says he was pushed. Peter Rabbit.*

'We need to talk to you.' A sharper voice. Nasal. The donkey woman. Bray of the clumpy body. Not that I can talk about anyone's appearance. Greasy hair and flabby thighs, pasty in the flashes showing from under my dressing gown.

'It's about Ava.'

Her words cut into my overheated brain, although I think that whatever they have to say, I'm way ahead of them. 'She isn't with any of her friends,' the policewoman continues, 'and they all claim they haven't heard from her.'

A crash and a curse come from another room. I don't like the thought of their rough hands on my baby's things. They need to remember that this is a victim's house, not a suspect's. I guess it's easy to get confused where I'm concerned.

No one ever sees me as a victim.

'We've been through her phone and iPad.' My eyes keep glancing over to the silent radio. I want it playing along with the TV. *Leave with me, baby, let's go tonight.*

'Lisa, are you listening?' The policewoman is speaking slowly and loudly as if she thinks I'm stupid. Trying to bash the words through my thick skull.

'She's been chatting to a man. There are Facebook messages. Lots of them. They'd arranged to meet on the night she went missing.' Her words, words I should be clinging on to, drift over me. I'm somewhere else entirely. My body is here, but my mind is scouring the past. We made a pact.

Cross my heart and hope to die.

Breaking those kind of promises wreaks vengeance. I should have known. I *did* know. I've always known. It's the cause of the fear that's eaten at me for so long.

Alison leans forward, obviously seeing how irritated the donkey is getting with me. 'It's *Jon*,' she says. 'He's the man Ava has been talking to on the Internet. But the things he's been saying. Well — they're not the sort of things a father would say to his daughter. Look.' She nods at Bray, who holds out a sheaf of printed paper. I frown as I take them, and look at Alison. 'What are you talking about?' Finally, I engage.

'Jon found Ava on Facebook. He's been messaging her for several months. But he hasn't told her he's her father. The messages have been of a more . . . ' she hesitates. 'Sexual nature. He's groomed her to run away with him.' She takes my hand as if we're friends and it's awkward for both of us. My palm is suddenly sweating, damp springing from my skin like the tears I can never cry. 'Have you heard from him at all?' she asks. 'He's not at his house. He told neighbours he was going travelling almost a year ago. The police are doing everything they can to find him — to find both of them — but they need your help. Is there anywhere he may have taken her? A place that was significant to both of you maybe? Or just to him? Somewhere you went on holiday? We can go through the files, but not everything will be in there.'

Drive away, baby. The rabbit. The photo smashed at the bottom of the stairs. It's all making a terrible sense.

I want the radio on. I may miss something vital. I zone out their words, Alison and the Braying woman still trying to speak to me. I cling on to the printed messages though. I'll study them later. I need to try and make some order out of all this if I'm going to save my daughter.

'She's not listening,' Bray says. 'We need someone who can get through to her. And she needs to ease off the meds for now.' She stands up and leans over me. 'Lisa.' I ignore her. 'Charlotte!' She barks the name, and I can't help but look up. 'Is there any way he could know where you were living?' she asks. 'Anything at all?'

'No,' I say, although even as I do, I know it's a lie. 'No. No way.'

Another piece of the puzzle falls into place. I

was young and stupid and it's the only piece that could fit.

Clever. So very clever.

I wish I could cry.

37

AFTER

2006

Her heart thumps as she licks the bitter glue of the envelope. She shouldn't send the letter. She *knows* she shouldn't, but although the world might think she's evil, if she can't forgive *him* for the thing he did, then how can she ever expect to be forgiven herself? She can't stay filled with hate. It's too exhausting. And he's sorry. He's done the best he can to prove that.

They can keep giving her new names — Lisa, she's now Lisa — but they can't so easily wipe out all the versions of her who went before. They are ghosts who live under the skin and one ghost loved him for a while. Even with how he was towards the end, and after what he did when they left, she still misses how she felt in the early days. And he gave her Ava — Crystal has a new name too this time — so how can she not forgive him now that he's done his best to make up for it all?

She physically flinches when she remembers the headlines — how he made their story, their life together sound so awful. How he blamed his drinking on her. How he said she'd ruined his life. All the tiny details of their relationship that she'd once treasured, he publicly trampled them and made them dirty.

At least they hadn't been able to print her picture. But still, there had been the relocation and another identity to be created, more taxpayers' money spent on someone most of the public would rather had been hanged for what she'd done. She was sure the team around her muttered at the ridiculous cost of it all and blamed her for being a lovesick fool who'd brought this on herself with her big mouth.

But over a year has passed and life has settled and now Jon's done this good thing which will allow her and Ava to have a better life. Alison — there's no more Joanne; a new town means a new probation officer — says that under no circumstances can she have any contact with him. They will pass on her thanks or any note or message she wants to send him. She's told them to do that, but she's also so very tired of everyone knowing everything and her life being under a microscope again. If she gives them the letter for him they'll read every word and some words, even *I forgive you and I wish you all the happiness*, should be private.

She stares at the envelope, the carefully printed address in stark black against the white. His mother's house, that's what the papers had said. He was moving there because his mother was sick and looking after her would help with his rehab. The papers said he wanted to start a fresh life away from his memories of *her*. Maybe he's not living there any more. But if his mother — Patricia, that was her name, Patricia of the over-sweet perfume — is still alive, perhaps she'll pass the letter on. She wouldn't, of course — she'd probably read it and burn it and curse the day her boy met Charlotte Nevill — but at least she will have tried.

She hasn't put any sender's address on the letter, and she's read it over and over to make sure there's nothing in it to give any clues as to where she is now. Not that she is worried about him. Not any more. She's doing the right thing. She owes the ghost of their love, and the very much alive spirit of their little girl, this much. This private moment. She needs to say thank you, and it needs to come on paper not sullied by others' eyes or touch.

Her decision made, she shoves the envelope in her pocket and smiles as she pushes Ava's buggy down to the little post office at the local shops. Stamp attached, she enjoys the whisper of paper as it falls into the box. It's done. Sent. It feels good, and she's smiling as she heads over to the small park with the swings and roundabouts Ava loves so much. She's closed a door on the past.

She doesn't for a second think about the postmark that will be stamped on to her carefully addressed envelope. It doesn't cross her mind at all.

38

NOW

MARILYN

Why did I say yes? Why? I'm only doing this for Ava, to get her back to safety. I'm full of anxiety for her, and exhaustion for me. I really don't need this shit. I breathe more condensation on to the window glass. It's one of those grey muggy days where rain has fallen but not enough, and damp hangs listless in the air soaking everything it touches. Even inside the car, my skin itches with invisible bugs.

Trees blur outside. At least the police hadn't gone to my house, but called my mobile after going to the office. From the look on Detective Bray's face when we'd met outside the hotel, Penny must have told her *something* of what was going on with Richard. I've never thought of Penny as a gossip, but then there's something about the police turning up that makes most people blurt out everything they know or don't know. Not only had she told them about my personal situation, it's clear she'd also mentioned the missing money. 'She thinks Charlotte took it,' Bray says, as we head to our *undisclosed location* to meet. 'Do you?' she asks.

I shrug, staring out at the countryside. 'What would I know? I thought her name was Lisa. I thought she couldn't harm a fly.'

She doesn't speak again until we finally turn down a narrow country lane and the car bumps over the uneven surface, my teeth clenching as each pothole makes my damaged ribs scream. 'She's here already,' she says. 'I must remind you that should you tell anyone at all about this meeting you could be hindering a police investigation and charged as such.'

I snort out a half-laugh. Like I'd tell anyone. Who would I tell? I don't *have* anyone to tell. My self-pity is bitter as bile. I loathe self-pity. I don't see the fucking point in it. 'I'm here for Ava,' I say. 'That's all.' Bray nods, satisfied. We're all here for Ava.

'Try to keep Charlotte on topic,' she says. 'She's . . . well. You'll see. Keep her talking about Jon.' She twists round in her seat as the car slows to a halt, and I see a fierce intelligence in her eyes. Not a donkey at all. 'There must be something she knows that can help us. Somewhere he might have taken Ava. Somewhere they'd been before. A place important to him somehow. We're going through the house again to see if there's anything there to help, but it may come down to what we can get out of her. What *you* can get out of her.'

'Why won't she talk to you?' I ask, carefully unfolding my damaged body from the unmarked car. We're outside a country cottage which should be pretty but instead looks bleak. The small front garden behind the low wall has been tarmacked and even from a distance I can see that the paint is chipped on the cracked sash windowsills, big strips of rotting wood now bare of colour. Even on a sunny day it would be depressing — under the thick grey sky it's virtually suicidal.

'Oh, she talks,' Bray says. 'But she doesn't make any sense. Chat to her. Try to relax her. We'll sift through what she says for anything useful. We haven't told her Ava may be pregnant, she's fragile enough as it is, so don't mention it. And don't try to talk about her past.'

Suddenly I feel sick. I'm going to see Lisa again, but it won't be Lisa at all. She'll be Charlotte Nevill wearing Lisa's skin. 'I have no interest in her past,' I mutter, as we trudge across the gravel to the gate. Talk about her past? How would I do that? *Hey, Lisa, I've had a shitty day at work. Fancy the pub? You can take my mind off it by telling me how murdering your little brother felt. For the lols.* Jesus, what a headfuck.

It's gloomier inside and has the kind of chill that settles in old houses when they've been left empty too long. A hollow cold, as if the bricks have given up waiting for anyone to come and give them purpose. A woman, about my age, in jeans and a sweater, hair pulled back in a loose ponytail, has let us in, and Bray quietly introduces her as Alison, Lisa's probation officer.

'Any problems?' Bray asks and Alison shakes her head.

'Once we agreed she could bring a portable radio, she was fine. She's still uncommunicative, but she's docile. Taken her meds.'

There's no time to process anything before I'm following the two women along a corridor.

The uneven floorboards creak under the thin carpet, and in the kitchen to my left, two men are drinking mugs of tea. They see us and one immediately refills the kettle, the screeching tap setting my teeth on edge. My heart is pounding but I keep moving and then I'm in the doorway of the sitting room, Bray nodding me in.

There's an old gas fire, all its panels churning out a headache heat, and she's sitting beside it, her back stiff, staring out of the window as the radio plays some old eighties hit. She's picking at the edges of her thumbs as she turns to face me. She does that at work when she's stressed. Picks and bites at the skin until it bleeds and scabs. They're bleeding now but she doesn't seem to notice.

'Hi,' I say. Bray and Alison disappear back into the corridor, giving the illusion Lisa and I are alone. My throat is suddenly sandpaper. There are dark hollows under her eyes and she's lost weight. Her hair, cut and coloured differently, surprises me. It suits her, I think, or it would if she was dressed to impress. She still looks like Lisa, but I can see Charlotte Nevill in her too. The picture from *then*, when she was just a child, has been in the papers everywhere for days and days, and she's still there. Under the older skin. In the bones of her.

'Lisa?' I say again. She's looking at me, but says nothing. I wonder if I should call her Charlotte, but I can't. Even though I know it's her real name, it doesn't sound right in my head. She looks so small and pathetic and I hate myself for pitying her. She's lost Ava. Whatever kind of monster she was or is, her daughter is missing.

'I didn't take the money,' she says. 'It was Julia. I'm not a thief. Not any more.' The words are blurted out, awkward, as if they're important, as if they can repair all this. As if I'm going to say, *oh that's all right then.*

'I know.' I think of everyone at work, blaming her, like she's a bogeyman, and I look at this tragic stranger in front of me who looks like my best friend, and my damaged bones scream as I feel tears welling up from nowhere in my eyes. Hers are dry, but she flinches as I try to blink mine away, my nose suddenly thick with snot.

'I didn't think you'd come.' Her voice is so quiet, I doubt Bray can hear her over the radio. 'You must hate me.'

'I don't hate you.' I don't know if it's a lie or truth, right now all I feel is sick. 'It's confusing. But we have to find Ava. That's the most important thing.'

Her face contorts a little, though her eyes stay dry. 'You'll help find Ava?' she asks, leaning forward in her chair.

'Of course I will. I love her, you know that.'

'The boy says he was pushed.' She's picking at her skin again, making it bleed afresh, and there's an electric energy coming off her as she gets more agitated. 'At the river.' She looks at me as if this is important.

'Maybe he was.' I am so out of my depth here and I can't bear feeling the weight of Bray's eyes on me so I get closer and take the other chair, although it's tired and musty and there are stains on the cushions. It's a relief to be sitting down.

The painkillers I took this morning are wearing off and my whole chest throbs.

'That's what I said,' she leans forward, as if I'm now her confidante. 'He *was* pushed. Because there was the bunny too. I found it in the street. Just like Peter Rabbit.' Her eyes are wide but bloodshot and her words come fast. I don't know what drugs they're giving her but she looks like she's not sleeping. This energy coming from her isn't good. I know it. I've felt it before when things have been bad with Richard. It's *survival* energy.

'What bunny? Did Jon buy it for Ava?' It's the first time I've mentioned him, but I need to get her on subject. I want to get out of here. Back to the hotel. To turn her into a ghost again.

'Peter Rabbit,' she says again. 'Before I found the photograph of Ava missing and the one of me and her smashed.'

I can't concentrate with the music playing, Rick Astley declaring he's never going to give us up, and I reach across to the volume button.

'Don't!' She snaps so loudly my hand freezes. 'There'll be a message in the music. Our song was on this show. There may be more. I can't miss them.'

'I won't turn it off,' I say gently. But I still turn it down so I can think and Bray has half a chance of hearing anything Lisa is saying.

'Was it your and Jon's song they played? Are you waiting for a message from Jon?'

Her fingers move more frantically on her skin and she frowns, her eyes darting away. 'I've been so stupid,' she says. 'I should have known this

202

would happen. And now Ava's gone.'

'And we have to find her,' I say, floundering.

'Yes, we have to find her.' She looks up at me. 'There was a deal, you see. Cross my heart and hope to die. You can't break a deal like that. You can't. I should have known.'

I frown and lean forward, despite the pain. 'You and Jon had a deal? What kind of deal? Is this why he's taken Ava?'

She stares at me, and tilts her head. 'Why are you asking about Jon? Jon never knew about Peter Rabbit.'

'Jon's taken Ava, Lisa.' I'm talking to her like she's a child. I don't know who she is but this broken creature isn't what I was expecting. 'And we need to find him.'

'Jon?' she sits back, looking at me as if I'm stupid. 'Jon didn't take Ava.' She pauses and when her eyes meet mine, for the first time they look clear.

'Katie did.'

I look back to the doorway, and see Alison's despair and Bray's frustration. 'Who's Katie?' I ask.

39

AFTER

1990 The Express, 18 March 1990 Evil incarcerated – psycho sister jailed

Twelve-year-old Charlotte Nevill, pictured left, was convicted yesterday of the brutal murder of her half-brother, two-year-old Daniel Grove, in October of last year. Nevill, who was only eleven at the time of the crime, has been sentenced to be detained at Her Majesty's pleasure. Daniel's body was found in a house marked for demolition in the problematic Elmsley Estate. He had been beaten with a brick and strangled.

At the end of a trial which has shocked and gripped a horrified nation, the jury of five women and seven men took just over six and a half hours to reach their verdicts for both defendants. Charlotte Nevill remained impassive throughout the summing up and sentencing, as she had throughout the entire proceedings, Mr Justice Parkway telling her. 'You will be securely detained for very very many years until the Home Secretary is satisfied that you have matured and are fully rehabilitated and no longer a danger to others.'

The second accused, also a girl of twelve years old, known only as Child B, was acquitted of all charges.

Witnesses testified that Charlotte Nevill had gained a reputation, from as young as eight or nine, of being a troublemaker and terroriser of the elderly and vulnerable on the beleaguered Elmsley Estate who was running wild and whose mother was no longer able to control her. As Mr Justice Parkway stated in his summing up, Charlotte 'was clearly influential over the actions of Child B, an easily led, emotional girl from a stable and perhaps over-protective family.'

Charlotte's jealousy of her innocent younger brother, perhaps because of her abandonment by her own father, was well known to the family, but no one could have predicted the terrible outcome of this cold-hearted killer's rage, one who has shown no remorse throughout the proceedings.

Full story inside, pages 2, 3, 4 and 6.

Feature article 'Nature vs Nurture: The making of a monster'.

40

NOW

LISA

I'm going too fast and she can't keep up. She looks so tired, and she glances back, confused. I see them in the doorway. Alison and Bray. Vultures waiting for me to spit out something from my rotten insides for them to hungrily gobble up. They see me see them and the terrible pretence that this is a secret meeting is over and they step inside the room.

'Katie's dead.' Alison looks at me, not Marilyn, as she speaks, slowly, as if I am simple. 'She drowned in Ibiza in 2004. We've been through all this.'

I shake my head. 'No. It's Katie. She didn't die.' I grab Marilyn's hand. I need her to hear me even if she won't believe me. I know her. She takes time, she thinks things over. Maybe, just maybe, something I say will lodge in her clever head. 'It's not Jon. It's Katie. And she *knows* me. She knows me *now*.' She frowns and tugs her hand away but I don't stop. 'Someone isn't who they say they are. Someone I know. She's found me and she's got Ava.'

Marilyn's looking at me like I'm a dangerous mad stranger which tears at my broken heart. She's my best friend. I'm her best friend. I'm both her friend *and* the evil killer she's read about. Charlotte is my shadow, my curse, my anchor in the black. She'll always be part of me.

'I still don't know who you're all talking about,' Marilyn says. 'Who's Katie?'

'Child B,' I say softly. 'They could only call her Child B.'

I see a hint of recognition in her eyes. A vague memory of another girl briefly mentioned in the recent spate of newspaper reports. But Child B was acquitted. No one cares about Katie, not then, not now. Katie didn't kill anyone. Katie wasn't the monster.

'Cross your heart and hope to die,' I whisper.

'We're not getting anywhere here. Sorry,' Bray cuts in. 'I'll take you back to your hotel.'

'Hotel?' I ask, and suddenly I see the details so much more clearly. The dark circles around the eyes. Imperfect make-up, so *not* like Marilyn. Clothes not quite what she'd normally wear. 'Why are you at a hotel?'

'Nothing,' she answers. A pause. 'Trouble with Richard.' Perhaps she feels there have been too many lies between us already, or maybe there's no point in lying to someone who you no longer consider a friend. She can't meet my eyes. This isn't my Marilyn, confident in her charmed life. 'Is it my fault?' I ask quietly. She looks for a moment as if she might say yes, as if she *wants* to say yes, but then she shakes her head.

'No. This is all his fault.'

'Come on,' Bray says, and all three of them turn away. I follow them to the corridor. Bray is talking about how they're searching Jon's house

207

for clues, and our old house, and they'll find Ava, but I'm not listening. I want to grab Marilyn and make her stay. Something is very wrong in her world and who can she talk to? Is it something new, and if not, why didn't I notice it? *You did. The migraines. The drinking. You were just too wrapped up in yourself.* I was a terrible friend even before she knew I was a monster. She's walking differently — *details, always details in my head* — carefully. Is she hurt? Oh, Marilyn, my Marilyn, what is going on with you? Ava gone, and you in trouble. What has Richard done?

'Who was Child B? This Katie?' I hear Marilyn ask as they reach the front door.

'Her name was Katie Batten. She was a sweet kid, by all accounts. Charlotte's best friend.'

41

BEFORE

1989

'You come back here, Charlotte Nevill, you thieving little bitch!'

'You fuck off, you old bag!' Charlotte laughs as she calls back over her shoulder, her feet confident on the wasteland littered with bricks and building debris as she runs across it.

'You're banned, you hear! Banned!'

Old Mrs Jackson still has one foot in the shop doorway. She can't chase after Charlotte, not with the Taylor boys over there on the wall, watching. They'd be in there and away with all they could carry before the shopkeeper had got halfway to the demolition site. Charlotte pauses, enjoying the rush of air burning in her lungs.

'See if I care! I'll burn your stupid shop down! Brick your windows in!' She reaches down and grabs one to illustrate her point, throwing it half-heartedly. She laughs again, and turns to run. It's the third week of March but the bitter wind that's owned February shows no sign of letting go. Charlotte doesn't care. She loves the way it blasts her skin and makes her eyes and nose run. It's wild. She feels free. She'll be in trouble again later but right now she doesn't care. She refuses to care. Nothing matters.

Katie is crouching behind the remains of a wall. She joins Charlotte as she comes by, and hand in hand they run laughing across the rough ground where houses have been knocked down but none yet rebuilt. Charlotte hopes that when they get moved out, they'll get a place near Katie. She knows it's a dream though. There aren't any shite council houses where Katie lives.

They run past the playground with the rusty slides, crappy seesaw and old climbing frames, and turn the corner. The bus shelter is there and they flop, as one, on to the worn seat inside, panting and giggling.

'That will never not be funny,' Katie says, and her eyes shine as she looks at Charlotte. 'I wish I could steal like you do.' Charlotte thinks her heart will burst with pride. Sometimes Charlotte thinks Katie is a living breathing doll. She's three inches shorter than Charlotte and a proper girly girl because her ma dresses her like that, but under the skin they're both the same. They both hate their lives, even though sometimes. Charlotte doesn't understand quite what Katie has to hate. Katie appeared like a dream, just *there* one day on the wasteland, and her life is like a dream too. Proper house. Posh car. Both parents. Music lessons, like the one she's supposed to be at now. Holidays.

Charlotte pulls the sweets she's stolen from the shop from one pocket and the sippy cup full of Thunderbird Red she's stolen from home from the other, and she takes a long swallow before handing it to Katie, who takes a smaller one. It tastes horrible but she likes the numbing heat of it. They eat the Caramacs and Discos and lean into each other, but that word sits between them today. *Holiday*.

'Where are you going again?' Charlotte asks, lighting a crumpled cigarette and blowing out the smoke. She doesn't like the taste but she's determined to get used to it. One of her ma's fags. It's stolen too. Not that her ma will notice. Or if she does she'll think Tony's been at the packet.

'You know full well,' Katie elbows her. 'The seaside. My grandfather's house in Skegness. Will be my mum's house soon. He's got the big C. He'll die soon. Not soon enough. He needs to get on with it. Sickness is so dull.' She pauses. 'Did I tell you he designed tricks for famous magicians? That was his job. You'd think someone who did that for a living would be fun, but no. He's as dull as my mother.' Charlotte could listen to Katie talk all day. It's like music, all posh and polite. Sometimes they try to talk like each other and it's the funniest thing.

'Oh aye,' Charlotte says. 'Skegness.' She's never been to the seaside. Her ma went to Grimsby once and saw the sea, but it wasn't the seaside like they have at Cleethorpes or Skegness. Fishing boats is all her ma saw. She said it stank. She was there for some man. Always for some man. It was a long time ago — before Tony — but Charlotte remembers it because she was left on her own. Her ma locked her in with some sandwiches and juice and crisps and told her to stay quiet and it was *just for one night*. One night that turned into two. She cried

211

a lot on the second night but it didn't make her ma get home any quicker.

'I wish you were coming with me,' Katie says, and leans her head on Charlotte's shoulder. 'It's going to be so dull. And I can't even go to the funfair. Mother won't let me on any of the rides in case I get hurt. Or dirty. I'm not sure which she'd think is worse.' She smiles at Charlotte and they both shrug. Katie's mother drives her mad with all her fussing. Katie says she doesn't let her breathe. She says her ma's *neurotic* although Charlotte doesn't know what that means. 'She'll be crying over Granddad the whole of Easter. So so boring. He's old and he's going to die. So what?'

'Maybe a pirate will save you, like in those old films.' Charlotte leaps up and pretends to pull a cutlass from the top of her worn-out C&A jeans. 'I'll be your pirate!'

'Yes yes!' Katie is on her feet too. 'They've locked me away in a cabin and you have to set me free. I've stolen a knife from the captain, and I'll gut her when she's not looking!' They are always fizzing with energy when they're together. Always playing pretend. Half in this world, and half in another. Movie stars, gangsters, always adventuring free and together.

'And I'll kill all the rest and we'll sail away!'

They swirl around for a while, the bus stop now the pirate ship and the estate an ocean full of monsters and other ships to raid. Afterwards they fall into each other, all breathless joy, slowly quieting as the real world settles in around them.

'I have to go in a minute,' Katie says. Her

music lessons are only an hour and a half long and Charlotte isn't quite sure how she gets out of them without her ma knowing, but she does and it doesn't surprise her. Katie can do pretty much anything.

'Me too.' She drinks more Thunderbird, acid in her hungry stomach to burn away the sadness of Katie leaving for two weeks. 'Daniel's birthday party. I should be there now.' Her face darkens and so does Katie's. Katie hates her ma and Charlotte hates Daniel. Perfect Daniel. The little shite who's made everything worse. Two today. 'I wish you didn't have to go away,' she blurts out and although she doesn't cry, her face contorts into anger and sadness and she punches the wall of the bus shelter three times, hard. She feels strong with Katie. All the rest of it doesn't matter when Katie's here. When she's with Katie she thinks she could go robbing from one of the empty houses like the men do and steal an iron bar or something and bash Tony and her ma and stupid Daniel in with it. Sometimes she sees it in her head. Her doing just that. Katie watching and laughing and clapping.

'Me too, me too,' Katie says and wraps her arms tight around her. 'I *hate* not seeing you.' She breaks away and rummages in her bag. 'But it's only two weeks. It feels like forever but it's only fourteen days.'

'One dole cheque,' I say.

'Exactly.' Charlotte knows Katie doesn't understand dole cheques any more than Charlotte understands music lessons, but she loves her for pretending.

'Oh!' Katie exclaims. 'I almost forgot. I brought you something.' She pulls it out with a flourish and thrusts it into Charlotte's hands. A Walkman. A good one. Small and metal, not some shite plastic thing. It's wonderful.

'Pirate treasure,' Charlotte says, because her emotions always get choked up in her throat and she never has the words for them, but the black clouds in her head disperse and the sun shines through and it's a better warmth than any amount of cheap booze can provide.

'For me?'

Katie nods. 'I'll say I lost it or broke it. They'll get me another one.' They sit close, side by side, and sniff in the cold as Katie shows her how to work it. 'There's a tape in there. A mix tape. I made it for you. Fourteen songs. One for every day I'm away. I've got one the same at home. See? We won't really be apart at all.'

★ ★ ★

'So there you are! Finally decided to show your face, did you? About bloody time.'

The party's in full swing when Charlotte gets home, and her ma is drunk and out of it on those pills she gets from the doctor for her back pain or whatever excuse she comes up with for the scrip. She glares at her from the doorway to the sitting room, and Charlotte barges through her, saying nothing. There's no bairns there but every seat is taken by someone off the estate. Jack from number 5 who spends all his time with those stupid pigeons, Mary who hasn't had a job

214

in a year and got no fella so will go the way of Ma soon enough and be in one of the rooms over the chippy opening up her legs, and a few others all clutching cans or paper cups of booze. No cups of tea. That's what Katie's ma would have, Charlotte reckons, for a birthday party. Cups of tea and jelly and ice cream. She doesn't look at Tony, holding forth from his armchair. He calls himself her dad. He's not her dad. He's part of the black angry storm clouds in her head.

Daniel sits in the middle of the carpet, and there's obviously been some cake because he's got a plate in front of him with icing and some crisps still on it, and as he looks up at her she can see chocolate crumbs around his mouth. He smiles and holds something up. 'Charrot!' he says, unable yet to pronounce her name properly. 'A rabbit, Charrot! Charrot!'

'It's Peter Rabbit, isn't it?' Tony's sister, Jean, is crouched on the floor beside him. 'Like from those books.' The rabbit's got dungarees on, and Charlotte knows right there that Jean made them. It's what she's like. She should probably live a life like Katie's. Probably would if she wasn't on the estate. But her husband is the foreman down at the factory and they're doing all right. Jean doesn't like Ma, that much is obvious, and she doesn't much like Tony, but she loves Daniel, just like everyone else.

'Charrot!' he says again, and his high-pitched voice, all sugar and innocence, makes her teeth grit.

'What's that you got?' Tony asks. He leans forward. 'You been on the rob again?' His eyes

215

have narrowed. Tony's not clever, not like school clever, or Katie clever, but there's something feral about him. He's clever like a hyena. He can sniff stuff out of you. She's still holding the Walkman, and her grip tightens on it.

'Found it,' she mumbles.

'You can give it to your brother then, for a present.'

'He's bloody two years old, what does he need a Walkman for?' She goes from a mumble to a raging shout, and anywhere else the room would fall quiet, but Charlotte's anger is nothing new. Letters from school, concern from the social, her mother swearing at her, they're all tired of Charlotte and her outbursts.

'Give it here,' her ma says, eyes blurred. 'You can have it back later,' she adds feebly, and Charlotte knows she'll be lucky to ever see it again unless Tony gets smashed and forgets about it. Otherwise it'll be sold on the estate somewhere when they realise Daniel's too young to care about it. She yanks the tape out and throws it at her ma. 'Take it then, you bitch!' She turns to go to her room, and Daniel is still calling after her, not so confident now. 'Charrot?'

He sounds like a fucking Chinky, she thinks as she slams her door and throws herself down on the mattress. All she really hears is *rot*. Like her life. Rotten before it's begun. Her stomach rumbles. Apart from the Caramac and crisps, she's eaten nothing today, but she won't go back out there for shite sandwiches and cake. Instead she finishes the rest of the Thunderbird, sucking it out of Daniel's dinosaur sippy cup, until her head spins and she feels sick. She falls asleep for a bit, or at least drifts into some drunken haze, because the next time she focuses, the house is quiet, and her ma is in the doorway.

'I'm going to work,' she says, her eyes defiant. 'Tony's going to the shop. Keep an eye on Daniel.' She doesn't wait for Charlotte to answer but calls out down the stairs that she's coming and to wait a fucking minute, and then the door slams behind them and Charlotte can let out a long breath. She gives it a moment to be sure they're gone before storming across the landing to grab her Walkman back.

'That's mine.' She snatches it from where it's sitting, untouched at the bottom of Daniel's cot, and although all his focus is on the soft bunny rabbit he's holding tight she makes him jump and the smile he had for her turns into a shocked frown and tears and the start of a quiet wail.

'Fucking shut up,' she mutters. The room stinks of dirty nappies and she can see one rolled up in the corner of the room where Ma obviously had thrown it and forgotten to bin it. At least he has clean nappies. He sobs and reaches one hand out for her.

'I said shut up!' She turns and leaves him clinging to his stupid rabbit, and by the time she gets back to her room, his sobs slow down to nothing. He's learning too, that there's no point if no one comes. Or maybe her ma's right. Maybe he's just *better* than Charlotte. *A happy baby. Not like Charlotte was. She was always a little bitch. Fucking hell, she was hard work. Full of trouble from day one. Daniel's always smiling.*

217

She knows what her ma means though. Daniel's dad didn't leave.

She carefully puts the tape back in and with a cautious glance at the door presses play, filling her head with Katie's songs. She knows most of them from *Top of the Pops* even though she's not as into music as Katie is and her ma never buys her any tapes or records. She hums along, imagining the seaside and being with Katie and their families disappearing in a puff of smoke. Then comes one song. 'Drive Away, Baby' by Frankie Vein, and she listens to the words, properly listens to them, before rewinding it and listening again. It's all about getting away. Going somewhere else. Leaving all the shit behind. It's their song, she knows that straight away. All their make believe, their fantasies, their thoughts of their families being murdered by an unknown assailant in their beds, everyone who's ever pissed them off disappearing, Katie's suffocating ma and stinky little Daniel, pulverised to dust like the old houses on Spring Street, everything is wrapped up in this song. It's why Katie's put it on there. She feels the same. They always feel the same. That must be what love is.

Play. Rewind. Play. Time slides. Tony doesn't come back for over an hour, the pub being too close to the shop to resist, and anyway *it's Daniel's birthday* and she luckily hears him coming up the stairs between plays, and quickly tucks the Walkman under her pillow.

He doesn't knock but pulls open her door and stands there, drunk and angry. It's a house full of simmering anger.

218

'You were supposed to watch the bairn! He's fell out of his cot. He's hurt his head.'

Charlotte says nothing. There's no point. From across the corridor, Daniel calls out for Ma. His voice sounds tired. How long has he been crying?

'You want to bring the social down on us? On your ma?'

He's pulling his belt off as he talks and his face is blotchy and she knows that's always when he's at his worst. *It's all Daniel's fault*, is all she can think as the first blow lands. *Everything's worse since the perfect child came along. No one ever hits Daniel. Why can't they love her like they love him? What's so fucking special about him?* She focuses on her anger and bites down on her cheek. It stops her crying. Tony's worse when she cries. It feeds the monster inside him. All his resentment at another man's kid taking food from his table.

⋆   ⋆   ⋆

She wakes up in the night, sore and bruised and her bed is soaking under her, and the familiar tang fills the room. She's wet herself again. She quietly strips the sheet off and scrunches it into a ball, stuffing it under the mattress. She'll have to wash it when everyone is out or when Tony and Ma are in bed in the afternoon. Ma said she'd get a plastic sheet if she kept doing it. She doesn't want that. Everyone will laugh at her if they hear about it, and everyone will because Tony's a big gobshite at the pub and all the parents from the estate drink in there. All the kids would know. No one would be scared of Charlotte Nevill if they knew she wet the bed, and the little 'uns being scared of her is all she has. And what would Katie say if she found out? What would she think of her?

The welts on the back of her legs sting and it's a cold night, but she hobbles to the window and opens it, hoping to blow the smell away by morning. She peels off her soaked underwear and wraps herself in the old parka jacket that's too big for her but she loves anyway, and lies on the floor, staring up at the ceiling. She thinks about Katie until she falls asleep. In her dream they're driving, fast and far, in a big pink convertible and laughing as they go. And in her dream they have blood on their hands.

42

NOW

MARILYN

It's nearly midnight and I'm wide awake, staring at the ceiling and trying to get my thoughts and feelings into some kind of order. Whenever I close my eyes, all I see is the flash of worry on Lisa's face when I told her I was having problems with Richard. As if she cared about me. As if we were still best friends. Ava's missing and she was concerned because I was unhappy. How am I supposed to feel about that?

Someone isn't who they say they are. Someone I know.

How crazy has Lisa become? Could she still be in love with Jon maybe, to come up with something that wild rather than think he took Ava? What sort of man is he anyway? Who would send those kind of messages to their daughter?

Too much thinking time, that's my problem. It's making the whole world murky and if I'm not careful I'll start to see conspiracy theories everywhere. I'm too tired for this. I need to go back to work. Penny texted earlier to say Richard had called a couple of times but hadn't caused any drama, and that there was some work to do on the Wharton account but if I wasn't up to it then one of the others could manage. My teeth clench at the thought. No one's stealing my client list.

Anyway, where else can I go? I can't hide forever. That's simply delaying the inevitable. If Richard shows up, I'll call the police. I'm tired of living a pretence. That thought leads me straight back to Lisa/Charlotte. Did *she* ever get tired of living a lie? Had she ever been tempted to tell me about her past? I'm glad she didn't. I wouldn't have wanted to carry that. Even if I was her best friend.

Her name was Katie Batten. She was Charlotte's best friend.

I give up on sleep and get up. I've got too many questions whirring around in my head to doze, and my broken ribs are throbbing, so I pull on some clothes, make a coffee in a takeaway cup in the machine, and pad downstairs. There's a business centre on the ground floor near reception and I head there, wanting a computer. The lights buzz brightly against the night outside and the man at reception gives me a perfunctory smile as I pass by. This is the best thing about hotels. There is always someone awake. You're never quite alone and it's all so comfortingly sterile and impersonal.

I settle down at one of the desks, not too close to the window, although the chances of Richard being out looking for me at this time of night are remote, and turn on the computer. There are things I need to know and thinking about Lisa's life is preferable to thinking about my own.

I search *Charlotte Nevill and Jon John Jonathan lover* and an archived tabloid comes straight up from early 2004. There's no picture of Lisa, but one of Jon, *Jon Roper*, sitting in a garden. He's thin and he's got an earring in, and he's scowling at the camera, no doubt as instructed, under the headline. *I fell in love with child murderer Charlotte and it nearly killed me . . .* He looks so young and there are dark circles around his eyes and his skin is unhealthy. It's a salacious piece, as I expected, but between the details of their life together, it feels like he's crying out for some kind of absolution. A lot of what he says is about Crystal — that must be Ava — and how when she was born the reality of Charlotte's crime hit him and he couldn't forgive her, and now he's lost his daughter too, all because he took up drinking too much to cope. According to the article, he'd moved back in with his mum to try and clean up his life and start afresh.

I know how you feel, I think. *If only it was so easy in your forties.* I read the article again, where he makes a big deal about their sex life and their drinking, and I wonder how much of it is true and how much he's embellished to make himself sound better. It all sounds so tragic and sordid. I almost feel sorry for him but for the fact he's taken Ava.

I flick through a few more results, but they're mainly different versions of the same article, and there's just a couple of other pictures. I can't find a Facebook account for him so I presume the police have shut it down already or whatever it is they do in these situations. Or maybe Jon himself deactivated it when he took Ava.

I start my next search. Katie Batten. Charlotte's best friend. 'Katie Batten drowned Ibiza 2004' takes me straight to the story. God bless Google in all but medical situations. My coffee is growing cold but I take a sip anyway.

The search has been called off for Katie Batten, a British woman missing in the Balearic party island of Ibiza. Ms Batten, twenty-six, was last seen going for a dawn swim on the beach near the bar where she'd been working since May. She had been travelling in Spain for most of the year after the death of her mother in 2002 in a car accident. Friends say she was coming to terms with her mother's sudden loss, but still had bouts of grief and has been described as nervous and fragile. Her colleagues stated that she spent much of her time alone.

On the night of her death, she was seen going into the sea, and two witnesses, a young German couple on holiday, who had been watching the sun come up in the secluded spot say they tried to call her back as she was weaving, and they thought she might be drunk. Miss Batten responded that she was fine. The young couple watched her swim out, but when they looked towards the rocks a while later, there was no sign of her. Despite the best efforts of search teams, Katie Batten's body has not been recovered. A verdict of accidental death by drowning is expected from the inquest.

There were a few other small news items but nothing with much more detail. Father had died of a heart attack several years earlier, after which Katie had cared for her mother who had struggled to cope with widowhood. Against another report of Katie's drowning, there's a picture, grainy, of a woman on the beach, long dark hair and sunglasses, tanned. Nondescript and taken from a distance. Was this the best they had?

Katie Batten's body has not been recovered. I re-read the line, over and over. Did she ever wash up? Is this why Lisa is so convinced Katie took Ava? Does she really believe she's not dead? Could it *be* her? But why? There's no reason. Surely she wouldn't want anything to do with Charlotte Nevill again even if she did find her? The newspapers have made it clear over the past few days that Charlotte's guilt wasn't in doubt. She was *seen* killing Daniel and she admitted it. Why would Katie want to come back into Charlotte's life now?

I have another sip of my coffee. It's Jon. Jon sent the messages from his Facebook. Jon is the one who's vanished with Ava. The police know what they're talking about. Trust them, not your crazy ex-best friend.

I close the computer down. Enough is enough. I've got my own problems. The police will find Jon and Ava. They will. I don't want to think about the nature of the messages he was sending her. Even the bright lights of the hotel can't dispel their darkness.

43

LISA

It's the sudden stiffness in Alison's spine that alerts me. She presses the mobile phone a little too close to her ear. It must be Bray and my head spins and darkness threatens the corners of my vision. *God no. Please, not Ava. Please, not Ava.* The fear is about to overwhelm me when Alison glances back over her shoulder to where I sit on the edge of my chair, gripping my mug of tea. She's furtive, not sympathetic, a wariness in her expression. A wariness of *me*. My fear for Ava's immediate safety is replaced by my own survival instinct kicking in. Something is wrong.

Alison gives me a tight half-smile and tries to look casual as she goes to her bedroom to continue the call. As the door clicks shut I dart from my chair and press my ear against the wood. For the first time since they moved me from our house to this awful flat, I'm happy about its cheap manufacture. The door is thin, and although I can't make out every word — she's speaking quietly — I catch some phrases *. . . will do . . . I'll be fine . . . No, she's the same as she has been. I'll lock the door . . . act normal until you get here.*

Shit, shit, shit. My face burns as my hands

cool. I'm all animal instinct now, and my instinct is telling me I have to get out of here at whatever cost. Something's happened and they're coming for me. What happens to Ava then? Will that be the game over? I can't risk it, and I can't risk being arrested. I am still Charlotte Nevill. They won't see a victim.

There's movement on the other side of the door and I am suddenly terrifyingly calm. I run to the kitchen and grab the kettle, the water inside sloshing heavy as I run back. The bedroom door is opening as I reach it, and Alison steps back a little, surprised to see me so close. Fear. I see fear.

'I'm sorry,' I say quietly. She barely has time to look confused before I swing the kettle around and hit her on the side of the head. The thump makes my stomach clench and she reels backwards, crumpling on to the carpet, dazed and hurt, a gasp of air *whoomping* from her chest. I don't hesitate but snatch the mobile phone and run to the front door, grabbing my old handbag and the keys from the table in the hall.

'Lisa, Lisa, don't . . . ' Her voice is quiet, an effort.

'I'm sorry,' I say again. My shaking hands pull the front door open before double locking it from the outside, the key almost dropping from my fingers as I hear her banging against the other side. *Too late, Alison, too late.* She's trapped inside with no phone. I still don't have much time. Bray is on her way here, I know it.

I run. I don't hear sirens as I jog towards the

227

town. Good. That's good.

I pray to a God I don't believe in before trying my debit card in a cashpoint, and I laugh with relief when it spits out the maximum two hundred and fifty pounds. In all this, they hadn't got around to closing my bank account down yet. I ditch the card, my handbag and Alison's phone in a nearby bin and quickly go to Boots and buy battery-operated hair clippers, pink and blue spray hair dye, make-up and black nail varnish. I visit three charity shops in a row and buy the hippiest, grungiest clothes I can find, along with an army surplus jacket and some second-hand Doc Martens that just about fit. I pick up a load of big junk jewellery of crosses and skulls and some leather bracelets. Sweat is slick on my skin and my heart is racing but my mind is clear. I've learned a lot over the years. They'll expect me to be mousy still. Maybe change my hair colour and put some glasses on, but no more. They'd be underestimating me. Be big and bold and hide in plain sight. Be someone new.

In Costa Coffee I go to the disabled toilet cubicle that has a mirror and sink and I work fast. When I'm done, even I don't recognise myself. I look younger, which is a surprise. Thirty at most. Thick kohl rises at points around my eyes, dark and angry. My lips are slashes of deep purple and my nails are black. My hair is almost gone; a buzz cut at the sides with a short pink and blue strip down the middle that leads to a narrow ponytail. The trousers are slightly too big and they hang on my hips, accentuating the youthful look. I've lost weight and the strip of belly that shows when I move is flat and taut.

I keep the make-up, dye, clippers and nail varnish, but stuff my old clothes into the sanitary bin and wash away all evidence of shaved hair down the sink. As I leave I find I'm walking differently. My hips are thrust forward and my shoulders are back. This woman doesn't take any shit. This woman does things her own way. She's hard as nails. This woman is my shadow and I know it. This is the Charlotte who could have been.

An hour or so later and I'm at the small services at the edge of the motorway. It's still light, but there's an edge of grey to the sky. I cruise up and down the rows of lorries that fill the car park until I find an occupied one. A driver, reading his paper, sipping from a flask, Burger King wrappers on the dashboard. All so ordinary. I tap on the side, smile, and he winds his window down to lean out.

'I don't suppose you're going anywhere near Calthorpe?' I ask. 'There or Ashminster?' They're both close enough to home. I can get a bus from either and be back in Elleston in less than an hour.

'I'm going to Manchester,' he says. 'So yeah I'm passing that way, but I'm parked up for the night. Done my hours. Sorry, love, but I won't be leaving until about four in the morning.'

He isn't an unpleasant-looking man. There have been worse men. I don't give myself time to think about what I'm doing but shrug and smile. 'I can wait.' No one will look for me in a parked-up lorry. I'll be safe there.

He looks at me for a long moment. 'What's your name, love?' His tone has changed. Almost nervous but also wily. He's sensing an opportunity. The sort of situation he's probably only read about in top-shelf magazines.

'Lily,' I say. It comes from nowhere and is at odds with my wild look but also kind of suits it for exactly that reason. Lily is a nice girl from a good family who rebelled and never went back. Her story is weaving together in my head as his eyes flicker up and down and I see his Adam's apple bob as he swallows.

'I'm Phil.' He opens the cab door and pulls me in. I'm relieved to find he smells clean and so does the cab. No cigarette smoke. No stale booze. Only leather and deodorant. It could be worse. *It could be much much worse.*

'I'll have to have a kip.' He nods back to where the rear seat is covered by a duvet. 'Sooner I sleep, the sooner we leave.' His eyes slide over me again. 'I normally have a wank, if I'm honest, but . . . ' He half laughs, as if he's making a joke, but his eyes are watery nervous.

'I guess I should pay for the ride somehow,' I say, knowing I sound like something from a cheap porn film but hoping it will make him come quicker. He's overweight and middle-aged and I doubt he and his wife do it often. Even if he gets a second wind I can make him finish fast. I'm thinking like Charlotte. I have to *be* Charlotte Nevill now. My old self. I need all her anger. All her strength. Ava needs me and I won't let her down.

I am Charlotte Nevill, I think, as I reach across to find his belt buckle under his gut. *I've done worse. I can do this.*

44

BEFORE

1989

It's May half-term for Katie but that doesn't mean anything to Charlotte. She barely goes to school any more and no one cares. None of the teachers want Charlotte Nevill in school. She breaks things. She swears. She hits the other kids. *There's no controlling her. She's getting worse.* The little ones are scared of her. Her anger is like a grinning wolf, gobbling up the bairns' fears to kill her own. Big bad wolf. Little Red Riding Hood.

'Charlotte? Are you listening?' Katie twirls circles in the empty shithole of a room, sending dust up in a cloud around her ankles. 'His skin was all grey and sort of baggy. Like he was empty. I could have stared at him all day.'

They're in one of the condemned houses on Coombs Street, stripped of lead by grasping estate hands, and now forgotten until the bulldozers get round to demolishing it which doesn't seem to be happening in any hurry as Mrs Copel next door keeps banging on about.

'Grey,' Katie says again, rubbing dust between her fingers. 'Like this.'

Katie's granddad died and she's only been back from the funeral a couple of days and she can't stop talking about it, which is good because it stops the words inside Charlotte's own mouth spilling out.

'Gross,' she says, as Katie flops down beside her. They're sitting on Charlotte's jacket in case Katie gets dust on her dress, but their backs are pressed against the wall and Charlotte makes a note in her dull, fuzzy head to check Katie's clothes before she goes home. She'd hate for Katie to get in trouble because that would mean she wouldn't be able to see her and right now, Katie is all she has to stop her from snapping completely.

'Yes, but wonderfully gross.'

Charlotte's never seen a dead body but sort of wishes she had. She wishes she'd seen it with Katie. 'Did he smell?' This house smells, damp and rotting, even though it's sunny and warm outside.

'No, not *bad* anyway. A bit like chemicals maybe. Like a science lab at school.'

Charlotte has no idea what that smells like but she *hmms* in agreement.

'Of course it's all made Mummy worse.' Katie lets out an exaggerated sigh. 'Doctor Chambers has given her some pills for her nerves but they don't seem to be doing anything much.'

Charlotte doesn't want to think about pills and leans in closer to delicate, beautiful Katie who's so strong inside, and drinks in her lyrical voice. 'She's obsessing about death. She thinks I don't notice, because they all think I'm a bit simple, but it's so obvious. Daddy says it's grief, but I don't see why she's so sad. He was old,

233

after all, and she's got the seaside house now so it's all rather good. *She* doesn't see it that way, obviously. When we got home she polished the stairs of our house so hard — to distract herself Daddy said — that she slipped down them! She said she nearly broke her neck!' She lets out a tinkling laugh with an edge of venom. Katie hates her ma. She hates her da too, but her ma the most.

'Of course then she got sandpaper and rubbed the shine away, worrying *I'd* fall down them. As if I would. She's making me take vitamin pills now. To keep me healthy. Honestly, Charlotte, she doesn't let me breathe. Daddy tries his best to make her see reason but she controls him too. At least he gets to go to work. Thank God the pills make her sleepy and I can come out and see you.' She smiles, so sweet and fresh, and Charlotte clings to her.

'I put one in her coffee today,' Katie says, impish. 'And she'd already taken one. She won't wake up for ages.'

'Maybe she should go to sleep forever,' Charlotte murmurs. Would that be so bad? To sleep forever?

'Yes!' Katie leaps to her feet. 'Maybe she should! What would we do then? Would we run away?'

All their games and fantasies start with running away — *drive away, baby* — who they'll be and what they'll do, and Charlotte leaps up despite her tiredness, despite her raw anger, despite the tears trapped inside that threaten to humiliate her. 'Bonnie and Clyde!' she says.

'We'll rob banks and shite people up! We'll be legends!' She feels stronger already, basking in the glow of Katie's admiration. Katie thinks she is wild and crazy and free. Katie thinks she is the big bad wolf, terrorising everyone in the estate. *The big bad wolf.*

'I'll be Bonnie and you'll be my handsome Clyde.' Katie pretends to fan herself with one hand, and pulls an invisible gun from her hip with the other. 'We'll be inseparable and people will envy our love.' She leans in and kisses Charlotte on the mouth and her lips are so soft Charlotte's face burns and contorts as the tears she dreads threaten to overwhelm her. She pulls a cigarette out of her top pocket and lights it, trying to control her trembling mouth.

'Charlotte?' Katie says, so full of concern. 'What's the matter? Has something happened?'

She shakes her head. 'Just shite with Daniel. The usual. Family. Nothing I want to think about.'

'You can tell me anything.' Katie holds Charlotte's face in both hands, not gently, like a girl, but strong.

'I know.' She can't though. This is not like Katie's over-protective ma. Instead, Charlotte breaks away and lets the cigarette hang from her lips as she stands in a pose she imagines a gangster would take. 'Let's go on the rob, Bonnie! There's a bank in town we need to hit!' She wiggles an eyebrow and holds out her hand and Katie laughs and claps her hands together and jumps up and down. Always so much energy. It feeds Charlotte and almost makes her feel better.

They clamber out of the house back into the sunlight and they run fast across the wasteland hand in hand. The bank will be old Mrs Jackson's stupid shop and their gold will be sweets and drinks that Charlotte will steal. She is the big bad wolf, she is, she is. She doesn't want to think about last night. She wants to run so fast the past can't keep up.

Stupid Daniel. It was all stupid little shite Daniel's fault. She can feel it, the memory of it, chasing her like hot breath on her neck. She runs faster, but she'll never be fast enough.

★   ★   ★

'Daniel's sick,' her ma says, standing in the doorway of her bedroom. 'I need to stay at home.'

'There's nothing wrong with him,' Charlotte growls and doesn't look up. 'He was fine earlier. He's fine now.' It's not totally true though and she knows it. He *has* been quiet and pale and not nagging at her to play with him since she got home. Just sat in a corner with Peter Rabbit, sucking on one of the ears. She feels a tug of something inside. Not love. She can't love Daniel. Everything is worse for her since he came along, but a tug of *something*. 'I'll watch him while you work.'

Ma shakes her head. She's like this whenever Daniel gets sick. Won't let Charlotte near him. 'It's me he needs.'

'So what're you telling me for?' She was never like this when Charlotte was small, when it was

236

only the two of them. She never stayed in for her.

'We need the money.' Ma isn't looking at her now, focusing instead on the listless toddler on her hip clinging to his rabbit.

'And?' Alarm bells are starting to ring in Charlotte's head. Her ma says nothing for a moment, chewing her bottom lip. Her eyes are glazed over, from drinking with Tony all afternoon probably. Red-ringed too. Has Ma been crying?

'You talk to her. I'll take him.' Tony appears and lifts the boy out of Ma's arms as her hands flutter to take him back. Daniel starts crying, little quiet sobs.

'Charrot come with me,' he says, and then he's gone.

'I'll come and tell you a story in a minute,' Ma calls after him. 'Little Red Riding Hood. Your favourite.'

Charlotte's racing heart hardens. There were never bedtime stories for her. No one looked after her when she was sick. Daniel's such a lucky shite and he doesn't even know it. Ma comes and sits, carefully, on the edge of the bed. This, this is something else. Danger tingles in every cell of Charlotte's body.

'You should take this,' Ma says. She holds out one of her 'back pain pills'.

'Don't want it.'

'*Just bloody take it!*' Tony's voice bellows from the corridor and both Charlotte and Ma flinch.

'Go on. It won't hurt you. It's a good feeling.' Ma half smiles but her eyes still slide sideways. 'I know you, Charlotte, you like a buzz.'

'Haven't got a drink.' *Delay, delay, delay.* It's all she can do, but she's cornered and she knows it. Daniel's crying sounds like it's coming from far away. There is only her bedroom and it's no longer her sanctuary. A can of lager is thrust in her hand and she takes it and the pill, and while wanting to scream with all the fear and the *knowing unknowing* of what she thinks is to come she swallows it.

'There's my good girl,' Ma says, and strokes her hair. Ma looks like she's going to cry which scares Charlotte more than anything. 'Don't worry,' she says. 'It'll be all right. It's always all right if you just don't think about it.'

'His nappy needs changing,' Tony says, appearing once again in the doorway. 'You do that. I'll get her down the chippy. She can have a wash there.'

Charlotte finds herself getting to her feet. She can't fight Tony. Ma doesn't fight Tony. No one fights Tony. Her legs are trembling. She won't cry. There's no point. She wonders how long it will take for her ma's pill to kick in and finds herself thinking *hurry up hurry up hurry up.* She turns to pick up her jacket.

'Only her mouth, yeah?' Ma whispers, and it's frantic, guilty, ashamed. Tony grunts in reply. 'I mean it, Tony. I mean it. She's only eleven.'

Charlotte thinks she might be sick, but she keeps her chin up. She has Katie. One day they'll run away. One day they'll fuck this fucking shite right off. Only when she gets to the front door does she glance back. Ma's at the top of the stairs, Daniel on her hip again.

'Once upon a time there was a forest. In the forest there was a little girl called Red Riding Hood. There was also a big bad wolf . . . ' She doesn't look down at Charlotte as she talks. Daniel does, though. Clutching Peter Rabbit with one hand, he gives Charlotte a half wave with the other. A small gesture. Just for her.

Fuck you, Daniel, she thinks, as she follows Tony outside. *Fuck you, you little shite.*

45

NOW

MARILYN

I'm shattered. What a day. What a mixture of a day. The adrenaline of being back at work and acting as if everything was fine at least kept me awake at my desk, and it felt surprisingly good to be back in the grip of humdrum normality.

That feeling lasted a whole hour before Richard arrived, unkempt and wild, banging on the glass doors, demanding to be buzzed in. I wasn't surprised. Not really. On some level, I knew he'd be watching the car park every day, waiting to see me arrive. If it hadn't been such a humiliation it would almost have been a relief.

When I went out into the corridor he did everything I expected. He begged me to come back. He pleaded. In the very predictable end, he threatened. Loudly. He slammed me up against the wall. *You're so fucking ugly no other man will ever touch you! Who the fuck do you think you are? I will fucking destroy you, you stupid bitch!* All so grotesque, the monster inside showing on his contorted face. I cried. I couldn't help it. Being pressed up against the wall hurt my ribs and all his anger hurt my heart. How did we come to this?

The noise brought Penny out in no time at all.

She wasn't going to take any of his shit and Richard knew it. Threatening and bullying his wife was one thing, but he couldn't play those games with Penny. She stood firm as he tried to swallow his rage and look reasonable, spit still on his lips from where he'd been screaming at me. She told him she'd call the police if he came back to the office again, reminding him that thanks to Lisa the police were quick to come to PKR when called. She told me *I* should get a restraining order. I straightened my clothes and told him I wasn't coming back. It was over. I'd be getting a divorce.

Penny escorted him to the ground floor and made sure the men at the front desk took him to his car and told them if he was seen again anywhere near the building they were to call her and the police.

The rest of the day was spent under a cloud of humiliation disguised as sympathy. Stacey was sweet in a *Oh God, I don't know how to deal with this* way. Toby puffed up and swore he'd beat the crap out of Richard if he dared show up again — which almost made me smile because I doubt Toby's ever had an actual fight in his life — and then there was Julia, the only one who in fact made me buck the fuck up because of all her faux sympathy and pity. Penny was nearly as bad, as if Richard's crazy might give her an excuse to demote or fire me at some point in the near future, and put all this 'Lisa business' behind her for good.

She and Julia are clearly thick as thieves already. Funny how things change. But still, I

241

went to work and I got work done, and after what happened when I got back to the hotel smug Julia's no doubt surgery-adjusted nose will be very much out of joint tomorrow.

Simon Manning had been waiting for me in the business centre downstairs. I'd thought he was going to ask me to leave, but instead he wanted to know if I'd be willing to take over his account at PKR — *Lisa's job*. He said I could stay in the hotel for a while and could meet prospective staff. It would give them — and me — a far better view of the ethos of the business and the work involved, and I could liaise with the heads of housekeeping and catering about the new build. Living in would give me more of an insight into the hotel industry, and he was sure I could work a few days a week from here to start. If I agreed, he'd call Penny right away.

If I agreed. I nearly fell to my knees in joy. Of course I wanted the contract. I was still blubbing my thanks when he walked away. And now here I am, flopped back on my big hotel room bed, a huge mixture of emotions. Relief. That's what I'm feeling mainly. I don't care if he's offered the work out of pity, I'll be good at it, and Lisa already had things underway.

Lisa. The day has been too full to think about her and I'm damned if I'm going to start now. This is *my* fresh start. Simon Manning has given me an out. My job is safe and I don't have to worry about finding somewhere to live yet. If the bank takes the house because the mortgage hasn't been paid, I can still survive. I need to get more of my things but that can wait and I don't want to go on my own. *No Lisa to go with you any more.*

I'm about to strip down for a shower before opening the bottle of wine, sandwich and crisps I picked up on the way home — funny how quickly *home* changes — when there's a knock on the door.

The police. Three of them. Bray front and centre.

'What's happened?' My stomach turns to water. 'Is it Ava?' My first fear is they've found her and it's not good, but I realise Bray's expression is too hard for that. I let them in.

'Lisa's escaped.' Blunt.

'Escaped?' I say. 'I didn't realise she was a prisoner.' There I go, defending her again, as if on automatic pilot.

'She's not.' She corrects herself. 'At least, she wasn't. But she's attacked her probation officer and run. We need to know if she's been in touch with you. Called you or emailed you. Anything.'

'Why would she run?' I sit back on the bed.

'Have you heard from her?' This time Bray's sharp and I shake my head.

'No. Nothing. Go through my phone if you want. What's going on?'

'Do you have a diary or calendar for the past year at home?'

'No. My life isn't that busy. Why do you want to know what I've been doing?'

'It's about pinning down Lisa's movements. I'm going to need you to try your best to give us a list of times and places you've been with her.'

I bark out a laugh. 'I can barely remember

243

what I did last week, let alone every day for the last year.'

Bray doesn't crack a smile and a weight drops in my stomach. 'Why are you so worried about Lisa?' *What's she done?* The question I'm too afraid to ask hangs in the air.

The policewoman sits on the bed beside me and I don't know if that's some attempt to befriend me or whether she's simply exhausted too.

'We searched their Elleston house again for any clues to where Ava might be now,' she says. 'We found Jon's laptop there, hidden under Lisa's mattress, and a set of keys we believe belong to a rented property in Wales.'

I glance from her to the two officers with her and they're all looking at me as if this is supposed to make sense. I frown. 'Jon was in their house? God. When? After all this . . . happened? How could he have . . . ?'

'No.' Bray cuts me off. 'We don't think Jon was there at all.'

'Just bloody tell me whatever you're trying to tell me!' I snap. 'In plain English.' I'm too tired for this and now my brain is spinning all over again.

'Jon hasn't been seen at his home for months. Neighbours say they thought he went travelling. He was made redundant two years ago. Only did odd jobs for a bit of extra cash now and again. He was quiet and no one really noticed him. He doesn't have a mortgage as he sold his mother's house and bought a flat outright when she died.

Inherited a tidy sum too. His bills all go out by direct debit.'

'And?' Why can't she get to the point? How bad *is* the point if it needs this much explaining?

'A neighbour said he'd had a female visitor before he left. They thought he'd met someone or had got back together with an old girlfriend. He seemed happier. More bounce in his step.'

'Who?' I ask.

'They didn't get a clear look. Only said she'd visited a couple of times. We found a cottage rental transaction on Jon's laptop and we've got officers on their way there now. Hopefully we'll find Jon and Ava there. Maybe Lisa too.'

'But why were his things in Lisa's house?' I know what she's driving at but I can't quite grasp it. 'You think Lisa was this woman? The old girlfriend? You think she and Jon have been in touch? That's why his laptop is there?' For a second, it makes a weird sense. Maybe they somehow rekindled a romance — *How, when she didn't have social media?* — but then I remember the messages Jon sent to Ava. The *kind* of messages. Lisa wouldn't let Jon send those. That's not the work of someone wanting a family reunion. Or didn't she know? Maybe Jon was sending them without Lisa knowing? It's tenuous at best, but I can't see Lisa going along with that. Hiding her past, yes, but this. This is *madness*.

'But it doesn't make sen — '

Bray's phone rings out, cutting me off, and she's straight on her feet, turning away to answer. I take a long breath, my temples throbbing. I *saw* the state Lisa was in when Ava went missing. She's broken. All the Katie stuff she said. She *couldn't* have known where Ava was. And those emails. She couldn't be part of that. She just couldn't. Could she?

'Jesus,' Bray says, quiet. 'I'll call you in five when I'm on my way.' Another phone starts ringing and Bray, her face grim and body stiff with energy, nods at her colleague to take it outside.

'What?' I ask her. 'What's happened? Oh God, are they . . . '

'Jon Roper is dead. His body was found in the cottage. There's no sign of Lisa or Ava.' Her words are blunt but they bounce off my tired brain.

'Dead? And Ava's not there?' I'm like a character from some cosy crime show, sitting there stunned, repeating words until they make sense.

'It's imperative you call me if you have any thoughts on where Lisa could have gone or if she makes any attempt to contact you.'

'Of course,' I say. 'But surely she wouldn't have . . . '

'Jon Roper's body is apparently in a state of extreme decomposition. He's been dead for months. Maybe even a year. Certainly longer than Ava's been getting those Facebook messages.'

'Was he . . . ?'

'Murdered?' She says the word for me. 'Yes. It would appear so.'

The world doesn't spin exactly but the straight

edges of the bed and walls curve slightly as all the colours brighten. I frown. 'But then who was sending Ava the messages? If Jon was dead?'

She looks at me as if I'm stupid. '*Charlotte was.* Lisa. Whatever you want to call her. The laptop was in *her* house. Even before this development, we were working on the assumption it was her.'

I feel like I can't get enough air into my lungs.

'I know it's hard to take in, but the most likely conclusion is that this is all her doing.'

'But why?' *Oh God, Lisa. Did I know you at all?*

'We think she's had some sort of breakdown. She's phoned Alison — the probation officer you met — at least twice in recent weeks paranoid she was being watched. The money theft at work could be symptomatic of her mental instability. We won't know until we find her. And until we do, we can't be sure Ava is safe. In fact, we consider Ava to be very much at risk. Do you understand, Marilyn?'

'But how could she — '

'When Ava ran away she'd been alone in the flat with Lisa. Lisa reported her missing the next morning when she woke up. Anything could have happened in those hours. Lisa could have left first to set up the meeting. Anything. Do you understand what I'm saying?'

I nod, slowly, my skull heavy. 'Lisa's dangerous.' I pause. 'Fucking hell. She's gone mad.'

Bray looks relieved that her point has finally sunk in. But this is easier for her. She didn't know Lisa. But then did *I*? Ever?

'I'll call you straight away if I hear from her.' My hands are trembling. Fuck, fuck, fuck. This is insane. 'If I think of anything else you might find useful, I'll ring.'

'Thank you. I know this is difficult.' Bray stands, eager to leave me and get to her crime scene.

'Ava's the only thing that matters.' My throat dries, as, in the midst of all this, a selfish thought strikes me. *And why not? I should get something out of this shitstorm.* 'Oh,' I say. 'There's one more thing, if that's okay.'

'Yes?'

'My husband. If you speak to him, be careful of what you say. He's been trying to get me to sell my story to the papers. I wouldn't trust him with any vital information unless you're ready for it to be shared.'

'Thank you. We were planning on seeing him, in case Lisa turns up there, so that's useful to know.'

'When you go there,' I try to sound casual, 'could you tell him to stay away from me and my work? It would be helpful. Until I start divorce proceedings. He can be . . . difficult.' I don't need to say more. She's a woman. We have an implicit understanding of what sentences like that really mean.

'No problem,' she says. And then they're gone.

I forget about the shower and the sandwich and go straight for the wine. I don't want to get drunk, but I definitely need one glass. My hands are trembling as I pour it and take the first sip.

Lisa. Has Lisa done all this? I remember Ava's sixteenth birthday, only a few weeks ago, but it feels like a lifetime. I'd asked Lisa about Ava's dad and if she ever heard from him. She'd shut me down as she always did. Had she already killed him?

This is different from trying to accept that my best friend had once been Charlotte Nevill. That was *past*. This is present. She did this while going to work with me, eating Chinese takeaways, idolising my *perfect marriage* and worrying about Ava's exams. How could she have been sending those messages to Ava? Killing Jon? All that while? Am I that stupid?

Someone isn't who they say they are.

Katie's body was never recovered.

No. No. No. Those thoughts will make me as crazy as Lisa, and she *is* crazy. Maybe she's had some kind of schizophrenic breakdown and is having episodes as Katie? Maybe living as a different person for so long, always afraid of being discovered, has snapped her? Maybe she's created a *Katie* to deal with the bad shit. Maybe it's one of those psychotic breaks like in the films, and she doesn't *know* when she's being Katie?

I like that thought. It gives me a little wave of relief. It's better than the alternative — that I didn't notice my sweet best friend was batshit fucking dangerous crazy. I can't get my head around the alternative at all. She couldn't have done it consciously. Could she?

It all pummels at my skull until I realise it's getting dark outside. It's ten p.m. and I'm still sitting here, holding the same glass of warm wine.

Fuck the shower. Fuck it all. Without even brushing my teeth, I crawl into bed.

46

LISA

I pretend to be playing solitaire with an old deck of cards, but my ears are locked on to the quiet sound of the TV in the corner of the communal sitting room. There are only two other people in here, sipping coffee and reading the papers. I figure everyone else has gone into town for the evening. That's what young people do, after all.

The lorry dropped me in Calthorpe and I got the bus to Ashminster from there, checking into this youth hostel for three nights, and paying the extra for a private room with a shower. First, I scrubbed myself clean, washing him off me until my skin was red raw, and then, despite the fear and nerves that have turned my guts into a painful acid tear in my midriff. I fell asleep for hours, a bleak, black empty sleep of non-existence.

When I eventually woke it was evening and I sprayed fresh colour into my hair, painted my face on and became Lily again. I think about the name. The flower of death. A mourner's bloom. Please don't let me be mourning Ava. Please let me have bought some time.

I'm on the news. Not Lily, but those other mes, Charlotte and Lisa. I was Lisa for so long.

It should hurt more that she's gone; but I've shucked her off like a snake's shed skin. After the last time I changed my name, after what happened with Jon, I think I knew she wouldn't be forever. Charlotte is harder to shake off. I have to die to truly end Charlotte. Maybe that's what this will come to, this battle of wits. But I'm not ready for that yet and Charlotte definitely isn't. I'm reclaiming the game as best I can.

It's the second time the news report has been on and this time I'm calmer and listen properly, pushing aside my grief for poor Jon who never did anything wrong apart from fall in love too young with someone who wasn't lovable. I try not to look at my face as it stares back at me from the screen, all Home Office anonymity deals off now I'm once again a murderer. I look so meek. So invisible. They've used the photo from my work pass. The newsreader says I now have shorter, blonde hair, and then there's a farcically bad Photofit that looks like a very non-sexy blow-up doll version of me with blonde hair added. It almost makes me laugh. It almost makes *Lily* laugh. She's tougher than me, whoever the hell I am. Lily's more Charlotte than Lisa. I'm only the husk they inhabit.

I glance at the photo on the screen again. It's nothing like me. Is that really the best the police can do? I wonder if *she's* watching. What's she thinking? This won't be how she expected it to go. She thought I'd be locked up by now. Game over.

The newsreader tells the world I'm wanted in

connection with the murder of Jon Roper whose body has been found in a rented property in Wales. After an overhead shot of the isolated cottage, the local reporter shares what they know.

'A man's decomposed body found on the premises is believed to be that of Jon Roper, the ex-partner of child murderer Charlotte Nevill and father of her sixteen-year-old daughter, Ava. As we heard earlier, police had been looking for Roper in connection with Ava's disappearance from a safe house where she and her mother had been staying after Charlotte Nevill's new identity and location had been exposed. But now, with Jon Roper dead and Charlotte Nevill having absconded, it seems this is a much murkier situation than at first thought and there is a real sense of concern here for the missing sixteen-year-old, who only last month saved a child's life.'

It's Bray's turn to take to the cameras, and she stands in front of the cordoned-off house, the wild wind blowing her hair around her face, dragging strands free from her sensible ponytail. She says I should be considered dangerous. She says if anyone sees me they should call the number at the bottom of the screen but should not approach me.

She's not telling the whole story. She's got something that very firmly makes them think. I killed Jon. I saw it in the stiffening of Alison's spine in the flat and I can see it in the serious guarded expression on Bray's face. I have survival instincts second to none. And I know my

253

enemy. My best friend. Two sides of the same coin. *Where are you, Katie? Where have you taken my baby?*

I clear up the cards as if I'm bored and throw the young couple on the other side of the room a smile as I get up. They give me a polite smile back, but there's no recognition. Nothing. How easy it is to become someone else. How easily people see only what they want to. All those years of fear that I'd be recognised were wasted time. No one sees anything at all. There was no anonymous caller to give me away after the photos in the papers. That was Katie. I *know* it. She set the whole thing up.

I go back to my room and lie on my bed. I can't do anything until tomorrow, except think. I've been blind too. I've missed someone right in front of me. I *felt* something, sure, and alarm bells were ringing deep inside me, but I didn't see you, Katie. Who are you? Anxiety bees buzz in my head and I want to curl up and cry for Ava, to scream for someone to get my baby back, but the only person who can do that is me, and I need to stay tough. To stay Charlotte.

Peter Rabbit. Drive Away, Baby. The missing photo.

Penny? No, Katie can't be Penny. Penny's been there forever. Marilyn? No. I can't even countenance that thought. Marilyn is my best friend, even if she hates me now, and as with Penny, ten years is a long waiting game for this. To have me in her sights all this time and do nothing surely isn't Katie's style. Katie was impetuous. Impatient.

But who else can it be? A stranger? No. She has to be someone I know. I think of the photos. Whoever it is has been in my house. Ava probably left the back door unlocked a million times. Maybe they found out about the spare key and took it? I think about all the occasions I've left my bag unattended at work. Or on the back of a chair in a pub. Could someone have copied the keys and put them back before I noticed? Stolen them temporarily from my handbag?

The thought of someone stealing from my bag makes me sit bolt upright. *Julia*. The thoughts follow in a succession of quick-fire bullets. She stole from Penny. She's new. She's sneaky and snide. She's older than she's made herself look. She's determined to turn people against me.

My breath comes in sharp pants and I take deep breaths to ease the pain in my gut. Is Julia Katie? Is this what she wanted? To make me a murderer all over again and then kill my baby, leaving me with all that grief? It should surprise me, but it doesn't. Deep down, I've always known she'd come for me.

Cross my heart and hope to die.

PART THREE

47

HER

Girl B. I never liked it. Sounds so second best. A tag-along. A pitiful runner-up. Like being the lesser half of a whole. Ironic, given how I'm the brains in this outfit and always was. Charlotte? God, how to describe *her?* She was brave. Strong. Wild and wicked. Yes, she was all those things, but I was always that bit smarter. I still am. But I haven't changed. Not like her.

You know what? I'm actually pleasantly surprised she's got this far in my game. I wasn't sure she had it in her to run. I'd hoped she would, I hoped those old instincts would kick in, but I wasn't banking on it. People change as they get older. That's the dull part of growing up. But there's changing and then there's *Lisa*.

The old Charlotte — my Charlotte — I'd have had no doubts about her. She'd have sensed what was coming and fled. She may not have been so smart but she was *feral*. This *thing* she's become, this ordinary middle-aged mother of yours, I thought she'd still be sitting there like a pathetic damp dishrag until they carted her off for Jon's murder and then she'd spend the rest of her miserable life locked up and wondering what happened to you while the world screamed at her to tell them where she'd left your body.

As a Plan B, I could have coped with that but it would have been such a disappointment. After all this time hiding and waiting to resurface. After all the planning. No, it would not have been a fully satisfying conclusion to our friendship. Certainly not quite the same as a proper reunion. She'd have been cheating herself too. She wants to see me. Of course she does. The question is, is there enough of the old Charlotte left to find me? To find us?

I guess we'll have to wait and see. Anyway, Ava, time for your medicine. You need to go bye-byes. I've got things to do.

48

BEFORE

1989

Everything has to come out somehow.

That's what Tony's sister Jean had said two years back when Charlotte had been puking with the measles. *It all has to come out somehow. Don't fight it. It'll make you better.* Maybe it does. Maybe that's why she shoved dog shit through old Mr Perry's letterbox and laughed at him, even though he's never done anything to her. Maybe that's why she sprayed her name big over the school wall with the can she found in the alley where the boys shoot up. Maybe that's how it's all coming out, all the rage that's wrapped around a bubble of something else, something deep inside she couldn't explain if she tried, something horrible and desperate.

They haven't made anything better though, these things she's done. They've just brought the police and the social and more warnings, and her ma screaming at her and Tony and the belt and always always, through the jumble of her thoughts, is the tight tear in her stomach since the chippy. It didn't turn out to be a one-off. It wasn't ever going to be. She should have known. More *special friends* and always a fish supper she feels sick eating after as if that makes it all normal. As if that makes it a *treat*. More pills, more often. Sometimes she feels like she doesn't know what's real or not any more. Surreal maybe. *Surreal*. A new Katie word she didn't understand and still doesn't even though Katie's tried to explain it. But she likes the sound of it anyway. Surreal makes everything sound cleaner. Safer.

Nothing is safe though. She's still sore from Tony's beating after the woman from the social left last Tuesday. The belt has left welts across the back of her thighs, and there was something different about it this time. Something animal in his face. It made her think of the chippy and she didn't like it at all. His face, the sound of Daniel crying and Ma soothing him. Her own shrieks and shouts as the belt came down, hating herself for making a sound. She didn't cry. Not even after, when she was alone. Instead she lost herself in their song, hers and Katie's. Playing it over and over, loud in the headphones.

She's out of the house as much as she can be despite what the police and the social say about school and happy families. Ma and Tony sleep late and she's gone by the time they wake. She shoves some milk or juice and bread at Daniel over the side of his cot and gets out. They can play their happy families, the three of them. That's what they want anyway.

Causing havoc or seeing Katie is how she spends her days. Katie. Oh, she lives for Katie. They have their den now, here in Coombs Street. There's blankets on the ground that Katie snuck out from home, some candles Charlotte nicked from the big shop in town, a couple of old cushions from the youth centre over on Marley Street. It's here she feels safest. She lights another cigarette as Katie speaks. Ma trouble, that's what Katie's got. The opposite of Charlotte's. Too much love, that's Katie's problem. Everybody loves her.

'Maybe I shouldn't smoke this around you,' Charlotte says, and laughs. Katie does too as she shakes the blue inhaler and squirts it into the air.

'I don't have asthma. Even the doctor knows that. I don't think he's put anything in this thing. He's probably given me an empty one to stop her going on and on at him. He said my lungs were fine. But did she listen? Of course not. It's her who stops me breathing. She's going to suffocate me soon. Wrap me up so tightly she'll never let me go.'

'How come you're not at school?' Charlotte's lungs are tight with smoke. She's smoking more. She wishes she had some booze but Tony only had two cans left in the fridge and she chickened out of taking one. She'd rob something later. From the shop. Or somewhere. Or maybe one of her ma's pills. She's getting itches for them a bit like the fags.

'Forged a letter. Family problems. It's easy. Summer hols start soon anyway. It's only sports days and activities left, and my mother won't let me take part in those if she can help it.'

It's easy for Katie. Katie's a good girl. If Katie had to go to the chippy and then told about it, people would believe her. They'd help her. No one would believe Charlotte. Or they'd say she brought it on herself. Maybe she did. Maybe she is a little bitch like her ma says when she's angry.

'Come on,' Katie says. 'Let's go for a wander.'

They clamber out the window, keeping an eye out that they haven't been seen and their secret den is safe. Charlotte holds the cigarette out for Katie, who takes it and puffs once before giving it back. She doesn't inhale. Charlotte would rip the shit out of anyone else for that, but she knows Katie only smokes for her. Because Charlotte does it. Not in a *trying to impress* way, but in a *being as close as they can be* way. Best friends. No, something more. There are no words for what this is between them. Charlotte doesn't want words for it. Words might break it.

They throw rocks at the wrecked houses just because they can, and for a little while they pretend they're the last two people on earth in the wasteland left after a nuclear bomb like in that programme on the telly a few years back that her ma still talks about sometimes because it scared her so much. Eventually, survival stories exhausted, they head towards the Rec and the crappy playground there.

They're inside the gates when Charlotte freezes.

'What?' Katie almost whispers it, so attuned are they to each other's feelings that she stills too. Charlotte feels Katie's hand slide into hers. She grips it. Her rock. Her strength.

'My ma,' she says. 'And Daniel.'

Katie gasps a little, and her eyes widen. Their real lives have always been *other*, Katie's in her big house and posh school, and Charlotte's in her scummy estate. But now, here, a door has been opened.

'Come on,' Charlotte grunts, tugging Katie backwards.

'But I want to see.' Katie pulls the other way, nodding Charlotte to the overgrown bushes on the other side of the railings. Charlotte glares at her. 'They won't spot us.' Katie leans in and kisses Charlotte's nose. 'Don't be a wuss.'

The word makes Charlotte grin almost as much as the kiss does, even though she doesn't want Katie to see, she doesn't want her shite life to be real to Katie. *Wuss.* No one around here ever says that. They have to move though, otherwise Ma will spot them soon enough. The Rec's not busy because the weather is crap and the bins haven't been emptied for ages so all the *good* mums take their bairns up to the big park where it's clean and sometimes there's an ice-cream van parked up, but Ma would never do that. Not without it being a special day and even then it would depend on her, or Tony's, mood.

They wriggle through the bushes, quietly giggling as the leaves and hard thin branches jab into them and snare their clothes, until they're both camouflaged behind the railings. Two pairs of eyes peering through shrubbery. Katie is alive with excitement, and Charlotte wonders how her family must seem to her. Ma, scrawny and in a cheap old anorak, her hair lank and pulled back into a ponytail. She probably hasn't had a wash. She looks like she got dressed fast to get out of Tony's way. A good job she hadn't nicked one of his cans, Charlotte decides, if Tony's in one of his moods. Daniel has Peter Rabbit tucked under his arm as Ma lifts him carefully into one of those swings with the safety rail, one leg on either side. She handles him so gently it hurts Charlotte's heart.

Once he's settled, he gives her a smile and chews on Peter Rabbit's ear as she pushes him, not too hard, just enough for him to enjoy. Tony used to push Charlotte on the swings, but he'd push her so high she'd be crying out in terror for him to stop. He found it funny. She's never seen him do that with Daniel.

They can't hear what she's saying but Ma's laughter carries on the breeze. It's sweet and soft and whatever she's saying to Daniel is full of care. Charlotte bites hard on the inside of her cheek, her mouth metallic as she breaks the skin. *It all has to come out somehow.*

She glances over at Katie. 'Can we go now?'

'She was never like this with you, was she?' It's a question but it isn't. Katie knows the answer. 'She really loves him.' Her voice is soft, talking to herself rather than her friend, but the words are like knives in Charlotte. She holds on to the imaginary steel slicing her. She'll make it part of her.

'Yeah, I wish he'd disappear,' Charlotte says, bitter, watching her ma lift him gently out and on to the ground, face full of concern.

'Imagine if he did,' Katie says, a half-smile on her face, lost to the fantasy already. 'Or if he died. Imagine how she'd feel. Maybe then she'd realise how much she loved you.'

It's a sweet thought, but Charlotte knows nothing can make Ma love her. Ma looks at her like she's bad and dirty and she *is*, but she only used to be bad. Ma can't look at her straight because of what she and Tony make her do.

'I'd run away,' she says. 'Leave them alone. With each other.'

'No.' Katie's voice is hard and she crouches, pulling Charlotte down too, so their knees are under their chins and it makes the welts on the backs of Charlotte's thighs burn fresh. 'No.' She shakes her head. '*We'd* run away. Together. We will.' She pulls the shell she brought back from Skegness from her jacket pocket and holds it up against Charlotte's ear. It's not the first time Katie's done this but it still seems like magic to Charlotte, the sound of the sea coming from it.

'We're going to make them pay,' she says. She leans in and presses her lips against Charlotte's. 'Your family and mine.'

Charlotte nods, Ma and Daniel behind her dissolving into nothing. 'We'll make them pay,' she agrees.

It all has to come out somehow.

49

NOW

MARILYN

I didn't sleep more than perhaps an hour's fitful dozing and by the time I get to work my head is thumping, my mouth is dry and my heart is beating too fast in that way that comes with insomnia. I spent all night thinking about Lisa and everything she's supposed to have done. She has a split personality, she must do. Maybe I should suggest it to the police — I'm fuck-all use to them for anything else. I can't even think of any dates from the past year that may matter. All my days run into a blur of work and home.

Lisa killed Jon. She sent Ava those messages. I remember how quietly happy she was about Simon. How obvious it was they liked each other right from the start — all those unnecessary meetings he arranged. And her nerves, like a teenager, when they were going for dinner. Could she really have been *that* Lisa and this crazy person at the same time? Even if I was too stupid to notice, surely Ava would? Maybe not. She's a teenager, absorbed in her own life.

The pregnancy test. Ava must have had a boyfriend. Have the police tracked him down? Is he relevant? He didn't matter very much to Ava. She was too fixated on her online love. It makes me sick, the madness of it all.

I dump my bag on my desk and try to stay breezy, but the excited chatter is loud. They're talking about it. Of course they are.

'I mean, holy fuck, she killed her ex. Murdered him. While she was coming in here and being all sweet and nice and normal.' Toby's rocking back in his chair, like some show-off teenager at school. 'Batshit crazy.'

'It's the daughter I feel sorry for. Where do you think she is?'

'Dead probably.'

'Julia!'

'Well, it's horrible but it's probably true.'

The women are in a huddle around Julia's desk, and none of them acknowledge my arrival.

'Penny in?' I ask, bright and breezy.

Heads turn, glances over shoulders as they quieten.

'She texted me earlier.' Julia, arms folded across her chest, all sharp eyes and confidence. 'Got a breakfast meeting so won't be in until about ten.'

Penny and Julia sitting in a tree T-E-X-T-I-N-G . . . Sly little Julia, a tapeworm in the guts of our world.

A phone rings. 'Don't, it's reporters,' Stacey says as I reach for it. 'They've been ringing since we got here. They'll probably turn up outside soon.'

'Poor Penny, having to deal with all this.' Julia turns inwards and neatly closes the circle again, me on the outside. 'She couldn't possibly have known. I mean, who would think a person could

269

be doing anything like that and still coming in to work every morning?'

Their chatter has a hysterical giggly edge to it and it makes me angry. So it's okay that Penny didn't know it, it's okay that Toby didn't have any suspicions, but somehow I'm still tarred with the Lisa brush?

'It's like Rose West or Myra Hindley,' Julia continues. 'Murdering all those people and carrying on with life like normal. Who knows what else she may have done? This could be the tip of the iceberg.'

Giving your age away there, Julia, I think. These kids have probably never heard of Myra Hindley. Or Rose West, for that matter.

'Gosh!' Emily's eyes widen. 'What if this was just the beginning? What if she was going to kill one of us next?'

'I thought that last night,' Julia, all glee, answers. 'Who knows what she's capable of? If she could kill her own daughter . . . '

'We don't know she's murdered anyone yet.' My rage bursts into flames, and I glare at them, all these young and not so young people so full of judgement and accusation.

'Oh, I think we do.' Julia turns, arch. 'What about her poor little brother?'

'You know what I meant.' My face reddens. My answer is weak.

'Oh, you meant we don't know whether she's killed anyone *this time*.'

Lisa *is* a murderer, but that was a long time ago. A different life. A different name. But it's so hard to believe she's got anything to do with the rest of all this crazy. Because she's *not* crazy, and even if she *is* crazy I'd still like her better than this grade-A bitch in front of me. She's smiling. This is exactly what she wanted. Well, fuck her.

'No, as a matter of fact, we don't. So why don't you get on with the work you're paid to do, and leave the police to get on with theirs.' It's not my finest ever comeback, but given that I'm a heartbeat away from screaming nonsensical swear words of rage and frustration into her smug face, it's not bad. It's not only her, it's all of it. Richard, Penny shutting me out, Simon being kind, Ava going missing and Lisa — I can't even begin there.

'I'm surprised you're not more worried,' Toby joins in, not wanting to be emasculated by Julia, the new power in town. 'I mean, you knew Ava pretty well, didn't you? I'd have thought you'd be more upset about her, instead of defending Lisa.'

I stare at him, this peacock of a boy who'll be bald and fat and unfuckable by the time he's forty. This boy who knows nothing. 'How dare you! How dare you presume to know my feelings?'

Red spots rise in his cheeks. He doesn't know whether to go forward or back.

'She stole the money.' A soft voice, barely there. Stacey. Sweet, dumb Stacey, defending her man. Julia's eyes dart back and forth, relishing every moment of this overdue confrontation. There's a long pause of held breaths, and then I don't disappoint as all the heat rushes out of me. A blaze of fiery words.

'God, you're all so fucking stupid!' I say. 'You can't see what's right in front of you! Lisa never stole any money! Jesus Christ, ten years she worked here and never a penny went missing! *Julia stole it!* Little miss resting-bitch-face over there. Yes, you! And you know how I know? Lisa *saw* you at the party. You took twenty quid out of Penny's wallet and bought her a thank you bottle of wine with it! You want to talk about crazy? Well, *that's* crazy!' I pause for a breath, my whole body shaking, as they stare at me.

'Yes, Lisa did something terrible a long time ago, and no, I'm never going to understand it, or get my head around it, but fuck you for thinking people can't change. Fuck you for being so quick to believe the worst because you're too young and too lucky to know what life can make you do, and fuck you all for being so stupid to think that girl' — my finger stabs at Julia — 'that *woman*, because she's my age if she's a day — is your friend!'

I finish my tirade to an applause of silence and wide eyes. Stacey looks about to burst into tears. Toby's mouth is hanging open but his eyes are gleaming with regret he hadn't videoed me on his phone. They don't get it. They'll never get it. But still, I'm feeling better already, as if I've just vomited up bad food, and then I see Julia's expression. Victorious even as she tries to look distressed. She's not looking at me. She's looking over my shoulder. My stomach sinks. Penny's arrived. Of course she has.

'Perhaps you should go and work from the hotel, Marilyn,' she says. Her smile is tight. Any other day and I'd be fired, I'm sure of it, but God bless Simon Manning. 'Feelings seem to be running a little high this morning and I know you have a lot to organise there.'

I nod. I'm like a scolded child and suddenly I want to cry. All I do is cry these days. I won't now, though, I'm not giving Julia the satisfaction. I don't trust myself to speak as I gather my things together. *Screw you too, Penny.* My eyes blaze into hers and the ten years of trust between us burns to ash.

'One more thing,' she says, as I head towards the door. I turn. 'Apologise to Julia. She didn't deserve that.'

Now all I want to do is laugh. Or applaud. Julia's certainly the ringmaster of this little circus. I stare at her and she stares back. Her eyes give nothing away. She looks truly hurt by what I've said. She deserves a bloody Oscar.

'I apologise, Julia.' It's clear from my tone I'm not sorry at all, but still she darts her eyes sideways in a Princess Diana *poor me* way, and tentatively smiles.

'Please,' she says. 'It's okay. I know it's been a difficult time for you.'

God, she's good, but I'm not buying it for an instant. My back is stiff as I walk out. *Fuck you, Julia, if you think this is over.* My hand trembles as I press the button for the lift. *If you think that, then you don't know me at all.*

50

LISA

Julia walks to work and back. If the thought hadn't woken me with a jolt, I'd probably have slept right through the day and maybe round to morning. All those pills they were giving me having a final assault on my system. It was two thirty in the afternoon when I got up, a whole morning lost. I felt brighter though. More together.

I showered, applied 'Lily', gathered my meagre belongings together in case I couldn't return, and was out of the hostel by three thirty and on the bus ten minutes later. Julia walks to work. She bragged about it on the first day and has said it more than once since. *It's a couple of miles or so but I enjoy it.* Julia Katie, Katie Julia. The names beat out the seconds and minutes of my journey and then, despite my sweating palms and palpitating heart, I headed towards PKR and grabbed a coffee in the cafe opposite, sitting in the window and pretending to read a paper. I was sure that at any moment someone would recognise me, or the police would swarm in and arrest me, but there was nothing. Not a single batted eyelid.

Finally, five o'clock came and within minutes

Julia emerged from work. I'd half-hoped to catch a glimpse of Marilyn, to see she was okay, but there was no sign of her. Once Julia had got a few feet ahead, I sauntered out and, keeping my distance, followed her. She didn't look back once. And so here I am. Still free. Still Lily, and also still terrified Lisa, desperately needing to save her daughter.

I hide under a tree and study the house. A sixties or early seventies terrace of four small homes in a row, a thin strip of grass — not nearly enough to be considered a garden — in front of each. Early council housing is my conclusion, and judging by the litter a little further along, this street hasn't been sold off to private owners. Surely she can't have Ava in there? There can't be much privacy — neighbours would hear any noise. A cellar, perhaps? Do these houses have cellars? I'm bemused. I'm not sure what I'd expected of Julia; probably something modern and soulless, but also practical and safe. Like the house Ava and I lived in.

And Katie? Katie of the big house and the piano lessons and the perfectly pleated skirts? Could she live here? *Katie could live anywhere*, the Charlotte inside me whispers. *Katie could do whatever it takes. Katie would pretend she was Charlotte. Games and fantasies and dares. Katie and Charlotte.*

I reach inside my jacket and grip the handle of the knife in the pocket. Youth hostels are so easy, so friendly. A knife from a kitchen drawer gone in a moment while asking for a teaspoon. Charlotte's old shoplifting skills served me well.

If she has Ava somewhere else, she'll have to go out and check on her. She won't have a partner in crime. Not Katie. That was always my role. My stomach tightens. She has my daughter. I want to peel her face off while she screams. But part of me wants to see her too. I'm sick. I must be.

I wait, unsure what to do — *you can wear as much make-up as you want, but invisible Lisa still has a hold* — as gathering storm clouds make the night darker than it should be in summer. Lights go on. Movement behind net curtains. *Who the hell has net curtains?* I move forward under the overhanging branches, and unable to take any more, sure I'm going to vomit where I stand, I decide this is it — I have to go and confront her.

Headlights turning into the road stop me. The car slows, pulling up on the kerb, and my breath catches as I shrink back into the gloom, khaki against bark. I know this car. It's Marilyn's car. What the hell is she doing here?

51

BEFORE

1989

'It worked perfectly!' Katie scrambles in through the window to where Charlotte is waiting in the stifling heat of the old house. 'You're so clever, Charlotte, you really are. How on earth did you know all that stuff?'

She shrugs. 'Read it in one of my ma's books.'

'Well, it went like a dream.' She holds out two large slices of chocolate cake. 'Mummy made it for me to take to Mr Gauci's house for him and his wife. I've got sandwiches too.'

They sit on the dusty mats and start their feast, Charlotte making sure to chew the thick white bread — no cheap thin doughy slices for Katie's family — slowly, enjoying the butter and mustard and proper ham.

'You should have seen his face,' Katie's eyes shine with the memory, 'when I told him that if he didn't go along with letting me out all day, I'd say he'd touched me. He went positively puce.'

Charlotte doesn't know what puce is, but it sounds a bit like puke so she figures Katie means green.

'He said no one would believe me, and so I said all the things you'd told me, the *detail* of what I'd say he did, and I swear I thought he might cry. I ended up pretty much comforting him. I did explain that no one would ever find out and he was basically getting paid for nothing, so why worry? I told him to take his wife out to lunch. And d'you know what I said after? Oh, Charlotte, you'd have been so proud!'

'What?' Charlotte says, smiling. Katie's joy is her joy. Katie is the sunshine. Katie leans in, their faces kissing-close.

'I told him maybe he should try some of the things I'd mentioned on her!' She bursts into laughter. 'Oh God, you should have seen it! I thought he might die!'

Charlotte tries to laugh but her smile is stretched too wide. Tearing at her like the sharpness in her gut. Those were things from the chippy that she'd given to Katie. She'd earned that knowledge not from a trashy novel, but from a small room reeking of hot fat and sweaty men.

'Anyway,' Katie waits until she's swallowed a bit of her sandwich before continuing to speak and Charlotte makes a note not to talk with her own mouth full any more. 'I did the work in about five minutes, so if Mummy asks when she picks me up, there's no need for suspicion. The summer hols are ours! Four hours a day, anyway.'

'Will she come to check on you, do you think?' Charlotte says, worried. It would be shite if Katie's ma caught her out. She'd lock her up all summer for it, to keep her safe.

'No. She's seeing the therapist and he told her she has to let me be during the tutor lessons. Death, death, death, worry. That's all she does. I

278

wouldn't mind if she was worried about her own — her death I could cope with — it's all being transferred to me. It's not fucking fair.'

That makes Charlotte laugh. Katie has given her *surreal* and *puce*. In return, Charlotte has given her *fucking* and *shite*.

'You wouldn't have had to have the extra lessons at all if you didn't play so soft and simple all the time.'

'Life is easier this way,' she says with a shrug. 'Why do you play so tough?'

'I don't *play* tough,' Charlotte grins and Katie smiles back, leaning on her shoulder. After a moment, she sits upright and frowns.

'You're getting boobs!' One slim finger pokes Charlotte's chest.

'Get off!' She pushes Katie's hand away, blushing and awkward. She's tried to hide it under a baggy shirt but her chest is getting bigger. She hates it. Ma said there was no point in getting a training bra because if she got big as fast as they did in Ma's family then in a couple of months she'd need a proper one.

Katie looks down at her own slight frame. Not even the hint of anything other than flatness under her shirt. 'That's not fair. I'm months older than you. If you get your period before me as well, I'm going to be so annoyed.'

Charlotte wrinkled her nose. 'Don't be disgusting.' She gets to her feet. She's itching to do something. She'd taken half of one of her ma's pills this morning but the haze is wearing off and she wants to rob some booze. She doesn't want to think about boobs and periods and the things she'd pretended to have read in a book. She wants to run away with Katie and stay like they are forever.

The curse, that's what Jean calls it. *She'll be getting the curse soon. You'd better make sure she knows what to use.*

The curse. Getting the curse. It's hanging over her, she can feel it. Of course she'll get the curse first. She's cursed already.

52

NOW

MARILYN

I bang hard on the door, the muggy heat fuelling my irritation. There's probably a bell but I can't be bothered to look. I don't care what she said in the office, I'm damned well going to have it out with her now. Apologise? Penny can go swivel. I've been quietly raging all day about her smug little face, and I'm going to get it out of her about the money even if no one will believe me. I want to know for *me*.

No one answers and I bang again.

'I know you're in there, Julia!' She doesn't get off so easily. There are lights on, I can see them behind the awful net curtains — she must surely be renting — so someone's home. The door opens as thunder rumbles overhead and the first drops of rain fall. She stares at me and neither of us speak.

'Who is it?' a voice calls from inside. A voice that grates with bitterness and cigarettes. 'Whatever they're selling, we're not buying anything!'

'What are you doing here?' None of Julia's usual cockiness. She looks tired, shoes kicked off on the thin carpet but still in her office clothes. Her blouse is untucked, the edges creased and her sleeves are rolled up.

'We need to talk.'

She glances behind her, up a flight of stairs. A chairlift is at the top and I can also see a pile of creased clothes on the landing. There's a wheelchair in the hall. 'It's for me!' she calls back. 'Someone from work to talk about the promotion I might be getting.'

'Promotion? What prom — '

She puts one finger to her lips, and I find myself falling silent as she nods me inside. I'm thrown by all this. I expected a sleek single girl's apartment. Small but blandly stylish. I come in from the rain and she closes the door behind me, signalling me into a downstairs room.

'Why would you come here?' she says quietly. Her cockiness is gone, it's all defensive aggressive now.

'You live here?' I ask. The room is too hot, central-heating-on-in-summer hot and there's a sharp tang in the air it takes me a moment to identify. Stale urine.

'My mother's house. Yes, I live here. What do you want, Marilyn?'

I'm so confused that for a moment I don't know why I *am* here. 'The money,' I say eventually. 'You're the thief. Lisa wouldn't lie about that. I just want to hear it from *you*.' I look around. 'I don't understand you. The veneers on your teeth. The fillers? You have them, don't bullshit me. But you live like this.' I wave my hand around. 'Why spend money on shit like that? Why steal money to spend on shit like that? Why steal money from Penny only to buy her something with it? I don't get it!'

It seems that there are many types of crazy in the world. Richard crazy, Lisa crazy — even though I can't quite bring myself to believe that — and now Julia crazy.

'Yes, I have veneers. Yes, I have fillers. And before you ask, yes, I have credit-card debts up to my eyes because of it.' She's angry. 'But what do you know about my life? So your husband beats you up and we should all feel sorry for you? More fool you for staying when you could have got out!'

Her words are barbed and they sting more for the truth in them. I *was* a fool to stay. To waste so much of my time.

'At least you could get out,' she continues. 'Have you tried getting care for someone on the NHS? I've been looking after *her*' — she stabs a finger up at the ceiling — 'for pretty much all my adult life. She's not bad enough for a full-time care home but bad enough to fuck up my life. I pay for someone to come in so I can go to work. I don't have a car. I don't have holidays. And it's *hard* to get a job when you're forty and tired and every minute of your sorry life shows on your face.' Now she's started she can't stop. All her containment gone.

'But now she's *dying!*' Her face shines with glee. 'A year at the most. And then I'll finally be fucking free. So yes, I've spent money trying to look younger. I have a whole youth to reclaim. And yes, I stole the money, and I used it to buy drinks in the pub and cakes for the office. Because I am going to have a better life and I'm going to have friends and people are going to think I'm smart and clever and important. And I'm not going to let you stop me. So fucking sue me or report me or whatever, but it will be your word against mine! And right now, your word means shit!'

She's breathing heavily, exhausted with the emotional effort, and I almost laugh because for the last few seconds I've barely heard a word she's said. Her diva moment, the confession I came here for, and it's like I'm hearing her under water.

'I'm sorry,' I mutter. 'I'm going to have to go.'

'What?' She looks like she's been slapped.

'I'm sorry I came. You've got enough going on. I won't say a word.'

'That's *it?*' Julia says. 'You don't *want* anything?'

'I really have to go.'

I leave her standing there, dumbfounded, and as soon as I turn away she dissolves into nothing in my head. My hands tremble as I drag the front door open and suck in rainy air that thankfully doesn't stink of stale piss. I don't care about Julia. I care about the person I just *saw*. I look to my left. She's hiding but I can see her.

The net curtains in Julia's sitting room didn't quite reach the sides of the windows and somewhere in the middle of Julia's rant, I'd seen a face, a clown face of running make-up in the rain, under blue hair shaved at the sides, pressed up to the glass. Our eyes met and it vanished. But I'd know her face anywhere.

Lisa.

'Get in the car,' I mutter, as I pull up by the tree and lower the window. 'Now.'

53

LISA

'It's not her.'

'What?' I can't focus. I'm trembling. I have been since I got into the car. Marilyn. She's holding the steering wheel so tightly as she drives, her knuckles are white.

'Julia.' She glances over at me. 'She's not Katie.'

'That's what you were doing there?' I stare at her. I can't stop staring at her as I try to process what she's saying.

'No, I was there about the money, but I'm presuming it's what *you* were doing there.'

'I was . . . I . . . ' I don't know what to say. 'How do you know?' I ask.

'It's definitely not her. Trust me.'

And I do. I do trust her completely. But inside I crumple. Here, with Marilyn, I'm Lisa again. Tough Lily is only a mask, and Charlotte is so long in the past she's a stranger. Ava, my beautiful Ava. I was so sure, *so sure* Julia had her, and now my hope slips like sand between my fingers and I can't grasp it. I've let her down. She hates me. She's going to die hating me and it's all my fault.

'Are you taking me to the police?' I ask.

286

It's her turn to stare at me. 'Given that they think you killed your ex and kidnapped your own daughter, I'm not sure exactly what that would achieve. So no. Fuck knows where we are going, and fuck knows what is going on in my head, let alone yours, but no, I'm not taking you to the police.'

'You believe me about Katie?'

She looks over at me, for so long I think we might crash. 'This probably makes me crazy, but maybe I do. I wasn't sure, but it goes around and around in my head and nothing else makes any sense to me. You wouldn't do that to Ava. I know you wouldn't. But we need to find Katie. We need *proof* of Katie. Then we go to the police and get Ava back.'

My throat is so tight with a rush of affection for her I can't say a word as the indicator ticks loud and she pulls off the main road on to quieter streets, heading out to the countryside. I think about Ava coming out here all full of love for a man who didn't exist. She was going to meet him down some lane. My baby alone in the middle of the night. What happened? *What did you do to her, Katie?*

'The thing I don't get,' Marilyn says, 'is why. Why would she do this? Is it something to do with Daniel?'

I've heard his name so many times recently, on the news, from the police, and yet still it's like a punch to my gut. 'I killed Daniel,' I say softly, as if the quieter I speak, the less dead my little brother might become. 'I wish I could say I didn't, but I can still feel my hands around his throat.' A flash of memory. *Surreal.* My thumping head, then and now. 'I can't talk about it.'

'And I don't want to talk about it, but if it's not that, what is her problem? All this must have taken planning. Finding you, killing your ex, setting you up. She didn't go to prison. She was free. So why does she hate you so much?'

I stare out at the darkness as rain smears the window.

'Because she loves me. And she can't forgive me for what I did.'

'Daniel?'

I half-laugh. A sorry, sad sound trapped in the past. 'No. After Daniel.'

I don't look at her, but I can feel her expectation.

'There was an anonymous call to the police that day. From a phone box down by the train station. Said two girls had taken a little boy into a derelict house on Coombs Street.' *You've got to hurry. I think summat bad has happened. He was crying and then he stopped. I think that Charlotte Nevill was one of 'em.* 'Said he was hurt.'

'And?'

'I made the call. It was me. I reported us.' My throat is burning and tight. 'I broke the deal.'

54

HER

Ava, if you keep crying you're going to drown in your own snot. I'm not taking the tape off. Not till it's food time. Jesus. I need you alive until Charlotte gets here. She's expecting you alive and one of us isn't a cheat. Unless the police catch her, then it's all over. But you know what? I actually think she'll make it. She's surprising us both, isn't she? So, for God's sake, stop snivelling.

Your mother, she never cried. Not after. Not before. Not even when old Mrs Jackson, nervous and trembling, took the stand in court and told what she'd seen through the broken window of our den on Coombs Street. How she'd been going home across the wasteland and heard a screech and then seen Charlotte hitting little Daniel with the brick. Charlotte didn't even flinch at the details being replayed. I always admired that about her. You could do with channelling some of those genes. Being a little more like her. I wonder how she feels, seeing herself all over the news again. Famous. Girl A — the star of the show, Girl B — totally forgotten. Clyde without Bonnie. Even she forgot me. When she told. She didn't think for a second how it would be for me. We were supposed to run away together. Start a new life. Be free. She got freedom of sorts. Yes, she got locked up, but she got what she wanted Daniel was gone and she was away from her family. Eight easy years later and boom, she's out on the streets a whole new person.

My sentence was longer and far worse. There are different kinds of prisons, trust me. You never met my mother. She was bad enough *before*. Inventing illnesses for me I didn't have so she could worry and over-protect me. The hoops I had to jump through to get out of the house to see Charlotte. All her neuroses foisted on to me. But after? It's funny, people think *acquitted* means you walk free and that's it. Girl B disappears into a sunlit future. What a load of bullshit.

There was court-ordered therapy. Years of it. Talking, talking, talking, and no matter how often I told them what they wanted to hear, there were more questions. Unpicking me, unpicking Charlotte. So much to remember. Lies are so much harder to embed in your head than truths, even for me, smart as I am. For a while, I just withdrew. Played the simpleton who'd served me so well. And it worked for the therapists, but it backfired into my life.

Sweet, simple, easily led Katie. Mother wouldn't let me go to school, of course not. What if I met another girl like Charlotte Nevill? So there were home tutors, specialist teachers, always with her sitting in. I had to keep playing dumb, of course, if I ever wanted the therapists to go away. So I didn't pass my exams — not well enough to go to university, and that was that. Life over. I was trapped. The little girl who never left home. Poor, fragile Katie Batten.

I knew I'd find Charlotte again after the news of her release broke. All I had to do was wait. I'd got used to waiting. I'd had to wait all those years for my mother to die, after all. People always leave a trail, and Charlotte was nothing if not impulsive. She'd make a mistake — threaten her new identity somehow — and I'd be watching.

She must have known I'd come back. I wonder if she ever believed — *truly believed* — I was dead? Our story couldn't end that way. Not apart. There was always going to have to be a reckoning, you see.

I thought she loved me. I thought she was my best friend. And we made a deal. We crossed our hearts and hoped to die and we sealed it with a kiss. We were going to be together forever.

Deals like that cannot be broken.

55

BEFORE

1989

It's the bleakest of days.

Rain falls, big heavy drops that splash inside their den from the roof with all its slates torn away, and run down the outside walls where the guttering has gone. The wasteland has turned to a sludgy mud of broken bricks and dirt and forgotten things, and their shoes are now caked in it. A rotten damp smell fills the room, and even with vodka and half of one of her ma's pills inside Charlotte, the blackness of the future can't be lifted. Not for her and not for Katie.

They huddle together although they barely feel the September chill, and for a while they're silent, their hands holding so tightly to each other Charlotte thinks they might fuse together as one. She wishes they could. She wishes it more than anything. This morning, with Ma and Daniel, was bad, and later, some instinct tells her, will be terrible, but Katie's news is the worst.

'I'll fucking kill myself,' she growls. 'I will.'

'Shh.' Katie rests her head on Charlotte's shoulder. 'Never say that. And let me think.'

Charlotte does, drinking in the exotic scent of Katie's shampoo but also searching for the *Katie smell* under it. She wants to breathe it in and she closes her eyes for a moment, imagining filling the emptiness inside her entirely with Katie. There's space now that she's let everything else out.

After Katie, glowering and angry and stabbing at the crumbling walls with a shard of glass, told Charlotte her news, it tumbled free from her mouth, all the crap she's held inside; Tony, Ma, the chippy, how her shite life is turning her to shite from the inside and how scared she is she'll end up buried in it. How it wouldn't be so bad if there wasn't always Daniel there, the loved child who makes her feel unlovable. How at least she had Katie, Katie was her lifeline, her beating heart, her rock to smash the world with, her one good thing.

But now there will be no more Katie. A few more weeks. Precious days that will trickle away too fast. The Battens are moving. Selling the house and taking Katie a million miles away, south to London. A void stretches ahead of Charlotte and she can feel herself on the edge of tumbling into it already. What will her life be without Katie?

Her ma took Daniel away for the weekend this morning. *A special treat for my little soldier,* that's what Charlotte had heard Tony say as she slammed her bedroom door. She didn't say goodbye. Why should she? Who would care? She could hear them though, Tony fussing over them both, speaking soft to Ma and giving her some money.

Charlotte had curled up like a fist on her bed,

holding her swollen stomach and staring at the pack of cheap pads her mum had given her the day before when the sticky brown blood appeared in her pants. She was wearing one now, a bulky betrayal. The curse. She didn't want it. She doesn't like it. She's still only eleven. She wants her changing body to go back to how it used to look, flat and hard like a boy. Like it was before Daniel came along. When things were better.

Ma has never taken her away for a weekend. She's never taken her anywhere. And now she's gone and left her with Tony for two whole days, maybe three, and as her head swirls with drugs and booze and feels heavy and thick on her shoulders, that worries her. It frightens her. Charlotte Nevill, the fearless girl. The trouble-maker. The bully. The little bitch.

'It's Mummy's fault,' Katie says, staring ahead, hard. 'Everything is always her fault. I wish she was dead.'

'I wish Daniel had never been born.'

'We can't let them do this to us,' Katie says. She sits up and swivels round so she's facing Charlotte, cross-legged, before taking hold of her hands again. They're soft and small and neatly manicured. Charlotte's, much bigger, with bitten-down nails and torn skin scabbing at the edges, look clumsy. Manly. She doesn't mind manly. Today she loves her hands.

'No, we can't,' Charlotte shakes her head. 'We won't. Let's run away. Let's do it.'

'Yes!' Katie says. 'We'll be free. Together forever.'

Charlotte grins and stands, spinning around like Katie does sometimes when she has too much energy for sitting still. 'Bonnie and Clyde, Clyde and Bonnie,' she says and suddenly she's giggling loud and from her sore gut.

'Just like them,' Katie says. 'In love and on the run.'

'You'll be on the run,' Charlotte says, her head swimming as she stops, part drunk, part high, part exhausted. 'But no one will come after me. They won't care. They'll all be glad to be rid of me. They can have their perfect family if I fuck off. Live in this shite estate, all happy without me.'

Katie pulls her back down, shaking her head. 'No, *we'll* be on the run.'

Charlotte waits for the world to settle. The half pill she took is kicking in hard. Maybe different from the others, she didn't look at the packet. She likes it, whatever it is. It makes her feel warm and floaty and sleepy. Like there's a blur between her and the rest of the world. Only she and Katie exist, like in one of their games. 'What are you on about?' She leans forward and smiles. 'Your eyes are perfect blue. Like the sky.'

'Concentrate, Charlotte! I'm being serious. This is important.' Katie shakes her shoulders and she tries to focus. She *does* focus.

'I'm listening, all right?'

'Good.' Katie is intense. 'Why should they get to be a perfect family? Why should they be happy when they've made you so unhappy? Why should I have to worry about Mummy ruining my life forever? She'll never let me go. Even if I run, she'll find me.'

'She should have died falling down those stairs,' Charlotte murmurs. She hates Katie's ma almost as much as she hates her half-brother. She hates anything that makes Katie unhappy.

'Yes,' Katie says. 'She should have.' She pauses. 'And she still could.'

A moment of stillness sits between them.

'And children have accidents too,' Katie continues, quietly focused. Slowly, slowly Charlotte grasps what her best friend is saying.

'There was the kiddie who electrocuted himself in Cairn Street,' Charlotte says. 'He nearly died. They reckon he did for a couple of minutes.'

'Exactly.'

The enormity of what Katie is suggesting is *surreal*, and yet Charlotte finds herself laughing. It's not a pleasant sound, but angry and bitter and filled with a hard joy. She imagines Ma in tears. Tony broken. No perfect boy and no dumb girl to send to the chippy.

'We'll kill them and run,' she says, breathless with the fantasy of it.

'On the same day!' Katie shines with excitement. 'I'll start stealing from my mother's purse. She never knows what she's got in there. And take some jewellery too. We could go to Scotland maybe.'

'Spain,' Charlotte says. 'Somewhere hot. Jean went to Spain once. She said all the buildings were white and that everyone was always happy because they sleep in the afternoons.'

Katie laughs, a sweet tinkle not like Charlotte's raucous uncouth noise. 'All right,' she says. 'If it has to be Spain then we'll get a boat. We'll go to my dead grandfather's house first. It's full of valuable things we could sell and they won't look for us there, not at first, not in all the shock. I'll get a key copied. And you don't need a proper passport to get to Europe. Just one of those cardboard ones from the post office.'

Charlotte hasn't got any sort of passport but who cares, Katie will take care of all that. In her head, they're on a boat, a big ferry, and shrieking together into the salty wind until they're laughing with tears running down their faces.

'When?' she asks. Everything seems better already. Even the rain is slowing down.

'Soon,' Katie says. 'Let me get enough money first.'

'I don't think I'll be able to nick much.' She hates her poverty. It's like grime under her fingernails she can't dig out.

'Don't be silly.' Katie takes Charlotte's face in her hands. 'You only have to bring *you*.'

'I love you, Katie Batten,' Charlotte says. 'My Bonnie.'

'I love you too, Charlotte Nevill. My Clyde. My partner in crime.' She smiles, still holding Charlotte's cheeks. 'We're definitely doing this, aren't we? Deal? No more playing?'

Charlotte nods. 'Cross my heart and hope to die.'

'Cross my heart and hope to die,' Katie whispers in agreement, before leaning in to kiss her.

56

NOW

MARILYN

It's dark by the time we get back to town and I can't risk taking her to Simon's hotel, so I check into a Travelodge near the centre of town, paying for two nights with cash on the off chance the police are watching my banking. Paranoia is catching. I also give Lisa a hundred and fifty pounds to keep on her at all times. She doesn't want to take it but I insist.

We make strong coffee and sit on the bed, Lisa cross-legged, the knife she's stolen from the youth hostel safely out of her coat and on the desk. With her strange blue hair and khaki clothes, she looks so much younger, barely in her late twenties, but this disguise also reminds me she's a woman who's *had* to survive. She's told me about her life before, about her plan with Katie. But the rest? Prison. Fear. Hiding. Who knows what she's faced during those times? But that life has given her skills which are ingrained, I think. And they could save Ava. I haven't told her Ava might be pregnant. There's only so much she can cope with.

'Poor Jon,' she says, as the TV plays the news again. 'He wasn't such a terrible person. He was just weak. He would never have taken Ava. And anyway, I knew it wasn't him. He didn't know about Peter Rabbit.'

'Peter Rabbit?' I ask.

'Daniel's favourite toy. He got it for his second birthday. His last birthday. Someone left one almost exactly like it outside the house. Jon couldn't have done that.'

Jon Roper's face comes up on the screen again, alongside one of Lisa — my Lisa — and the shock of seeing her there still jolts me.

'He gave us all the money he made from when he sold the stories to the papers about us. Exposing me. His mother had made sure most of it went in the bank so he wouldn't drink it away, and when he sobered up, I guess he felt guilty. It wasn't a fortune but it was enough for a deposit on the house and I could finally put some roots down for Ava and me. I could never hurt him, just as he would never hurt his little Crystal. It's Katie. I knew from the start it was Katie. It was always games and make-believe with her.' She swallows some coffee and stares into its rich murky brown. 'Until the deal.'

'Why didn't you mention the deal in court? It would have made sure Katie got in trouble too.' I'm trying to form a clear picture of the past she's kept boxed up. She told me most of it in the car but it's still a whirl in my head. Who she was. Who Katie was.

'I didn't *want* Katie to get in trouble. And anyway, I didn't say a word about anything. Not one. I stayed silent throughout the whole trial. And before. I only spoke three words. *I killed him*. It was all there was to say. Katie cried and whispered and looked around nervously as she said whatever it took to get herself freed. I sat there like stone. None of it mattered.'

'Because Daniel was dead?' I phrase it carefully, not *because you killed Daniel*.

'Because it was all for nothing.' She stares into space, a window opening into a past I can't even imagine. Her voice changes too, a hint of an accent, an edge of the north, Charlotte's accent. 'I'd been so wrapped up in myself. In all the shite of my own life. My jealousy of him ate me up. All those treats, how carefully Ma handled him. God, I hated him. I couldn't see the truth though it was right in front of me.'

Her eyes are brimming and I think of the girl they reported in all those newspapers, the monstrous girl who never cried. I've never seen Lisa cry either. Are we only ever transfers of adulthood pasted on to our childhoods? How much has she been holding inside? 'What didn't you see?' I ask.

'When the pathologist's report on Daniel's body came back it showed evidence of several injuries received over a long period of time. *Sustained*, I think was the word. I didn't know what it meant at first, like it was a new Katie word. Of course everyone presumed it had been me and I let them believe it by my silence. I didn't care by then. I *wanted* them to use it against me. Because I should have seen. I should have known.'

'It wasn't you.'

'No. All those times he wanted my attention. My *affection*. When he followed me. He didn't want to be alone with Tony and Ma either. Tony was hurting him too. I should have run away with him. Told the social worker. He must have been so scared and alone and I was his only hope, but I was too blind with my own anger and pain and fear, and the pills and the booze, to *see*. I should have protected him.' Her breath hitches. 'But instead I killed him.'

Her shoulders start shaking and the sobs come thick and fast. Snot runs from her nose as she breaks, wailing quietly with the terrible grief of it all. I wrap her up in my arms, not caring how my ribs hurt with the pressure and rock backwards and forwards, soothing her.

'Hush now, hush now, it's okay,' I say, although I know it can never be okay, this terrible thing she carries inside her. 'We'll find Ava.' I can't talk about Daniel, I can't make it better with platitudes and I won't try. But Ava is alive and I love her and I also love my best friend regardless of her past. You can't rule your heart and my heart beats for these two.

'We'll find Katie,' I say, with grim determination. 'And we'll save Ava.'

57

LISA

It's not long past dawn but Marilyn is up and ready to go. Neither of us have slept much. 'I want to get back before Simon turns up,' she says. 'I'll shower there. Leave my hair a bit damp so it looks like I've just got up. Maybe it's over-cautious, but we can't take any chances, can we?'

She amazes me, this woman. All the shit going on in her own life, everything she knows about mine now, and yet she's still here, *with* me.

'I'll make my excuses as soon as I can and get out,' she continues. 'Meeting at the bank or something. Hopefully I'll be back by lunchtime. You going to be okay?'

'I've got stuff to get on with.' On the small desk in the corner is notepaper with everything we *know* about Katie scribbled down on it — not much — and now it's up to me to draw up a list of people in my circle, people she could be hidden amongst.

'My number's on there too.' Marilyn is at the door, hesitant to leave me alone. I want to reassure her that despite last night, I can do this. I'm Charlotte Nevill as much as I am the Lisa she knows. 'I'll pick up a pay as you go phone on the way back, but for now, use the hotel phone if you need me, okay?'

'I'll be fine.' I get up and hug her gently. 'And thank you. Thank you for everything.'

'That's what friends are for, right?' She grins, despite her tiredness and her pain. Maybe helping me is helping her, giving her strength.

I wait until she's gone, put the *Do not disturb* sign on the door and then sit for a moment as the coffee machine gurgles. I feel different. All those tears, years of tears, a lifetime of them, suddenly bursting free, have left me feeling stripped back to the bare bones of whoever I am, clean and refreshed. And I have a kernel of hope. I have Marilyn. She loves me. I am not unlovable. Whatever happens next, I will have been loved.

We slept together in our underwear, all our damage on show. The marks of our hidden lives. Faded-to-white cigarette burn scars on the backs of my knees from the worst part of those days immediately *after* when I wanted to hurt myself, and the fresher, larger bruises on Marilyn's skin. Once the lights were out and we were safe in the darkness, she told me about Richard. About the slow decline in his behaviour, how over the years, irritation turned to rage and then, more recently, to violence and how she always hoped it would never happen again, all the *shame* of it. This time it was my turn to listen and wonder how someone could hide a thing like that as a stumbling, stuttering story was told in the night.

We're strong this morning, both Marilyn and I. We've found that in each other. And I'm calm.

Cool-headed. Katie won't hurt Ava — not yet. She's many things — crazy clearly amongst them — but she's not a cheat. She's taken Ava to lure me and she'll want to see that weakness in me when we reunite. This is like some forties gangster film fantasy we would play on the wasteland. She's Cagney, holed up somewhere, hostages for leverage, and I'm the FBI goon coming for her. We age, but we never really grow up. We never really change. I know Katie.

When Marilyn asked me, later last night when all the quiet talking was done, what I thought Katie wanted from all this, I lied. I said she wanted what I'd promised. That we'd run away together. Be free and on the run all at the same time. I don't know if she believed me but she didn't say any more. What could she say? Katie isn't real to her, she's just a bogeyman. A wicked figure from my past. And maybe she is, but back then, she ruined me and saved me all at once. Those days *before* were some of the best days of my childhood. How can I ever explain it? How I'd never loved anyone like I loved Katie and how I'd never been loved by anyone the way Katie loved me? How precious it is to be loved in this mess of life. I close the door on those memories, running hand in hand across the wasteland, but I remember the deal. The intensity of her gaze. Yes, I know what Katie wants. She wants to kill me. I owe her. A mother for a mother.

Maybe she will kill me. As long as Ava is safe, I don't care what happens to me. In some ways, it would be a relief. Justice for Daniel and freedom from the heavy constant guilt that has become my lifetime companion. At least he wouldn't be alone in the cold any more. So, yes, maybe she will kill me, and I'm not scared by the thought. I feel Charlotte's steel in my backbone as I go to the bathroom. I may not be afraid to die, but I don't intend to make it easy for her. Maybe I'll kill her. I've already killed once. How hard can it be to do again?

By eight I'm showered and dressed and staring at our notes. We've got very little to go on with Katie. Never married. No kids. Cared for her mother. Fragile. No job. There were also no photos of any use. She could be anyone in them. She's a few months older than me, so around forty now, but the few pictures we found were so grainy and so old, they're no help.

I wonder about the lack of images. Did she hide from cameras, like me? Even though her identity had never been revealed — the papers never had her name or photo — did she worry the world would somehow *know* and she'd be guilty by association? No, I realise. It was always for this moment. For when she could find me. She needed to stay a ghost, invisible and unknown. She needed to stay hidden as much as me.

I sip the strong coffee. Well, she found me and now I'm going to find her. The circle of fucking life. I crave a cigarette — Charlotte once more coming to the fore, old habits dying hard — but instead I pick up a pen and chew on the lid, like a child, as I start to write.

The list of names is depressingly short. My life

305

as Lisa has been private; fearful and small.

Penny. Highly unlikely. Julia. Not her. I list the various other people I come into contact with through work and none of them strike me as potentials. Too old, too young, been there too long, too dull. Mrs Goldman? Does she have a nurse or friend who comes to see her? I've never seen anyone but her family and they don't visit often. Someone perhaps when I'm out at work? I put lots of question marks next to her name. Maybe Marilyn can go and talk to her. She's a lonely old woman, she would talk easily.

Under the heading 'Ava's teachers' I start a new list, but from the names I remember from parents' evenings I can't see anyone on it who's new to the school or who has overly befriended her. A teacher would probably be able to get into her bag to steal her keys. And they'd know where we lived. They're all possible, but it doesn't feel right. Teachers have background checks, degrees, etc. How much could Katie fake? *Don't underestimate her*, I tell myself. *She was always too clever for her own good.*

Ava's friends go under another heading. This is the biggest grey area. I have done my best to know as much as I can about her life, but as she's grown older it's been harder. Alison was constantly telling me I had to let her be a normal teenager. *Well, so much for that, fuck you very much, Mrs Probation Officer.* Secret Facebook messages. How many people did Ava know who I never met? People who could learn about me through her?

The swim club girls I know, and I cross them

off my list. Katie didn't have any children and there are no wicked stepmothers newly arrived on the scene. I'd have heard.

I stare at the page, stumped. She found me through Jon. Maybe I should start with him. Go there and talk to his neighbours. I know I can't as soon as I have the thought. The police will be all over his place and any woman turning up and asking questions will get picked up straight away. I wish I had Marilyn's phone. At least I'd be able to look up news reports on him. See if there's anything we've missed that's not showing on the TV.

The list blurs before my eyes I'm concentrating so hard. Katie, Katie, where art thou? *She wants you to find her,* Charlotte reminds me. *This is a game. She won't be a total stranger. There will be clues.* Something jars in my memory and I frown. Something I really need to remember.

And then I see it. Plain as day. I know who Katie is.

58

HER

It's hard to disappear completely. I should know. I've done it several times. You have to plan. A lot. And well in advance. Small amounts of money moved around at first. Yes, there may be paper trails, but generate enough paper and it causes a mess that no one can be bothered to dig through. Most of planning is waiting. I've become very good at waiting. My mother finally died — some accidents happen more easily than others if you use a drunk mechanic to fix something — and I put my plans for my carefully invested inheritance into action.

I travelled. Foreign bankers are always less stuffy about the rules of cash bank accounts if you know how to persuade them. I sold property to offshore companies deep in the web of assets I owned. I sold companies to various of the identities I forged, ready for when I might need them.

You're looking at me like I'm crazy, Ava. So I didn't go to school or university, but I never stopped learning. I slept with the kinds of criminal and white collar people who could teach these things and when I'd taken all I could from them, I'd vanish. Probably a relief to both parties. I've never been overly lovable. Mother would tell me so in her later years. When she'd started to see *me* rather than the princess she'd always wanted.

Charlotte always longed desperately to be loved. I didn't. I'd had her and she was enough. Charlotte though, I knew she'd always need someone. And the thing with people, as you know, little Ava, is that they *talk*. The bigger the secret, the more likely it will eventually burst free gloriously loud, telling everyone at once, and that's what happened with your father.

I read the story in Spain. I got the newspapers every day after Charlotte was released, and never missed a day. You have to be meticulous if you want to find someone. How could I risk a tiny detail or photo evading me that could lead me to her? As it turned out, she was all over the front pages when it happened. When he *told*. I devoured every word. All those ridiculous details he made up to make himself sound better and her sound worse. I knew that whatever happened I'd have to kill him one day. Just for being so pathetic, if not because I needed to, and as it turned out he came in far more useful dead than alive. Everything ties up so nicely.

Anyway, where was I? Oh yes, the story he sold. The waiting was much harder after that. God, it was hard. What if he died? Drank himself to an early grave? Had a car crash? Life never seems more fragile than when your success depends on someone else staying breathing a few years longer. But lack of patience destroys plans. People get sloppy. I had to focus on what I needed to do and hope fate would stay on my side with Jon. I had to wait for years. But I had plenty to keep myself busy.

The first thing I had to do was kill Katie Batten off. It was easy. If you're unloved, no one asks questions or looks for you. Certainly not the Spanish police with their hands full of drunk and high teenagers. Who's going to waste time looking for some drowned English woman's body? So, once she was dead I activated one of my other dormant identities — the government aren't the only people who can create those — and bided my time. I couldn't put myself in Jon's world straight away. He needed to forget her, you see? He needed to be over it. To have her words vague in his head. To have forgotten all mention of Girl B. Time and space were required.

I still checked the papers, of course, every day like clockwork, but after Jon's betrayal, your mother was obviously much more careful. And she had you to focus on. To love. To keep safe. She'd want to stay settled. Give you the childhood she never had. A big heart, Charlotte. Damaged, but big.

After a while, I moved into Jon's area, got a job — supermarket checkout girl — and waited some more. I let a life build up around me. People believe *lives*, as if they're the truth of a person rather than the window dressing. You only have to look at Facebook. All those miserable people trying to outshine each other with holiday photos and humble brags and #feelingblessed. Adding people they've never met and thinking they somehow *know* them from the shit they share. One random friend in common. Your father didn't like social media. After his experiences with the press, I think anything with *media* in the name was a turn-off. But he was lonely and sober and he made it so easy to get close to him. Slowly, slowly I let him fall in love with me. Well, not with *me*, but with Anna. Anna the shopgirl. Sweet and giving.

They say women are the softer sex. The more emotional. Which fool decided that? A man in love is weakness personified. A man in love will tell you anything. Share anything. Give you everything. And he did. Once I turned on that tap inside him, the whole story poured out. He loved you, you see, in his own weak way. He showed me the letter your mother sent him back in 2006 when he'd given her the money. He'd kept it.

He said they'd called you Crystal, but he thought she'd change your name to Ava. She'd always wanted to call you Ava but he hadn't let her. He thought it was an old woman's name, but now he thought it was beautiful. He whined and whined about wishing he knew you or knew where you were and hated that you probably knew nothing about him. Nothing good. He wanted you to know he loved you.

I had to bite back a laugh, if I'm honest. What is it with men? They create their own misery and then act as if it was somebody else's fault. So much self-pity in their genes. Or in their jeans? He wanted to find you but he had nothing to go on and he'd tried to contact the probation services about it but they'd told him he'd have to wait until you were eighteen. What did he expect? He'd cost them a whole new identity and I for one know that's not cheap.

I told him to forget you. I told him it wasn't healthy and he should move on. I said his future was with me. He was weak — always weak — and agreed. I took the letter, of course. It was *dwelling in the past*.

He didn't deserve to keep that letter — he hadn't seen the clue to where you both were, right there in front of his eyes. The small faded postmark on the envelope. I did though. I saw it very clearly indeed.

59

MARILYN

It was a good job I came back early because I wasn't long out of the shower when Simon rang up to my room and said he'd arranged a meeting room for some things he wanted to go through with me. He's pale and the slump in his shoulders screams tiredness and I don't need to ask why.

'You look a bit under the weather,' I say, my heart sinking as he thuds a pile of printouts and training manuals down on the table and turns the projector on. There's a plate of pastries there too, but neither of us takes one. 'I'm sure there are other things I could get on with today.' *Like continuing to help a suspect on the run.*

'I'm fine. Not enough sleep.' I don't need any further explanation. Lisa's *the* news story of the month and although the police haven't revealed any fresh evidence that's not stopping all the news channels continually talking about her and digging through her past. Might be useful for Lisa and me, but probably less so for Simon.

'Anyway,' he continues, 'I want to go through the various training programmes and reward schemes we have in the Manning group for both contract workers and full-time staff. I like to make sure everyone has a chance to achieve their potential.'

'That's the sort of thing Lisa would say.' The words are out before I can stop them. 'Sorry, I shouldn't have — it's just — well, whatever she did or didn't do, that was her philosophy when hiring people and I don't have any reason to think she was faking it.' I speak defensively, and part of me is challenging him to fire me. If he did, my life would be fucked, but at least I'd be out there helping to find Ava.

I expect him to snap at me, but instead he glances up as if wanting to say something, yet not knowing how to. 'It's odd, isn't it?' he says, eventually. 'I mean, *odd* isn't a big enough word, but it is odd.'

'What do you mean?' My heart thumps. Is he trying to catch me out here? Has Penny told him about my outburst yesterday and he's trying to figure out how crazy I might be?

'What they say she did. What she did. I don't know.' His jaw is tight. 'I told her once that I'd made mistakes in my past. Did things I shouldn't have done. I was involved in — well, I guess illegal activities would be the truth. They say never ask anyone how they made their first million. I wouldn't want to have to answer that question. Not honestly, anyway.'

'We all do things we regret.' I don't know what else to say, but I want to keep him talking.

'I'm a good judge of people. I always have been. I've *had* to be at times.' He looks at me, direct. 'And all these things in the press, this new murder, her ex, and Ava . . . it's so hard to

314

believe. I can't get my head around it. I mean, could she *really* have done all that? The . . . the *thing* in the past, well it's awful and terrible and I'll never understand it, but it was a long time ago. This new stuff? Another murder? While we were around her? It doesn't feel right. Not at all.'

There's a brisk knock at the door and a woman in her fifties in a smart suit bustles into the room to join us, a sharp efficient smile on her face. 'Karen Walsh. Head of in-house staff training. I manage everything across the leisure and hotel range. You didn't have to join us, Simon.' She smiles at him, but it's clear that his presence is unusual.

'I like to keep my hand in,' he replies, and whatever moment we had to talk about Lisa has passed. I want to punch the woman in the face for interrupting. Does Simon think Lisa's innocent of Jon's murder too?

He turns his attention back to the paperwork. 'These are the presentations the new staff will all be seeing on our training days. We have very high standards that have to be exact across all the hotels so it's important there's nothing unclear. Penny tells me you're pretty much seconded to me for now. You may as well know as much about the business as you can absorb.'

Oh great. So Penny *has* told him about my outburst. I look down at the long and tedious list of things they want to work through. This is going to take hours. 'Let's get started,' I say, through gritted teeth. 'Sooner we begin, the sooner we finish.' *Why today*, I think, as he turns the main light out and starts the projector. *Why,*

315

when Lisa needs my help? I look at him. He's staring at the screen but his mind's not on it. He's too tense. A different knot is untangling in his thoughts. I know how he feels. I've been through it myself.

At the front of the room, Karen Walsh starts talking through the first presentation, and although I try to focus, I can't. My head is buzzing. What if Lisa gets seen? What if she can't figure out who Katie is? What if we don't get to Ava in time? And could Simon be an ally?

60

LISA

I didn't spray my hair but just ponytailed it, and kept my make-up light. This is a nice part of town and, although I'm sure they're not all curtain-twitchers, for now the brash look isn't going to suit me. As it is, the streets are quiet, people either at work or maybe away on long summer holidays, months in France or Spain, the kind the people who own these large detached homes take as a reward for burning themselves out to pay the mortgage.

The curtains are open but there's no sign of life through the large front windows and I'm not surprised. This isn't an endgame location, not for me and Katie, only a stepping stone along the way. Still, my palms sweat and my mouth is dry and I like the reassuring feel of the knife in my jacket pocket. I can't call the police or Marilyn — not until I'm sure. Even then, I can't tell the police until I know exactly where she is. I can't risk my baby. They're not looking for Katie, only Charlotte. They'll throw me in prison and Ava will be lost forever.

Down the side of the house the high gate to the garden is unlocked. She knows I'm coming. Why make it difficult? The lawn at the back is slightly too long and out of keeping with the sterile neatness of the building. *Not had time, have you, Katie, you busy little bee?* My jaw aches with tension, a mixture of rage and fear settled there.

The patio door slides easily open and I'm inside. I know straight away that I'm right, that there's no one here. It's too silent. The house itself is asleep, its purpose served. There's no *life* here. No day-to-day clutter. If I'd been in here before I'd have seen it for what it is. A facsimile of a home for someone who only needs it to fulfil a purpose.

A packet of cigarettes and a lighter sit on the breakfast bar, jarring against the blandness of everything else, and I pick them up. They're for me, after all. For Charlotte. All part of bringing Charlotte back. I pocket them and head into the hall.

I hold a breath when I reach the stairs and any fragment of doubt that I might have guessed wrong evaporates. Katie's been here. Katie's left me some clues. Oh, Katie, always with the games.

Katie is Jodie's mother, Amelia Cousins. This I know now.

Always working away, the boyfriend in France, all that time to deal with Jon, the child who lived with someone else for the first years of her life. Easy to say she never had children if no one's been paying attention and there was no body found to examine. Did she manipulate her daughter to get to me through Ava, so she could be nearby without getting too close?

318

I look again at the stairs. Small shells have been placed on each cream step, like a breadcrumb trail to a witch's house, and I carefully follow them until they lead me into the main bedroom. It's a flamboyant gesture — as if I'd come this far and not look upstairs — but it screams of Katie enjoying herself. On the neatly made double bed lies the prize.

The first thing I see is the conch and immediately the memory of a shell pressed against my ear assails me, the sound of the mysterious sea, Katie's small hand holding mine, the determined set of her expression. I know why the conch is here. It's a symbol of my betrayal.

I pick it up and move it aside, using the tips of my fingers as if somehow she might emerge from its inner curls — *Listen, Charlotte! Isn't it wonderful! The sound of the sea. Sounds like freedom, doesn't it?* — and my hand trembles as I pick up the tape box it's been sitting on. The plastic casing is cracked and worn, any shine roughed away over the years, and inside, written on folded exercise book paper are the words, *'K & C's Top Tunes!'* filled in with brightly coloured felt-tip, the writing careful but with the boldness that only comes in childhood. Katie's copy of the tape she gave me — *Leave with me baby, let's go tonight* — kept all these years. It feels too light and I open it up.

The first thing I see is a small note. The writing on it is precise and tidy — adult. 'Don't look for Jodie, I've sent her on holiday.' I stare at it. What does she think I'd do? A daughter for a daughter? Is this what she thinks of me, that I'd go after her daughter because she's got mine? *I owe her a mother, not a child, but still she's mentioned hers.* Is this the tiny weakness in Katie's armour? Maybe I would go after Jodie if I thought it would help me find Ava. Of course I would. But would I hurt her? No. I couldn't hurt a child. Not again. Never again.

I tuck the note into my pocket even though it's not evidence of anything. She's worded it carefully. It could be an innocent message she meant to post through someone's door to let them know Jodie wasn't around. There's nothing in it that could turn the overwhelming tide of evidence the police have against me.

There's something else in the box, tucked into the cover paper, and I pull it out. My heart thumps and I let out a small involuntary gasp as it unfurls. The missing photo of Ava. My baby. She smiles out at me, her face from years ago but her face just the same. I press the image to my mouth as if I can somehow breathe her in, smell her, feel her. Ava. My baby Ava. I can taste the strange plastic of photo paper that was so familiar to me all those years ago when I first left prison and when I met Jon. Circles of my life coming around, tightening, threatening to suffocate me. I can't be weak now. I can't give in to my self-pity. Ava, Ava, Ava. She needs me. Her life depends on me.

Still holding the photo, I take a second to gather myself and look again at the clues. Our escape tape. The seashell. It's not very subtle, but it's not supposed to be. She wants me to find her.

The seaside. Skegness. Her grandfather's house. But where is it? How am I supposed to know where to go? I put the photo down for a second, although it hurts my heart to let go of my little girl, and look in the tape box again for anything I might have missed. Nothing. Frustration nips at me. She wouldn't lead me here only to let the trail grow cold. I grab the shell and shake it, but there's no paper curled up inside waiting to be pulled out, and I throw it back down before sitting heavily on the bed. I can't be this stupid. There must be something.

It's then that I see the neat writing on the back of Ava's photo. *The Crabstick Cafe, Brown Beach Street.* My heart soars. I grab the phone by the bed and call for a taxi to the train station. Skegness. My baby is in Skegness. In the ten minutes I have to wait I try ringing Marilyn but it goes to answerphone.

'I know who Katie is,' I say. 'Jodie's mother. I'm going to find her. I'm going to . . . ' I pause, my self-preservation kicking in, not wanting to share anything too obvious yet ' . . . where we were going to run away to. She's waiting for me there. I'll call you when I have an exact address.' I want to tell her I love her, and that she's the most amazing person in the world for believing in me but I don't, the words tangling inside me, and so I just hang up. She knows I love her. She's my best friend.

Within twenty minutes I'm at the station and ten minutes later I'm on a train. I'll be in Skegness in under two hours. I sit back in my seat, Ava's photo gripped tight in my hand, and stare out at the countryside rolling backwards through the window like it's returning me to my childhood.

It's time to end all this. I'm coming to find you, Katie.

61

BEFORE

1989

She needs to find Katie. Only Katie can make her feel better. Katie will be waiting for her. But to get to Katie she has to leave her bedroom. She's been curled up on her bed, mattress wet with piss, a chair up against the door, all morning. No one's tried to come in. Her head thumps. The pills don't make her feel good any more, just as if she's somewhere behind a glass wall away from the rest of the world and her thinking is foggy. She wants to take another one anyway. She's got a packet stashed in her jacket pocket. Ma will have to get some more, but fuck her. Nothing can get any worse.

Ma has been at Jean's house overnight. A girls' night and then shopping today for her birthday, that's what Jean told Tony when she came over yesterday. She said it in her 'no arguments' voice. Jean's the only one who can do that with Tony. When he started to complain she said Charlotte could look after Daniel — *Won't do the girl any harm to have some responsibility, she's off the rails, any fool can see* — and even though Ma protested a little, that was that, a bag was packed, and they were gone. No one argues with Jean.

If Ma had been here, the *thing* with Tony wouldn't have happened. Ma might be a bitch but she wouldn't stand for it. Not for Charlotte but for herself. It's hazy in her head and if she wasn't sore and bruised, she'd wonder if it was some horrible dream.

It was late. It was dark. She was asleep. She'd shoved Daniel in front of shite cartoons with beans on toast before retreating to her room and drinking some of the cheap vodka kept hidden under her bed, bought with money Katie had given her. Katie was worried about her. Katie wanted to help make it better. Katie warmed her more than the alcohol ever could but Katie wasn't around often enough and Charlotte needed the booze to get through the days.

There wasn't much left in the bottle. What had been a *sometimes* thing had now changed into a habit but she didn't want to think about that either. Anyway, everything would be different when she and Katie ran away. She wouldn't *need* the drink then, they would have champagne in glasses like those Babycham ones, and it would be for fun and not to squash all the stuff that was burning to come out. *Better out than in, dear.* There wouldn't *be* anything to come out when it was only her and Katie. Everything would be perfect.

There would be no more nights like last night. She doesn't want to think about it but she can't stop thinking about it. She needs to leave her bedroom but she's too scared. She needs Katie. She shuts her eyes against her headache but that sends her straight back to the darkness of last night. To what happened. Then, despite herself, it's replaying in her head.

For a moment, when he'd opened the door, there'd just been a shape against the hall light. She remembers the sudden brightness and thinking *What shite is this, Daniel, what do you want now?* before her brain woke up and realised that the figure there was far too big to be her little brother. Daniel was still sleeping safely in his cot. Daniel, always safe.

The door closed, leaving her with the terrible grunting, grumbling monster in the darkness. Sweat. Stink. A crushing weight. Hands, so many hands. His mutterings as his breath got faster. The shameful pain. The breath on her face. It was like the chippy, but worse, so much worse, because it was home and the monster in the dark was Tony, and he was doing *it* and they never did *it* in the chippy even if they wanted to, just all the other stuff, and *it* was so much worse than she imagined and if he was doing *it*, then who would stop them doing *it* there?

It didn't last long, and then he was gone and she was left breathless and shaking and alone in the dark. She pissed herself after. Not even asleep this time. She just couldn't move. She still can't move. But she has to. Katie is waiting. She takes half of one of Ma's pills and drags herself up. Her wet pyjamas are on the floor, the bottoms torn. She doesn't look at them as she pulls on some pants and her jeans and jumper. She doesn't look at her body either. She wants to scrub herself down to nothing, but not here, not if he's in the house.

Dressed, she takes the vodka from under her bed and swallows two long mouthfuls, letting it burn her clean from the inside. She moves the chair and opens the door quietly. She's afraid and she hates being afraid. She tries to turn it into anger, and she knows that will come, but not until she's outside and away. It's hard to be angry feeling so small.

She can hear the TV's on, some horse racing programme, and her legs shake as she comes down the stairs, slowly and carefully, staying quiet *and where is Ma if only Ma were here even if she was calling me a little bitch and a pain in the arse she'd be here* and wincing at any creak in the floorboard that might cause Tony to shout out to her or worse.

Her heart in her mouth, she peers into the sitting room. Beer cans on the floor. A takeaway box. Legs, dressed, stretched out on the sofa. A low growl of a sound. Snoring. Relief floods through her, a rush better than anything the pills can give her. Asleep. He's asleep.

'Charrot?'

She's at the front door when the small voice stops her, and she turns to see Daniel, clutching Peter Rabbit, in the doorway of the sitting room.

'Where you going, Charrot?' he asks again. His voice is quiet but not quiet enough.

'Out.' It's a whisper. Irritated. She wants to be gone.

'I come?'

'No.'

His chubby face crumples and she sees tears well up in his big eyes and she knows that any minute now he'll start crying and then Tony will wake up and who knows what will happen.

'All right,' she says, *shut up shut up don't cry you little shite,* 'but be quiet.' Daniel breaks into a joyous grin, all thought of tears forgotten, and does what he's told and sits carefully on the bottom step and clumsily pulls his shoes on while she gets his blue thrift shop coat that's too big for him. She tugs his arms into it and then, one finger across her lips, quietly opens the front door and they creep out into the October cold.

Daniel looks as though he could explode with excitement as he holds his hand up, Peter Rabbit tucked under his other arm. She takes his small warm palm in hers and pulls him quickly down the street. She doesn't want him with her. What will Katie say? Why couldn't he have stayed where he was? Why does he always have to be the centre of everything?

He's humming to himself, and sniffing, his nose running, as she eventually slows down to go at his pace and they pick their way across the wasteland, his clumsy feet stumbling occasionally. What if Ma comes back while they're out? That makes her smile. Tony asleep and Daniel gone would fuck Ma right up. They'd fight then. Let them worry. Go down to the swings and look for him. She can imagine Ma's panic and Tony's defensiveness and she wants to laugh and run and get drunk.

They can shite off. All of them.

And there it is. Her anger. She holds on to Daniel's hand a little tighter.

62

MARILYN

Finally, *finally*, we finish. It's been an interminable morning, and even Simon's feet were tapping under the table by the end of it. At least he hasn't planned anything for the afternoon. If I move fast I can be back at the hotel with Lisa in half an hour or so. I grab my bag from under the table and check my phone. There's a missed call from a number I don't know. Shit.

'Do you want to grab some lunch?' Simon asks. 'Just to talk. Not work. All this stuff on the news, it's . . . '

I hold up my hand to stop him as I hit the message button, gripping the phone to my ear. 'Sorry, give me a minute,' I say. The message kicks in. It's her, Lisa. I listen, and find I'm pacing.

'Oh my God, oh my God.'

'What is it?' Simon's staring at me. 'What's happened?'

'She knows who Katie is. Jodie's mum. She knows. She knows where they are!' I play the message over again. 'Ava. She knows where Ava is.' My breath is rapid. She's being cautious in her message *where we were going to run away to*, but she knows.

'Who knows?'

'Lisa.'

He stares at me, pink blotches appearing on his neck. 'Lisa? That's Lisa? You have to call the police.'

'No, I can't. It's not so simple. Look, she found me. Last night. She — '

'Jesus, Marilyn!' He steps up close. 'You've seen her?'

Neither of us notice Karen Walsh leaving the room as I start to talk, the events of the past twenty-four hours spilling out of me in a random mess of words. I'm vaguely aware of the door closing but I'm intent on telling him as quickly as possible. I can't hold it in any longer and I *need* him to believe us.

'It wasn't Lisa who killed Jon and took Ava. The police have got it all wrong. It was Katie Batten. Girl B. She faked her own death in order to find Lisa. They had a pact and Lisa broke it and now she wants some kind of crazy revenge or something . . . ' I'm breathless as I speak and his eyes get wider.

'Slow down,' he says. 'Katie Batten?'

'We need to find her.' I don't want to talk. I want to get to Lisa. She's out there alone somewhere. She didn't wait for me and I can't blame her for that with her daughter missing, but anything could happen to her. I said I'd help her and I have to. I'm all she has.

'And we will,' he says. 'But you need to explain. Who is Katie Batten?'

'She was Lisa — *Charlotte's* — best friend,' I start. And then it's all coming out of me and he listens, without saying a word, as I tell him about their childhood friendship, about how her life was as a child, even about little Daniel's bruises found after his death and how they crushed Charlotte with the realisation that his short life had been as shit as hers.

I'm still talking when the door opens. We both look up and I see my surprise shining back from Simon's face.

It's the policewoman, Bray. Why is she here? Her anger is like a haze around her brisk efficient body as she and the two men with her sweep into the room. She takes my phone from me before I've had a chance to speak.

'Bag it,' she says, passing it back to a constable. 'We need to talk to you at the station, and if you refuse, I'll have no option but to arrest you — '

'Arrest her? She hasn't done anything wrong!'

'Where shall I start?' Bray snaps. 'Accessory after the fact? Aiding and abetting?' She turns to me. 'Where is she, Marilyn? I can't believe you'd put that girl's life at risk. You told me you'd let me know if you heard from Lisa and I put my trust in you.'

How does she know all this? How does she know I've spoken to — and then I see *her*, Karen Walsh, standing further back outside the open door. The bitch rang the police.

'No, it's not like that,' I say. I see a flash of black plastic in Bray's hands and realise in horror what she's holding. Are they really going to handcuff me and lead me out of here like a common criminal? What do they think I'm going

330

to do? 'It's not Lisa. She didn't kill Jon. Jodie — from Ava's swim club — her mother is Katie Batten! Lisa found out and she's gone to find her.'

'She's conned you,' Bray is almost growling at me, looking at me as if I'm the world's biggest fool, the beaten woman once again duped by someone. 'We've found Lisa's hair and other DNA in both Jon's flat and the cottage where his body was found. Even her fingerprints are there.'

'How do you know it wasn't planted?' Simon stands alongside me.

'Jesus Christ, this isn't an episode of *Morse*. Are you buying into this bullshit too?' She glares at him. 'We spoke to all of Ava's friends and their parents when she went missing. There was nothing suspicious about any of them, and for the last time, Katie Batten is dead. Marilyn, you're coming with us to the station. We've wasted enough time and I need to know everything. You could have placed two further people at risk with this craziness: Amelia and Jodie Cousins.'

I look at Simon, helpless.

'I'll send a lawyer down straight away. Don't worry.'

I hug him, a sudden movement too fast for anyone to stop, and before he breaks away, I whisper in his ear, 'Find Katie.'

'*Now*, Mrs Hussey.' Bray takes my arm but Simon gives me a tiny nod as they lead me to the door.

'Can you tell me one thing?' he asks. 'When you spoke to this woman, Jodie's mother, and her daughter, was it face to face?'

'No,' Bray says, after a pause. 'It was on the phone. Amelia Cousins is in France and Jodie is on holiday in Spain.'

And then I'm gone, my face burning as she leads me out through the building, sending men up to search my room as we go, and I feel naked and exposed and humiliated and I'm once again in the back of a police car. Simon. All my hope now rests on Simon. It's only as the car moves away that I remember where Katie and Charlotte were running away to. The seaside. Her grandfather's house. *Skegness.*

63

LISA

It's grey and raining in Skegness, the kind of fine drizzle that comes at an angle and gets in every pore. It suits me fine. No one is looking up, all either head down against the water or hunched under an umbrella. The sea churns a dirty blue to my left as I walk briskly along the seafront and the air is filled with salty spray. I dreamed of this as a child, being here with Katie. And now here we finally are.

The Crabstick Cafe isn't on the main strip and I have to turn down three side streets before I reach Brown Beach Street, having flipped through an *A-Z* at the train station to find it, imprinting the directions on my lazy brain so used to having technology do this stuff for me. I sit at a table by the window and order a coffee. It's the height of summer and the place should be busier, but the Formica tables are tired and chipped and the few customers look like broken, lonely people, reading papers and drinking tea because they can't face the four walls at home any more. Residents, not tourists. No one looks my way.

There's a TV on, up on the wall in the corner, a portable that must have been there for years, and behind the counter is a large hot-water urn. Further over, beside a noticeboard, is a pay phone. This is like a cafe from decades ago. Did Katie choose this place on purpose because it's so old-fashioned? Is this part of her bringing us back to that moment in the past? And I'm here, so what now?

The waitress, a thickset woman in her mid-fifties wearing a housecoat, brings me over my mug of coffee and I stare out through the window. There's a games arcade over the road, with a small group of teenagers huddled, bored, outside. Where is Katie? Is she in there watching me? Where is the next clue?

I feel sick with nerves. I need to find out where she's got Ava and then call Marilyn. She can tell the police where to find me to get them. I don't care if they shoot me on sight as long as they get Ava out safely. She's the only good thing I've ever done with my life. They can do what they want with me.

I've drunk half my coffee, my impatience with Katie rising with every sip, when the noticeboard catches my eye again. It's the kind that used to be in every supermarket before the Internet took over, little cards pinned on them advertising everything from second-hand cots to gardening services. I stare at it. A message board. Of course. I get up and go over to it, mug in hand to try to look casual.

'Turn that up, love,' a man grunts somewhere from a table behind me, and the waitress duly raises the volume on the TV. I'm not listening, but scanning the rows and rows of carefully printed adverts. The fragile care in some of the handwriting makes me think of old people and my heart squeezes with an emotion I don't understand. Lost people. I know how they feel.

Finally I see it. Black ink on a blue card. My heart leaps to my mouth as I take it down.

Clyde! Call Bonnie! Let's catch up! And underneath, a mobile number. My hands tremble. I'm so close. Katie is a phone call away. *Ava* is a phone call away. I scrabble in my pocket for some change for the phone. I need to call —

' *. . . is believed to be Marilyn Hussey, a co-worker of Charlotte Nevill's . . .* '

Marilyn?

I look up at the TV.

' *. . . the police have made no statement at this time but our source tells us Ms Hussey was taken in for questioning from her place of work and has been harbouring the missing child murderer Charlotte Nevill, although it appears no arrest has been made there.* '

A humming starts up in my ears as my heart races. Oh God, Marilyn. My lifeline. And now in trouble because of me. Will she tell them where I am? Will she even have figured out where I've gone from my message? As I stare at the screen and feel the blue card softening in my hand as I squeeze it, a calm settles over me. I have only me to rely on now. I could still phone the police. Once I've spoken to Katie and got some idea of where she and Ava are, I could ring them and they'd come so fast thinking they were going to arrest me. But how can I be *sure* of where they are until I've seen my baby? What if the police go charging in looking for me and she's not there? Katie will kill her. I know it. One betrayal too many.

My heart slows down to a regular steady beat and my skin cools. I can't do anything to help Marilyn and I should never have involved her, but she'll be okay. At worst, she'll look like a fool, but I'm not sure how far they'll want to go with prosecuting a woman just out of an abusive relationship. If this all goes wrong and they come for me, I'll tell them I made her help me. They think I'm still the monster I used to be, they'll believe it.

Maybe this is how it should be. Me and Katie. Finishing what we started, one way or another. I go outside and light a cigarette in the rain. A few moments of quiet before making the call. The smoke is harsh and it makes my head swim but it feels like coming home. Everything does. The anger and fear simmering inside me, the smoking, the being entirely alone with no one to believe in me.

It's a perfect mood for Katie.

64

HER

The thing with your generation is you're all so needy. Narcissistic. Instagram or it didn't happen. But even with all that it took me a while to find you. You'd be surprised how many Avas of your age there are in Elleston. But I worked my way through them, all those little details of life casually given away, making it so easy to track someone down, and once I saw you with your mother, I knew I'd struck gold. It wasn't the way she looked — I defy anyone to recognise a woman they knew as a child, we're all masters of disguise — it was the way she *was*. Nervous. Hunted. Edgy. Alone.

The waiting was over. I bought the house, and brought passport number three to life. Let a new identity build, watched you both and slowly integrated. Placed myself in the perfect position for studying Charlotte. Easy as pie. Of course this was when I really needed Jon. Not *him*, obviously, but access to his life. I knew he wouldn't have changed much — they're all creatures of routine, aren't they, and he didn't have the spine for reinvention — and he was so pitifully glad to see me again. Not for long, obviously.

Once I'd got into your house it was so easy. I took fingerprints from glasses and stole strands of her hair from the bathroom and planted them at Jon's so the police would think she'd been there. The same with the cottage I rented via his laptop and disposed of him in. I know he was your father, but don't look at me like that. The man was both weak and a fool. You'd have been disappointed in him, trust me.

I set up a Facebook account for him, liked some of the same pages as you, and, when I was ready, started messaging you. Dear God, you were easy. So needy for love, little Ava. So determined to be a grown-up. You wanted romance. Passion. All that crap.

I wound your mother up too. Little surprises I knew would make her paranoid. Drive her to call her probation officer for reassurance while looking a little bit crazy. And then, when the time was right and the stage set, all it took was one shove of a toddler into the river and boom, a picture in the paper and an anonymous phone call saying I recognised her as Charlotte Nevill.

And here we are. Still waiting. She'll call soon, I know she will. So, let's get you into position, shall we? Ready for the show.

65

LISA

'It's me.'

For a moment there's nothing at the other end. I'm gripping the receiver tight to my ear and I've pressed myself into the corner of the cafe so close to the glass that there's instantly a mist of condensation across it from my hot breath, coating the grime.

'Charlotte,' she says. 'You made it.'

'I want to speak to Ava.'

'And you will. When you get here. To our hideout. Bonnie and Clyde, finally on the run.'

'We're not children any more, Katie. I don't want to play these games. Let me speak to my daughter. I want to know she's safe.' *I want to fucking smash your face in, you crazy cunt.*

'You sound like you're in one of those terrible straight-to-DVD thrillers.' Her tone is light. Still so well spoken. So Katie. Pristine and perfect. 'Lighten up. She's fine. Looking forward to seeing me?'

'It's been a long time,' I say.

'Not for me, I've been seeing *you*,' she answers. Her voice drops, becomes deeper, all humour gone. 'I'm going to give you an address. If you come here on your own I'll let Ava go. I promise you. She doesn't interest me. But I swear to God, Charlotte, if you tell anyone else, she'll be dead before they get through the door. Do you understand?'

I absolutely believe her. Everything she's put into this, she won't fall at this hurdle.

'I understand,' I say.

'Don't dawdle, Clyde,' she says, after she's given me the address and told me the front door will be unlocked. 'It'll make me suspicious. And aside from that, I can't wait to catch up.'

'Oh, I'm coming, Katie,' I say. 'You can count on it.'

66

MARILYN

I feel like I've been in here for hours, the same questions, the same answers, going round and round in circles. I've given them everything I can tell them — about Lisa, at least. The lawyer Simon sent in said it was for the best and it probably is. I told them she got into my car and that I rented her a hotel room. I told them her thoughts on Katie. I haven't told them about Skegness. If they found Lisa there before she had a chance to find Katie, then Ava is dead. We've had ten minutes of peace while Bray was called out of the room, but now she's back. What next, I wonder? What have they found?

'My client is aware she made a serious judgemental error by not contacting you immediately Charlotte Nevill approached her, but she fully intended to call you today. Ava Buckridge's wellbeing is her primary concern and she acted with that at heart. I feel, given her personal situation — a woman who's been through a serious domestic trauma as well as dealing with the fallout of Charlotte Nevill's new identity being exposed — there's nothing to be gained in charging her. She is absolutely remorseful for her actions, which were brought about by impaired judgement from emotional exhaustion and misplaced loyalty to someone she believed to be a best friend.'

'She has seriously impeded my investigation,' Bray says. 'Charlotte Nevill is a dangerous killer.'

'It's not her,' I say, for the thousandth time, despite the glare from the lawyer. 'It's Katie. Katie isn't dead. There was no body. She's Jodie's mother. I keep telling you. If you'd seen Lisa, you'd know. She's convinced.'

'I'm sure she is,' Bray says. 'Perhaps she believes it to be true. Perhaps there are two personalities at work here. Perhaps she's Charlotte *and* Katie now. But we've searched Amelia Cousins' house thoroughly and there is nothing to raise suspicion. There is, however, evidence Charlotte has been there. A tape with her and Katie's initials on was found on Amelia's bed, alongside a large seashell. Is Lisa headed to a seaside town, Marilyn?'

'I don't know,' I answer. *Skegness* sits on the tip of my tongue. 'But maybe Katie left them there as a message for Lisa?' I won't call her Charlotte. She's Lisa to me.

'Or Charlotte could have left them there as a false lead.'

'Have you spoken to Amelia Cousins?'

'Both her and Jodie's phones are switched off or out of signal range. We knew they were both away. Amelia said she may travel to join her daughter in the finca she's at in Spain. That's hardly suspicious.' She leans across the table. 'I'm trying to be patient with you Marilyn, I really am. But you need to accept you may have put Ava in danger with your actions. Maybe Amelia and Jodie Cousins too. You need to help us.'

'While my client believes this version of events to be true, she *is* doing everything she can to help you.' His voice is dry. Calm and measured against Bray's irritation and my exhaustion.

'Let's go through it once more. From the beginning. Every detail. There must be something we've missed. Start the tape again.'

I take a deep breath and sigh. It's going to be a long afternoon.

67

LISA

I expected the house to be near the beach. In those long hours as a child when I'd fantasise about being there with Katie, my only lifeline in the shite of my existence, I'd always imagined the front door opening straight on to the sand with the sun blazing down as if on some tropical island rather than an English seaside resort where the air smells of salt and cheap fried food. It's not near the sea though. It's not even in the town proper, but out towards the countryside.

The drive up is more of a track and the house looms ahead of me. It's stylish, large and almost deco. More modern than it should look given its age. When was it built? Maybe 1920s? I pause, and consider my options. *The front door will be open.* What's she afraid of, that if I ring the doorbell and she answers, I'll thrust a knife into her chest before she has a chance to speak? She wouldn't be wrong, but I'm not planning on stabbing her fatally. I just want to disable her, to be sure I can find Ava.

From where I'm standing, a little to the right of the building, I study it for signs of cameras marking any movement. I can't see any. Maybe she's got one over the door so she'll know when

I'm here. The windows, black pools in the gloom, give nothing away. Perhaps there are closed blinds or curtains on the inside; I can't tell from this distance. There's no way around to a back door, the garden cut off by a high fence. She's given me no choice. Go in, following her instructions, or go away and call the police. If I go in, she's going to try to kill me. If I leave, she'll kill Ava. Katie, the ringmaster. Katie the planner.

My hands are sweating. Ava's in there, I know it. Ava and Katie, waiting for me. She promised she'd let her go, I tell myself. It's not Ava she wants. I think about Daniel. About what I did. About the weight I've carried all these years. Saving Ava is all that matters. If I have to die in the process and end all this, so be it. Still, I pull the knife out and grip the handle tight.

It's eerily quiet as I come up the drive, just the patter of rain in the bushes around me and the hushed whisper of my shoes on the gravel. My eyes dart everywhere, looking for something or nothing. A threat unseen. *She won't kill you straight away*, I tell myself. *She wants to talk. She has catching up to do.* This is my advantage. I know it. If I can rush her, get my knife in her, *weaken* her, then I have a chance.

There are three pale steps to the bright white front door and I take a deep breath and reach forward to push it open. I tentatively cross the threshold, leaving the door open behind me. It's cold inside and although the wooden floorboards are polished and sleek, the empty, abandoned scent of the building takes me straight back to the house on Coombs Street. A few pictures, some abstract modern art, are still hanging, and a dresser is pushed up against one wall, but they are forgotten items, uncared for. More expensive than the debris of the ruined house on Coombs Street, but the same. Time is folding in on itself. No, I correct myself. Time is always folded in on itself, the past like shadows we can't shake off, and now I feel them surrounding me, wraiths drawing in to choke me. *Katie, Daniel, Tony, Ma*.

It's a large open hallway, a room of its own, made more vast by the lack of furniture. Up ahead, a staircase climbs into darkness. The windows are shuttered, only splinters of grey light coming in from outside. I can hear my own breath. What now?

I take a step forward, and then another. No figures lurking in the corners. No one here with me. Should I go upstairs? *Where's the next clue, Katie? What are you expecting from me here?*

She appears so suddenly, a shimmering figure in front of me, that I gasp and stumble backwards. Katie, but as she was as a child. A ghost of my Katie there on the bottom step. *What is this?* is all I have time to think before the floor somehow disappears beneath me.

A magician's house, remember? Katie's voice whispers in my head. *Full of tricks.*

I walked straight into it. Dumb, stupid Charlotte. I feel a web around me and then a sickening thud as my head hits concrete and the world goes black.

68

MARILYN

They've kept my phone but at least I'm out.

'Thank you,' I say. Simon Manning is there, waiting with the car. I wonder how much this afternoon has cost him for the lawyer. I could cry with gratitude. 'They still may charge me, but for now, I'm a free woman. I've told them I'm staying at the hotel. That's all right, isn't it?'

'Of course. Get in.' He looks past me at Bray, who's come outside and lit a cigarette. 'Don't worry. She won't be absconding.'

'I'm sure she won't. We've got people going through CCTV from Elleston train and bus stations looking for Charlotte. Hopefully we'll find something in it and this fiasco won't cost any more lives.'

I can hear them, but I'm not listening. Something else has got my attention. Another car, parked discreetly across the road, a figure in the shadow behind the wheel. Richard.

'All I want is a long shower and to sleep,' I mutter, turning back to them. 'So can we go?'

Richard. This is all I need. How did he know I was here? He doesn't get out of his car, but as we pull away, so does he.

'Does anyone know the police took me in?' I

try and make it sound nonchalant.

'Everyone, I'm afraid.' He glances over at me. 'It was on the news.'

I groan and lean back in the seat. 'How?'

'It wasn't Bray. She wanted it kept quiet in case Lisa got in touch. I think it was Karen Walsh, that stuck-up bitch. Don't worry, she's all but fired already.'

'Thanks for this,' I say. In the side mirror I see Richard's car weaving along behind, staying close but not too close.

'I've been busy too,' Simon says. 'I've got a team of forensic accountants, lawyers and private detectives working at digging into the Batten family and specifically what Katie did with their assets. Turns out there is a mess of paperwork. Identities hiding behind a maze of offshore companies and accounts. They were pretty well off, but not so much anything like that was necessary. Anyway, one thing this amount of paper trail tells me — someone is hiding something.'

'Like the fact they're not dead?'

'Exactly.'

'Skegness,' I say. 'Katie's family had a house in Skegness. I think that's where Lisa's gone. I didn't tell the police. I didn't want them to get there and find Lisa before she got to the house. I know it's stupid but they don't — '

'It's okay. I believe you. I believe *her*. I'll find . . . ' He pauses, glancing sideways, catching my eyes straying nervously to the mirrors.

'What is it?' He frowns. 'The police?'

I shake my head. 'Worse. My husband.'

He says nothing but his jaw tightens as he slows the car, turning off the main road.

'What are you doing? Ignore him.' I'm panicking and I don't know why. *Ignore him.* Like it's that easy. Simon's still slowing and as soon as a lay-by appears, he pulls into it.

'Don't,' I say, my voice a nervous whine I detest. 'Let's just go to the hotel. Come on.' I don't want Richard to hurt him. Richard's done enough damage.

'Wait here.' He doesn't look at me as he gets out of the car.

I want to shrivel into my seat, but I have to look, opening the window and twisting around to peer out. Richard's out of the car, a bundle of rage. I know the stance of his body, I know the look on his face when the mask falls away.

'Are you fucking my wife?' His words are clear and I cringe as he squares up to Simon, who's walking casually towards him. His fists are balled tight. He's going to lose it completely. 'I said, *are you fucking my fat bitch of a wife?*' My stomach turns to water and I want to throw up. He's going to kill Simon and then he's going to drag me out of this car by my hair and kill me.

Simon moves so fast, I can't register what's happening. He doesn't speak but suddenly his hands are out of his pockets. Richard barely has time to look surprised as the precise blows to his ribs and gut hit him, short and sharp and powerful. He crumples, gasping for breath. Without saying a word, Simon turns and returns to the car at the same steady pace.

I stare at him, almost as breathless as my

husband lying on the tarmac a few feet behind us.

'Now *he* knows how it feels to have a few broken ribs,' he says calmly, the car purring away beneath us.

'Where did you learn to do that?' I ask. *And can I have lessons?*

I look at his hands properly for the first time. Rough skin. Toughened over years.

'I never went to prison,' he says, turning back on to the main road. 'But I should have done. How do you think I know how to find people? The best people to know how to find people are those who've learned to distance themselves from their pasts. Who've learned to hide the source of their income. We know the tricks.'

'We've got to find Katie,' I say. 'The police won't.' I look out at the gathering clouds overhead. 'And we have to be quick.'

69

LISA

I almost laugh when I open my eyes and see her. Of course. I should have known. Stupid Charlotte, always one step behind. A wave of nausea hits me and my head thumps as I try to stand.

'You fell badly and hit your head,' she says, smiling. 'Trapdoor. One of Grandfather's little tricks. How to make a person disappear. Slightly cruder than my methods, but effective. You only half-landed in the net and then dropped. I forgot how clumsy you are.'

How did I not see it before? Her smile. That delicate movement as she tucks hair behind her ears. All my wariness of the world but I thought the threat would be from strangers. The newspapers. My guard was up the wrong way and the serpent slipped right into my nest.

My throat feels raw and my body is like lead. She's given me something, a pill forced down my gullet while I was out. I can feel it lodged somewhere in my chest. It's dark and I'm squinting in the gloom when she turns a small desk lamp on. 'That's better.'

A whimper comes from the far corner and now, although my vision is blurring, I can see her. My baby. My Ava. She's lying on a dirty mattress on the floor, hands and feet tied, her mouth gagged. Her eyes are wide and full of tears and I want to run and hug her. I gaze at her and I want to tell her everything will be all right, but I won't give Katie the satisfaction. I have to stay strong. The only slim chance I have of beating her is being Charlotte again. And Charlotte was tough. She didn't let people touch her heart.

'You said you'd let her go.' My words are slurred, a jumble, whatever clarity they have in my head losing form by the time they reach my mouth. What the fuck has she given me? I try to move my sluggish body and only then notice the fluffy cuffs she tied me to the chair with. Like something from a sex shop. I wonder if I'm tripping out but she laughs. The curious Alice in Wonderland tinkle of sound I used to be fascinated by. Now I want to punch her in the throat and kill it dead.

'Ridiculous, aren't they? But I don't want anything to leave a mark. Can't have all this to end up with you looking like you might have been in trouble.'

My mind is too spacey to acknowledge the panic somewhere deep in my system, and instead I wonder where my knife is. Eventually I see it, over on a long bench with something that looks like a coffin on it. A coffin? Is that what she's planning for me? To bury me alive? *Katie, Katie, what is your game?* I look around. There are no windows. Underground, we're underground. A strange clock stands in the corner, the numbers in the wrong order. Some contraption with a camera in another. A glass box, man height.

'This is where my grandfather worked on his illusions,' Katie says, leaning back on the table, her narrow hip by my knife. 'A hidden place. He was nothing if not paranoid about someone stealing his ideas. He made a fortune designing illusions for the showmen to take on stage. Totally soundproofed, obviously. I had to gag Ava, though. She wouldn't stop yelling and screaming for help. It was giving me a headache and I doubt it was doing her any good.'

I'm mesmerised by her. Katie. After all this time. I'd never have recognised her, but I guess that was the point. She's had work done. A lot of work. Her nose is much smaller, button-like. I'd never have told her, but when we were kids her nose was too big for her face. It took her from beauty to simple prettiness. Maybe that helped her when we went to court. No one wants to believe in beautiful girls, but pretty ones are harmless.

'Let her go,' I mumble again. 'You said you'd let her go.'

'Let's not get ahead of ourselves.' She smiles, her eyes bright and sparkling. Katie in full game mode. She pushes the table she's sitting on and it slides in half, the coffin cut through the middle. Not a coffin at all. An illusionist's trick.

'I never liked him, if you remember. God, he was dull. An old desiccated dying man. But I can respect his meticulous mind now. I've learned to have an eye for detail myself. It was hard work persuading my mother not to sell this house. But

then I had years to stay on top of her, didn't I?'
She looks at me, something like fondness in her
eyes. Regret? 'We were going to come here,' she
says softly. 'Weren't we?' Her voice hardens: 'If
you hadn't ruined everything.' She takes a deep
breath. A controlling breath. 'But we're here
now. I can hardly believe it. I've waited such a
long time for this.'

The world is spinning again. Is it the
concussion, or the pill she gave me? As the
darkness closes in again, I realise it's irrelevant.
Whichever it is, I'm going to pass out. My head,
too heavy to hold, drops forward. Katie starts to
fade.

'Charlotte?' Her words come at me from
under water. 'Charlotte? Oh goddammit, you
used to be better than this.'

And then I'm gone again.

70

MARILYN

'Thank you. That's great.' He hangs up the phone. 'We've got it.'

I sit up straight, all tiredness and frustration falling away. 'You're shitting me.'

'Grandfather on her mother's side. Harold Arthur Mickleson.' He slides the piece of paper he's scribbled the address down on across the desk as proof. 'Skegness.'

'Bloody hell.' I pick it up and stare at it. 'Your people are good.'

'My people are the best, but it's time to call the police in.' It's hot in his office where the two of us have been holed up waiting for calls since getting back from the station, and I can see sweat at the edge of his hairline. It's been two long hours. It feels like forever. My whole body aches with tension.

'Lisa's in trouble and we both know it,' he says. 'If this Katie woman has gone to these lengths to track her down, she's no match for her.'

'I agree. I'll call Bray.' I reach for the mobile phone he's given me while the police have mine, but he shakes his head.

'It can't be you. They won't listen to you.'

'Fine. You do it.' I don't care who makes the call as long as they pay attention. He dials and my foot taps under the table as I listen in.

' . . . No, this has nothing to do with Marilyn. She's taken a pill and gone to bed. I've been digging into Katie Batten to satisfy my own curiosity. Yes, it is an advantage of being rich, but I'm now sharing what I've found so I've saved your resources. You should at least check the house out. It's empty. It was going to be turned into a museum, apparently — he was some kind of famous illusionist — but it never happened. Just like the new owner never materialised. Someone's hiding behind a lot of paperwork, Detective Bray, and whether that's Katie or not, I think there's a good chance Lisa will have gone there, to Skegness. It's somewhere she and Katie would have talked about, surely? Katie's grandfather died earlier *that* year and if they'd been planning to run off together, an empty house might be a good place to hide out for a day or so? What's it going to hurt to send a couple of officers to check it out? On a case like this you could have people there in ten minutes, surely?'

There's a long pause and our eyes meet. Finally, he nods, triumphant. 'Thank you. Yes I will. And thank you again.'

It's a long wait and we sit in silence, tension humming between us. I wonder if he realises he's in love with Lisa. He thinks he's doing all this to vindicate his own judgement, to make his attraction and flirting and dating her slightly *less bad* than it's made him feel, but this is more.

356

This is driven by something deeper, even if he doesn't know it yet. I love Lisa too, even knowing everything about her past. That's a truth I'm going to have to learn to reconcile too. Someone can do a terrible unforgivable thing, and yet you forgive them if you love them. The heart is such a strange thing.

Finally, Bray calls back. Simon listens, and then, after a few perfunctory minutes, the call is over. I can tell it's not good news from the slump in his shoulders.

'There's no one there. The place is deserted. The only oddity was that the front door was unlocked. They're going to try to contact the owner to get a locksmith out in the morning, but there's no sign of anyone having been hiding there, and no sign of Ava.'

'They're missing something,' I say. She has to be there. I can feel it in my gut.

'They're looking for a killer.' He slumps down into his chair. 'They'll have been thorough. They can't be there. We're back to square one. Let's hope the searches into Amelia Cousins come back with something. Until then, there's nothing we can do. Running around like headless chickens without information isn't doing us any good.'

I stare down at the paper I'm still holding with the address on it. I don't care what he says, they've missed something. A clue at the very least. Katie drew Lisa to that house. It wouldn't be for no reason.

'You look exhausted. Maybe you should go upstairs and have a shower and a rest. Some food, if you can manage it. If Bray decides to show up here to ask me what I'm up to, it probably wouldn't look too great to find you with me.'

I'm still looking at the paper. 'You're right,' I say, with a wan smile. 'It's late and this headache is killing me. Maybe a lie down for an hour will do me good.'

I pick up the mobile from the table. 'Your number's in here, right? I'll text you if I think of anything that might be useful.'

He nods and tells me everything is going to be all right in the way men do to women, as if we're all children, as if we don't know for ourselves how very often things don't turn out right, as if they can somehow protect us from all the wickedness in the world, so much of which we suffer at their hands. He's right, I am tired. I'm tired of a lot of things. I'm tired of being a victim. I'm tired of being reliant on men. I'm tired of waiting.

'I think I'll be out like a light,' I say, as I reach the door. 'But call me if you find anything useful.'

'I will,' he answers. I wait until he turns away, and quickly take something else from the desk by his coffee cup before leaving.

Minutes later, I'm in his car, punching Katie's grandfather's address into his top-of-the-range satnav. I'm not stupid, I knew the police had someone watching my car, parked out at the front of the hotel, so I went out through the back, past the kitchens, to the staff car park. No one was watching Simon's car. How long before he realises I took his car keys from his desk? An hour maybe? More, if I'm lucky. I'm not going to let Lisa down. Skegness is only an hour or so's drive away, less at this time of night. I'm not going to wait around for a man to save the day. Fuck. That. Shit.

71

LISA

My throat is bone-dry and it hurts to open my eyes despite how little light there is in the room.

'Drink this,' she says, and I take a long swallow. The sudden burn makes me cough and splutter. *Not water.* For a moment I think it's acid or something equally lethal but then the memory kicks in. *Vodka.* Neat. Cheap. The shock wakes me up and I shake my head, ignoring the pain.

Katie takes a sip and grimaces. 'I never could understand how you drank this.'

'It did the job,' I answer.

'You always did like to be numb. To dull all your energy.'

I look over to the mattress and Katie sees my alarm. Ava is covered with a blanket, head to toe. *Oh God no, please no —*

'Don't worry, she's not dead.' She turns her head. 'Wriggle for your mother, Ava, let her know you're alive.'

The blanket squirms and I hear a whine. I'm glad to hear some anger mixed in with the terror. *That's my girl.*

Katie leans in, conspiratorially. 'She's had some vodka too.'

'When are you going to let her go?' I ask. My voice is clearer now. I slur on purpose. Let her think whatever she gave me is still knocking me out a bit. 'You said you would.'

'I did, didn't I?' She pulls a chair up close to me. All the plastic surgery she's had done is one thing, but why didn't I recognise those eyes? The over-bright sparkling joy at the world that I should have, even back then, known was touched with madness. 'But people change their minds, don't they, Charlotte?'

'I know I broke our deal,' I say. 'I'm sorry I let you down. I'm sorry I called the police. But I did that, not Ava. This is nothing to do with Ava.'

'You betrayed me and you don't even know it. I loved you and you betrayed me.' Tears prick at the corner of her eyes. 'And for what? This life? We could have had everything. We could have been *glorious*. But look at you. Such an ordinary mouse of a woman.'

I let my head loll a little and pretend to drag it upwards as if I can't quite hold it myself. Something she said jars in my head. 'What do you mean, I don't even know it?'

'What do you remember, Charlotte?' she whispers, pulling my hair back hard and tipping another slug of vodka down my raw throat.

'I don't remember,' I say. I know I did it so why would I want to remember it? I've spent a lifetime not remembering. I don't want to think about it. Ever.

'Of course you do,' she purrs. 'You just don't remember it right.'

72

THEN

1989

Katie isn't at all unhappy to see Daniel. He's shy and clingy but eventually settles down on the floor with Peter Rabbit and plays with some old bricks Charlotte brought in from outside. His eyes are wide and nervous though, and Charlotte doesn't like looking at them. They make something inside her squirm. Maybe she should have left him at home.

She drinks more vodka, and Katie produces another half-bottle, and a couple of her own mother's pills, some anti-anxiety or anti-depression shit. 'Been carrying them around for a special occasion,' she says, smiling. 'Let's get high together!'

'Play with me, Charrot,' Daniel says, carefully balancing one brick on top of another. 'Building a fire station.'

'I'm talking to Katie,' she says, taking a pill and swallowing with booze. 'Play by yourself. Here, have some of this.' She holds the bottle out to him and he takes a small sip before she swipes it away. He's coughing and for a moment looks as if he's about to cry and then stops himself. Maybe he's learned already that being a crier in this family doesn't get you very far. Maybe he knows Charlotte well enough to know she won't cuddle him better. 'Don't like it,' he says.

Somehow his reaction gives her some satisfaction. 'Then shut up and play quietly.' It's a growl and she doesn't look at him. She doesn't want to feel sorry for him. She only wants to feel sorry for herself.

Katie's mood is electric as the world starts to spin a little too disconcertingly for Charlotte. They drink more and Katie plays their tape on her pink double cassette player, the music tinny in the damp, cold house. A breeze comes in through the broken window, and it makes Charlotte shiver pleasantly.

'I can't believe we're doing it,' she says.

'Doing what?' Charlotte is having difficulty focusing. It feels good though, this chemical warmth inside her. She can't feel the soreness down there from last night any more. Just a little throb inside, like her heartbeat. Even her anger feels good. Katie leans against her, and takes another sip of vodka before passing it over.

'Our pact!' Katie huddles in close. 'That's why you brought him here, isn't it? We're going to do it today!'

Charlotte frowns. Is that why she brought him here? Does she want that? 'He just followed me,' she says. 'I haven't stolen anything. Got no money.'

'I've got all we need. And we'll go to my granddad's house and hide there for a couple of days. I know the perfect place.' Katie squeezes her arm. 'Let's get drunk and do it. Then we'll go and do my mother when she's home this

363

afternoon. After that, we'll be free! Bonnie and Clyde!'

Charlotte thinks about it for a moment. There's nothing she wants more than to be away from here with Katie. No more Tony. No more Ma. She looks at Daniel, muttering away to Peter Rabbit as he plays. She hates him. She knows she does.

'Maybe we should just run away,' she slurs. 'Forget the other shite. Fuck them.'

'They'll never let me go,' Katie is slurring too. 'My mother will keep me forever if she can.' She rests her sweet-smelling head on Charlotte's shoulder. 'And we had a pact. Cross my heart and hope to die. Remember.'

'Cross my heart and hope to die,' Charlotte murmurs. 'Let's get drunk first.' She doesn't want to think about their plan. It was a game that now feels too real. 'I want to get out of my face.'

When the pills hit, they hit hard and for a moment she has a blind panic she's taken too much. She fades in and out of darkness, a haze enveloping her, almost lifting her out of her body.

'What is this?' she tries to say, and for a moment it looks like Katie is smiling and *glowing* at her, and then she's slumped asleep against the wall. She has no concept of time, drifting in and out of confusion. Everything is a blur.

'Charrot?' Daniel's face suddenly looms large in front of her. His eyes, Tony's eyes, fill her distorted vision. 'Feel sick, Charrot.'

Is he feeling sick or is he asking her? Whichever, she doesn't want to see him. Doesn't want to think about him. 'Shut up, Daniel,' she mutters, although her words are thick on her tongue. Too much. She's drunk too much with these pills. She closes her eyes, even as she's aware of Daniel tugging at her.

It's all his fault, a voice in her head says. *Everything. The chip shop. Your ma not loving you any more. Tony and his belt. None of it was there before he was. They didn't realise how little they loved you until they loved him and that's the truth of it. It's all his fault.*

She drags her eyes open, the voice confusing her. It's in her head, it must be her voice. Daniel is still in front of her. He looks hazy too. Has she given him more to drink? She can't remember. Maybe. She can't remember how much she's drunk herself. Is it all his fault? Yes, she thinks. Yes, it is. She knows it is, like the voice in her head is saying, but he's only a baby and it can't really be his fault. He looks scared, sucking the corner of Peter Rabbit's ear. She doesn't want him to look scared. It jars something inside her.

The voice in her head is still talking, reminding her of all the love and care her ma has given him and all the pain she's had to suffer. How if something bad happened to Daniel it would punish Ma as she deserves. How this is what she wants. It is what she wants but also not what she wants. She doesn't know what she wants. She wants to pass out. To sleep. To forget about everything. But the voice won't shut up, needling her from inside her own mind. *He's a little shite and you know it. He's spoiled. He's a brat. He's the reason they hurt you.*

Everything fades to black, hazing out — *Do it, try it, squeeze his throat and make everything better.* She sees her hands on his neck, feels his soft skin under them, the voice in her head is raging, and his little eyes are wide, and she's not quite sure what's happening. Blackness again. She's here and yet not here. She's doing it and yet not doing it. Her brain won't work properly and her body feels all wrong. At some point there's the thump of a brick. And then nothing but swimming in the darkness.

When she opens her eyes next, her vision is clear but her head feels like it's going to explode and her stomach roils with puke waiting to happen. What the shite kind of pills does Katie's ma take? She doesn't want any more of those, never again. Katie is passed out beside her, slumped up against the wall, her legs splayed out at a very non-Katie angle. 'Katie?' she says, and the world spins slightly again with a wave of nausea. 'Katie, you awake?'

Peter Rabbit catches her eye, abandoned on the floor by her feet. A flash of something comes to her: *hands, neck, Daniel.* A dream? The nausea fades with a wave of something cold. Dread. A small shoe in the corner of her vision. A leg very still. She doesn't want to look, oh she desperately doesn't want to look, but she can't help herself.

Oh shite, Daniel. His face is turned away, but there's blood on the ground and he's not moving at all, and he's dead she knows he's dead and she thinks she might scream or —

'Oh my God, Charlotte.' Katie is dragging herself upright, eyes blearily widening. 'You did it. You actually did it.'

Charlotte's shaking, her whole body trembling like she's standing next to one of those stupid pneumatic drills they've been using up on the high street, and *it's so surreal, it's all so surreal and he can't be dead, not really dead, not like we talked about, hands around his throat, oh God Daniel you little shite I'm so sorry,* Katie takes her cold hands and holds them up to her face.

'Look at me, Charlotte.'

She does. She wants to look anywhere but at little Daniel and *oh God what will Ma say,* and so she stares straight into Katie's perfect eyes. 'It's done,' Katie whispers, hot breath on her cold face, *Daniel will never breathe again, oh shite oh shite.* Katie kisses her gently on her open mouth. 'You've done it. It's the beginning, Charlotte. We can be free! I can't believe you did it, but you did. Oh, Charlotte, you're my hero. There's no going back now. Next, my mother. Then we run. We fly like the wind. Just us. You and me, forever. No going back.'

Charlotte's teeth are starting to chatter. It can't be real, how can it be real, it was only a fantasy, a crazy game. Everything is too bright, too real, and yet at the same time too *surreal.* No going back.

'I need to go home first,' she hears herself saying. 'Make things look normal. If Ma's home I'll say I'm going to look for Daniel. Then come to you. They don't know about you. They won't look for me with you.' How does she sound so normal? So calm. 'We'll do your ma and go, right?' She kisses Katie back although her own mouth tastes sharp and bitter. *Rotten.*

'Half an hour? At mine?'

Charlotte nods. She needs to get out of here. She needs to get away. Where is her anger now? Where did it all go? *Into your hands and round little Daniel's neck, that's where it went and oh shite no going back.*

'I love you,' Katie says with a smile as they clamber back out into the cold October air.

'I love you too,' Charlotte answers, her own smile a sickly grimace. And maybe she does. She *does*. But everything is broken now. She's broken now. *Daniel's broken can't be fixed never be fixed oh God oh God.* 'See you in half an hour.'

They go their separate ways and Charlotte knows she'll never see Katie again. Not like this. She throws up around the corner, vodka and bile spilling out on to the dirt and leaving her empty. Hollow.

She looks back at the house, a wreck, unloved and unlovable. She doesn't want to leave Daniel there alone with only Peter Rabbit for company. He'll be afraid. He won't understand. *He's dead you stupid shite cunt, he will never understand anything again because of you and your pills and your stupid voice in your head and your stupid hands and your stupid anger and he never hurt you, not really, Daniel never took you to the chippy or beat you or did the thing Tony did last night.* Why is everything so clear now? Why is she always one step behind?

She knows what she has to do. The only thing she can do. *No going back*. She runs, faster than she ever has before, all the way to the train station. There's a pay phone there. Her breath is raw in her chest. Her head is still spinning with the booze, the pills and the numbing shock, but her trembling fingers punch in the 999. *I'm sorry, Katie*, she thinks, when the call is done. *I'm so sorry, Katie*.

Daniel. I'm so sorry, Daniel.

She wishes she could cry. She wishes she could die. Instead, she goes home on numb legs with a numb heart and waits until she hears the sirens. It's not long before Ma is wailing too, pushing Tony away.

When they take her to the police car, she doesn't look back.

There'll never be any going back.

73

NOW

MARILYN

I park up on the secluded road, away from the house, a black shape in the darkness up ahead, and get the torch from the boot of the car. I keep it turned off for now, walking carefully on the uneven track. My feet are invisible, no street lights to cut through the heavy darkness of the night. It's not raining but the air is damp and heavy with pressure, the clouds hanging low under their own weight. As I turn into the drive I can't see any other cars, certainly nothing resembling a police car, and for once I praise all the recent government cuts. No lights on. No sign of life. If they're here, Katie's dumped whatever car she's been using out of sight. Without hesitating, without giving myself time to chicken out and turn around, I climb the steps. No police tape, no boards nailed across the door. No sign the police have taken this lead seriously at all.

When I push the door open, I understand why. The house is empty. In its soul it's empty. I turn the torch on, a pool of yellow in blackness. There's not much to see; wooden floors and pale walls and then a wide modern staircase that turns on a landing, before heading up to the next floor. I can hear nothing but the hum of my own body in my ears.

There's no furniture to speak of, most rooms empty, but as I methodically search from top to bottom, there are some items that have been left behind. A mirror with no reflection in one room gives me a start. *Illusionist*, I remember. Was this part of a trick or was it put here to frighten guests? Some books still in the built-in bookshelves in one of the sitting rooms. Some crockery in the cupboards in the kitchen. If this was going to be a museum, where was everything else? In a lock-up somewhere? And surely it was all too bland and modern to attract any visitors? It could be a banker's house, or a businessman's. Not a magician's.

I make my way back to the hallway and let the torch methodically search. A rug on the floor. An old projector of some sort high on the wall above the door, boxed in wood painted white to match the walls, an illusion to hide it. Sneaky. Like grandfather, like granddaughter. So far, though, no clues.

I find the door to the basement past what might have once been a utility room, and I open it carefully, listening out for any sign of life. Nothing. *Not a creature was stirring, not even a mouse.* I shiver involuntarily. I'm a grown woman. It's only a cellar. I'm about to head down into its depths when the phone in my pocket starts buzzing. Shit. Simon.

'Where the hell are you?' he asks. 'I thought you were going to bed. You took my car?'

For a moment it could be Richard, demanding

371

and annoyed, and my first instinct is to apologise, but I don't.

'I'm in Skegness.' I'm speaking quietly but the sound is almost too loud in this mausoleum of a house. 'At the house.'

'You're where? Jesus, Marilyn, if the police — '

'The police aren't here. No sign of them. But I can't sit around and do nothing. And this house is part of it, I'm sure. A clue. It has to be. But if I can't find anything, then I'll drive straight back. No one will know I was even here.'

'I don't like you being down there on your own. I wish you'd told me. I'd have come with you.'

Not like Richard at all, I realise. This isn't irritation, it's concern. Same coin, different sides. Richard used to hide his paranoia as concern. *Don't wear that dress today, you know what men are like.*

'But listen,' he says. 'We've got something. I'm about to call the police with it. Amelia Cousins . . . '

'You can track her back to Katie?' My breath catches in my throat with the sudden speed of my heartbeat.

'No, not quite, but her history doesn't add up. Not if you go back a few years. It's paper-thin — and trust me, there's a lot of paper. But it's not that.'

'What then?'

He pauses. 'I think Katie was pretending to be *two* other people.'

74

AVA

Jodie. The fucking bitch. A small sob escapes my gag. Jodie. I trusted her. She was my friend. She was my best friend. My head hurts and I'm horribly drunk and it's making it hard to think. No, she was never my friend. She was *Mum's* best friend. Katie. Girl B. Whatever.

I'm going to die here, I know it. Me and Mum together. Jodie's going to kill us, because Jodie isn't Jodie and she's batshit crazy and I'm so ashamed and I feel sick and I'm so sorry Mum is going to die here with me and I keep thinking about the baby inside me and that's going to die too and this is not its fault. Maybe it's dead already. Fresh tears threaten and I fight them back. I can't breathe when I cry. I'm scared to cry. I'm scared to die. I'm so scared and I just want my mum to make it all okay, but I don't think she can. I'm not even ashamed any more. The stupid Facebook messages feel like a lifetime ago. I was different then. I was stupid then.

My face is sore from snot and tears and my jaw aches from this gag and I hate myself for being so helpless. I should have fought back. I should have known something was wrong when I saw her at the car, but it was so fast, and I was so confused. Before I knew it there was the cloth on my face and the darkness and then I woke up here, bruised and sore.

I don't hate Mum. I love her. I want to tell her. She's going to die thinking I hate her. I can't let her die thinking I hate her. She thinks everyone hates her. I want to be sick. I can't be sick. I'll choke. The blanket is heavy on my face and I try to shake it away but I can't. I want to see my mum. She's being so tough. Not like my mum at all. She came here to die for me. She loves me that much. I've had long days of hearing about her life as Charlotte. My mum before she was anyone's mum. She wanted it all to be better for me and whatever she'd done, *the awful thing she'd done*, I was selfish and thoughtless and awful and now I feel five years old again. Pathetic. I'm pathetic.

I can hear Crazy Katie talking to her. She's talking about the day Daniel died. She doesn't care about me now Mum's here. It was all about Mum. I'm nothing to her. Worse than nothing. I was a pawn and now she's going to knock me off the board. All that time at swim club, *MyBitches*, the Fabulous Four, all the shit she gave me about weird mums club, how I looked up to her, how we all kind of looked up to her — none of it was real. A bubble of anger bursts through my self-pity. How fucking dare she do that to us?

She doesn't care about me now Mum's here. The thought repeats itself in my hazy brain. *She can't even see me. I'm under a blanket.* When did she last re-tie my hands? A day ago? More? Less? Time has lost all meaning. It wasn't recently anyway. I wriggle my fingers to see if there's any give. It's hot under here and I'm sweating. Sweat is good. Sweat is a lubricant.

75

MARILYN

My mind is too distracted with what Simon's told me to have any fear of the cellar. I shine the torch on the stairs and creep down. Jodie Cousins never attended Allerton University. She registered, went through the process to get all her documents and her student card etc., but never showed up to any courses. By the time Ava went missing it was the summer holidays, and so the police never went there to ask her any questions. They probably just got her number from one of Ava's school friends or the swim club. Jodie would have given them her mother's number — always away working or with her boyfriend — and that was that. After all, the girls weren't suspects.

Katie was both Jodie *and* Amelia Cousins. Mother for buying the house and setting up the bills and then vanishing off to an imaginary life in Paris and becoming the daughter for insinuating herself into Lisa's life via Ava. No one ever *met* Amelia, only Jodie. I think about Jodie. Slight, never in any make-up, a hard trim boyish body. Short. Quiet. In the background. You see what you want to see. You believe what's in front of you. Another thought strikes me.

Katie supposedly died by drowning. A strong swimmer. She must have thought her luck was in when she found out Ava was a swimmer too. *Fate*.

The basement is quite cluttered and dusty. Old furniture stacked up against a wall. A dresser, probably worth a fair bit, covered with a sheet. Boxes of knick-knacks. Scraps of a life with no one left to remember it. If there's a clue in here it will take me a while to find it.

Still, something feels odd. I sweep the torch around, looking into the corners and nooks and crannies. The plaster of one wall is damp and cracked. *That'll need looking at*, I can hear Richard saying. I look at the wall on the other side, furthest from the stairs. The plaster matches. I move closer and shove some of the boxes that are up against it out of the way, not caring as their contents spill. It *almost* matches. There are no cracks though and the surface is slightly smoother. I spin round and look at the space again, fresh eyes this time. *It's not big enough. It should be far bigger than this. An illusionist's house.*

I run up the stairs and back to the scullery. As soon as my phone shows service, I'm dialling Simon.

'You need to get the police here. Now.' I cut short his protests and questions. 'There's another room. A secret room. Underground somewhere.' I'm breathless with the realisation. *They're here. So close to me.* 'That's where they are. I need to find it. Get the police here now. I don't care how, say I'm here with Lisa or

377

whatever. Just get them here!'

I hang up and my face burns as I look around me. A house of tricks. There's a doorway here somewhere. And I can't wait for the police to arrive to find it.

76

LISA

I'm drunk and there's some shite drug in my system slowing everything down, but I'm not as wasted as Katie thinks I am. I've been on a lot of pills over the years. Anti-anxiety meds, anti-depressants, Valium, sleeping pills — you name it, I've had it. And it's paying off now. In all her planning, Katie thinks I need the same dosage as I did when I was eleven. Not so perfect Katie. I slump slightly in the chair and let my eyes drift in and out of focus. Here but not here.

'You think you betrayed me by calling the police?' She looks at me wide-eyed. 'Oh yes, that was part of it. But you'd done the damage before then. I tried to make it better, but you wrecked it.'

'What are you talking about?' I ask.

'You changed your mind.' She spits the words out, disgusted. Her tone constantly changes on a whim, light and entertained becoming hard and bitter between breaths.

'I know. I'm sorry. But that's not Ava's — '

'No you don't know! You don't know at all!' I flinch as she barks the words out, and her face draws close to mine and she whispers, 'All the things they did to you and you still couldn't do it.' She sees my confusion. 'You didn't change your mind after. You changed your mind *before*. You didn't kill Daniel.' She smiles but her eyes are cold. 'I did. I did it for *you*.'

For a moment, everything is frozen. What is she talking about?

'No,' I say, my heart racing. She can't be right. I murdered my little brother. It's a fact. It's the bedrock truth of my whole sorry life. 'No,' I say again. 'I remember my hands round his throat. All my angry thoughts.' I pause. 'And Mrs Jackson from the shop. She *saw* me. She saw what I did while you were asleep.'

She snorts. 'Oh come on. Mrs Jackson *hated* you. And there was no way my parents were going to let there be even the slightest chance that I could get dragged down with you. Not their little angel. Mummy made Daddy talk to her. They came to an arrangement. Mrs Jackson was more than happy to make sure you went to prison.'

'No.' My head is spinning. 'No, that can't be. It can't . . . ' Nothing is making sense. The Battens paid the shopkeeper to lie in court? 'But I remember . . . I . . . '

'*He's only a bairn, Katie. We didn't mean it, Katie, did we? We can't really kill anyone.*' Her voice is a mocking whine. 'Ring any bells?'

The words echo somewhere deep in my subconscious. There's a weight of *real* about them. 'But,' I say, as my whole existence, everyone I've been, shimmers and cracks. 'I was so angry with him. I remember my hands on his throat.'

'You remember what I made you remember. Gullible Charlotte. Always a victim. You were so out of it. You think I was too, but I wasn't. I've never liked being out of control. Anyone can do anything to you when you're out of control, Charlotte.'

'No,' I mutter. 'I killed him. I know I did. There were all those thoughts in my head . . . '

'*I* was the voice in your head, Charlotte. Those words were mine. You put your hands on his throat for barely a second before laughing it off as a joke even though we'd *sworn* to do it, and you'd brought him along. You were all *We didn't mean it, did we Katie? He's only a bairn. We can't really kill anyone.* Can you imagine how you made me feel? You were weak. But it wasn't what was best for you. It wasn't what was best for us. I forgave you, Charlotte, but I had to put it right. We had a plan. We'd made a deal.'

She's pacing now, the memory or whatever this is either irritating or enlivening her, I can't decide which. I don't care much either. I can barely think straight with what she's saying. My whole life is unravelling and somehow it terrifies me.

'You changed your mind and I played along until you were out of it,' she continues. 'I pretended to pass out while you were still aware of what was around you, and then as you slumped into your stupor, when I knew you couldn't tell real from false, I was the voice in your head. Prompting, cajoling. But still, you wouldn't do it. You chose *him* over me. Do you know how much that hurt? How much pride I

381

had to swallow to overlook it? After everything you'd said, everything we'd planned, and suddenly you didn't want to go through with it?'

She stares at me. Mad. Quite, quite mad. 'I knew you couldn't *mean* it.' She shrugs. 'So I did it for you. He was sleepy and scared. He didn't like the drink. He was worried about you. It was easy to get him to come to me. And that was that. Afterwards, I squeezed your hands around his throat again, and then I picked up the brick and made sure it was done. I whispered some more into your ear, planted all those seeds of what you'd done, made sure you'd gripped the brick hard enough to leave marks, and then faked being asleep until you woke up.'

All the threads of who I am, unravelling. I didn't kill Daniel. Can it be true? Can I dare to think it? Is this just some drunken, drugged-up hallucination? Am I more out of it than I realise?

'And after all that,' she snarls through gritted teeth, 'you still let me down.'

I didn't kill Daniel. I didn't. I don't know how to process this. I don't know if I can.

'Let Ava go,' I say. 'You don't need her.'

'Ah, but I do!' Her face lights up again and my stomach sinks. *What game now, Katie, you crazy cunt? What have you planned now?*

'You're going to do it again, Charlotte.' She smiles at me as she grabs my hair and tips another slug of vodka into me. 'Just like before. Poor Charlotte Nevill, cracked and killed her ex then killed her daughter exactly as she did her little brother all those years ago. It'll be Broadmoor for you, forever. You can say

382

whatever you like about me, no one will believe you. Katie Batten is dead. You're the crazed child-killer. I think it's the justice you deserve for what you did to me, don't you? Left me with my mother. All those fucking years.'

My eyes are blurring now and the world spins and it panics me. I may be used to the pills, but my alcohol tolerance is non-existent. I can't pass out. I can't.

'And you know the best bit?' she whispers. 'Ava's pregnant. And you *do*, after all, owe me a mother. I get to kill two birds with one stone.'

My eyes close and my mouth drops open slightly. 'Are you still with me, Charlotte?' she asks. 'You go to sleep if you need to. I can take it from here. It's time to get started. We're going to need your fingerprints on her neck, of course. The devil is in the detail.' She digs a key out of her pocket and starts to unlock one of my cuffs.

I didn't kill Daniel. I didn't kill Daniel. Slowly, slowly the truth of it is sinking in. My whole sorry life has been wrapped around a lie. *Oh yes, Katie, I think*, as my anger tightens into a ball of fire in my gut, but I force myself to go limp. *It's time to get started.*

77

MARILYN

Think, think, think. I'm running from room to room, looking for anything I may have missed. I find what looks like a trapdoor in the hallway floor, but there's no leverage for opening it and it feels solid under my feet. Does it lead to the secret room? Is it part of another trick? How the fuck am I supposed to open it? I try every light switch to see if one of those is a hidden lever, but nothing happens. No electricity. No lights, no opening door.

It opens from the inside, is the only conclusion I can draw. This isn't the way down. I try the cellar again, but that's too obvious. Time is ticking away. Lisa and Ava's time. *Maybe they're dead already.* I don't entertain the thought. I don't think it's true, just my panicking mind leading me to the darkest of places. If they were dead, Katie would be out of here, cleaning the place up and gone. And if they were dead, she'd want their bodies found. Displayed. She's set a stage and this is the big performance. She's an illusionist of a different, deadlier kind than her grandfather, but this is a set piece all the same. She wouldn't want them somewhere hard to find. She wants the world to see whatever fucked-up shit she has planned.

I still have time. I take a breath. *Think, think, think.* Use your brain. The torch streaming light ahead of me, I go back to the pantry and stare down at the tiny cellar. It's a wide staircase though, which implies to me a big basement. Space. I've always been good with spaces. Look at the *space.* What ground-floor rooms should the basement run under? Not going to be the kitchen. When the house was occupied, it would have been too cluttered and busy for secret doorways. Especially if there was a cook or housekeeper or whatever the fuck those old posh families had. Somewhere else.

'I'm coming, Lisa, I'm coming,' I mutter as I follow the walls and corridors, tracing my fingers on them and tapping, listening for anything that might not be right. Nothing. I go into a sitting room, and there it strikes me. I almost smile.

The bookshelf. Those old books haven't been left there for no reason. If you were going to design a house with trickery at its core, a secret doorway would have to be in a bookshelf.

Heart racing, I pull the various books free, throwing them to the ground, clearing the ledges. One refuses to budge as if it's glued in place. *Part of the shelf.* I pause, breathing heavily, and shine the torch on it. Very carefully, I push it forward. Something clicks and the whole shelf swings inwards. My mouth drops open as the cool rush of air hits me.

I've found it.

I think I hear a distant wail of sirens. The

sound is barely more than the hum of a mosquito. If it's the police, they're still some distance away. My feet are hot in my shoes. My whole body itches with impatience. All I have as a weapon is my torch. I should wait for the police. I *know* I should wait for the police. To go down there unarmed is fucking madness.

But as a shriek from below carries up the stairs, I find myself doing it anyway.

78

LISA

She wanted me to be Charlotte again. But I'm not. I *was* Charlotte. Now I'm Lisa. I have my own rage but I have Charlotte's too, and as the second cuff comes off I channel *all* of it, shaking my faux sluggishness off in an instant and shrieking as I lunge at her.

'You fucking bitch!' My words spray in her face as I shove her backwards. 'You fucking shite bitch!' There's so much I want to say, to scream at her, all that grief, all those years of guilt, what she did to me, what she did to Daniel, but these are the only words I can find.

She thuds heavily into the table, and I reel sideways, more unsteady on my feet than I was expecting. I stop moving but the world doesn't. *Shit*. Katie's surprise and shock turns to a sneer, and as nausea threatens to drop me, I see why. *The knife. My knife.* She grabs for it and I lunge to stop her but she's not drunk and drugged and she lithely turns and then it's in her hand. She smiles, triumphant, as I sway, trying to focus.

'Never could keep up,' she says.

'Fuck you.' Behind her, I can see movement under the blanket. Not panicked wriggling but more focused. I need to keep Katie distracted. I

387

need to stay alive long enough for my baby to get away. 'So you're going to stab me? That screws your perfect plan, doesn't it?'

'I'll improvise something,' she says, but I see the irritation. More movement under the blanket. Does Ava have one wrist free? 'I'd rather you went to prison, but if you're both dead I can live with that.'

She lunges towards me and I manage to stumble out of the way. She laughs and I realise with a sudden despair that she's playing with me. I can barely stay on my feet.

'Lisa?'

The voice is so unexpected, I turn automatically. She's standing in a doorway behind us, her eyes wide, shocked, a torch limp in her hand by her side. *Marilyn*. Marilyn found us. I let out a small sob at the sight of my best friend, my true best friend, but she's suddenly leaping towards me, the torch dropping useless to the ground as she shoves me sideways, hard.

I spin, falling backwards to the ground, in time to see Katie, her face ugly with all her crazed bitterness, slice the knife down into the space where a second ago I had been standing. The space Marilyn now occupies.

I hear Marilyn gasp. It's not pain but utter surprise. She looks down. The handle is embedded in her chest. For a moment, there's a perfect stillness, and then her head turns to face me. She's trying to smile. Her mouth moves, attempting to form a word, and from where I am on the floor I can hear the liquid rattle of her breath.

'Run,' she finally says, before, like a puppet whose strings have been cut, she crumples to the floor.

I don't run. I can't run. I am done with running. I drag my eyes from my beautiful friend's broken body and then I'm screaming. I hear the noise and I know it's me, but it's like it's coming from somewhere else, someone else, somewhere far outside of me. I have no rational thought. I am a weapon of pure pain and I leap up, no unsteadiness in my legs now, and launch myself at Katie, my bodyweight taking both of us to the ground, the weight knocking the wind out of her under me. My hands grasp at her throat and I start to squeeze.

Marilyn. Daniel. Me. Ava. All those years. My whole life. She's struggling but my grip is a tightening vice on her slim neck. I see the fear in her eyes and I revel in it. 'Fuck you, Katie Batten,' I say through gritted teeth and as tears spring up at the back of my eyes. 'Fuck you, you crazy bitch.'

She's choking, awful sounds coming from her crushed windpipe, and she desperately struggles to breathe, but still my grip tightens, the muscles in my hands starting to scream with the effort. I'm going to kill her. I know it. And it feels good.

'Mum, no!' Hands on my arms, scrabbling at me, trying to pull me off her. 'Don't. Mum, don't!'

Ava. My Ava. She's dirty, snot- and tear-stained and her hair is lank and knotted, but her eyes are clear as she grabs my face.

'You're not a killer. Don't let her make you a

389

killer. I love you, Mum. Don't do it.'

I stare into her eyes, so much like Jon's but also, behind the facade of colour, in the depths of who she is, so much like mine. My baby.

'Please, Mum,' she says. 'Please.'

I feel my grip loosen. Underneath me, Katie starts to cough as I let go, my arms unable to be so close to Ava and not hold her. I pull her to me and we cling to each other, crying into each other's hair as I murmur, *it's okay, it's okay, baby, Mummy's here now, it's over, it's over* and from upstairs come voices, feet on stairs and I know we're safe.

Katie tenses beneath me and attempts to push herself upright. I break free from Ava, and in one swift movement, punch her hard in the face. She doesn't try to move again.

Epilogue

There are still nightmares. There will probably be nightmares for a long time, for all of them, but they are different now, and she reminds herself they are only dreams. Katie is locked away. Katie won't escape and find them. They say Katie writes her letters, but she doesn't read them. She's told the prison staff to burn any correspondence. She has no interest in any of Katie's words.

She is Charlotte again now and she finds she's okay with that. This time the therapy has been good, although she finds it hard to let go of a lifetime of guilt and shame. They talk about her childhood a lot. They talk about Daniel. She cries.

When she's not having nightmares about Katie looking for her, she still dreams of holding Daniel's hand. She thinks the dreams are here to stay. But that's okay too. He's inside her and always will be but she's made her peace with him. He's gone and nothing can change that. It's time to look forward. To live. To embrace new life. She has to try to be happy. She can *be* happy now. She has every right to be. Today, she is happy. Today she is filled with hope.

Ava, pale and beautiful and awestruck, is holding the baby, so tiny and fragile and new, and Charlotte thinks they are the two most beautiful creatures in the whole world, this young daughter of hers and her new child. They are her strength. They will always be her strength. Courtney has gone home from the hospital, somewhat shell-shocked and bewildered, but Charlotte thinks he'll be okay. He's a good boy and she has a feeling that, with enough help, he'll be a good father. This baby will not be short of people to love him.

'He's beautiful,' she says, tears stinging her eyes as she smiles at her daughter. Tears come easily these days. Funny how things change.

'I brought Jelly Babies!' The hospital room door opens, and Marilyn comes in, waving the bag of sweets with her functioning arm. It's been a long road for her too, but she's a fighter. She's had to be. Her natural glow is returning, slowly. Her smile is no longer forced. She has nightmares too. Charlotte hears her cries in her sleep. After coming out of hospital it seemed natural for Marilyn to move in, and what was supposed to be a short-term arrangement has turned into an unspoken permanent one. Charlotte, Ava and Marilyn; an odd little family, but one she would not change. They are survivors together. They will survive this together. The rest of the world can wait. She knows Simon wants to take things further, but isn't sure that will happen. Maybe one day. It will depend on his patience.

'So, we've got a little man moving in with us,' Charlotte says, sitting on the edge of the bed. She wriggles her finger into one of the baby's tiny wrinkled hands, fascinated by the gorgeousness of him. There was never going to be an abortion. Ava couldn't do it, and Charlotte wasn't going to fight her decision. Another time and another life, maybe. But not hers or Ava's.

'Do you have a name yet?' Marilyn asks. Charlotte looks up, curious. Ava's kept her name choices close to her chest all through the pregnancy, not knowing if the baby was going to be a boy or a girl. Ava nods, sweaty hair clinging to her face.

'Daniel,' she says. 'I want to call him Daniel.'

The baby's tiny hand grips tight on Charlotte's fingers, and her tears come hot and salty and fresh as he refuses to let go.

Daniel. It's perfect.

Acknowledgements

Thanks as always to Veronique Baxter my agent at David Higham, and also Grainne Fox at Fletcher & co. You ladies rock — and stop me from rocking backward and forward too much! Big thanks to the entire team at HarperFiction UK, especially Jaime Frost, and of course, always, to my friend and editor extraordinaire — Natasha Bardon. Also big thanks to David Highfill at William Morrow in the US for loving the book so much and bringing me further into the global HarperCollins fold.

Thanks also to all my family and friends who spur me on and keep me going, and don't care that I dress like a scruff and rarely change my dog-walking clothes all day. I owe you all wine.